*"So rack 'em up, cowboy.
But first take off your shirt."*

His smile was briefly interrupted with surprise, and she took satisfaction in that. No point being too predictable, since she was becoming a new Emily.

Nate sailed his hat onto the glass coffee table, leaving his black hair tousled, then slowly pulled off his shirt, his gaze fixed on her. Her mouth went a little dry at all that lean muscle earned working hard for a living. Even though he had the faintest farmer tan on his lower arms, it was obvious he worked without a shirt when he was overheated.

Speaking of overheated . . . she felt suddenly too warm beneath his smoldering gaze.

Romances by Emma Cane

A TOWN CALLED VALENTINE

EMMA CANE

A Town Called VALENTINE

AVON

An Imprint of HarperCollins*Publishers*

AVON BOOKS
An Imprint of HarperCollins*Publishers*
10 East 53rd Street
New York, New York 10022-5299

To my Mom, Renee Kloecker, who nurtured a budding romance writer in the best ways. I wrote my first manuscript when I was sixteen, a Western. Guess I liked cowboys even then. For the love scene, not having any personal experience of my own, I gathered info from my favorite romances. My mom very calmly pointed out that although she liked my writing, I should take out the love scenes because I was too young. To this day, it makes me smile. Thanks for believing in me, Mom.

Acknowledgments

I'm indebted to Virginia Aubertine, James Callen IV, Jeffery McClanahan, Maggie Shayne, and Christine Wenger, who graciously answered my research questions. Any mistakes are certainly my own. *A Town Called Valentine* wouldn't have existed without the Packeteers and the Purples, who helped me in so many ways, from brainstorming, to emergency meetings, to the overwhelming generosity of their friendship. To my husband, Jim, for making sure I have everything I need, especially him.

To my agent, Eileen Fallon, who has believed in me for so many years. There are no words to express how much your dedication and friendship have meant to me.

And thanks to my editor, Amanda Bergeron, for falling in love with Valentine Valley and giving me all the support, advice, and editorial skills an author could ever want.

A Town Called
VALENTINE

Chapter One

The car gave one last shudder as Emily Murphy came to a stop in a parking space just beneath the blinking sign of Tony's Tavern. She turned off the ignition and leaned back against the headrest as the rain drummed on the roof, and the evening's darkness settled around her. The car will be all right, she told herself firmly. Taking a deep breath, she willed her shoulders to relax after a long, stressful day driving up into the Colorado Rockies. Though the trip had been full of stunning mountain vistas still topped by snow in May, she had never let her focus waver from her mission.

She glanced up at the flashing neon sign, and her stomach growled. The tavern was near the highway and wasn't the most welcoming place. There were only two pickups and a motorcycle beside her car on this wet night.

Her stomach gurgled again, and with a sigh, she tugged up the hood of her raincoat, grabbed her purse, and stepped out into the rain. Gingerly jumping over puddles, she made it beneath the overhang above the door and went inside. A blast of heat and the smell of beer hit her face. The tavern was sparsely furnished, with a half dozen tables and a long bar on the right side of the room. Between neon signs advertising beer, mounted animal heads peered down at the half dozen customers. A man and a woman sat at one table, watching a baseball game on the flat screen TV—at least there was one other woman in the place. Another couple men hunched at the bar, glancing from beneath their cowboy hats at her before turning away. No surprise there.

When she hesitated, the bartender, a man in his thirties, with shaggy dark hair and pleasant features, gave her a nod. "Sit anywhere you'd like."

Smiling gratefully, she slipped off her raincoat, hung it on one of the many hooks near the door, and sat down. She discovered her table was opposite the only man at a table by himself. He was directly in her line of vision, making it hard to notice anything else. He was tall, by the length of his denim-clad legs. Beneath the shadowing brim of his cowboy hat, she could see an angular face and the faint lines at the corner of his eyes of a man who spent much of his day squinting in the sun. She thought he might be older than her thirty years but not by much.

When he tipped his hat back and met her eyes, Emily gave a start, realizing she'd been caught staring. It had been so long since she'd looked at any man but her ex-husband. Her face got hot, and she quickly pulled the slightly sticky menu out from its place between a napkin dispenser and a condiment basket.

A shadow loomed over her, and for a moment, she thought she'd given the cowboy some kind of signal. Maybe her presence alone in a bar late at night was enough.

But it was only the bartender, who gave her a tired smile. "Can I get you something to drink?"

She almost said a Diet Coke, but the weariness of the day overtook her, and she found herself ordering a beer. She studied the menu while he was gone, remembered her lack of funds, and asked for a burger when he returned. Some protein, some carbs, and with lettuce and tomato, it made a pretty well-rounded meal. She had to laugh at herself.

"I didn't know the menu was that funny," said a deep voice.

Not the bartender. Emily glanced up and met the solitary cowboy's gaze. Even from one table over, she could see the gleam of his green eyes. His big hand lifted a bottle of beer to his lips, yet he never stopped watching her.

Was a cowboy trying to pick her up in a mountain bar? She blinked at him and tried to contain her smile. "No, I was smiling at something else," she said, trying to sound polite but cool.

To her surprise, the cowboy simply nodded, took another swig of his beer, and glanced back at the TV. She did the same, drinking absentmindedly and trying to pretend she liked baseball. Her ex-husband had been a fan of the San Francisco Giants, so she'd gone to an occasional game when one of the partners couldn't attend.

By the time her hamburger arrived, she'd finished

her beer. The cowboy was watching her again, and she recklessly ordered another. Why not? Though she hadn't eaten much today, the burger would certainly offset the alcohol. Hungrily, she dug in. The two men at the bar started to play darts, and she watched them for a while. The cowboy did, too, but he watched her more.

She studied him back. "Don't cowboys have to get up early? You're out awful late." What was she doing? Talking to a stranger in a tavern?

But she was away from home, and everything she'd thought about herself had gone up in flames this past year. Her belly had warmed with food and the pleasant buzz of her second beer. Emily Murphy would never talk to a man in a bar—but Greg had made sure she didn't feel like Emily Murphy anymore. Changing back to her maiden name would be a formality.

And then the cowboy gave her a slow smile, and she saw the dimples that creased the leanness of his cheeks and the amusement hovering in those grass green eyes. "Yes, ma'am, it's well past my bedtime."

She bit her lip, ready to finish her burger and scurry back to her car, like the old, properly married Emily would have done. But she wasn't that person anymore. A person was made up of what she wanted, and everything Emily had thought she wanted had fallen apart. She was becoming a new woman, an independent woman, who didn't need a husband, or a mother, to make a success of her life.

But tonight, she was also just a single woman in a bar. And who was that hurting if she was? She could smile at a man, even flirt a bit. She wasn't exactly dressed for the part, in her black sweater and jeans, but the cowboy didn't seem to mind looking at her. She felt a flush of reaction that surprised her. How long had it been since she'd felt desirable instead of just empty inside? Too long.

"You'll hear this a lot if you stick around," the cowboy continued, "but you're a stranger around here."

"Yes, I am," she said, taking the last swig of her beer. Her second beer, she thought. "I've just driven from San Francisco."

"Been here before?" he asked.

She grinned as she glanced at the mounted hunting trophies on the walls. "Not right here. But Valentine Valley? Yes, but it's been a long, long time. Since my childhood in fact. So no one will know me."

"Don't worry," he said dryly. "Everyone will make it their business to fix that."

She eased back in her chair, tilting her head as she eyed him. "You don't like that?"

He shrugged. "It's all I've ever known." Leaning his forearms on the table, he said, "Someone waiting for you tonight?"

"No." A little shiver of pleasure stirred deep in her stomach. She wouldn't let herself enjoy this too much. She was a free woman, flirting in a bar to pass the time after an exhausting day. It didn't mean anything. The bartender brought over another beer, and she didn't protest. "None of my family lives here anymore."

For a moment, the cowboy looked as if he would

question that, but instead, he glanced at the bartender. "Tony, since the dartboard's taken, mind if we use the back room?"

Emily gaped at him.

The cowboy grinned as if he could read her mind. "Pool table. Do you play?"

She giggled. Oh, she'd really had too much to drink. But it was dark and raining, and she had no family here, and no one who cared what she did. She got to her feet and grabbed her beer. "Not since college. And I was never good. But if you need a reason to stay up past your bedtime . . ."

His laugh was a pleasurable, deep rumble. As she passed his table, he stood up, and for the first time she got a good look at the size of him, the width of his shoulders thanks to whatever work he did, the flannel shirt open over a dark t-shirt, those snug jeans following long legs down to well-used cowboy boots. *Damn.* He could really work a pair of jeans. And who would have thought she'd find cowboy boots hot? She'd always been drawn to a tailored suit and the subtle hint of a well-paid profession.

The back room was deserted on this stormy night. Low central lights hung over the table, brightly illuminating the playing surface but leaving the corners of the room in the shadows. Emily set her beer down on a nearby table, and the cowboy did the same.

He chose a cue stick. As she was pulling her hair back in a quick ponytail, he turned and came to a stop, watching her. His hungry gaze traveled down her body, and though she realized her posture emphasized her breasts, she didn't stop until her hair was out of her face. It had been so long since a man looked at her with admiration and desire and need. Surely she'd be flustered—if it wasn't for the beer.

She took the cue stick from him and smiled, saying, "Thanks," knowing he'd chosen for himself.

He laughed and put several quarters in the table to release the balls. She watched him, drinking her beer and having a handful of mixed nuts from a basket on the table. Normally, she never would have eaten from food that could have been sampled by anyone. Tonight, it didn't matter. She was a new woman.

"Do you have a name, cowboy?"

He'd been leaning over the table to rack the balls, but he straightened and looked at her from beneath the brim of his hat. "Nate."

No last names. She felt a thrill of danger. "Emily."

"Pretty."

Though she normally would have blushed, this new, adventurous Emily smiled. "Thank you. But then I had no say in it."

"I wasn't talking about your name." His voice was a low drawl, his eyes narrowed and glittering.

Had it gotten warmer in here? she wondered, unable to stop looking at him. Though there were several windows, they were streaked with rain, and it would be foolish to open them. Her sweater felt like it clung to her damply.

"So, Nate," she said brightly, "are you going to take me for all my money?"

"I'm a high roller," he said. "I might bet all of a dollar."

She snorted, then covered her mouth.

"Or I might bet a kiss."

She stared at him, still smiling, playing his game and not thinking. She was so tired of thinking. "Is that the prize if I win or what I owe if I lose?"

He chuckled. "Depends, I guess. Am I worth it?"

She couldn't seem to take a deep enough breath. "I don't know. Guess we'll have to play and find out."

They didn't speak during the game, only watched each other play. Emily had to be honest with herself—she was watching him move. She liked the way his jeans tightened over his butt, how she could glimpse the muscles in his arms when he stretched out over the table. He took his hat off, and the waves in his black hair glinted under the light. The tension between them sizzled, and she wouldn't have been surprised to hear a hiss. They walked about the table, about each other, as if in a choreographed dance of evasion and teasing. This was flirtation as a high art, and he was far better at it than she'd ever been.

But the beer was helping. When it was her turn to lean over the table to line up a shot, she knew he was watching her hips, knew what, as a man, he was thinking. And although she would *never* have sex with a stranger, the thought that he desired her gave her a heady, powerful feeling. This new Emily, in the next stage of her life, could be lusty.

But not with a stranger, she reminded herself.

And then she lost the game, as she knew she would. She still had so many balls on the table as he sank his last one and slowly straightened to look at her.

"I'll take that kiss," he said, coming around the table.

Oh God. She was breathless already, looking up and up into those narrowed green eyes. He stopped right in front of her, her breasts almost touching his chest. She could feel the heat of him, the tension, the tug of danger, but it wasn't exactly him she was afraid of. She was drunk enough that she was afraid what she might do if she tasted him.

But she was also drunk enough to try it. As she stepped forward, their bodies brushed. His inhalation was sexy in itself, letting her know that she could affect him. She waited for him to lean down over her, arched her neck—and then he put his hands on her waist. She gasped as he lifted her off her feet and set her on the edge of the pool table. With wide eyes, feeling breathless, she watched him, unaware that she kept her legs pressed together until he leaned against them.

He smiled, she smiled, and then she parted her knees, holding her breath as he stepped between them. Their faces were almost level.

He leaned in and very lightly touched his lips to hers. "Breathe," he whispered, softly laughing.

She did with a sudden inhalation. What was she supposed to do with her hands? She was beginning to feel nervous and foolish and that she was making a mistake. And then he put his hands on the outside of her thighs and slowly slid them up, past the roundness of her hips to the dip in her waist.

"So delicate," he murmured huskily, and kissed her again.

Part of her had expected a drunken kiss of triumph,

but he took his time, his slightly parted lips taking hers with soft, little strokes. Soon she couldn't keep herself from touching him, sliding her hands up his arms, feeling each ripple of muscle with an answering ripple of desire deep in her belly. Her thighs tightened around his hips, she slid her hands into his hair, then, as one, they deepened the kiss. He tasted of beer, and it was an aphrodisiac on this lost, lonely night. The rasp of his tongue along hers made her moan, and he pulled her tighter against him. She was lost in the heat of him, the feel of his warm, hard body in her arms. He tugged the band from her hair, and it spilled around her shoulders. She had no idea how long they kissed, only reveled in feeling absolutely wonderful. It had been so long.

He leaned over her, and she fell back, body arched beneath him, moaning again as he began to trail kisses down her jaw, then her neck. His big hands cupped her shoulders as he held her in place, her own hands clasped his head to her as if she would never let him go.

Deep inside, a whisper grew louder, that this was wrong. Another languid voice said no, they both wanted this, just a little while longer . . .

His mouth lightly touched the center V of her sweater; his hands cupped her ribs, his thumbs riding the outer curves of her breasts. The anticipation was unbearable; she wanted to writhe even as his hand slid up and over her breast as if feeling its weight. His thumb flicked across her nipple, and she jerked with pleasure. His hips were hard against hers, her legs spread to encompass him . . .

On a pool table, where anyone could walk into the

back room and see them. The thrill of danger and excitement receded as guilt and worry rose up like hot bubbling water.

She was leading him on; he probably thought he could take her home and—

Torn between passion and mortification, she stiffened. "No," she whispered. Then louder, "No, please stop."

His hand froze, his head lifted until their eyes met.

She bit her lip, knowing she looked pathetic and remorseful and guilty. "I can't do this. Our bet was only for a kiss."

As he let his breath out, he straightened, pulling her up with him. He stayed between her thighs, watching her mouth. "Are you sure?" he whispered.

When she nodded, he stepped back as she jumped off the table. She stood there a moment, feeling shaky and foolish.

"I should go," she said, turning away and heading back to the bar.

At her table, she couldn't bear to wait for her bill, knowing that the bartender and the two dart players might have heard her moan. Her face was hot, her hands trembled, and she prayed that the TV had been loud enough. She threw down far more money than was probably necessary, but she just couldn't face the bartender. Grabbing her raincoat off the hook, she ran out into the rain, jumped into her car, and sat there, feeling so stupid. She'd never done anything like that in her life. That man—Nate, she remembered—must think her the worst tease.

After a minute's fumbling in the depths of her purse,

she found her keys and slid them into the ignition. The car tried to turn over several times, but nothing happened. Emily closed her eyes and silently prayed. *Please, not now.*

She turned the ignition again, and although the engine strained once or twice, it wouldn't start. She stared out the rain-streaked windshield at the glowing sign for Tony's Tavern. She couldn't go back in there. Her brain was fuzzy from too much alcohol as she tried to remember what she'd driven past when she left the highway. A motel perhaps? She'd been so worried about her car and the pouring rain and her growling stomach. How far could she walk at midnight in a strange town in a storm?

With a groan, she closed her eyes, feeling moisture from the rain trickle down her neck.

Chapter Two

Nate Thalberg felt perfectly steady on his feet, though still hot under the collar, as he turned off the light in the back room and reentered the bar. Three pairs of eyes fixed on him. Tony De Luca's were the first to drop as he smiled and continued to dry a tall glass before hanging it on the rack above the bar. The other two men, twin brothers Ned and Ted Ferguson, plumbers for Sweet Construction, were a good ten years older than him and long past their pickin'-up-women-in-bars prime. But they still snickered.

Nate ignored them and sat down at the bar. "Another Dale's."

"You might as well head to Aspen if you're going to drink that stuff," Tony said, his usual response. He set the bottle before Nate without another word.

Nate was grateful. He was still aroused and embarrassed and feeling like a fool, all at the same time. He hadn't behaved like that since college, and that was almost ten years ago. Of course, he hadn't left Valentine Valley much since then, and he was careful about picking up a local woman in a bar. He knew them all, and all their relatives. A little fun wasn't worth what would happen the next day, the assumptions of what he owed them, the way they'd look at him as if he were their newly acquired property. Nope, when he went out with a woman, and that happened regularly enough, she knew exactly where she stood with him. And it wasn't on the road to any sort of relationship.

But he'd come into Tony's after a long day riding in the White River National Forest checking the herd. Once it would have been enjoyable to hang with his brother and talk about nothing and everything. But lately, he and Josh had clashed over minor things, and every physical exertion ended up being a contest of wills. It made for a long, frustrating day.

Tonight Nate had needed some peace. He knew Tony could be quiet, at least when he didn't have a hockey stick in his hand. So he'd come to the tavern to enjoy the rest of the baseball game.

Until *she'd* shown up. Emily. Every other man at Tony's had stared at her, however briefly, and he hadn't wanted to be one of those. But she'd had this pink rain-coat on, and when she'd taken it off at the door, her black sweater had ridden up an inch at her waist, and her long strawberry blond hair curled damply near her neck. She was short and curvy in all the right places, and when she'd looked around at the nearly empty bar with wide but tired blue eyes, something in him had paid a bit too much attention.

Remembering how he'd stared at her, unable to stop, he took another swig of beer in disgust. He was weak.

"That should be your last," Tony said, leaning back against the shelf near the cash register. "You have to drive."

Before Nate could take offense, Tony glanced with a frown at the door. "Maybe I should have stopped her, too."

"Emily," Nate said without thinking.

Tony grinned. "At least you got her name. Or did you get more?"

Nate winced and sighed. "Nope. Shouldn't have been trying for more."

"She seemed willing to me."

"And tipsy. I shouldn't have—"

The door jangled, and Nate automatically turned to look. Emily stepped back inside, rain dripping down her coat, her fingers gripping her purse.

Without looking at Nate, she said coolly to Tony, "My car won't start, and I'm not certain who to call for a tow. Could you please give me a name?"

Tony walked to the end of the bar. "Sorry, but Ernie won't come at night if it's not an emergency."

"Oh."

Nate thought she looked blank for a moment, as if it never occurred to her that there were parts of the country where you couldn't have what you asked for twenty-four hours a day.

She took a deep breath, still not glancing at Nate. "Then if you could call me a taxi, I'd appreciate it."

"It's too late," Nate said quietly.

"Pardon me?" She met his eyes at last.

He felt a jolt of need. Damn, but she still affected

him even though he regretted their little game and his lack of control. And then she bit her plump lower lip, making everything worse.

"Only one taxi driver in Valentine Valley," Tony explained with a shrug of his shoulders.

"Let me guess," Emily said with a touch of bitterness. "He only comes at night if it's an emergency."

"She," Nate said reluctantly.

Her posture seemed to slump as she tucked a loose strand of hair behind her ear. He'd smelled that hair, tasted the skin on her neck. He stirred on the barstool, wishing he could adjust himself. And it had been his stupid idea to head back to the pool room.

"Since you're not from around here," Tony said, "there's a motel just down the block."

Nate could see her jaw clench from across the room.

"I own a building in town," she finally said. "I need to get there."

Tony and Nate shared a surprised glance. Both of them knew just about everybody—and every building—in town. Who was this Emily?

"I can drop you off," Nate offered. It was the least he could do.

She studied him, wariness in her narrowed eyes. "If you can tell me how to get—"

"You can't walk there in this," Tony interrupted. "You can trust Nate to take you, regardless of what happened in the back room."

Her eyes shut as she grimaced. Ned and Ted Ferguson gave another matching set of snickers.

Nate frowned. He could see Emily's blush like

a beacon. He glared at the brothers, and they both hunched their shoulders and turned back to the game.

"But first," Tony continued. "I've just brewed a fresh pot of coffee. Nate, how 'bout something to eat?"

He was just about to protest that he was not drunk, but then he remembered kissing a woman he didn't know a thing about. "Sounds good."

· Emily perched on a chair closest to the door. "Thank you. I'll wait."

Tony served him some fajitas with the coffee, and although Nate offered her some, she didn't leave the safety of her chair, making him feel even more like a monster. After a half hour, he quietly said, "Guess it's time to leave, Tony."

Tony smiled and glanced at Emily. "I might have to call you tomorrow."

"There'll be nothing to report." He stood up and slid on his jacket.

Emily waited by the door, wincing as she peered out at the rain.

He opened it and gestured. "After you."

He ran toward the pickup as rain dripped off the edges of his hat. He followed her to open the door, but she veered toward her own car first and tried to lug a suitcase out of the trunk. He grabbed it out of her hand, opened the truck door, and slid it onto the rear bench. She was short enough that she had trouble getting up inside, and he almost boosted her up by the ass but figured she wouldn't appreciate it. He ran to his side and hopped in, and the slam of both doors echoed in the rain-drumming silence. He started the pickup and quickly rolled up the partially opened window, swearing again at the rain that streaked the inside of his door.

At the soft "woof" from the backseat, Emily gave a little cry. Scout stuck his black-and-white nose over the seat and sniffed at her. Nate held back a smile as she sagged against the door with a shudder.

"Afraid of dogs?" he asked.

"No, but he startled me." She eyed Scout. "Does he like strangers?"

"Yep."

She put out her hand, palm up, and within a second, Scout turned traitor and happily licked her before settling down again next to her suitcase on the bench seat.

"What's his name?" she asked.

"Scout."

With a sigh, Emily buckled herself in, then sat facing forward, hands in her lap. When Nate didn't put the truck in gear, she glanced at him with a frown. He could sense the tension as if it were a force field around her.

"So where are you going?" he asked.

"Sorry. Two Oh Four Main Street."

Damn, he knew that building. His luck had definitely run out tonight.

"I'm sorry if I didn't appear grateful for the ride," she began, speaking quickly. "It's just that—"

"You don't know me. I get that."

She didn't look at him, didn't say anything more. He didn't blame her. And she was about to find out some bad news.

Two Oh Four Main Street was less than six blocks away, so the drive didn't take long. In the rain-soaked darkness, he could see nothing but the blurry image of lights along the street, and the flat-fronted buildings nestled side by side along each block of Main Street. There wasn't even a traffic light to slow them down. He pulled into the alley behind the two hundred block. Of the four commercial buildings, three had lights shining above the door to help—but naturally, hers was out. He knew this building, knew it had recently been a small restaurant that had closed down just a few months before.

"Is this it?" she asked, obviously trying not to sound disappointed.

"You really haven't been here since you were a kid?"

She shook her head. "This used to be my grand-mother's store. I was eight when she died. My mother never brought me back after that."

"Did you have the electricity turned on?"

She sighed. "No. I had planned to arrive during the day."

"There's a motel back—"

"No, I need to go in." She unbuckled herself.

With a sigh, Nate brought a flashlight from beneath the seat. She gave him a quick, grateful smile, then jumped down into the rain. Nate glanced over his shoulder at Scout, who panted and watched her curiously.

"I know what you mean, buddy," Nate said. "I'll be back."

When he joined her, she was already shivering, trying to enter a code in a numeric box next to the door. The flashlight helped, and soon she'd removed the keys from the box and was able to unlock the door. He followed her into a little hallway with two doors. He assumed one led upstairs to an apartment, like most of the buildings on Main Street. She used another key on the door directly in front of her and stepped inside. The place smelled musty and unused, but before he could even shine the flashlight around, he heard the squish of his foot stepping in water. *Uh-oh.*

Emily felt the last hope she'd cherished dissolve inside her. As Nate slowly moved the flashlight around the room, she saw that they were in the kitchen of the restaurant. The stainless steel gleamed dully from counters and appliances, and she winced as she saw a splash of paint spattered down the door to the walk-in refrigerator. Holes gaped in the walls, and the sink, with a slow stream of water coming from the tap, had overflowed, leaving the floor wet, although a drain at her feet took the worst of it. Garbage was strewn everywhere, and shelves had toppled.

"Let me check in front," Nate said. "Wait here."

Offended by his peremptory attitude, she reached to take the flashlight, but he didn't see her as he walked away. She gritted her teeth, put her hands on her hips, and waited in the dark until he returned a minute later.

"No sign of a break-in. The restaurant owners were your tenants?" he asked.

"Yes."

"Guess they were mad at you."

"I had to raise the rent after my mother died." She didn't owe him any explanations, especially not since he seemed angry with her over their mistake earlier in the evening.

"They weren't from here," he said.

Maybe he was thinking *Outsiders,* and that she was one, too.

"What did you plan to do here?" he continued. "Open another business?"

"God, no. I need to sell it, but I certainly won't get a good offer like this. I won't be leaving as quickly as I'd hoped."

He remained silent, probably disappointed.

"You can go, Mr.—Nate."

"Thalberg. Nate Thalberg."

"Emily Murphy," she said, knowing their formal introduction was a bit too late.

He hesitated, then said, "I can't leave you like this."

At last she turned to him. His face was in shadows, since the flashlight beam was aimed away from him, but she could see the gleam of his eyes.

"Of course you can leave." She spoke more sharply than she'd intended.

"You're going to *stay* here?" he demanded.

"It's mine." *The last thing I own,* she thought. But it was *hers.* "There's an apartment upstairs."

"And you think it will look any better?"

"Guess I'll go see. Can I use the flashlight?"

He handed it over, then crossed his arms over his chest, obviously planning to wait.

"If I could borrow this until morning . . ." she began.

"The apartment won't look better, Emily, but go ahead and check. I'll wait here."

She went back to the hallway off the alley, used another key while holding the flashlight under her arm, and went upstairs. The smell alone already convinced her, and the debris was just as bad, if not worse. Piles of furniture and boxes were toppled around her, and she couldn't even get a sense of the apartment. It felt like a horror-movie set, where she didn't know what she'd find when the lights were eventually turned on. *What am I supposed to do now?*

Without answers, she trudged back down and found Nate in the hall, waiting for her. She couldn't see his face, with that cowboy hat hiding everything.

"Let's go," he said quietly.

She frowned and opened her mouth to protest.

He took the flashlight back. "I shut off the water. There's nothing else for you here tonight. You can come back tomorrow and see the rest of the damage."

She felt exposed, vulnerable, and suddenly so weary. He'd seen the mess in the restaurant, just as if he'd seen the mess in her life. She couldn't waste the last of her money when she was going to need every dime to fix this place.

"Listen, cowboy," she said firmly, "I know this looks bad, but it isn't up to you to make my decisions for me."

"Is that right?" He tipped up his hat to look her in the eyes.

She suddenly noticed that his drawl had disappeared, and he spoke in crisp, cool tones.

"Well, it's a shame you didn't tell me what you were doing here from the beginning because I could have saved us all this hassle. I do have a say in your decisions"—he briefly looked past her—"or at least my father does, because you don't own this property outright. My dad lent your mother money, and he has a lien on the place. She'd been paying him back over time."

Emily gaped at him, still standing a step up so he couldn't crowd her in the tiny hallway. "You've got to be kidding me."

"I wish I was. I'll tell my father about your arrival and word of your mother's death."

"She died last year!"

"We've been receiving regular payment through a lawyer. If you don't believe me, I'll bring the papers to show you." He sighed. "He would never stand in the way of you selling the building—to an appropriate business, of course."

She felt her face heat. "Excuse me?"

"With how land is selling in Valentine Valley," he continued as if she hadn't spoken, "you'll have no problem getting a decent price, and you'll be able to keep most of it."

Swallowing, she knew it was best to keep her temper until she saw those papers. She'd thought she was on her own, independent at last, and now to find out someone else controlled her, after everything that had happened in her marriage . . . To her mortification, she felt her eyes sting. Thank goodness for the darkness.

Nate was still watching her. She stiffened and met his gaze with what she hoped was a look of cool defiance and a tilt of her chin.

"I'm glad you're being calm and reasonable about this," he said. "That means you'll also understand that you can't stay here tonight. It may be spring, but the nights are cold in the mountains. I have a place you can stay." When she drew in a furious breath, he held up both hands. "Not with me. My grandmother has a boardinghouse for her and all her friends, and I do occasional work for her. There's an empty room right now, and you can stay there until you figure things out."

For a crazy moment, Emily wanted to refuse, to kick him out, to hunker down in the only place that was hers. But common sense intervened at last, and she let out a frustrated breath. "I guess I don't have a choice. I'm sorry you're forced to help me once again."

He didn't answer, just stood looking at her. She was suddenly very conscious of the quiet, of the lateness of the hour, of how very alone they were. Without thinking about where she was, she took an instinctive step back—and hit her heel on the next step and started to fall backward.

He caught both her arms and briefly steadied her. Even that little touch brought back those hot moments when he'd stood between her thighs and kissed her.

"Let's go," he said gruffly, and walked out of the building into the rain.

Emily took a few minutes to lock both interior doors, then the outside one, before running back to the pickup. She received a sniff to the back of the neck from Scout, but she'd been prepared this time.

Without a word, Nate drove slowly down the alley and out onto a street. Within a few minutes, they left behind the twinkling lights of Valentine Valley, and she got the impression of immense darkness rising on one side of the pickup. They were driving closer to the Elk Mountains, if she remembered her map correctly, and they must blot out the stars. After crossing a bridge, they turned and followed the creek for several hundred yards before pulling up in front of a huge old three-story Victorian home. Lights illuminated the wraparound porch, and she could see decorative gingerbread trim. A huge, cheerfully lettered sign read, WIDOWS' BOARDINGHOUSE.

Emily glanced at Nate, raising an eyebrow.

"I didn't name it," he said impassively. "They think it's funny."

Except for the porch lights, there was no illumination in the house. With a glance at the dashboard clock, she realized it was past one in the morning.

"Nate . . ." she began.

"Most of them wear hearing aids, and your room is on the first floor in the back."

"But—"

He got out of the pickup, and this time Scout followed him to do his business at the base of the sign before bounding up on the front porch to watch them alertly. Emily at last got a good look at the dog, all black-and-white irregular patterns in his furry coat, a cute pointed nose that almost looked delicate, and eyes that watched Nate with adoration and readiness.

Like every woman he met, she thought with sarcasm. Herself included.

"Stay, Scout," Nate said, pulling her suitcase out of the pickup and closing the door.

"I can carry my own—"

He strode past her. With a sigh, she followed him onto the porch and all the way around to the rear of the house. After letting himself in with a key, he led her through a neat kitchen, lit only with a dim light above the sink. She thought she could smell the lingering scent of pumpkin pie, and it gave her a stab of home-sickness for the world she'd left behind. She didn't have time to examine the kitchen, her favorite room in any house, but had to follow him through a door and down a small hall to another door. He opened it and turned the light on, leading the way into a small sitting room.

He pointed to a key ring on a table next to the door. "A set of keys for this room and the outside doors. You don't have a private kitchen—this is more of an 'assisted living facility,' or so I've heard people call it. The widows share the kitchen. A woman comes in to do their laundry and the general cleaning. There's a bed-room through that door, and a bathroom beyond. The linen closet will have sheets and towels."

He set down the suitcase and turned to leave.

"Nate!" She caught his arm, and he stopped, look-ing down at her. Her mouth seemed to dry up every time those green eyes captured her, and such weakness made her furious. She'd conquer it if it were the last thing she did. "Thank you, but your grandmother—"

"I'll leave her a note. She'll be tickled pink."

She almost smiled. " 'Tickled pink'?"

"Her words, not mine. We're only about a mile from Main Street, so you'll be able to come and go until your car is fixed."

When he turned away, she called to him once again. "Nate, please!"

He stopped, but only glanced over his shoulder.

"You don't know me," she said tensely. "Why are you doing this?"

"For the sex, of course."

Her mouth fell open.

He sighed and shook his head, looking amused for the first time in several hours. "You're gullible. Hard to believe you're the one from the big city."

"Be serious," she said harshly.

His smile faded. "If my sister found herself in this predicament, I'd want someone to help her. Now go to sleep. You look exhausted."

And, like a stupid teenager, she put a hand to her hair in distress, but he was already gone.

After preparing for bed, she lay a long time staring into the darkness. She didn't want to remember the evening, but every time her eyes drifted closed, she saw the intensity in Nate's face, the hungry way he'd looked at her, like she was the only one who would satisfy him. She could still remember his hand cupping her breast and the pleasurable ache he'd roused in her.

Even though she was ashamed by her drunken behavior, part of her was relieved. At least her ability to feel passion hadn't died with her marriage.

Chapter Three

Nate loved the privacy of the log cabin he'd renovated on the edge of the Silver Creek Ranch, which had been owned by his family for generations. He'd torn down walls, creating a large open living space with a bedroom at the back, and a loft above for his office. Though he spent most of each day at the ranch, his free evenings were in his own private sanctuary, where he seldom invited women.

But the cabin had one drawback: it was within a half mile of the boardinghouse, and tonight that was too close. He was already imagining Emily getting ready for bed, and wondered what she wore, or if she wore anything at all . . .

Stop it, he told himself.

Scout took up his customary perch on the back of a couch up against the window, where he could look out over his domain. Nate smiled and ruffled between the dog's ears, making Scout pant and look up at him with adoration. A dog only wanted affection, and that was so easy to return.

With a sigh, Nate turned away. He should get to bed,

for the next day would be another long one. He was getting less and less sleep each night. Preparations for the Silver Creek Rodeo, run by his family, were heating up, and there were always the day's chores at a cattle ranch. Instead, he paced, remembering Emily, and the way she'd insisted on going to her building instead of a motel. She really would have stayed in that unheated mess if he hadn't insisted she leave. And all of that told him she was desperate, with little money and nowhere else to go. When he felt his sympathy being churned up again, he should have run the other way.

Instead, he'd put her with his grandmother and her friends, the town busybodies. They knew everything and everyone. Certainly, they could inform Emily all about her mother's family. But they could also discuss Nate. And he didn't want to be a topic of conversation, especially not after the way he'd behaved tonight at Tony's Tavern.

After undressing, he stepped into the shower to remove the tantalizing scent of Emily still on his clothes, on his skin. If only cold water could remove memories.

It was still dark when Emily awoke at the beep of her cell-phone alarm. She didn't hit snooze but sat right up. For just a moment, she'd thought she was at home, but she didn't have a home anymore. Greg had remained in their elegant apartment in San Francisco, close to his law firm in Nob Hill, and she'd found a temporary little sublet across the bay. She'd been so furious with him, so disappointed and heartbroken at his betrayal, she hadn't wanted to be tied to him in any way, so she'd refused alimony—his guilt money.

Sometimes it seemed like *every* decision she made led to a mistake. She'd fallen in love with Greg, a law student, while she'd been in college, and when he graduated, she quit school to marry him. She'd never enjoyed school although she'd gotten good grades, and had only gone to college because it seemed the thing to do. After her crazy upbringing, all she'd ever wanted was to be a wife, to make a home, to have a family. She still had warm memories of her father, Jacob Strong, the scent of his aftershave when he hugged her, how special she felt when he exclaimed over every art project she brought home from school. She'd dreamed of re-creating those simple but heartfelt moments for her own family.

But after her dad's death, her mom had spent most of her time on her new age shop and the various men in her life, making Emily feel . . . inconvenient. It was how she had first discovered she loved to cook, for fast food or late meals had grown irritating. Delilah often forgot to come home to make dinner after work. But at least she always spent nights at home, and never at some guy's place. It had taken Emily until adulthood to appreciate that. Her mom always said she wished she'd been born early enough to be a hippie, so she lived the life, from practicing reiki to insisting Emily call her "Delilah," not Mom or even "Dorothy," the name she'd been born with.

It had all come to a head for Emily on the opening night of her school musical. She had the lead, the youngest ever at fifteen, and thought for sure she'd given her mom a reason to be proud of her, a reason to care. But her mom hadn't remembered to come. Every other kid had a parent—hell, a whole family—meet them backstage with flowers and hugs and praise. Delilah could charm a forget-me-not blossom and keep it in her purse to remember a date with a man, but her daughter's musical was not that important. Emily had stood alone, feeling as if the last joy in her accomplishment was crushed beneath her mother's indifference. She was achingly alone, would always be—until she made her own family. That had become her guiding force through the rest of high school and into college.

She thought she'd succeeded with Greg, a man whose extended family made her feel included. For several years, she'd given elegant dinners for their friends and the partners at Greg's firm. Greg's family lived on the opposite coast, and year after year, he couldn't find vacation time to visit them. At first, she pretended not to see that she'd exchanged one lonely life for another. She volunteered at the local hospital, crocheted blankets for premature babies, and occasionally worked as an emergency backup for her friend's catering business by baking desserts and pastries, waiting for the day she had a baby.

But that day never came, and her marriage fell apart in ways that still hurt too much to think about, a well of grief so raw it was a physical ache. She'd lost her baby and her husband and her dreams all within a week. Emily had known she had to find a way to support herself, but each day she could barely get out of bed. She was skirting the edges of depression, replaying the tragedy of her marriage and Greg's cruelty over and over again in her mind. Her money running out had finally awakened her to the pitiful excuse her life had become, the way she wallowed in self-pity. Though Greg was gone, she was still letting him control her. She didn't need a man to create her own family.

But she did need a career, something she'd so conveniently ignored when she was head over heels in love with Greg. College just hadn't seemed important—but it was important now. She'd already registered for the fall semester back at UC Berkeley. She had to find a way to support herself even though she didn't have a clue what to major in. That was what advisors were for. Perhaps her two years' worth of credits would still count for something.

When she sold her mother's building, she'd use that money to pay her tuition. Once gainfully employed, she would save enough to adopt. She'd gone the husband route, and it had failed. But there were plenty of children around the world desperate to be part of a family.

She thought she'd taken control of her life by coming to Valentine Valley, but on the first night, she made out with a stranger, her car wouldn't start, and she had found that her building was severely damaged. It was as if life was giving her a good kick for her efforts.

She wasn't going to let "life" get away with it. Sitting up, she threw back the covers with determination. She'd had a couple setbacks, that was all. She would lay out a plan to repair her building as quickly as possible. Her future was waiting for her.

But in the present, she was a stranger in a home with elderly women who hadn't even been consulted about the arrangement. Nate Thalberg had made decisions for everybody.

But he'd also given her a place to stay for the night, and she would force herself to feel gratitude instead of resentment that she hadn't been able to do that for herself.

As for the ladies, she only had one way to show her gratitude, and that was in the kitchen. After a quick shower, she dressed again in a long-sleeve t-shirt and jeans. After reading the note Nate had left for his grand-mother in the formal dining room—it was short and to the point, but didn't make her sound too pathetic—she went to take stock of the pantry. The kitchen itself was full of windows to let in the rising sun, a little break-fast nook, oak cabinets that gleamed, and a decorative theme of . . . cows. There were bowls of fruit deco-rated with black-and-white cow spots, two lowing cows held up napkins, horns sprouted near the back door for hanging jackets. Cows everywhere. It made Emily smile. If Nate was a cowboy, perhaps his whole family was involved.

The house remained quiet as, from memory, she began to assemble muffins and banana bread on the spacious granite countertops, then started a pot of coffee while they baked.

With twenty minutes to spare, she stepped outside onto the porch, rubbing her arms at the brisk chill, then catching her breath in wonder. The mountains loomed above her, so high and magnificent and close that they didn't seem real. Snow dusted the peaks even as spring had brought out the green below the tree line. During the drive up, she'd gaped up at the towering peaks and narrow canyons, finding it difficult to concentrate on her driving. But now she was in a wide valley between two mountain ranges, carved out over time by the Roaring Fork River, according to her map. The Silver Creek in Valentine joined with the river down valley. She could see farm fields with high stalks of some kind of grain stretching off into the distance, and a glimpse of what might be a red-roofed ranch house, but no cows.

Emily let the beautiful scene bring her a moment's peace, then went back inside, knowing she had a long day ahead of her. To her shock, the baking was a disaster. She should have realized something was wrong when the batter seemed too thick. The muffins were flattened when she pulled them out of the oven, and the bread was still batter at the bottom of the pan, though the top seemed done.

She was glaring at her creations when she heard someone enter the room. She turned about, and to her relief, it wasn't Nate but three elderly ladies, one leaning on a walker, another clapping her hands together with excitement, the third holding Nate's note.

"Good morning!" said the cheerful one with the note. "I'm Grandma Thalberg. You must be Emily."

Emily smiled cautiously. "How nice to meet you."

Mrs. Thalberg had the reddest shade of curly hair Emily had ever seen. She wore a battery of makeup, though skillfully applied, and a colorful housecoat and slippers. She introduced her companions. Mrs. Ludlow, the trim, white-haired lady leaning on her walker, was already dressed for the day in slacks and a bright blue blouse. Mrs. Palmer, plump and vibrant in a paisley dress, pearls, and what must be a blond wig, nodded at Emily and began to wash dishes.

"Oh no!" Emily said quickly. "Breakfast is my way of thanking you for allowing me to spend the night. You mustn't clean up. Not that I've made much of a treat . . ." She trailed off, embarrassed.

Mrs. Thalberg glanced at Emily's failed muffins and banana bread. "Oh dear, let me guess—you've never baked at altitude before."

Emily smacked her forehead. "I never thought of that! I've seen it mentioned on boxed mixes, but I never cook with those."

"They'll still taste lovely," Mrs. Ludlow said kindly.

"Not the banana bread. It's practically batter at the bottom."

Mrs. Palmer broke out the aluminum foil. "We'll cover it and cook it a bit longer. Next time, use a tube pan. We swear by it!"

Emily stared around her as the ladies—widows all? she wondered—began to bring out china and silverware. She didn't know where anything was, so she brought out the milk and butter.

Then they sat down at the table in the sunny corner of the kitchen and looked at her expectantly. Emily sank down opposite them. They exclaimed over her flattened muffins until at last Emily tried one. They weren't horrible, but she was known for her baking talents, and this was just upsetting.

Mrs. Thalberg gave a kindly smile. "I'd love to give you the little baking tips we mountain dwellers have learned from childhood."

"That's so kind of you, Mrs. Thalberg, but I won't be in town very long."

Mrs. Ludlow elegantly patted her lips with a cloth napkin. "Where are you in such a hurry to return?"

"San Francisco, ma'am. I was born and raised there, and I'm going back to college this fall."

"Good for you. Nate says your mother was born in Valentine Valley." Mrs. Thalberg shook her head even as she clucked her tongue. "But he didn't say her *name,* the silly boy. Yours is Murphy, but that's not familiar to me."

"I'm divorced," Emily said, trying not to feel humiliation, her constant companion these last six months before she'd realized her future could only begin with her. "My mother's maiden name was Riley."

Mrs. Palmer, who kept straightening things on the table as if she couldn't sit still, now froze. "Agatha Riley was your grandmother?"

Mrs. Thalberg gasped, and Mrs. Ludlow put a hand to her heart.

"Yes." Emily felt a sudden warm glow as she realized these ladies had known her grandmother, and it was as if they had opened up a connection to a past when she still had a family. "She died when I was eight, so I don't remember her well."

"Agatha Riley was such a treasure," Mrs. Thalberg gushed, patting Emily's hand. "You look like her!"

Emily felt a flush of warmth.

"That lovely shade of strawberry blond hair," Mrs. Thalberg continued. "I was always so jealous."

Emily hid a smile as she regarded the flaming color the old lady had chosen.

"She was a teacher before she married, and loved children," Mrs. Thalberg continued. "I always thought it such a shame she only had one herself. When her husband died, she took over the general store and seemed to find a new calling."

Mrs. Ludlow sighed. "A shame she sometimes had such terrible arguments with her daughter." Then her eyes widened as if she suddenly remembered she was discussing Emily's mother. "Oh dear."

Emily smiled. "I know everything about my mother, Mrs. Ludlow, so you're not offending me." She wished she could change the subject, for thinking about her mother was something she seldom did. She didn't want to imagine Delilah growing up in this town, worrying her own mother endlessly. However, had Delilah discovered her passion for a Wiccan lifestyle in Valentine Valley?

"We often wondered how she supported herself," Mrs. Thalberg said quietly. "She left Valentine at such a young age."

"But don't you remember?" Mrs. Palmer said, waving both wrinkled hands. "Agatha told us that Dorothy started her own business. Imagine that!"

"She changed her name to Delilah," Emily said, shaking her head.

"How exotic!" Mrs. Palmer exclaimed.

For the first time, Emily thought of her mother from

someone else's viewpoint, and knew that with little education, her mother had provided for her, and in an expensive city, no less. But that didn't make up for the simpler things she'd lacked, a mother's love, an interest in her life. There were no school paintings taped to the refrigerator at the Strong house, at least not after her dad died. He'd left his favorites up so long—the Hall of Fame, he'd called them—that they yellowed at the edges. Emily still had a vivid memory of her mother throwing them away, stone-faced, right after her father's death.

"Nate wrote that your mother died, and you've come back to sell the family building," Mrs. Thalberg said, watching her too closely. "How did she die? She was far too young."

"A car accident," Emily replied, feeling a twinge of regret. "It was very sudden, but she didn't suffer."

They offered condolences, then sat for a moment, nodding, their silence respectfully spiritual, as if they were kneeling in church.

"You lost her too soon," Mrs. Thalberg said, "but it's obvious she raised a fine girl."

Sometimes Emily believed she raised herself, but she wouldn't say that aloud. She'd been doing her own laundry by the time she was eight. At least it made her self-sufficient.

"We were sad that Dorothy—Delilah—didn't return when she sold this house," Mrs. Palmer said.

Emily stared at her. "Excuse me?"

"Ah, then you don't remember visiting here at all?"

Mrs. Thalberg chimed in. "This was Agatha's home while she lived."

"For some reason, I thought she lived above the store," Emily said slowly.

"No, no, she rented out that apartment," Mrs. Ludlow said, picking up the tale. "After she died, your mother arranged to sell this old house to the Thalbergs."

"I always liked it," Mrs. Thalberg said in a confidential tone. "Agatha and I were close neighbors, of course, and time and again I told her if she ever wanted to sell, she should come to us."

Close neighbors? Emily thought, not remembering seeing any houses on the near side of the creek. "Oh, the ranch!" she said, smiling. "So that's your family ranch behind us?"

"The Silver Creek Ranch," she said with pride. "My husband's grandfather came to Colorado when they were mining silver in the 1880s. Someone had to provide food for all those miners, so he started running cattle. When the silver went bust, it was the ranches and farms that kept this valley going."

"And then Aspen became so popular," Mrs. Ludlow said with a sigh. "Things changed around here. Lots of new people."

"Things always change," Mrs. Palmer said firmly. "We change or die."

"But Renée, the price of land!" Mrs. Ludlow protested. "My granddaughter works in Aspen, and she can't even afford to live there."

"So she lives in Basalt, which is closer to us, Connie."

Mrs. Thalberg patted her friend's arm. "And isn't that a blessing?"

Mrs. Ludlow gave a slow smile and whispered to Emily, "Don't tell my granddaughter that I agree with Rosemary about anything."

Emily smiled, then turned to Mrs. Thalberg. "It was very kind of Nate to allow me to spend the night, but you ladies don't know me, and I feel like I'm imposing."

"Nonsense!" Mrs. Thalberg said with a grin. "This house is as much his as mine since my son owns it. And not know you? You're Agatha's granddaughter, and that's good enough for me. Nate must think you're special to bring you here."

All three women leaned toward her, and Emily almost leaned back. "We only met briefly last night. I stopped for dinner, and then my car broke down. Nate took me to the building, but . . ." She trailed off, not knowing how to explain the condition in which she had found things.

Mrs. Palmer's eyes narrowed. "That little restaurant closed without any notice. I never did trust those people. They didn't make friends—"

"Which is very foolish for a restaurant needing customers," Mrs. Ludlow interrupted. "And they would set trash outside their back door rather than take it right to the Dumpster. Unsightly."

"Well, they weren't nice people," Emily said, "judging by the condition they left the building. I'll have a lot of cleaning and repairing to do before I can sell it."

"You don't want to keep it for yourself?" Mrs. Thalberg asked, studying her. "Or rent it out again?"

"That's too difficult from San Francisco. And I need

to finish my degree, so the money will come in handy."

All three ladies nodded.

Then Mrs. Thalberg's eyes twinkled as she said, "Nate lives just down the road."

Back to Nate again, Emily thought, forcing a smile even as she was trying to control a blush. If these sweet old ladies knew what she'd been doing with him on top of a pool table . . .

She excused herself to remove the banana bread from the oven. The top was overdone, but when she cut several steaming slices, it didn't look too bad. She sat down and offered everyone some, then buttered herself a slice.

"Connie," Mrs. Thalberg said to Mrs. Ludlow, "did you know Nate remodeled this house all by himself?"

"I did not," Mrs. Ludlow exclaimed, blinking with feigned astonishment. "He's very talented."

As if Mrs. Thalberg would ever keep that a secret, Emily thought, biting her lip to hide a smile. She kept her gaze innocent and polite.

"And when you see that boy on a horse, you know God meant him to ride."

Mrs. Palmer nodded solemnly. "He's so devoted to the family ranch."

And he gets drunk and tries to seduce strange women, then gets mad when he's rejected, Emily thought with a touch of sarcasm. She sighed, knowing she'd been "strange" enough to allow it. And not just allow, but participate with hungry enthusiasm.

"He renovated the cabin, too," Mrs. Thalberg said, nodding. "It's one of the original buildings on the ranch, and he made it so cozy."

"And he takes such good care of us," Mrs. Palmer intoned solemnly.

They might as well call him Saint Nate.

"But he doesn't only work hard," Mrs. Thalberg continued, oblivious to Emily's discomfort. "He knows what it's like to enjoy himself."

Emily coughed on a piece of banana bread, and Mrs. Palmer whacked her on the back.

"He snowboards, of course—don't all the young people?" Mrs. Thalberg beamed. "And he still rides a bike—up on that mountain that towers over our heads! Ever since high school, where he played so many sports, it's like he's a daredevil. Now it's climbing rocks." She shook her head, tsking.

"They do what makes them happy," Mrs. Ludlow said with a sigh. "Look at my granddaughter—she drives a snowmobile too fast!"

The discussion degenerated into the dangerous mountain sports each of their grandchildren participated in, and Emily used their distraction to finish the dishes and find plastic containers for the food. She needed to escape the Nate festival, and she desperately wanted to see her building in broad daylight.

When at last the ladies noticed that she'd come to stand next to the table, Emily said, "Mrs. Thalberg, I'm going into Valentine today. Are there any errands I can run for you ladies? I don't know what time I'll be back . . ."

"I'll drive you!" Mrs. Thalberg insisted, rising to her feet in her housecoat and slippers.

"No, ma'am, I truly need the exercise. And it's not far, not even a mile."

"Well, that's true . . ." she said, still looking concerned.

"It's a beautiful day, and I'll enjoy being outside before being cooped up for the rest of the day."

They still looked concerned when Emily emerged from the small apartment with her purse and a backpack with a few supplies.

"Promise you won't work too hard." Mrs. Thalberg offered her a bottle of water.

Emily took it and smiled, already enjoying the company of these three women. "I won't. And thank you again for welcoming me into your home. I promise to look into a room at the motel today, too."

"No!" all three ladies said at once.

"We will not hear of it," Mrs. Thalberg said firmly, in the tone of voice of a woman used to being in command.

Emily remembered that she'd probably been actively involved at the ranch for many years.

"We're enjoying getting to know Agatha's granddaughter," Mrs. Ludlow added smoothly. "You cannot deny us that."

"Every day is always the same." Mrs. Palmer spread her hands.

Looking at the ladies, Emily doubted that. "Then I insist you allow me to pay rent."

Mrs. Thalberg smiled in triumph. "We'll think about it. Have a good day!"

With a wave, Emily went out the back door, shaking her head at how easily they'd maneuvered her. As she walked down the driveway to the gravel road, she glanced about worriedly, wondering if she could see Nate's cabin—if he could see her. But wherever it was, it was well hidden. She relaxed, letting the scenery bring a moment's peace. Silver Creek rushed along, muddy and turbulent, close to the height of its banks. This was springtime, and the runoff from the mountains must affect every river and stream. Across the creek, she could see the buildings of Valentine Valley, most only one or two stories tall. Between the creek and the town, a park ran along the banks, scattered with picnic pavilions, playgrounds, and a couple hundred yards down, a large white gazebo.

As Emily reached the bridge, the road she was on continued sloping up toward the mountain, and across the green rise were scattered the jutting gray headstones of a cemetery. She was tempted to go peek at the dates on the stones, then reminded herself that she had a purpose. After crossing the bridge, a couple blocks ahead of her she could see the tall stone building with a clock tower that must be city hall. With its back to the towering cliffs of the mountains, it presided over the town. When she reached it, she saw she was on Main Street, and turned down toward her building.

She walked past the storefronts butting against one another for several long blocks. A beautiful old theater marquee advertised a forties movie festival that weekend. Clapboard storefronts with bay windows on each side of front doors alternated with sandstone edifices with arches rainbowing over windows. Planters over-flowing with spring flowers lined the sidewalks, and US flags hung from the antique light poles in a long line down the street. She passed a local history museum, a toy and gift shop, restaurants, and the Open Book, a corner bookstore that made her peer longingly in the windows. She could see the beautiful white steeple of a church rising from behind the Main Street buildings.

Villagers swept the sidewalks in front of their stores and greeted her, leaving her a little surprised. In San Francisco, no one looked at passersby, and now she felt on display, as if everyone knew her secrets. For all she knew, Nate Thalberg could have bragged to his buddies about the fun time he'd had at Tony's Tavern. But no, that was too cynical of her, especially toward a man who'd given her a safe place to stay. Surely the businesspeople of Valentine Valley thought her just another tourist, and there were plenty of those, people taking pictures of the town hall framed by the Elk Mountains, or of the long row of flat-fronted stores painted various pastel colors. Young lovers—and those not so young—were everywhere, holding hands and looking about with delight. In a town named Valentine, she saw plenty of hearts and cupids and red accents.

Her own storefront restaurant was shuttered and dark, looking so forlorn between Wine Country and Monica's Flowers and Gifts. It was still too early for them to be open, so she took a moment to admire the Hotel Colorado across the street, three stories with arched columns running the length of the block, like a grand old duchess, with sparkling glimpses of its youth. She tried to imagine all of this in the nineteenth century, when the wide dirt street would have been teeming with mule trains, and the hotel full of newly rich miners, come down from the mountains to enjoy themselves. Okay, so she'd done her research before driving up.

But she couldn't delay any longer, regardless of the sunshine and the beautiful spring day. She had to face something ugly and deliberately ruined, and she reminded herself that this was not an omen of her future. It was like her marriage, something she could eventually put in the past as a bad memory. Taking out her keys, she tried the front door. The lock turned with a little effort, and she went inside, tripping almost immediately over a toppled table in the gloom. She opened one of the shutters partway, not wanting people to be able to see the disaster.

And then she sighed. A corner bar that would have once served drinks was now spattered with paint, as if someone had just tossed an open container. Every upended table and chair seemed to be missing legs. The mirror that lined one wall to make the room seem more open had giant cracks running through it, like an ancient face. And someone must have taken a sledgehammer to the walls. Even the trim and baseboards had been gouged. The security deposit they'd forfeited was miniscule compared to all this.

Emily could have cried.

But she was done crying. It had gotten her nowhere, solved none of her problems. She didn't even know where her tenants had gone, and she could hardly afford a private investigator to find them. She could do this on her own; she'd pull out her notebook and start her lists: jobs to be done, supplies to be purchased, repairs to be made. She didn't have the money to hire someone, so she would do it herself. With access to the Internet, she could learn how to do anything.

But first, the electricity. She placed a call, glad that her cell phone worked, when she knew reception could be spotty in the mountains. To her dismay, the power company couldn't give her an appointment for another three days, much as she tried to explain the circumstances. They compromised on two days, but that was it. At least the days were growing longer, so she could work when the sun was up.

She took out her notebook and spent an hour cataloging the damages and making her to-do lists. After discovering a Dumpster in the back alley, she began dragging out the worst of the garbage, trying to clear a path from the front of the restaurant to the kitchen. She was so engrossed in her chores, she didn't hear the front door open until a dog's bark alerted her.

She whirled around in surprise and saw Nate Thalberg grimacing as he looked about, and Scout, off leash, nosing into a pile of garbage. Nate's cowboy clothes had been replaced with loose shorts, sneakers, and a t-shirt that outlined his biceps as he held the door open. She could berate herself for the previous night, but damn, she couldn't fault her choice of men. Yet he'd seen her at her worst, offering herself to him in a way she'd never done with any man before. And he'd accepted it all, as if he was used to women throwing themselves at him. He made her feel flustered even though she was sober. She'd never been nervous around people, always the gracious host and volunteer. But with him, she didn't know how to behave or what to say.

Stiffening, she tried to think about being polite and neutral, hoping he'd leave. She looked a mess after all, sweaty, disheveled, and covered in dust and dirt. But then his eyes locked on her, and suddenly she was back in the bar, his mouth on hers, his hands making her feel like a woman once again.

Chapter Four

*Nate hadn't thought the destruction in the old restau-*rant could look any worse in the daylight, but he'd been wrong. It was as if a demon had been set loose. He was tempted to haul Scout back by the collar. But there was Emily, wide-eyed and lovely, the dirt streaking her face evidence of the work she'd already put in that morning.

And there was that thin t-shirt, clinging to her damply.

Emily lifted a hand before he could speak. "You don't need to remind me. I promise to be out of your grandmother's hair quickly. Now you can go on and"—she tilted her head and spotted his mountain bike leaning against the front of the building, helmet dangling from the handle—"ride your bike, knowing you've put the fear of God into me. Is this how cowboys get around in the mountains now?"

He frowned. "Grandma likes to meet new people. She called me right after you left to say you'd been *so sweet* to them. Hard to believe right now."

He hadn't meant to antagonize her, especially since he felt uncomfortable about all the work she had in store for herself. But from the moment he'd laid eyes on her, she'd drawn him like steel to a magnet, and he knew he had to pull away. Her building wasn't his problem—*she* wasn't his problem, he reminded himself.

Her chin came up, and those sky blue eyes glittered. "Your grandmother is a lovely person."

Unlike you, seemed to be her unspoken words.

"And I am grateful to her for agreeing to let me *briefly* stay there," she continued. "I have offered to pay rent."

He rolled his eyes.

"You think I haven't?" she asked icily.

He held up a placating hand. "No, I just know my grandmother. Taking care of you will make her day."

"I don't need to be taken care of."

He said nothing, hoping that was true.

She put her hands on her hips. "Did you just come by to annoy me or to watch me work and have a good laugh at my expense?"

"I haven't laughed," he said. She was touchy, but he couldn't blame her. This was damn awkward between them.

"So you meant to annoy. Why are you checking up on me? Here are the details, if you absolutely need them. My building is a disaster that will take weeks to repair and keep me here even longer. They can't turn the electricity on for two days, so my hours are limited, further lengthening my time in Valentine Valley. Oh— and my car needs to be towed. Does that satisfy all your questions?"

Nothing the two of them said to each other was

going to work after their abrupt encounter last night. "Look," he said with a sigh, "I didn't come to check up on you. I just wanted to tell you I had your car towed to Ute Auto Repair, which is at the gas station at the end of Main Street back by the highway. They'll give you an estimate. You can trust them."

He was at least gratified to see her hostile expression turn wide-eyed before she winced at his news about her car.

"Let me get my purse and pay you for the towing. I don't want to owe you after last night."

"Owe me?" he said in disbelief. "You think I'll hold that little bit of money over your head to get something out of you?"

She looked so mutinous, he knew he'd hit the nail on the head. And he deserved her suspicion.

"Look, I'm sorry about everything. I've got to go ride my little bike up into those tall mountains and try not to slide on my face in the springtime mud. But you have a pleasant day."

Then he turned around and strode out the door, whistling for Scout.

Emily clapped both hands over her face, wondering how many times her own behavior could mortify her. He'd done her another favor, on top of all the others. This, after he'd been so angry that she'd turned him down last night. She must be giving off a very needy vibe. She didn't want to be that woman!

Or had he simply been drunk and angry, just like she'd been drunk and a tease? She didn't want to contemplate that, didn't want to think too nicely about

him. She wasn't in Valentine Valley to make friends
with men.

"Hello?"

Emily gasped and stumbled over a broken chair.

"I'm so sorry!"

Emily looked up to see a pretty, young, black woman
with shoulder-length curls framing her elegant face
like sunbeams. With her high cheekbones and slightly
slanted eyes, she could have been a model. Instead, she
was dressed casually in capris, sandals, and a sleeveless blouse, as if she was anticipating summer to arrive
momentarily.

The woman reached toward her as Emily stumbled
over another chair. "Can I help you?"

Emily pushed the chair aside. "Only if you want to
get filthy."

The woman grinned. "I wouldn't mind a little dirt
for a good cause. But what I really want to do is meet
the person who put that thundercloud on Nate Thalberg's face."

Emily felt her cheeks heat up. "It wasn't exactly in-
tentional, but I can't seem to help it. We . . . don't get
along." She sighed. "I'm Emily Murphy."

"Monica Shaw. I own the flower shop next door."

"Monica's Flowers and Gifts. I thought your window
displays looked adorable, all decorated for spring. The
crocheted flower baby caps were an inspired idea." And
had made her positively ache, remembering her own
baby's kicks, the way she'd held her belly between both
hands, as if she were already trying to protect the little
girl. But she hadn't been able to protect her from what-

ever whims of fate had chosen to curse Emily. And there would never be another baby inside her. After a shaky start, Emily was dealing with it the best way she could.

"The crafts are part of the 'and Gifts,' " Monica continued. "Tourists are really into the romance thing in Valentine Valley, and babies are a natural result. I take in local craft products on a consignment basis."

"Another inspired idea," Emily said, stepping over junk on the floor to approach the other woman. Though she had work to do, she wouldn't rudely ask the woman to leave.

"They sell," Monica said with a smile and a shrug. "My craft partners and I all end up happy. Wedding-bed quilts are my number one selling item—after my flowers," she added self-deprecatingly.

"I only just arrived last night, so I haven't had a chance to wander around. Guess wedding items make sense for tourists in Valentine."

"Oh, you have no idea. We're sort of famous around here for romance. Many a love affair has blossomed here. Haven't you seen all the lovers holding hands?"

"I did notice a few."

"And the proposals? Girl, I swear there's one every other day at the gazebo, or the stone bridge in the Rose Garden. The demand for Valentine Valley postmarks on wedding invitations keeps our post office over-worked. And luckily, they always want flowers. I'm not complaining, you understand."

"I understand." Emily reluctantly smiled, feeling more and more lured in by Monica's cheerfulness.

"So you only arrived in town last night?"

Emily explained her plans to sell the building.

Monica looked around sympathetically. "Those people were assholes, and I didn't need to see this disaster to know that. They had flower arrangements for their tables shipped in from *Aspen*! Like I can't get flowers just as good thirty miles down the road. More expensive in Aspen, that's for certain. No wonder they went under."

Emily didn't mention the slight increase in the rent.

"Sorry to see you have all this work ahead of you," Monica said. "Are you hiring help?"

Emily hesitated. "Not right now."

If Monica grasped Emily's financial predicament, she didn't give any indication of pity, which Emily appreciated.

"You'll do a fine job of it," Monica continued.

"You can tell that already?" Emily sarcastically spread her hands wide, indicating the state of the building.

"Come on, let's sit outside. My break is almost over, and I want to enjoy the sun."

Emily knew she shouldn't, but her back was aching, along with her feet, so she followed Monica outside. There were wrought-iron benches beneath the plate-glass windows on either side of the front door, perhaps meant for customers waiting for a table. Emily sat down beside Monica, stretched out her legs with a sigh, and lifted her face for the sun's warmth.

"So how do Nate and his bad mood come into this?" Monica asked.

Emily glanced at the woman, noticing her amusement, praying that the story of her conduct hadn't spread beyond the tavern. She didn't want to discuss her business with a stranger but found the words tumbling tiredly from her lips. "I stopped for a meal at Tony's Tavern when I got in late last night. Then my car wouldn't start. Tony vouched for Nate, who offered me a lift. I tried to go to a motel—"

"With Nate?" Monica interrupted, then clapped a hand over her mouth, eyes wide.

"No!" Emily said too fervently, praying she hadn't started a new rumor. "Just me. But he insisted on taking me to the Widows' Boardinghouse, where there's an extra room."

Monica grinned. "You know that's practically a senior living home."

"I do," Emily said. "But they were very kind to me, and since they knew my grandmother, they're insisting I remain there while I'm in Valentine. But once the upstairs apartment is ready, I'll be moving in here."

"Your family is from here?"

Emily briefly explained about her grandparents owning the building and her mother leaving right out of high school. "Once my grandmother died, we never came back. I don't remember much at all about the town." She refixed her ponytail in anticipation of returning to work. "So anyway, that's my only connection to Nate. Now I should get back inside—" She started to rise.

Monica whistled. "He's some kind of man."

Sitting back down, Emily willed herself not to blush

and tried to find a noncommittal response. "Is he?" She sounded a little too sarcastic.

Monica's focus on her sharpened, but she only said, "Every girl in town has been after him at one time or another. There aren't many who catch him, and when they do, it's brief and fun and over."

"Including you?" Emily pressed, unable to help herself.

"No way. Sadly, I got brother vibes from him the moment I was old enough to notice my own brother's friends."

Emily couldn't help smiling, even as she told herself to leave. But the sun's warmth seemed at last to be settling in her bones, and being with Monica was strangely relaxing. In San Francisco, she'd been so wrapped up in Greg that she'd never made time for girlfriends. Her college friends had been too busy being single and pursuing school, making it hard for them to understand the choice she'd made to marry. Greg didn't have time to go out "with the girls," and her excuses soon no longer were necessary. At the time, she thought she'd been making the right decision to let her friends go, so that they wouldn't feel guilty when they attempted to reach out. But she'd made a terrible mistake. A woman didn't need just a husband, she needed friends, people to rely on or to comfort in turn. And she'd foolishly taken those friendships for granted. It made her almost wistful for what she'd missed. Not that she'd be here long enough to make friends.

On the sidewalks, the tourists had multiplied in the last few hours, and she now paid attention to the couples since Monica had pointed it out. Valentine Valley had its own specialty theme just from the name.

Emily almost groaned as she turned her feet in little circles, stretching her aching ankles. "All those people in love must flock to your store to buy flowers."

"They do," Monica said with an exaggerated sigh, then grinned. "And I love it. Hey—have you had lunch yet?"

"No, I haven't. Perhaps you can recommend a casual place." A cheap place. There must be a grocery store someplace close to buy sandwich fixings.

"We'll do lunch one of these days, I promise, but I can't go out today. I'm manning the store alone."

"Oh, I'm sorry!" She couldn't start doing lunch, but at least that was an excuse to get back to work. "Here I've kept you away."

"Trust me, I've had my eye on the store the whole time. No customers at the moment. They're probably all eating lunch. Care to join me?"

Emily opened her mouth, not wanting to be rude, but not knowing how to escape the kind offer. "Oh, but you only made enough for yourself. That would be a terrible imposition."

"Nah, I made a big salad, and I always keep cheese sticks and almonds in the store for emergency snacks."

"Oh, but here comes a customer," Emily said with relief. It would be too easy to get caught up with someone as friendly as Monica.

Monica turned her head and saw the hassled-looking young man enter her store. "I'll take care of him, then bring out lunch. The day is too beautiful to waste."

Emily was about to object, then had a change of heart. What was the point of being rude? She had to eat, didn't she? She forced each muscle to relax one at a time after the stress of the last few days. When Monica returned, they spread out the feast between them and began to eat.

"So why are you working alone today?" Emily asked, after pouring ranch dressing across the top of her salad. "Surely you're busy this time of year."

"Spring and fall aren't usually the busy seasons up in the mountains. We get a lot of tourists during the winter and summer. They tend to avoid our muddy seasons between. Besides a teenager working after school, I usually get by with Mrs. Wilcox, my part-time help, but she's getting old, and the poor thing has been having to call in sick more days lately."

"That's too bad."

"We rely a lot on retirees for seasonal help here. And believe me, lots of people retire to Valentine Valley. It's away from the big city of Denver, yet not in overly priced Aspen. You'd be surprised at the backgrounds of many of the locals. Not all are residents for generations like the Thalbergs, even though we *are* nestled in the middle of several ranches."

Emily had heard enough about Nate and decided to keep the conversation on Monica. "So you were born here, too? What was it like growing up in such a small town?"

"Claustrophobic."

Emily reluctantly shared her laugh.

"But you never feel alone," Monica continued.

Emily had occasionally felt alone in San Francisco with Greg's long hours, which was why she filled her days as much as possible, deluding herself that when she had a baby, Greg would spend more time with her, with their little family. The old pain hadn't dulled, she realized, setting down her fork because of the lump in her throat.

Monica thoughtfully bit into a cheese stick and chewed. "Pretty quickly, you do feel like you've met every man. We often used to drive into Aspen to meet all the rich guys. But you know, most of them only wanted one thing from local girls. And let me tell you, there weren't a lot of brothers on the ski slopes."

Emily smiled. Both of them glanced toward the street as a commercial van pulled up next to them, the power company advertised on the side. A balding, middle-aged man in jeans, work shirt, and boots came around to them and smiled.

"Hey, Monica," he said, nodding to her.

"Charlie," she answered back. "Tell your wife those napkin holders decorated with hearts are hot sellers."

"Great!" He looked at Emily. "Are you Emily Murphy?"

Surprised, she straightened up from her lazy slouch. "I am."

"I'm Charlie Bombardo. I hear you were scheduled to have your electric and gas turned on in a couple days. Nate Thalberg knew I was working in the area, so he gave me a call." He smiled. "He has a way of getting a person moved up the list."

Damn, had she been so pitiful that he'd done her *another* favor? How was she supposed to rely on her own strengths when people kept assuming she couldn't?

Monica laughed and shook her head. "That Nate. So what did he promise you?" she asked Mr. Bombardo.

"Lunch and a beer. I'll be collecting during the Colorado Rockies game next weekend."

"I—I don't know what to say, Mr. Bombardo." Emily heard herself stuttering, knew she hardly sounded professional. "Surely, I should be the one to owe you for this favor."

"It's Charlie. And no, don't worry about it. I'm happy to help. And it's hardly a favor—you'll be paying the company for the service." He grinned. "It'll just take me a few minutes to make sure your hot-water heater and furnace turn on."

"Perhaps I should be your guide," Emily said ruefully. "The last tenants left a mess."

"I'll find what I need."

After he went inside, Emily saw Monica regarding her thoughtfully.

"Well, well," the other woman said.

Emily held up a hand. "Don't even think it."

"Think what?" Monica countered, cocoa brown eyes wide with innocence.

"Anything to do with Nate."

"He's doing you a lot of favors."

Emily pressed her lips together. She might as well be a heroine tied to the railroad tracks the way she inspired Nate to rescue her.

"So you noticed, too," Monica said. "Whatever he

wants for it will be more than worth it if my girlfriends are telling the truth."

Wanting to clap her hands over her ears, Emily concentrated on her salad.

After a long day of hauling junk to the Dumpster—and no end in sight—Emily washed her face in the blessedly warm water in the restaurant ladies' room. Miraculously, the plumbing still worked.

She felt bone weary and full of new aches, wondering if her thirties would now feel different than her twenties. She'd heard that the altitude could make her tired and out of breath. Since Greg had left her, she hadn't made time for exercise like she used to. That would have to change.

Tomorrow. Tonight, the only exercise she'd get would be the walk to the mechanic to hear about her car. She changed into a clean shirt and repacked her backpack before locking the door. Early evening in Valentine Valley echoed with chirping birds and the occasional quiet laughter from open windows.

She walked tiredly down Main Street but still managed to notice the rest of the shops. The scent wafting from Carmina's Cucina on the other side of Monica's smelled divine, but she could also have eaten Mexican, or at a diner or a tearoom. And there were so many more ways for tourists to amuse themselves: a gift emporium, art galleries, and a portrait studio to have old-time photos taken. A huge sign advertised an outdoor tour company, and she imagined they did a brisk business in these mountains.

Hal's Hardware was a welcome sight, and she knew she'd be frequenting it. Perhaps they gave lessons, or had books she could study. At the boardinghouse that morning, she'd seen an old computer with a big square monitor in a corner of the dining room. Were the widows even connected to the Internet? she wondered. They might still have dial-up.

The mechanic at the service station had had a chance to look at her engine and told her that the car would need about five hundred dollars' worth of work. Emily winced at the thought. Since she didn't need the car right away, the mechanic agreed to store it for a couple weeks, without charge, until she was ready. As she walked away, she felt embarrassed and frustrated—and grateful for his kindness. She wasn't used to having so little money and reminded herself that perhaps she'd been spoiled during her marriage—maybe even by her mother. Though Emily had waitressed as a teenager, it had been for spending money, not the essentials.

The grocery store was on Main Street, too, and after stopping there for supplies, Emily walked back to the boardinghouse. The mountains were an impressive blackness rising up against the starlit sky. Then she heard several howls in the distance and picked up her speed, looking at the lights of the Victorian house as a beacon in the night. Only upon reaching the porch did she feel herself relax.

The widows were waiting in the kitchen, all flustered that she hadn't called them, that she'd been out so late. She refrained from pointing out that she didn't have their number, but they were ahead of her, giving her the number of the boardinghouse, and insisting they have her cell number in return. She felt uncomfortably tied to them.

"I have my own cell phone," Mrs. Thalberg said with pride. "My grandkids insist on checking up on me."

"And she hates that," Mrs. Palmer said with a roll of her eyes. "I have a cell phone, too, you know, but you don't see me braggin'."

"My family knows where to reach me," Mrs. Ludlow said calmly. "I just don't see the need." She nodded toward her walker and spoke without bitterness. "It's not as if I drive anymore."

"She has other skills that more than make up for it," Mrs. Thalberg said, washing her hands at the sink. "Wait until you taste this pot roast she made."

"Oh, no," Emily insisted, setting down her bags. "I refuse to allow you to feed me when you've been so good to let me stay here." Although the kitchen did smell incredible.

"Nonsense," Mrs. Thalberg said. "We all take turns cooking. Today, I was at the ranch, and I knew I'd have a wonderful meal waiting."

Emily studied Mrs. Thalberg's corduroys and padded jacket. "Do you go to the ranch often?"

"Though I used to live there, I find I don't miss it so much, what with my husband gone to his reward. I went to help my daughter-in-law Sandy weed the garden."

Emily hoped her surprise didn't show, but Mrs. Thalberg laughed.

"I'm still good for an occasional workday, Emily Murphy. Don't forget to ask if you need help."

She didn't want the widows to see her chaotic building, so all she did was raise both hands to placate them. "I promise I will. Now if you're going to be so kind as to feed me, I want a place on that cooking schedule."

She spent a surprisingly enjoyable hour with the widows, received her first baking-at-altitude lesson, then was graciously permitted to use the computer. Though the desktop looked old, with a big, boxy monitor, the Internet connection was pretty good, and she was able to do some research on the work she'd need to do. YouTube had an amazing amount of how-to videos. Hal's Hardware even had its own website with a complete database of their products online. That seemed rather strange for a small town, but she shrugged her curiosity away.

When she almost fell asleep at the desk, she knew it was time to turn in. Since she'd showered before dinner, she barely remembered hitting the pillow. At dawn, her cell-phone alarm jarred her awake, and just shutting it off made her wince. Sitting up in bed, she circled her shoulders, feeling the aches and knowing it would be a long day. But that was no excuse for not running, she firmly reminded herself.

After dressing in shorts, Nikes, and a zipped sweatshirt over her t-shirt, she went outside just as the sun was rising. Once again, she came up short, staring in wonder at the imposing mountains that seemed so unreal. Would she ever get used to the sight?

Warm-up stretches made her muscles feel a bit

better, but her first hundred yards at a light jog almost made her change her mind. Doggedly, she pushed herself a little faster, and this time, when she reached the road that led over the bridge, she went the opposite way, following the fence along the field. Mrs. Thalberg had told her last night that the field was hay to feed the cattle through the long winter, and they'd be harvesting it next month. Then the old woman had said Emily'd better see Nate while she could because come haying season, he'd be working dawn to dusk to get the hay in before the weather could ruin it.

She hadn't told the widows that Nate had dropped by her building yesterday. She could only imagine what they'd make of that.

With the mountains towering on one side of her, and the rolling green hayfields on the other, she tried to clear her mind and concentrate on nothing at all. In the distance, across the fields, she could see several buildings that must be part of the Silver Creek Ranch. She made out horses and riders, but couldn't see what they were doing. Yet after a while, even the scenery couldn't distract her from feeling light-headed, and queasiness followed soon after.

She wasn't that out of shape, she told herself. But she couldn't seem to catch her breath. Stopping to lean a hand against the fence, she found herself panting, head bent, wondering if she was really going to be sick.

And then she heard the sound of a horse's hooves thudding on the dirt road. Still breathing too fast, she glanced up and knew in a moment that it was Nate riding down the road toward her, a cowboy fantasy come to life, his body moving in perfect rhythm with the horse, that dog running behind.

Oh God. He'd seen her drunk and loose, vulnerable and poor, angry and defensive. Was he now about to see her lose the banana she'd had for breakfast?

Chapter Five

Nate drew back on the reins, and Apollo obediently came to a halt. The horse nickered softly, gesturing with its head at Emily.

"I know what you mean, boy," Nate murmured, his earlier curiosity at the sight of her running toward him, having turned to exasperation.

She looked clammy and pale, with her breathing coming too quickly. He reached into the saddlebag for a bottle of water, then dismounted. Apollo contentedly bent to graze in the grass beside the road, while Scout danced excitedly at his side, panting from the run.

Emily frowned at Nate, but before she could open her mouth, he held out the water, and said, "You're not used to the altitude yet. Take some slow, deep breaths, and you'll start to feel better."

She winced but did as he ordered, and he could see when she gradually regained control of herself. After a couple sips of water, the color began to return to her face.

"Don't you work enough at the building all day?" he asked. "Why are you pushing yourself so hard?"

The annoyance faded from her expression as she studied him. "Why do you care?"

He found himself smiling. "Because you're being nice to my grandmother. And I'm regretting getting her that cell phone because she's suddenly calling me more than once a day and manages to get your name in there."

She rolled her eyes, but there was a reluctant grin on her lips that reminded him too much of the woman she'd been at the tavern, the one who didn't seem to exist except when she'd had a couple beers. No, the real woman had problems, lots of them, and that was pealing like a warning bell in his mind.

"Look, I'm sorry your grandmother is annoying you," she said, bending down to pet a very grateful Scout, who leaned against her legs and gazed up with adoration. "I like her a lot, but I won't overstay my welcome. She should leave you alone after that. And about Charlie from the power company, you shouldn't have done that. I can take care of myself just fine. You may get a thrill out of rescuing women, but—"

"Rescuing women?" he countered, chagrined to realize that she saw right through to part of his biggest flaw. If it was only about rescuing women, maybe he could have conquered it already. "I saw him passing on the street and knew you needed a break. And as for right now, if I hadn't come along, you might be planted facefirst in my hayfield."

She grimaced. "No more favors, Thalberg."

His cell phone began to beep, making him grateful for the interruption. Pulling it out of his pocket, he glanced at the screen. "I have to take this."

"Thanks for the water."

She walked away at a brisk stride. He didn't let his annoyance with himself stop him from watching her. For a short woman, she had legs that were long and shapely, and she obviously took care of herself.

Then he swore as he realized his cell phone had gone to voice mail. Before he could call the supplier back, he heard the arrival of another horse and glanced over his shoulder to see his sister, Brooke, bearing down on him, looking past him to Emily.

With a sigh, Nate patted Apollo's neck and mounted to meet his sister at eye level, which wasn't difficult when she sat in the saddle almost as tall as he did. Her brown hair was hidden by her cowboy hat, but he knew a long braid trailed down her back, and although it got in the way sometimes, she didn't cut it. Those intelligent hazel eyes finally settled on him.

"So who was that?" Brooke asked. "I didn't recognize her."

"Emily Murphy. She just came to town to see about some old family property she inherited."

Brooke's amused eyes suddenly focused on him with new light. "I see."

He didn't stiffen, knowing how easily she could read him. "What do you see?"

"Grandma Thalberg was here yesterday."

He wanted to wince. "Then you know everything I do. I'm sure Emily will be gone soon enough, and we can go back to knowing just our regular neighbors' business."

It was bad enough he couldn't get Emily out of his mind, but he certainly didn't need his sister or brother to know that. Although with the way Josh had been picking fights, maybe rumors of woman trouble would distract him.

"So what happened to Ashlee?" Brooke asked.

Nate frowned. "What do you mean? Is something wrong with her?"

"Oh, Nate, you're hopeless," Brooke said with a groan. "No, there's nothing wrong with her. Although shouldn't you know that since you've been dating her?"

"*Was* dating her. We cooled it off."

"You mean *you* cooled it off. Had she reached the ten-date limit?"

He guided Apollo back down the road, away from town. Brooke's gelding ambled alongside, while Scout trotted beside them, occasionally pausing to stick his nose in a hole.

"I don't have any dating limits," he said mildly, then remembered that Josh had first come up with that supposed rule.

"Oh, please. Every girl in Valentine knows your dating rules. I think Ashlee let her hopes get too high."

"No, she didn't," Nate said patiently. "She sensibly asked me if I'd like to take our relationship deeper, and I regretfully said no. No tears, no recriminations." Ashlee and all the others like her were safe from him—he knew when to stop himself from getting too involved, saw the warning signs a mile away—except where Emily was concerned.

"She knew the score, like every woman in Valentine Valley." Brooke glanced over her shoulder as if she could still see Emily. "But this woman's new. Someone will have to explain how it all works to her. You can't trust Grandma Thalberg for that. If it were up to her, we'd each be married already."

"Married?" He smiled. "You have a barrel-racing career to advance."

She snorted. "You know I'll be lucky to win at our rodeo, let alone take my meager talents on the road."

With a laugh, he said, "Don't worry about Emily. She doesn't seem to be the tenderhearted sort. She's fixed on repairing her property, selling it, and leaving."

"Your ideal woman."

"Will you stop it?" he demanded with exasperation. "You can find out the truth all by yourself the next time you see Monica Shaw. As I was leaving yesterday, I saw her curious face peering out at me. You can bet she's hightailed it next door already."

Brooke's face lighted up at the mention of her best friend. "Then I know who I have to visit today."

"We're going out to inspect the irrigation ditches at Cooper's Mine. Dad and Josh are waiting for us up at the barn. I think we have some holes that need plugging. That could take all day."

"Don't worry, I'll bring my hip boots. That'll help me wade through the bullshit you always spout."

With a tap of his bootheels, he had his mount dancing up against hers, and laughing, they took off at a gallop for the barn, Scout chasing them with eager excitement.

The Silver Creek Ranch was a sprawling complex of a half dozen buildings beside the main house on its thousand acres. They even had a bunkhouse for use mostly during calving and branding season, when neighbors and extra help could stay the night. The ranch was a family business, manned by Nate and his parents and siblings. They had been self-sufficient for generations, and proud of it.

But the last thirty years or so, things had changed in the Roaring Fork Valley, as skyrocketing land prices made selling out family ranches far too easy to do. But the Thalbergs stood for tradition in Valentine, and Doug Thalberg had wanted to do what his father and grandfathers before him had done, run cattle.

And Nate had been able to continue his father's family traditions, with a little smart investing, and he'd never been prouder. And it hadn't taken anything away from the job he did day to day on the ranch—he made certain of that.

Josh and their dad were just leading a saddled horse out of the barn. Ducks quacked and scattered out of the way, heading back to the pond. Josh would be driving the ATV in case they needed extra supplies quickly. Doug Thalberg squinted out over his land with the narrowed, gray-eyed gaze of a man who knew the worth of what he did. He had the same brown hair as Brooke and Josh, but his was going gray, along with his mustache.

Josh, as usual, looked like he'd just rolled out of bed, rumpled and unshaven, but always alert and ready for whatever the weather and the ranch would bring that day. His eyes, so similar to their father's, saw the world kindly, but lately he'd been focusing too sharply— needlessly—on Nate.

"Nate, did you get word about the part for the swather?" his dad asked, all business. "The hay won't cut itself."

"And the cattle won't feed themselves this winter," Brooke added, grinning at their father's oft-repeated phrases.

Josh smiled at their sister.

"He just called," Nate said. "I'll head to the office and call him back right now. You all go on ahead, and I'll meet up with you."

"Take your time," Josh said. "We can handle the dams."

"Nope," Nate said briskly. "I won't be long at all."

"Afraid I'll move my dams quicker than you will?" Josh taunted, grinning.

He sounded completely good-natured, but Nate knew a challenge when he heard one. Lately, every-thing with Josh ended up with a challenge.

"Not a chance," Nate said. "I always do my share."

Josh studied him, then shook his head. "I know you do." He headed for the truck shed where the ATV was parked.

Brooke and their father mounted and rode off, sev-eral ranch dogs chasing them, but Nate stood with his hands on his hips, watching until Josh disappeared inside the shed.

Lately, Josh had this crazy idea that Nate was trying to do too much, spreading himself too thin, and Nate was mightily offended. He'd spent years juggling the ranch investments, his own, as well as his ranch chores. Nate tried to ignore Josh's concern rather than confronting him outright, partly because he didn't want their father to think something was wrong. When Nate had insisted on going to Colorado State while his parents would have preferred he go to school closer to home, things had changed between Nate and his dad. He got the feeling that Doug Thalberg thought he was going to leave the ranching business—much as he'd always told Nate he could choose whatever career he wanted. A subtle tension had worked its way into their relationship even though Nate had majored in animal sciences along with business.

When Nate was young, there was always a part of him that wondered if Doug could think of him as a real son because he'd been adopted. Nate's biological dad had married his mom, then abandoned them when Sandy had been diagnosed with multiple sclerosis. Nate, only four at the time, had brief memories of his mom's sorrow, and that perhaps things had been hard, but his mom made sure he never knew it. A year later, Doug had fallen in love with Sandy, and when he married her, he adopted Nate. True to his word, the adoption had been a pact between them, and Nate didn't think his dad could possibly love him or his mother more.

College had seemed to change something between them, and it had taken years to work itself out. They were fine now, and he didn't want Josh upsetting things. Nate had the ranch's best interests at heart, and he knew what he was capable of—Josh didn't. So many mountain ranching families couldn't make a living and had to sell out, but Nate had found a way to bring more money in. His wide variety of investments—rodeo stock, organic farms, even a winery at lower altitude— were a challenge to manage, and he'd certainly never imagined the pleasure he'd take in coordinating so much, including the Silver Creek Rodeo, a month away.

That reminded him—after his phone call with the parts supplier, he could check out the online registration and make sure all the program advertising was in place.

There was always so much to do, enough to keep thoughts of Emily Murphy at bay, to his complete satisfaction.

As Emily got dressed after her shower, thoughts of Nate kept interfering. He'd looked so damn good riding toward her like a cowboy out of a Western movie. She had no idea cowboys still wore chaps, but they'd covered his jeans, fringe flapping at the edge. He'd worn a heavy work jacket, gloves dangled from his belt, and even had a scarf about his neck as if he'd need to cover his face in a dust storm. A dust storm in the Rockies? That almost made her smile.

But she hadn't been smiling when she'd seen him. She'd been panting, and not out of lust but out of stupidity. Of course she'd heard about taking it easy when exercising at altitude. She'd just totally forgotten. Did he think she'd done it on purpose to get his attention? After all, she'd been jogging on his family land. But she'd stuck to the road. She'd been all ready to be upset at the implication she couldn't take care of herself, and once again, he'd simply thanked her in regard to his grandmother. Nate Thalberg was making it too easy to forget what they'd done together that first night.

No, that was a lie—she couldn't possibly forget. She still woke up in the middle of the night remembering how good she'd felt in his arms.

Maybe he wanted her to forget. She was living with his grandmother, after all. He was hardly going to proposition her under those circumstances. It had taken alcohol to make him do so in the first place, she thought with a sigh.

And there she went, downplaying her own sexiness. He'd thought her sexy enough that first night. Now she was just an annoyance, and it was better that way. Her indebtedness to him and his family—both father and grandmother—felt like another anchor around her neck as she struggled to stay afloat in the pursuit of her new life.

At least they hadn't threatened her with foreclosing on the property, she reminded herself as she went into the kitchen. She would soon be able to repay it, once the building sold.

She hoped.

The widows were all in the kitchen as if waiting for her. Mrs. Thalberg seemed dressed for another casual day on the ranch, jeans and boots this time, and her red vest perfectly matched her hair. Mrs. Palmer was as colorful as a tulip beneath her blond wig, and Emily had realized that the prints and patterns in her dresses were just like her personality, big and vibrant. Mrs. Ludlow, dressed conservatively in tailored clothing, certainly didn't let using a walker interfere with her self-respect.

"So let's taste those muffins you made last night," Mrs. Thalberg said brightly. "While we eat, you can tell us how you're feeling. Nate called to make sure you got home all right."

The word "home" struck her with a moment of sadness until she realized Nate was part of the same sentence. She smiled through gritted teeth, hating that she inspired anyone's concern. "He felt the need to check up on me?"

"Of course he did!" Mrs. Palmer said sternly, with a hint of her Western drawl. "You could have full-blown altitude sickness, you know. You gotta take that seriously."

"But I'm fine, and Nate could see that." Emily turned to Mrs. Thalberg. "You know he wouldn't have let me go, otherwise."

It was true. He obviously liked to take control of every situation.

"Now let's taste those muffins," Emily said, changing the topic.

They weren't perfect yet, so next time she'd alter a different ingredient, sugar instead of baking powder. Mrs. Thalberg said you just kept experimenting until you got it right. But the apple tarts, now those had turned out pretty good, and Emily carefully packaged plenty to take to Monica to thank her for lunch.

At her building, Emily had already cleared the beginning of a path through the downstairs restaurant and kitchen though now it looked like the maze of paths in a hoarder's house. Braving a peek in the basement, she found more junk, but it could wait. Deciding to begin hauling out the garbage in the apartment, she headed upstairs until she heard a bell ring at her back door. Through the door window she could see a handsome, middle-aged man dressed stylishly in a sport coat and open-necked shirt, as if he'd just left a boardroom meeting in New York City. When she opened the door, he took off his sunglasses, his eyes widening as he looked past her.

"Good morning," he said when he'd recovered. "I'm Cal Carpenter. Are you Emily Strong, granddaughter of Agatha Riley?"

She nodded curiously, but didn't offer her married name. "What can I do for you, Mr. Carpenter?"

"I used to be with a law firm in Aspen although I live here now in blissful semiretirement."

His toothpaste-commercial grin said he was more than enjoying himself in "semiretirement." He seemed tanned and fit, as if he spent a lot of time outdoors.

"Your grandmother hired me before she died to take care of some legal matters."

She blinked at him in surprise. That had to be over twenty-three years ago. "You mean her will?"

He nodded. "Among other things. Obviously, the

will has long since been settled, but she left something for you." He reached inside his breast pocket, withdrew a long envelope, and handed it to her. "Have a good day, Miss Strong."

"Wait!" she said, before he could do more than begin to turn away from her.

He paused, eyebrow arched. He was so impeccably groomed, she wondered distractedly if he had those perfect eyebrows plucked.

"Why wasn't I given this before?"

"I was under orders not to have it sent to you until you came to Valentine Valley to deal with this building."

"And what if I never did?" she demanded with exasperation. "What if my mother sold it before she died?"

"I had other directions to follow." He grinned. "But that didn't happen, did it? And you still would have received the letter on your thirty-fifth birthday. Your grandmother said she was giving her daughter a chance to tell you herself."

Emily felt a chill sweep over her. "What do you mean?"

He shrugged. "I wasn't given all the details. Your grandmother was a private woman, even toward her own daughter."

She couldn't think straight, her mind was tumbling. But practicality intervened at last. "But—do I owe you something for your services?"

"No, it was all taken care of. Enjoy your day." Then he glanced past her again and winced. "Or at least try to get out of here occasionally. Spring can be beautiful around here—as long as you don't mind the mud."

"Mud?" she said blankly.

"On the trails up in the mountains. At least I can still use my snowmobile farther up." He smiled at her, then nodded toward the envelope. "Hope that's good news."

When he was gone, she stared at the envelope, tracing the faded lettering of her name. The handwriting was firm and bold, and she wished she'd thought to ask Mr. Carpenter if it was her grandmother's. She had a faint memory of a warm kitchen smelling of pine from the nearby Christmas tree, and rolling out cookie dough with her grandmother. She was surprised to feel a sting of tears, and knew it wasn't truly for the grandmother she couldn't remember but because the homey memory made her long for a simple life. She'd chased that memory and longing through her life, first with her distracted mom, then in her marriage, but she'd never made it work.

With a sigh, she sat down on the only unbroken chair in the restaurant and opened the envelope. There was a single sheet of paper dated the year of Grandma Riley's death, and it was addressed to her.

My dear Emily,

You're a sweet little girl as I write this, knowing nothing about your history here in Valentine Valley. But I'm worried that your ma's eagerness to forget the past will blind her to how lies hurt. She kept things from you—and from me—that were easier for her to forget. She was always free-spirited, and doing things without thinking.

It usually didn't hurt her. But she left town so fast after her high-school graduation, then married barely four months later to a man she just met. When she came home with you, I confronted her and she finally admitted the truth—Jacob Strong wasn't your father.

With a gasp, Emily reread the last sentence over again. Her grandmother was saying her entire childhood was a fabrication.

She'd never questioned her mother's impulsive decision to marry her father after knowing him so briefly. Since Delilah consulted the stars for so many things, it was hard to find more . . . grounded reasons for what she used to do. Half the time, Emily thought Delilah had picked her dad for his last name since she always said she liked how "Delilah Strong" sounded. Emily's memories of him were of a warm, patient man who loved her and put up with her mother's flitting in and out of their day with resignation mingled with affection.

But . . . he wasn't her biological father.

Chapter Six

Emily felt as if she'd reached the crest of a roller coaster, her stomach heaving as she wished desperately to stop time. But that couldn't happen, and all her thoughts tumbled about in her head while she sat motionless in the disaster of her kitchen.

Another piece of her past was unraveling all because of her mother's screwups. Did Delilah even love Jacob Strong, or had he been a convenient husband? That had been her worst fear growing up, that her mother hadn't truly loved her dead father. Stumbling to her feet, Emily leaned heavily against a dull counter and stared around the kitchen wide-eyed. This had still been a general store in the early eighties, and her mother had worked here part-time. Teen pregnancies had still been somewhat of a scandal to most people. Had Delilah stood in this very spot, wondering what she'd do with her life, feeling unable to confide the truth in her own mother until forced? It made Emily wonder what kind of relationship they truly had. Delilah's desperation must have forced her to flee Valentine Valley—leaving her family, and whoever Emily's father might have been. Perhaps he hadn't even known. Or perhaps her mom hadn't known his identity. The way she'd gone through men, never being without one long, spoke a lot about her behavior.

She scanned the rest of the letter.

If Dorothy did right by you, this won't come as a shock. I pray she came to her senses and told the truth, understanding that you deserved to know. But sometimes she gets it in her head that she's right, damn the consequences. If you didn't know—I'm sorry, child. Forgiveness is one of God's graces, but he makes us work hard for it. I ask for your understanding on my own behalf, too, for not being able to reach my only child. It is a failure I pray over every night. Rosemary Thalberg says I obsess too much, that I did my best, that the next generation will heal the mistakes of the past. I tell her she's a busybody, full of too much sunshine and rainbows. But deep in my crotchety old heart, I hope she's right.

I pray for you, too, my little Emily. Your past may have some heartache, but only you can determine your future. And may it be a long and happy life. You have all my love.

Grandma Riley

A tear slid down Emily's cheek, a wry smile twisted her lips. The letter sounded just like the grandma she remembered, the one who liked to walk in the rain wearing big rubber boots, who stubbornly spent hours in her garden even though vegetables refused to grow for her.

Part of Emily still didn't want to believe Grandma could be telling the truth about her dad. And with everything going on in her life, it seemed too overwhelming to think about. Perhaps she didn't even want to pursue it. What would it matter? All those important years after Jacob Strong died had been spent without a father, and looking for one at this late date seemed almost selfish. She might disrupt an entire family.

A family she should have been a part of. But it was too late.

And perhaps her mother had actually been protecting her from a man who didn't deserve to be a father. Instead, Delilah had given her Jacob Strong, kind and wonderful, his memory still a balm when she needed to be soothed.

Hands shaking, she folded up the letter and thrust it into her purse, as if it were a live snake she didn't want to touch again. She went back to relentlessly bagging garbage in the apartment, exhausting herself so she didn't have to think, only taking a break when it was time for lunch. She pulled the container of apple tarts out of her backpack, then realized she'd left the lunch she'd packed back at the boardinghouse. Apple tarts would have to do.

She locked up the building—was that even necessary in broad daylight in Valentine Valley? But she was a city girl, and it just seemed wrong not to be careful.

Forcing herself to look cheerful, she went next door and found Monica rearranging a display of crocheted baby afghans and looking relieved for the distraction.

Emily set the plastic container on the main counter. "I brought us something a bit more decadent to share than a salad. Dessert."

"Oh, I haven't eaten lunch yet," Monica said, looking hungrily at the container.

"I already did, so I'll leave you to finish yours." She didn't want Monica insisting on sharing two days in a row.

"Don't rush off." Monica lifted the lid, wafted the container under her nose, and groaned. "Ohh, it smells divine. You baked this?"

"Apple tarts."

"Crust from scratch?" she asked, eyes going wide. "I thought everyone bought theirs nowadays."

"Not me. Never have. But baking up in the mountains is tricky although you probably already know that."

Monica snorted.

Emily reluctantly smiled. "I've been taking lessons in high-altitude baking from the widows, and this is one recipe that turned out okay the first time."

"So you're not experimenting on me?" Monica teased.

"Cross my heart." Emily had to admit that it was nice having a conversation instead of spending too much time keeping dark thoughts at bay.

The bell above the door jangled, and they both turned to look.

Monica broke into a big grin as a young woman entered. "Brooke, just in time for lunch—or should I say Emily's fantastic dessert?"

Brooke's gaze focused on Emily with recognition as if she'd already heard about her. What is it with small towns? Emily wondered wryly. Brooke was a good half a foot taller than she was, her lean build shown off in tight jeans, cowboy boots, and a button-snapped Western shirt with a fleece vest over the top. She carried a cowboy hat at her side along with a small cooler, and in the other hand a paper bag.

"So you're Emily Murphy," Brooke said, a smile slowly forming. Then she lifted a brown paper sack. "You forgot your lunch."

Emily gaped at her momentarily, trying to put together some sequence of events that could explain this.

Monica elbowed her. "Hey! You told me you already ate lunch."

Emily stared at the smirking Brooke as she answered Monica. "If I'd have told you I forgot it, you'd have offered to share again, making me feel like an idiot. I had tarts, didn't I? With healthy apples in them." She took the bag from Brooke. "Thanks. Should I ask how you got my lunch?"

Brooke put out a hand. "I'm Brooke Thalberg."

"Ah," Emily said, as all the lightbulbs went off in her head. They shook hands, and she noticed Brooke's firm grip, her skin rougher than most women's. "Nate's sister—and Mrs. Thalberg's granddaughter. Did she call you?"

"Of course not. She called Nate."

Brooke and Monica exchanged a knowing grin, then

both women started to unpack their lunches. Emily hesitated, knowing she should make excuses and leave instead of being drawn into temporary friendships. But it just seemed too rude, so she reluctantly sat down on a stool.

Emily told herself she was glad Nate hadn't shown up with her lunch himself. She didn't have time for his sort of distraction although she was curious about his reaction to his grandmother's call. While Monica helped a couple customers with an emergency birthday bouquet and long-stemmed roses for a dinner date, Brooke kept grinning at her, as if reading her thoughts.

When Monica returned to eat lunch, Emily said to Brooke, "I'm sorry you got drawn into this."

"I'm not," she answered cheerfully. "I wanted to meet the woman Nate brought to the Widows' Boardinghouse. And he couldn't help out with your lunch because he was having a tough time getting hold of a part we need."

"I know I shouldn't have imposed on your grandmother," Emily said, after swallowing a bite of her turkey sandwich. "But Nate was pretty persuasive and . . ." Her words died off as she realized they were both watching her with speculation.

Brooke shook her head. "I don't know if I want to hear how my brother was persuasive."

Emily knew she was blushing when the women started to laugh. "It wasn't like that!" she protested. "I tried to stay in my own building, but the heat wasn't on, and he wouldn't let me."

"Damn, I thought there might be a better story than

that," Brooke grumbled, before taking a bite of her chicken drumstick.

Emily concentrated on her sandwich for a moment, controlling her tone, before saying, "Nope. But your grandmother is absolutely wonderful."

"Thanks. And she really likes you. She says it's a shame you're leaving in a couple weeks."

Emily explained about selling the building and moving on with her life.

"Doing what?" Monica asked.

Emily chewed a celery stick thoughtfully. "College. I'm enrolled at Berkeley for the fall semester. The first time I went, I was so in love, I dropped out to get married. It didn't end well," she murmured, and was grateful when the two women nodded with sympathy instead of asking questions. "Although I'm in liberal arts, I'm determined to find a more specific major that interests me."

"You don't sound like you did that before," Brooke said.

Emily shrugged. "I didn't. I'm hoping a school advisor can help me. Maybe take some kind of aptitude test or something. It's sad to be thirty years old and not know what you want to do with your life. Monica, did you always know the flower shop was what you wanted?"

"No, I went to college. I took a lot of business courses because I knew I wanted to be my own boss. I'd always been creative—I used to draw and paint—so I tried interior design. That was when I realized it was the flowers I was drawn to more than the furniture or wallpaper. And luckily, the owner of the flower shop here in Valentine was ready to retire, so I assumed the lease. I keep taking classes, studying books, learning new things. And I love it."

Emily was glad to hear that someone else had to figure out her career path—until Brooke spoke.

"I always knew what I would do."

Monica groaned. "Isn't she wonderful."

"Hey, it's a family business," Brooke protested. "When you're in the saddle by age three, guiding cattle to pasture by eight, and helping birth calves at fourteen, it's kinda in your blood."

Emily gaped at her. "I was playing soccer at fourteen—and even that seemed too complicated. Wow."

"It's not that impressive around here," Brooke said with a shrug. "You smell like cow shit a lot. We were thigh deep in muddy irrigation ditches today, and I'll be heading back there after lunch."

"I bet Nate was there," Monica said, using her carrots to scoop up a creamy dip even as she eyed Emily.

Emily ignored her.

"We all work the ranch together. My mom takes care of the books and keeping everyone fed. My dad and my two brothers work outside with me." As they divided up the apple tarts, Brooke turned to Monica. "I saw your sister on TV last night."

Emily glanced in surprise at Monica, who frowned.

"Oh, she likes being famous," Monica answered flippantly.

"She's a journalist at CNN," Brooke explained.

"She's often out of the country covering whatever big disaster or battle is hot."

"She likes the big-city life," Monica said at last. "And I don't. Kind of strange, for twins."

"Twins?"

"Fraternal. We don't look alike."

"Sure you do," Brooke said, rolling her eyes. "Like sisters, anyway. Okay, so Missy knows how to glam herself up."

"Melissa," Monica countered. "Let's not forget that 'Missy' doesn't sound professional. Doesn't matter that's what we all called her."

"I'm sorry you and your sister aren't getting along," Emily said.

Monica smiled. "Thanks. You're sweet. We used to. I never thought anything would separate us. We went off to college together, and afterward, she chose the big city, and I moved back home. Over the years, we seem to have . . . lost our connection."

"I can't believe that. You're sisters."

"Hey, you never know," Brooke said, using her finger to swipe another crumb from the container. "I always thought my brothers got along great, but lately, I've sensed . . . I don't know, tension or something."

"Not Josh and Nate," Monica said dismissively. "So they had an argument."

Brooke shrugged, her eyes focused far away. So Fantasy Cowboy had some human weaknesses after all, Emily thought. It was a lot easier to hear about other people's family problems than consider her own.

* * *

Nate knew he shouldn't go anywhere near Emily's building, but Valentine Valley was a small town, and on his way to the feed store, he ended up driving his pickup past her block. He glanced down the alley—being cautious, he told himself—and saw Emily dragging a huge stuffed chair a couple inches at a time toward the Dumpster. Once again, he got that immediate sensation of awareness and interest and concern that didn't bode well.

He took the next corner and came to a stop. He shouldn't have driven that way. She was pretty upset that he was doing her "favors," and he knew he should stop, knowing what happened when he got involved. But the chair looked heavy.

He pulled into the alley. Emily straightened and frowned. Her jeans and t-shirt had some dirt stains, and that strawberry blond hair of hers was falling down the back of her neck. *Damn, but she looks good.* He got out of the truck.

She put her hands on her hips. "This can't be a coincidence. Didn't I just see you this morning?"

"I'm on my way to the feed store. What am I supposed to do when I see a woman in distress? My mom would beat me if I didn't stop. Now move aside."

He brushed past her, and she seemed to quickly get out of his way. She was being smarter than he was. He hefted the chair off the ground and walked the final twenty yards to the Dumpster. She raced ahead of him to open the lid, and he got to watch her jeans-clad butt as she stood on tiptoes to reach the top.

He tossed in the chair.

Wide-eyed, she said, "Okay, that was impressive."

"That couldn't have been a compliment. After all, I was rescuing you again."

"So your mama raised you right. Thank you for your help."

As she walked by him, she stole a glance at him that he couldn't quite read. It wasn't angry or defensive or affronted. So what was it?

He found himself walking beside her. "Did you get your lunch?"

She snorted, and he was surprised she wasn't too ladylike for it.

"Do you doubt your sister?"

"Nope. Just checking up on her. Although now that I think about it, she did rave about some apple tarts. So I guess she had those with you."

She climbed the couple stairs to her building and glanced at him over her shoulder. Luckily, he'd stopped checking out her butt in time.

"You don't sound like you listen to your sister very well."

He realized he'd lost track of the conversation. *Damn.* He climbed the first step, unaware she'd stopped until he almost bumped into her. Their eyes met and held for a moment before she glanced away. He found himself wanting to gather her wayward hair into his hands and . . . fix it for her. Not . . . caress it or anything.

"You brought up the apple tarts for a reason," she said. "You country boys probably need to check out a woman's cooking."

"You baked them yourself?"

"Don't sound so disbelieving," she shot back.

He raised both hands. "Just surprised."

"I like to cook." She lifted her chin, as if daring him.

"Then I better try one," he said, trying to remain serious when a grin was eating at him.

The kitchen was still a mess, but a lot of the junk was off the floor, and it had been swept.

"You've been working hard," he said.

"Thank you." She picked up a container and continued to walk into the restaurant. "Now that I have paths to the doors, I've been focusing on the apartment—so I don't have to impose on your grandmother," she added over her shoulder.

"You know she doesn't consider you an imposition."

"But you do."

He didn't know what to say—it had seemed true. And he was no longer certain why. After all, it wasn't like he was forced to see her every day.

"No, you're not an imposition. Not if you can cook, anyway."

He thought she might have smiled, but since she was still ahead of him, and he was still focused on her butt, he wasn't certain.

"There aren't enough usable chairs in here," she said. "We'll sit outside on the bench."

"So you're not handing me a tart and sending me on my way?" he asked dryly.

"I considered it. But you're Brooke's brother, and I like her."

But not me, he thought. He tried to tell himself that was a good thing, but already his mind was slyly protesting that she'd liked him well enough a couple nights ago. Damn, he shouldn't have let his thoughts go there. Before he knew it, he was noticing how close they had to sit on the bench, and that when he sat naturally, his leg touched hers, so he pulled back. But he'd almost lingered.

She handed Nate a tart on a napkin. When their fingers touched, he didn't pull away too quickly. She blushed, and he knew she was remembering Tony's Tavern, too.

He took a bite, and as the sweet and tart flavor oozed across his tongue, he made a humming sound of approval.

"Thank you," she answered, just as if he'd spoken.

"Oh, you're good," he rumbled, after swallowing.

Another answer that could be taken two ways.

She didn't meet his eyes but let out a deep breath. "Look, there's been this . . . tension between us since that first night." As she glanced at him, her big blue eyes looked determined. "I'm going to be here for a couple weeks, and it's a small town, and I'm living with your grandmother, and I'll probably keep bumping into you." She stopped, as if realizing her mouth was running away with her.

He kind of liked it. She was nervous about him.

"It's silly for us to . . . go on like this," she continued. "I just wanted to tell you I'm sorry I drank too much and let things go too far between us. Regardless of what you might think, I've never done anything like that before, and when I realized what I was doing, I had to stop it. I don't just . . . give myself to a guy I just met."

He smiled. " 'Give' yourself? That sounds pretty old-fashioned."

"You know what I mean," she said with exasperation.

She was watching him, looking anxious and hesitant, as if she cared what he thought. Something inside him eased.

He tipped his hat to her and grinned. "Apology accepted. I feel bad that things have been awkward between us. Regardless of what you might think, I don't normally drink and proposition women in bars. But you were sitting there so . . ." His voice drifted into a soft rumble.

She was staring at him wide-eyed, fresh and innocent and embarrassed.

"Drunk?" she offered wryly.

"No. Pretty. Pretty and relaxed and funny. I'm a sucker for funny. But I apologize for going too far. I've been pretty mad at myself these last couple days for taking advantage."

She blinked at him. "I thought you were mad at me."

"For saying no?" He snorted. "Hardly. It wasn't your fault."

She smiled at last and kept glancing at him as if she didn't know whether to believe him.

She stuck out her hand. "Could we start over? I'd like it if we could be friends."

He slid his hand around hers, noticing how small and fragile it was, that he had to be careful not to squeeze too hard and hurt her.

"Friends," he said, his voice too husky.

This was a bad idea, but he couldn't stop himself.

Chapter Seven

Emily knew they were connected too long. His hand was so big and warm and rough from working hard on the ranch every day. His hat shadowed his face in the afternoon sun, but that only made his eyes gleam even greener.

A car slowed down as it went past them, and even that didn't stop them—until she noticed the twin smirks from the two men in the car, men she'd seen that first night at the tavern. She pulled her hand away.

"Don't worry about them," Nate said. "It's just Ned and Ted Ferguson. Guess plumbing doesn't keep them amused enough."

"So you don't mind being on display for the whole town?" she asked skeptically.

"On display? You make it sound like we're doing something dirty rather than enjoying the sun."

"And the mountains," she said at last, relaxing back on the bench, reluctantly enjoying the sexiness of his drawl. "It's so beautiful here."

He took another bite of the apple tart and savored it.

It had seemed like forever since a man had appreciated her cooking. But that memory took her back to her marriage, and she wasn't going there.

"Nate," she began, then hesitated. "Just so you know, I'm not interested in dating anyone while I'm here. If you had other ideas, I'll understand if you don't keep dropping by."

He chuckled, exuding all that smoldering sexuality that seemed so unconscious on his part. But she would learn to be unaffected if it killed her. She reminded herself it had taken alcohol to make him respond to her.

"I appreciate honesty in a woman."

And then he took another bite of her tart. She wasn't sure he'd agreed to her conditions, but she let it go. It was a tentative, temporary friendship. It wasn't as if she was tempted to confide in him about her grandmother's letter. No, that was personal and none of his business. But of course, her mother must have been close to his father to ask for a loan—not the way you'd treat a man you were hiding a pregnancy from, thank God, because the thought of being Nate's sister made her feel icky.

Nate studied the play of emotions on Emily's face, from happiness to hesitation to determination. She was telling the truth about not wanting to get involved with a guy, and he understood that. He wasn't a getting-involved kind of guy, especially not with someone with her vast array of problems. And he'd already been so drawn to her, it was wise to keep anything from going further. She was right about his liking to rescue women. But it was more than that. He wanted to help people—too much. And then things went bad in ways he never intended, and people ended up resenting him.

Like Lilly, his girlfriend sophomore year at Colorado State. She was his first real clue that he had a dangerous weakness. He'd fallen in love so fast, his head spun every time he looked at her. And that was a lot, because they spent all their free time together. She'd been a freshman, from a small town like he was, so lost her first few weeks of college that it had been easy to give her some suggestions—good classes to take, professors who'd go easy on her. He'd been a shoulder for her to cry out her homesickness, and he'd stupidly felt all puffed with pride, glad he could be there for her. A week or two before midterms that semester, her dad had gotten sick, and Nate ended up helping her study and get organized when she could barely think straight. They were both overwhelmed, but he was determined not to be like that sorry excuse for a man, his own biological father, who'd run out on his mom at the first difficulty. In hindsight, he could see now that he probably spent more time trying to keep Lilly afloat than having a good relationship. He didn't seem to know how to do both. What poor woman would want a man who tried to do everything for her?

To make it up to her, he'd stayed on campus with her during the break, but a freak snowstorm hit early up in the mountains, while his family was trying to gather the herd to bring them down to the ranch. Brooke accidentally let slip how many cows were missing and feared dead, and Nate felt awful, like he'd let everyone down when he should have been there. He rushed home to help, even though he knew Lilly felt abandoned by him right when she needed him most. Though he loved her, she thought he was putting his family first. Furious about being on her own, she floundered in her classes, dropped out of school and out of his life. He hadn't realized how he'd undermined her, but that was no excuse. It was a lot longer before he learned his lesson.

"Good morning, Emily and Nate!"

They turned to see Mrs. Ludlow, dressed in a tailored skirt and blouse, limping toward them with the aid of her walker. Her granddaughter, three or so years old, if Nate remembered, held on to one of the metal bars. He got to his feet and tipped his hat as Mrs. Ludlow came to a smiling stop.

"Well, it's so pleasant to see you both," she said with a smile.

To Nate's surprise, Emily knelt right down on the sidewalk as if her bones had melted and smiled at the little girl.

"And who are you?" Emily asked.

The girl pulled her thumb out of her mouth, said, "Miri," and popped it back in.

"It's short for Miriam," Mrs. Ludlow said with pride. "She's one of my granddaughters."

"Aren't you so pretty?" Emily clapped her hands together.

The little girl giggled.

Emily glanced up at Mrs. Ludlow with such a sweet, happy expression, it was like a reality kick in the gut to Nate. He didn't need a billboard sign to tell him she was the marrying kind of woman.

As the two women discussed Miri's dress, hand-made by Mrs. Ludlow, and Emily fingered the lace, he saw a pale line on her ring finger. Had she already been married? Or was she still?

Her background was none of his business.

Emily offered part of an apple tart to the little girl, then boosted her onto the bench to eat it.

"You're just the kindest girl," Mrs. Ludlow said, a bit too loudly. "You fit in well at the boardinghouse. We have a mission, I'll have you know."

"A mission?" Emily echoed. "Sounds mysterious."

"Nothing political, of course," Mrs. Ludlow said firmly. "But we take pride in Valentine Valley, and we like to make sure it stays true to its small-town roots while still encouraging the right improvements, the kind that preserve the history of our buildings for the enjoyment of our residents and visitors."

"You mean tourists," Nate said dryly.

"There is nothing wrong with tourists," Mrs. Ludlow scolded.

"You don't like visitors?" Emily asked him sweetly.

He knew she was amusing herself at his expense. He let his eyes remind her just how welcoming he'd been to her, a visitor. She blushed.

"I like visitors and tourists just fine," he drawled.

"Others don't," Mrs. Ludlow said. "But we simply can't let our historic buildings fall down around us—or allow an inappropriate business to give people the wrong idea. Rosemary, Renée, and I oversee the Valentine Valley Preservation Fund."

Nate didn't like where the conversation was heading.

"A preservation fund sounds very worthwhile," Emily said politely.

"And the town has been the better for it. We're the ones who encouraged businesses like Back in Time Portrait Studio to open here."

"Mrs. Palmer just likes dressing up in costumes like his customers do," Nate said dryly.

"She's loyal to our roots here in the West," Mrs. Ludlow insisted.

"She goes around like a pioneer woman on the Fourth of July," Nate said to Emily in an exaggerated undertone.

"What a wonderful idea," Emily said. "I bet the tourists love it."

Mrs. Ludlow smiled with superiority at Nate, before continuing, "Main Street's flourishing, more and more Aspen tourists are taking a day to come relax with us, and our little Victorian gingerbread houses don't stay on the market more than a day."

"And some would say the prices are getting pretty high," Nate volunteered.

Emily's glance morphed into skepticism as she studied him.

"Beautiful craftsmanship always draws the connoisseur." Mrs. Ludlow lifted her nose in the air.

Nate lifted both hands, palms out. "I know all about a free-market economy. I studied it in college."

"I think it's a wonderful thing you're doing," Emily said to the old woman. "How does it work?"

As Mrs. Ludlow explained the application process, and the widows' coordination of donations and grants, Nate waited with resignation for her to mention his connection. Much as he tried to keep his business private, that was hard to do in a town the size of Valentine. To his surprise, she left him out of it.

"I think you should apply for yourself," Mrs. Ludlow finished.

Emily blinked. "For myself? But Mrs. Ludlow, I'm selling the property as soon as I can. I don't even know who'll end up buying the place. Surely the funds should be used by those who intend to stay and be a part of the town."

She didn't jump at the offer of money, and Nate respected her for it. Eventually, Mrs. Ludlow and Miri were on their way, and Emily was perched on the edge of the bench. She shielded her eyes from the sun as she looked up at him. He sat back down.

"Brooke said your whole family works on the ranch," she said. "You raise cattle?"

He nodded.

"I didn't see any cows when I was jogging—or should I say trespassing—on your property."

He gestured with his head toward the mountains. "They're in summer pasture, grazing our allotment in the White River National Forest."

"So you have to ride up *there*"—wide-eyed, she pointed to the same mountains—"to check up on them?"

"We drive pickups pulling horse and ATV trailers, then we ride around to check up on them."

"Not very Old West of you," she said wryly. "But I love steak as much as the next person, and I certainly don't want it to be even more expensive."

"I prefer being on a horse although Scout might disagree. He likes to perch behind me on the ATV."

She smiled. "I'm very relieved that you project a traditional cowboy image. The hat's important, of course, and you don't fall down on the job there."

"Complimented on my hat," he said dryly. "That might be a first for me."

She rolled her eyes. "I think you'll take compliments where you can get them."

"Now you're implying I'm desperate."

"Oh, your grandmother doesn't think so. She thinks women are too easy on you, lining up to be your casual dates."

He leaned back on the bench, lowering his hat over his eyes. "I knew taking you to the boardinghouse would be a mistake."

She laughed again, and it made him feel too good to take her mind off her troubles—he glanced at her bare ring finger again—whatever they might be.

"About that preservation fund," she began. "So the widows try to keep certain businesses out?"

Nate's shoulders relaxed. "That sounds worse than it really is. We have a McDonald's by the highway, right? It's not just the widows—everyone wants the locals to benefit the most from tourists. And what tourists will be drawn by chain restaurants and stores they can find anywhere?"

Emily smiled. "So you're not talking about censorship or favoritism."

"God, no."

"You know I didn't mean to imply that your grandmother would be a part of something so . . ."

"Don't worry, I won't tell her what you were thinking," he said in a confidential tone.

She rolled her eyes.

"She's sharp as a tack, my grandma." He shook his head. "She deals with the paperwork of the committee, handling the behind-the-scenes stuff, preparing the grants for the committee and the investors. Mrs. Palmer, in all her Western-drawl glory, is the public face, the one at every opening, the one who delivers the good news and the bad."

"Why does that not surprise me?"

He grinned. "Mrs. Ludlow handles the legalities, attending the mayor's press conferences, or sitting in on corporate board meetings, anything involved with the investors. Those three women are pretty formidable when they're all together. Once, they chained themselves to a broken-down old house that had been a mining-town brothel."

"No!" Emily clapped her hands to her cheeks, eyes wide with humor.

"The mayor wanted to tear it down, but they claimed it stood for women's history since Chinese immigrant women had been the original whores—uh, prostitutes."

"Good thing you corrected yourself. I can't hear naughty words."

He didn't want to like her, but he couldn't help himself. "I was a teenager at the time, but I can still remember Mrs. Ludlow calmly setting her walker to one side and putting manacles on her wrists."

She laughed aloud, and he saw more than one man look her way appreciatively.

"So what happened to the building?" she asked. "Surely they didn't drag three old women away."

"Nope, they came up with a grant that enabled the building to be renovated into a B&B down by Silver Creek. It's called Connections now."

"Connections?"

"The B&B is one of the ways we're connected to Valentine's past."

They smiled at each other, and he felt his own begin to fade as he contemplated the joy in Emily's eyes. A man could look at that every day.

She slapped her hands on her thighs as she rose to her feet. "I think it's time for you to go, cowboy. I have work to do, and I suspect those cows need you, too."

He followed her back inside the restaurant and through the kitchen. He saw again the holes in the walls. "You going to hire someone to repair all this?"

At the back door, she turned and put her hands on her hips. "Why does everyone ask that? I'm a hard worker."

"No offense, but there's some skill involved."

"What I don't know, I'll learn, so thanks for your concern."

He passed her to go out into the rear hall. Without even touching her, he could feel the warmth of her body, smell the faint hint of floral perfume beneath the odor of Spic and Span. Whatever he told his brain, his body was paying attention to other signals.

"Tell Scout I missed seeing him," Emily said, holding open the door to the alley.

She was a dog lover, too. Nate took the steps down to his truck before he could linger, but Emily had already shut the door.

Emily locked the alley door behind Nate and locked away any more thoughts of him. She was glad the awkwardness was finished. Well, most of it. She returned to the front of the restaurant and stood near the door's glass window. Though she still kept the shutters drawn because of the mess, she could see out enough to admire how the town had made the best of its location and history. The perfect example was the Hotel Colorado just across the street, where a steady stream of cars loaded and unloaded near its front door. She imagined that the preservation-fund committee might have had an active part in that, too. Except for her own building, she hadn't seen a business on Main Street that looked in need of repair; but then again, she hadn't walked the side streets, something she'd have to rectify. It was hard to make the time when she needed to finish the building before she could get on with her life.

She idly wondered about the donors to the preservation fund and their opponents, the people against bringing in tourism. Which side did Nate really come down on? His family was well entrenched, and it would be easy to imagine that they didn't want things to change.

Thoughts of Mrs. Ludlow's fund made her remember the lady's granddaughter. Seeing the little girl with her curly pigtails had made Emily's heart just about tighten up in her chest. It used to hurt every time she walked past a stroller or a school bus or a ball field. But she couldn't keep living in that constant state of depression, or she might never come out of it. She had a future, a good one. She was doing something about her wish for a family, beginning with the repairs on the building. It wouldn't happen overnight, but she could be patient, waiting for the day she had enough money to adopt. She'd spent too many weeks and months of her life wallowing in the wreck of her marriage and dreams, as if she didn't have the power to change things.

Just looking around at the restaurant made her realize she'd already made a dent in the chaos. And she was doing her Internet research each night on putting up drywall and ripping up damaged flooring. It didn't look too hard, she told herself. Nate might be unconvinced, but she would show him what she was capable of.

No, he wasn't her motivation. She would show *herself*.

Over the next few days, Emily spent most of her waking hours focused on the building. Occasionally, the widows dropped food off to her at midday, as if they didn't trust her to remember to feed herself—or if they thought she wasn't spending her money on that.

And they were right. The longer Emily remained

in Valentine, the more she realized she was going to
have to look for part-time work soon. Yet she took the
time to put flowers in the planters out front, so that her
bare building wouldn't hurt any of the other businesses
nearby.

She'd become acclimated to the altitude at last, and
found some wonderful hiking trails up behind the town
hall. Running brought her such peace in this beautiful
mountain country, leaving her feeling stronger than she
had in a long time.

She didn't see Nate at all, and told herself that was a
good thing. Brooke occasionally mentioned how busy
they were at the ranch, with the stress of haying season
coming up in June. If they didn't harvest a good crop,
they'd have to purchase hay at the end of winter to feed
the cattle, cutting into their profit.

Monica and Brooke were proving to be a welcome
distraction, occasionally insisting she accompany them
to a movie or out to eat. Brooke dragged them to Outlaws, the local honky-tonk bar, where Brooke fit right
in with her cowboy boots and hat. She did a mean line
dance, but Emily felt like she had two left feet though
she gave it a try. Her ex didn't like to dance, so they
didn't. Why had she been so stupid as to let that stop
her? Because she'd let go of her high-school and college girlfriends, that was why. She'd been a fool.

At Outlaws, they were each drinking beer, turning
down requests to dance until they could get their breath
back. A Kenny Chesney song was blaring in the background. Even though Emily was only wearing jeans
and a shirt over a camisole, she noticed more than one

admiring glance, and as the evening went on, her spirits lifted. She watched the crowd, a mixture of young and old, and found herself focusing on the older men, gathered in a booth near the back, playing cards.

Could one of them be her father?

Angry with herself, she took another swig of beer and glanced at Monica, who was picking the label off her bottle absently.

"Is something wrong?" Emily asked.

Monica glanced up with a jerk. "Sorry. Guess I got distracted."

Brooke studied her. "With what? Everything okay at the store?"

"Busy, and Mrs. Wilcox was sick again today, so I was alone."

"Poor old lady," Brooke murmured. "What about Karista?"

"She's still in high school, remember? She's only evenings and weekends. But that's not the real problem." Monica heaved a sigh. "My sister's coming to visit."

"Isn't that a good thing?" Emily asked.

Her friend shrugged. "It should be. But sadly, Missy always manages to make sure I know she thinks I'm wasting my life."

"She *says* that?" Emily was aghast.

"No, not in so many words. But I know. She thinks you can only feel 'fulfilled'—her word—with an important job in a city."

Brooke smiled without amusement. "You can only imagine what she thinks about me."

"No, she really doesn't think that way about other

people," Monica insisted. "It's just me. I'm her sister—her twin. Somehow, she thinks we're supposed to want the same things."

Mention of Melissa had brought down the mood of the evening. Emily had always wanted a sister or brother, and it made her sad to see sisters not getting along.

"When is she coming?" Brooke asked.

"I don't know the exact date. She's in the Middle East right now. When it quiets down a bit, they'll give her some free time."

"It sounds like an exciting job," Emily said, then realized she sounded too wistful when Brooke gave her a warning frown. "I mean—"

"Emily," Monica interrupted with a smile. "I'm not *that* sensitive, whatever Brooke thinks. Of course Missy's job is exciting. But it's not exactly glamorous most of the time, especially when she's covering earthquakes and tsunamis, and people are dying right in front of her. Sometimes she can't get a lot of food because it might make her a target for starving, desperate people. But if it sounds interesting to you, then you should talk to her about it. She'd *love* that," she added dryly.

"That's the problem—I don't know what sounds interesting to me." Emily clenched her beer bottle in frustration. "I know going back to college is the right thing to do, but I didn't enjoy it the first time, and I have no clue what to study. Although I think I'll rule out international journalism." She grinned at Monica. "Too much travel."

"You don't like to travel?" Brooke asked in surprise.

"I do, but I want to have a family, and that would be difficult." She smiled shyly. "I'm going to adopt."

"That's a great plan," Monica said. "You're not waiting for a husband to share it with?"

"I tried that, and it didn't work. I'm getting too old to wait around for the right man, especially since I'll have to save up adoption money."

"You might not know what you want to do for a job," Brooke said, "but you've got a plan, and that's important."

"You must have been a cheerleader in high school," Emily said.

"Bite your tongue. I was a barrel racer, and the high-school girls' champion of Colorado."

"I'm impressed, and I don't even know what it means," Emily continued. "You ride horses around barrels?"

"Something like that. I'll show you sometime."

"Speaking of plans," Monica said cheerfully, "Emily, you mentioned needing some furniture in your apartment. What do you have?"

"I don't need much since I won't be here long. There's a bed frame, but I wouldn't feel comfortable using the mattress."

Brooke visibly shuddered, and they all laughed.

"What size bed?" Monica asked.

"Looks like a double, since the bedroom is pretty small."

"Let me see what my parents have."

Emily frowned. "What do you mean? I certainly can't take your family's furniture."

"They've been talking about remodeling the guest

bedroom for the longest time. Now that Missy's coming home, I'm sure my mom will jump right in."

"I detect sarcasm," Brooke murmured.

Monica briefly stuck out her tongue.

"I don't know if I feel right about this . . ." Emily began.

"Quiet. What else do you need?" Brooke asked.

"There's already a table and two chairs. With those and a mattress, I'll have eating and sleeping covered. That's all I need."

The two women looked at each other doubtfully, and Emily prepared herself to insist, but nothing more was said about furniture.

Brooke set her empty beer bottle down with a thump. "Guess it's time to go. I need to be up before dawn."

Monica shuddered. "You work long hours. I don't know how you do it."

Brooke shrugged. "It has to be done. Emily, can I drop you off on my way home?"

Emily gladly accepted, no longer feeling guilty about it, since the boardinghouse really was on the way to the ranch. After letting herself in the back door, she came up short when she found Mrs. Thalberg, dressed in a housecoat and slippers, sitting at the kitchen table with papers spread out before her.

Mrs. Thalberg lifted her head and smiled. "Did you have a nice evening, Emily?"

She grinned. "I did. Brooke taught me a line dance, and I wasn't too terrible. But why are you still up at midnight?"

"I just wanted to prepare our new applications for

the committee meeting tomorrow. Now that I don't have to get up before dawn, I do some of my best thinking at night."

Emily found herself picturing the redheaded grandmother chained to a brothel, and barely held in a laugh.

"When it's not so late, I'd love to hear all about your work. It sounds really challenging." Emily suddenly noticed a man's jacket on the hook by the back door. "Uh-oh, someone might be cold tonight since he left that behind."

"That would be Nate's. He dropped by to see you."

Emily stiffened in surprise.

"He fell asleep on the couch," Mrs. Thalberg continued, shaking her head. "That poor boy works too hard. I think you should go wake him since he brought a box he says is for you."

Two beers must have been too much, for Emily felt a pleasant little zing of warmth traveling through her veins.

Chapter Eight

Emily walked slowly through the dark dining room, wishing Mrs. Thalberg would've come with her. But the old woman had mentioned Nate, then disappeared up the back staircase, wiggling her fingers good-bye. Emily saw a box on the dining table, and much as she wanted to open it, she kept on going. The living room—or the parlor, as the widows enjoyed calling it—was decorated in country-printed fabrics and seemed to be the focus of whatever crafting talents the women possessed. There were crocheted pillows and afghans, needlepoint scenes on the walls, even a pile of rocks glued together—surely the talents of someone's grandchild. But beneath the country charm, she could see modern touches: brand-new windows, newly stained floorboards, and elegant trim.

It was homey and feminine, which was why the sight of Nate sprawled across the too-small couch seemed out of place. His legs dangled over one armrest, and his hand rested on the floor. The ever-present cowboy hat was perched on his chest, rising and falling with his even breathing.

Emily tiptoed closer and stared down at him. Without her being able to see the knowing look he often wore, he seemed younger, more relaxed. The lines fanning out from his eyes were less evident. She found herself wanting to touch his unruly hair, straighten it.

And then he opened his eyes, and she jumped back with a gasp.

"God, you scared me!" she said in a loud whisper.

"I could say the same thing." He swung his feet to the floor and sat up, setting his hat beside him and running his hands through his hair.

"It's still sticking up," Emily said, unable to help herself.

He rolled his eyes even as he absently fingered it again. Glancing at the grandfather clock standing guard in the corner, he said, "It's past midnight."

She folded her arms over her chest. "Your point?"

"My sister's cranky when she doesn't get enough sleep."

"She's a big girl."

He rose to his feet, six-plus feet of him, taking her breath away with his lean, rangy height and all that masculinity.

"You smell like beer," he said.

And suddenly she remembered what had happened the last time she had a beer with him. The bar had had the same dark shadows as now enfolded them in the parlor, making her feel like they were alone in the world.

"I was much more careful this time," she said.

The corners of his lips turned up with a touch of bad-boy humor.

"Do you dance as well as your sister?" she asked.

"Is that an invitation?"

The awkwardness she'd been hoping to avoid returned with a vengeance. "Sorry, I was only teasing."

He ran a hand down his face. "No, I'm sorry. I shouldn't be flirting. It's a habit with me and the female of the species. You'll have to break me of it."

She laughed. "You're probably not thinking straight, having just woken up. I guess I should've called your grandmother to let her know how late I'd be."

"No curfew at the Widows' Boardinghouse. That Mrs. Ludlow likes to party all night long."

Emily covered her mouth although a snort of laughter escaped.

"I decided to hang around," Nate continued, grinning. "There's always something that needs fixing."

"Really?" She wandered away from him, toward the front hall and the beautifully carved woodwork of the staircase banister. "From the way your grandmother talks—and from what I've seen myself—you did a superb job the first time you worked on this house. You really did it all yourself?"

He shrugged. "I grew up helping my dad in his woodworking shop."

"There must be a lot of things to fix on a ranch."

"I like making things work."

She leaned against the banister even as Nate came

closer, standing beneath the arched entrance of the parlor. "What did you work on tonight?"

He pointed to the banister behind her head, and she jumped away with a wince.

He laughed softly. "No, I was just teasing. That's solid and well over a hundred years old. I sanded and stained it a couple years ago, but that's all. The kitchen faucet had a leak. You didn't notice this morning?"

She frowned and shook her head. "I was baking, too, so I think I would have . . ." She trailed off in realization.

"Yep. I think Grandma does it deliberately to get me over here. Makes me feel like a bad grandson," he said with bemusement, "that she thinks I need to be coerced to be here."

"No, don't think that," she said, laying a hand on his arm.

They both went still, and he looked down at her hand before meeting her eyes.

She patted him briefly and let go, glad of her outward calm even though her heart had picked up speed. "She's very proud that you and Brooke and Josh call her on her cell phone. She knows you pay attention. Maybe she just likes seeing you."

They looked at each other for a moment, and when Emily felt like she could get lost in his green eyes, she cleared her throat, and said, "Your grandma tells me you brought me something?"

"Oh, yeah, follow me." He led her into the dining room, turned on the old-fashioned chandelier—that gleamed with newness despite its design—and gestured to the box. "You know how this house used to be your grandma Riley's? When I remodeled, I found mostly junk in the attic, but I collected a few things that I thought someone might come looking for someday."

She looked up at him in surprise. "Why, Nate, how sensitive of you."

"Just too lazy to throw anything more away." He folded his arms across his chest and frowned. "I think it was Grandma's idea."

Though she doubted that, she didn't dispute him, seeing how uncomfortable he was. It was hard to hide a smile, but she made the effort. "What's inside?"

"Go ahead and look."

She slowly unfolded each tab of the box, reminding herself that she wasn't worried about the past, that her grandmother was just too sensitive where Delilah was concerned. But would she find something here that would change how she thought about everything? And did she want to discover it in front of Nate?

But the box was open, and she let herself explore like it was Christmas morning. There was a jewelry box with several pieces of costume jewelry that might make a cool vintage statement in San Francisco. Her feelings of Christmas became even stronger as she found some homemade tree ornaments that made her gasp with delight. An empty carved wooden box must have meant the craftsman had been close to her grandmother.

And then she found more modern items, childhood toys from the sixties, several of which had images of the moon, which she knew had always captivated her mother. Even when in a hurry, if they stepped outside under a full moon, Delilah would raise her face to it for a moment's peace. She never preached to Emily about the things she believed in, another private part of herself that she kept distant. Emily never knew if Delilah didn't want to be ridiculed or didn't care enough to teach her daughter.

She shook off her memories and went back to the box, finding high-school yearbooks from the early eighties, and even the fifties, a legacy of her grandparents to add to the few other mementoes she had of theirs. Lastly, there were clothbound books that might be diaries. Her mother's diaries? she wondered, feeling both intrigued and dismayed. Did she want to be sucked into her mother's life again, to learn secrets that might hurt her even more? Although what could hurt her more than hearing that her father had been a lie? Had the poor man even known?

"You don't look happy," Nate said quietly.

Startled, she glanced up, having almost forgotten he was there. He was watching her too closely, as if he could read her thoughts.

She forced a smile. "I was just remembering my mother. We didn't get along well."

"Sorry to hear that."

She cocked her head as she watched him. "I hope you don't understand what that's like."

"I don't," he answered simply. "My mother helped my father raise us even when she suffered her worst attacks of MS."

"She sounds wonderful and brave. I'll have to meet her sometime."

To her surprise, he didn't respond, even out of polite-ness. Protective, was he?

He gestured to the box. "Well, good night then. Hope you find something in there you're looking for."

She wished him the same and briefly watched him walk into the kitchen. She was staring at the box again when the back door opened and closed. The box couldn't contain anything she was looking for because she wanted the future, not the past. She folded it shut.

The next morning at dawn, Nate was working side by side with Josh in the horse barn, raking dirty straw and loading it in the back of a flatbed. The barn was still cold before the spring day could warm it, and the horses occasionally neighed to one another, or butted Nate's arm when he passed. Scout moved in and out of the stalls, yipping at the horses as if greeting old friends.

"So have you been to Outlaws recently?" Nate asked. "It's been a long time since you offered to be my wingman."

Josh laughed, for neither brother ever needed help approaching a woman. Nate tended to be more open and sociable, filling time with words instead of having to answer questions, while Josh let the soulful-cowboy thing work for him.

Josh stepped out of an empty stall and regarded him with interest. "Funny you should mention that. I was at Outlaws, and saw Brooke and Monica with that new woman everyone's talkin' about."

Pretending nonchalance, Nate looked at the time on

his phone, then put in his earpiece. The calls would begin soon. He realized Josh was still watching him. "Brooke didn't mention seeing you."

"I didn't want to be noticed by my sister," Josh said dryly.

Nate chuckled.

He leaned on the end of his rake. "Nice dodge, big brother."

Nate shoveled a pile of straw into the wheelbarrow. "Dodge?" He didn't want to talk about Emily. But now she was there in his mind, her expression full of hesitation and hope and even wariness in the shadowy dining room looking at the box from her past.

And then his phone rang on his belt and relief washed over him. He tipped it toward him to read the ID. "Give me a sec. It's about the grandstands for the rodeo." He kept the conversation brief, then tapped his earpiece to hang up. "So what happened at Outlaws?"

"It's amazing how you go from one thing to another without missing a beat." Josh smiled, shaking his head, and took his towering wheelbarrow outside to shove onto the flatbed.

Nate piled his own wheelbarrow a bit higher than his brother's had been.

"You have an amazing mind," Josh continued, returning to lean against the empty stall, "able to do so many things at once—too many things. You can't possibly keep functioning this way, doing everything, being everything to everybody."

"Josh, you sound like I'm an old man who needs to slow down. I'm in my prime, boy!" he said, keeping his voice light, even though Josh was irritating the hell out of him.

"I'm glad about your new girl, really I am."

Nate kept his face impassive. "She's not my girl."

"Tony De Luca said you met her the first night she was in town. That's good. She might help you remember there's more to life than work."

Nate turned his back. "I played some pool that night, and that was all."

"Really? Besides Tony, there were others doing some talking."

Nate rubbed his forearm across his perspiring face. "Let me guess—Ned and Ted."

As Josh gave a knowing grin, Nate's phone rang again. The strangest expression came over Josh's face. Nate let the phone ring.

"Get that," Josh said seriously. "It's important to you."

"Everything's important to me. And I treat it all that way."

Nate answered, continuing to rake while he talked to Joe Sweet about Valentine's organic farms co-op. Joe was a fellow rancher whose family also owned the Sweetheart Inn. As if Joe didn't have enough to do, he'd gotten involved in coordinating the distribution of organic produce to restaurants in Aspen and the rest of the Roaring Fork Valley.

When he hung up, Josh was coming back in with the empty wheelbarrow. The phone rang again, and Nate silenced it without looking.

Josh sighed. "I know you. You'll regret not taking that. You try to be there for every fence post we put in a hole, every horse that needs to be shoed—and every report about the winery or the farm. You can't keep this pace up. Maybe this woman will help you see that you have to make *choices,* Nate."

"That's enough," Nate said shortly.

"For now," Josh shot back, and stalked out of the barn.

Emily slept a bit too late for a long run, so she decided to walk through Valentine Valley for her exercise. On leaving her room, she glanced at her mother's box, then away again. It seemed to stare at her as she left. She was being an idiot. Remembering the lunch she'd packed the night before, she realized she would have to do another grocery run soon, further depleting her savings.

Rain had fallen through the night, making everything glisten with the morning sun, like the world had been sprayed with glitter. The Silver Creek was running even higher as she crossed the bridge, flecks of foam spraying into the air. She walked the streets parallel to Main, enjoying that they were all named after women: Nellie Street, Clara Street, Grace, Mabel, and Bessie, names that must have been popular in the late nineteenth century when the town was new. Past the town hall, an inn gleamed with old-fashioned elegance, perched on the slope of the Elk Mountains. She'd heard more than once that she should try the restaurant there, the finest dining in town, but that would be too big a strain on her wallet.

A landscaped rose garden made up a city block, complete with a fountain and a stone bridge over a fish-pond. Four bed-and-breakfasts presided, one at each corner. Monica had called them the Four Sisters, and with the cupolas, gingerbread trim, and wraparound porches, they were elegant reminders of another era. A van was parked in the driveway of one of them, unloading tables and chairs, and Emily imagined an outdoor engagement party or wedding reception.

And everywhere, even at midmorning, were the lovers. She spotted them kissing under vine-covered trellises or biking side by side. At the rose garden, she was asked to take a couple's picture on the bridge, and they confided he'd asked her to marry him on that same spot fifty years ago.

As far as love was concerned, Emily felt even more ancient than they were. How did a relationship last so long?

She was feeling a little down by the time she approached her building, turning into the alley. She came up short on seeing Nate's pickup, dismayed to find herself feeling a jolt of interest. Oh, this wasn't good.

And then Brooke came out of Monica's Flowers and Gifts, keys dangling from her hand, and noticed her arrival. "Hey, Em, you're just in time. Give me a hand with this mattress."

Em? Even her mother hadn't been so casual with her, so . . . familiar. She kind of liked it.

Brooke pulled down the rear door of the pickup, and Emily saw a plastic-draped mattress.

"It's the one Monica mentioned. Mrs. Shaw was thrilled to get rid of it without a fuss. I borrowed Nate's pickup."

"But—what do I owe her?"

"I asked, and she said it was twenty years old, and she hoped you wouldn't ask for money to take it."

They smiled at each other.

"Let me unlock the doors and set down my backpack," Emily said, suddenly eager.

Between the two of them, they dragged the mattress upstairs and plopped it into the frame. Emily was breathing a little hard, but Brooke only wiggled her eyebrows and made a muscle with one arm to emphasize her strength.

After hearing someone come through the door, they left the bedroom to see Monica.

"Hey, this is just like my place," Monica said, smiling.

Emily looked around her, trying to see the apartment as others did, now that the garbage had been removed. It still needed a good cleaning, of course, and scuffmarks and nail holes decorated the white walls. The two bedrooms—one larger than the other—and bathroom were in the rear of the apartment, overlooking the alley. The main living area was open, with a view of Main Street. The galley kitchen had a small window set in the wall between it and the living room, and a table and two chairs sat nearby. But the big front window let in a lot of light. The place had promise, and hopefully whoever purchased the building would agree.

The only other piece of furniture was a couch with torn cushions, sitting forlornly in the middle of the dull wood floor.

"You don't plan to use *that*," Monica began doubtfully.

Emily shook her head. "No, but I needed another person to help move it."

"Then let's go," Brooke said.

After it had been removed to the Dumpster, Emily led the way into the restaurant kitchen, saying, "Come on in for a soda."

As they drank, Brooke walked around the place, peering into the dining room. "Hey, what's this?" she called, walking to the front entrance. She bent down and picked up something that had been slipped under the door. "Guess this is for you."

Emily's name was scrawled across a Deering Family Real Estate envelope.

"I was wondering when Howie Junior would get to you," Brooke said, shaking her head.

" 'Get to' me?"

"Brooke, that's not fair," Monica said. "It's his business to discuss property that's for sale."

"Shouldn't I be talking to him?" Emily asked.

Brooke sighed. "I dated him in high school. He liked to kiss and tell."

"He's grown up since then." Monica shook her head. "Brooke just doesn't like her private life discussed."

Emily almost said *Just like her brother,* but she stopped herself in time.

"And I'm certain she kisses better now," Monica added solemnly.

"You people all know each other!" Emily said with a laugh. "Is there anyone in town who doesn't have a story to tell about someone else?"

Brooke and Monica shrugged at each other, then said in unison, "Nope."

"I took a walk around town this morning, and although people were all friendly, sometimes I felt like everyone was staring at me, just waiting for me to do something worth talking about."

Monica bit her lip. "Girl, I think you already did. It seems the plumbers—"

"Ned and Ted Ferguson," Emily interrupted.

"Well, they told Bill Chernoff at the post office, who told Sally Gillroy from the mayor's office—"

"The mayor!" Emily cried.

"No, she's the clerk, but she told my mom, who's a receptionist for Doc Ericson, who told me."

"Told you what?" Emily asked with a sigh. Rumors could transform into ugly things.

"That you and Nate got a little drunk the first night you were in town."

Brooke gaped at her. "And you didn't tell me?"

"So I'm supposed to tell you about your brother?" Emily threw her hands wide. "Anything else?"

"That you went into the back room to play pool, and a half hour later, you came hurrying out red-faced, and Nate looked angry."

Well, at least the whole town didn't know how far things had gone. "This is embarrassing."

"You don't need to tell us if you don't want to," Monica said soothingly.

"There's nothing to really tell," Emily insisted. "We bet a kiss on the pool game, and in the middle of the kiss, I stopped it. I've never drunkenly kissed a stranger before, and I was just mortified."

"That's all?" Brooke said, obviously a little disappointed.

"Well . . . there might have been some groping." She closed her eyes with a groan when the two women glanced at each other and chuckled. "I don't want to talk about my horrible behavior that night. We've since apologized to each other, and we're friends."

"Groping friends," Monica mused thoughtfully. "Maybe I should try that."

"We're not groping anymore," Emily shot back.

"Sorry if we're too nosy," Monica soothed. "Neither of us is dating anyone, so even hearing about drunken groping sounds more exciting than our lives have been lately."

"Believe me, I understand," Emily said wearily. "It's just that . . . I've recently come away from a terrible marriage, and I'll be leaving in a few weeks, and dating would just be too complicated. Nate's been a friend."

"That's my brother," Brooke drawled. "Nooo self-interest there."

"We're not dating!" Emily insisted. The merest thought of trusting a man again, especially now that she'd put her own future first . . . no, she had new priorities, things to accomplish on her own. "Now can I see the envelope addressed to me?" she asked sweetly.

Brooke handed it over. Emily scanned the contents, written in a cheerful manner by Howard Deering—

though she could only think of him as Howie Junior, thanks to Brooke.

"Someone is interested in my building!" Emily said, grinning at her two friends.

Monica smiled. "Good for you. Do we know the person?"

"Howie—Mr. Deering—didn't say."

"It's kind of strange that he wouldn't mention the buyer," Brooke mused.

"I'll call." Emily dialed the real-estate office and reached a receptionist, who gave her Howie's cell phone. To her surprise, he hesitated about revealing the interested party, and when at last he did, she understood his reluctance. After hanging up, she put on an innocent air and took another sip of her Diet Coke.

"Well?" Brooke demanded.

Emily laughed. "You're going to love this. The name of the company is Leather and Lace. They have another store in San Francisco, and they're beginning to branch out. Take a guess what they sell."

"Leather and Lace . . ." Brooke mused. "Decorated saddles?"

"You would go there." Monica rolled her eyes. "S & M?"

"Close," Emily said. "Naughty lingerie."

"Ooh." Monica looked thoughtful. "However will I concentrate on work with *that* next store?"

"They're very sexy, and apparently run the gamut from *really* naughty to tasteful. And who says I'll accept their offer?" she added. "They're not making one until they see the building. And I'm not letting anyone see *this* disaster for a while."

"You think they'll fit in here?" Brooke asked. "This can be a conservative town."

"*Valentine Valley,*" Emily emphasized the name. "Isn't it all about romance? And what says romance better than honeymoon clothes?"

"I like it," Monica said firmly.

"We'll see if anyone else does." Brooke looked doubtful.

"Don't be pessimistic," Emily said. "Someone has an actual interest in the building, and in this economy, I'll take what I can get. Now if someone else is interested, and they start a bidding war . . . maybe I'll have my college tuition paid for with lots to spare for a baby." She hugged herself, pushing back her doubts and worries. "Back to work. I have to get to the hardware store."

"And Mrs. Wilcox is probably panicking without me," Monica said glumly.

"And Nate threatened to whip me if I didn't help take care of some fences in the horse pasture."

When Emily was alone, she let the peaceful happiness of friendship wash over her. Already, she felt like she could tell Brooke and Monica anything, and they'd understand and sympathize, or even tell her she was making a mistake. She realized, to her delight, that girlfriends were family, too.

Emily walked the one block to the hardware store, feeling cheerful and positive. She browsed in the windows of the Vista Gallery of Art, admiring its beautiful mountain landscapes, then inhaled the aroma from the coffee shop Espresso Yourself. She didn't like coffee, but she loved the scent that drifted out the door when someone went inside. Several people sat outside at little wrought-iron two-person tables, even though the day was overcast. Emily nodded and smiled as people did the same to her. It still surprised her how friendly everyone was.

Hal's Hardware, a clapboard structure built on a corner lot, rose three stories, a rarity in Valentine. Inside, she stopped in amazement at how much was crammed in each aisle, floor to ceiling. The first thing she saw was the paint department, where a large table was placed near a coffeemaker. Three men sat around the table, and turned to stare when she closed the door behind her. They were in their sixties and older, but it was hard to tell with men who spent their working lives outdoors.

Feeling as on display as a butterfly pinned to a board, Emily forced a smile. "Good morning."

They all smiled back, to one degree or another, but the interest was obvious.

"Hey there, girl," one grizzled old man called, taking off his cowboy hat as if to see her better with steel blue eyes. He wore a well-used tan Carhartt jacket, open over his overalls. "You lost?"

"Not if this is the hardware store," she said pleasantly.

She glanced at the clerk behind the cash register, an older man who wore glasses above a beard laced with white like his sandy hair. His pleated denim shirt was monogrammed with the name "Hal." Not a clerk then.

Hal smiled. "You've come to the right place, Miss . . ." He trailed off.

All the men seemed to wait in fascination for her identity, but before she could say it, another man at the table, balding, wearing the blue shirt of the US Postal Service, spoke up. "Emily Murphy."

One of the men nodded as if his suspicions were confirmed, and the other seemed to cock his head to study her.

"Bill Chernoff," she responded to the postal clerk, remembering what Monica had told her about rumors spreading.

He reddened, and the man in the Carhartt jacket guffawed. "How do you know my name?"

She put one hand on her hip. "Rumors fly, but I guess you already know that."

Behind the counter, Hal snorted. "She's got ya there, Bill. I'm Hal Abrams, Mrs. Murphy."

So he knew she'd been married—but of course, that made sense, since everyone in town knew she didn't have her mother's last name.

"Your grandparents were good people," said the third man, wearing a down vest over his flannel shirt. His gray mustache was twirled up at the ends, and he had bushy eyebrows to match. "And we're doin' nothing but confrontin' you. I'm more polite than these cowpokes. Name's Francis Osborne, of the Circle F Ranch, and this here's"—he gestured toward the man in the Carhartt jacket, who nodded, even as he briefly said something into a cell phone before hanging up—"Deke Hutcheson of Paradise Mountain Ranch."

"Nice to meet you, gentlemen," Emily said politely. She glanced at Hal. "I guess your coffee's better than the brew at Espresso Yourself next door."

Deke shuddered. "Naw, this tastes like horse piss, but the company's not bad."

Bill Chernoff patted his slight paunch. "No Sweetheart Inn cookies to tempt me."

She narrowed her eyes in puzzlement. "Sweetheart Inn cookies?"

"That's where Suzie gets her coffee-dippin' cookies next door."

"I see." She glanced at Hal and smiled. She was about to ask him where the drywall was, when Deke spoke.

"Never did get to eat at the restaurant that rented your grandma's store. What are you doing with the place?"

All four eyed her, suddenly serious.

"I'm selling the building and returning home to San Francisco."

"But your people come from here," Francis said, bushy brows lowered in confusion.

For just a moment, she thought about asking questions about her mother even though these men were older than Delilah. But this was a very public forum— and she didn't want to know, she reminded herself. "I wasn't born here, but thanks for including me. It would have been nice to be raised in such a beautiful place."

"It's hard work keeping it beautiful," Bill said. "You'll find out when you put the building up for sale. Only certain stores fit in."

Was he on the preservation-fund committee? she wondered with amusement.

"You never know who wants to move here," Francis said, shaking his head. "Big-city folk from Denver want everything left 'unspoiled,' they say, as if our hundred-year-old ranches don't belong here."

"And then there's the tourists," Deke practically spat.

"They look harmless to me," she said, "holding hands and taking pictures and eating at your restaurants."

"But then they rent their ATVs. Punk-ass kids take down my NO TRESPASSING signs and ride through my hay like it's just grass in a meadow."

They all seemed to grumble under their breaths, nodding in agreement.

"Strangers bought up that house my boy's been saving for," Francis said. "Cash money, too."

Hal shrugged at her, his expression regretful, as if he knew she had better things to do at his store.

The door jangled, and she glanced over her shoulder, stiffening as Nate Thalberg walked in, Scout at his heels. He had work gloves tucked into his belt and a scarf around his neck as if he'd just come from the ranch.

Deke patted his cell phone on the table. "These little things can be handy."

Chapter Nine

She wanted to groan. Why had Deke called Nate?
Then she saw all four older men grinning at each other,
and she remembered that they had all probably specu-
lated on what she and Nate had been doing in the back
room at Tony's. She tried to keep a smile on her face,
knowing they thought they were teasing her but not ap-
preciating being the butt of their joke.

The amused glances they shot at Nate made her realize that perhaps she wasn't the target. Yet she couldn't
miss the fondness in the old ranchers' eyes when Nate
ambled over to shake hands with everyone. After
nosing her hand, Scout went from knee to knee, wrig-
gling in canine delight at each petted greeting.

"Moved the herd to the next pasture yet?" Francis
asked, stroking his mustache with interest.

Nate began to talk about conditions up on their grazing lands and asking about the health of everyone's
cattle. He might be the son of their fellow ranch owner,
but they treated him with the respect of a contempo-
rary.

Though the conversation was interesting, Emily had work to do. She turned away and began to examine the racks behind her stocked with patching supplies, writing down some prices. But it was hard to concentrate when they started talking about an upcoming local rodeo, because images of Nate on horseback kept intruding on her thoughts. Would she be able to watch him compete? No, no, she'd be gone by then, she reminded herself sternly.

She wasn't certain how much time had passed until Nate spoke right behind her. "A different brand is on sale at the end of the rack."

She gave a start, then glanced over her shoulder to see him grinning.

"Concentrating, huh?" he said. "Such dedication."

"Gee, thanks."

"So what do you need?" He looked over her shoulder at her growing list. "Drywall. Yep. Don't buy all those tools on your list. I have plenty you can borrow."

Once again, he was trying to do her a favor, and though part of her bristled, the practical side of her was reluctantly grateful for anything that saved her money. "Thank you." She picked up the patching compound that he'd shown her was on sale, trying not to feel embarrassed at revealing even more of her financial problems. But then again, the way Valentine Valley worked, the mechanic had probably told him she couldn't have her car repaired, and Nate had already known she couldn't afford to stay in a motel. To cover her embarrassment, she babbled, "When I was looking up the hardware store on the Internet, I was shocked that a small-town store had its entire inventory online."

"Hal's not the only owner," Nate said. "His partner has plenty of money to put into the business. You'll find that a lot around here."

"Silent partners with plenty of money?" she said dryly. "That could sound suspicious."

"If we weren't so close to Aspen. People are always looking for investments. Or else they've moved here from somewhere else to semiretire."

"Like the lawyer, Mr. Carpenter?" she said without thinking.

He shot her a surprised glance. "Cal? Where'd you meet him?"

"Oh, around," she said, trying to sound nonchalant. "He introduced himself, just like everyone does around here."

When he accepted her explanation without comment, she quietly let out her breath. He didn't need to know about the ache in her heart over her father. He unsettled her, made her babble when she should choose her words carefully. But he had a lot of experience with home repairs, so she'd take his advice, regardless of what it cost her in pride or composure.

She wasn't there to buy, only to make lists and plan her purchases. Nate followed her around the store, mentioning the extras she hadn't thought about, filling in details that the videos online hadn't. He didn't seem to care that the two of them were a source of amusement to the men hanging out in the paint department.

She did pick up some cleaning supplies, and as she took them to Hal at the counter, she overheard Deke grumbling to Francis.

"A restaurant for raw fish? Isn't that what sushi is? Who needs it?"

"The diner is just fine," Francis shot back. "And when I want fancy, there's the steak house at the Hotel Colorado."

All the men nodded.

"And about that other place," Deke continued. "What does 'new age store' even mean?"

Though she'd brightened at the thought of sushi, now she winced, having spent her life hearing variations of that question. There was a new age store in Valentine Valley?

"The owner's a woman," Francis said. "Maybe 'new age' is code for bein' younger."

"Or maybe she's a witch," Deke shot back.

That made everyone guffaw.

She could be a witch, Emily thought mildly, but if she tried to explain the Wiccan religion to these old guys . . .

"She did have witch books," Bill insisted.

"So you went inside?" Francis asked incredulously.

"Naw, saw it through the window. She had a sign about getting one of those card readings. Who the heck believes in telling the future?"

"Why does it matter?" Emily heard herself asking. She might have distanced herself from her mother's interests, but the store had put food on her table.

She was suddenly the focus of all the male attention.

She shrugged. "People have a right to open any business they choose, and only the customers can decide if it will succeed. How long has this store been open?"

"A year," Deke gruffly answered.

"Then she has customers."

"Tourists," Francis snorted.

"Just tourists?" Emily smiled. "You sure none of your wives and daughters have stopped in?"

A couple of the men frowned, a couple looked shocked.

"Oo-kay," Nate said, smiling at Hal. "We're ready to check out."

By the time he escorted her out of the hardware store, Emily was almost enjoying herself. "My, you're sensitive," she said, when they were out on the sidewalk. "You practically yanked on my arm to get me out of there. No healthy discussions in the paint department?"

"The old-timers have their own problems," Nate said, taking the bag out of her hands.

She tried to tug it back. "I can carry my own bag."

"And what would my mother think if she drove by right now and saw that I was empty-handed?"

She was tempted to answer that since she hadn't met his mother, she didn't know—but that would sound like she *wanted* to meet his mother, that she wanted to get to know him better. Bad impression. She began to walk up Main Street, and Nate fell in at her side.

"So the *old-timers* don't like anything new or different moving to town?" Emily asked. "That kind of leads to stagnation, doesn't it?"

"Whatever they think about mystical stuff, they know that modern technology has revolutionized ranching and can save them money in the long run. They aren't against new ideas."

"Unless they can make fun of them."

"Why are you so quick to defend a store you know nothing about?"

She hesitated, then found herself saying, "Because my mother owned a new age store."

He shot her a surprised look. "I didn't think anyone from Valentine Valley had such free-spirited ideas."

"Why do you think she left?" Or that's what Emily had always been told. Her grandmother's revelation rose unbidden in her mind. "Delilah was born too late to be a hippie though she'd have fit right in."

"Delilah?"

"She liked me to call her by her first name. I always thought she felt too young to be a mom. She was only nineteen when she had me." So young and hotheaded. Delilah fled Valentine rather than admit to her own mom that she was pregnant. "Her real name was Dorothy, but she changed it in San Francisco."

"Part of her new age image?"

Nate seemed curious rather than condescending, and she felt herself relax as they slowly strolled down Main Street. "Or her image of herself. She had different ideas about everything, from the Wiccan religion to tarot readings."

"But not you?"

"No, I'm more practical, like my dad." She'd thought about him with love and fondness for so many years, she was surprised to feel her eyes sting. "He died when I was seven. He loved my mother, and didn't care what her beliefs were, as long as they made her happy." Had he loved her so much he could accept another man's baby? Oh, why couldn't she forget about that?

"So if you're practical like your dad, it sounds like maybe you and your mom didn't get on real well."

She eyed him even as she came to a stop outside her building. "We didn't understand each other. She was happy with her popular store and her succession of men."

"But not happy with you?" he asked in a teasing tone.

She couldn't answer lightly. "No."

His smile faded. "Sorry if I'm prying."

"It's okay. She didn't understand how I could drop out of college to get married. Frankly, I think we disappointed each other."

"You were practically a baby when you got married."

"I know. But I was in love, and people in love can make the wrong decisions." She was revealing too much. "So that's why I know all about new age stores. Honestly, I'm as surprised as the old guys that you have one here. Your preservation-fund committee didn't have a problem with it?"

"They don't control the town," Nate said, then sighed. "And Mrs. Palmer likes to read tarot cards."

She was delighted to hear him almost sounding annoyed. "I'm glad they're not too conservative since I just discovered that an unusual company is showing interest in my building."

"Unusual company?" he echoed.

"Uh-huh. It's called Leather and Lace."

"I don't suppose it specializes in Stevie Nicks stuff," he said, arching an eyebrow.

"Nope. It's a lot better than that. But I am impressed at your musical knowledge." She grinned.

He sighed. "So what's the store?"

"Naughty lingerie. They want to see the building when I'm done." His wince made her laugh aloud. "I wouldn't have taken you for a prude, Nate Thalberg."

"You of all people know I'm not."

She choked on her laugh.

"But Valentine prides itself on being family-oriented," he said. "A store like that might get some protests—not from me, of course."

"Of course. But Valentine is a romance-focused town, after all. Brooke told me the B&Bs host wedding showers all the time. Lingerie is the perfect gift. Besides, I'm sure the window displays will only hint at what's inside. And is this about the preservation-fund committee?"

"They'll be overly interested," he said with a sigh. "And I'll get to hear all about it."

"Oh, I see. So you have a personal motive for your complaint."

"Well, I can hardly object to the store itself, and call myself a red-blooded man."

"This isn't a chain store, so they can't object to that. This will only be their third store, and they're all owned by one person." They had reached her building, and as she unlocked the front door, she took the bag from him. "Thanks for your help, Nate, and your offer to lend me tools. I'll let you know when I'm ready." She went inside and closed the door behind her, giving him a little wave through the glass.

Emily spent the next two days scrubbing the upstairs apartment until it was ready for her to move in. It was mindless work, so it gave her far too much time to think. The new age store had triggered memories of her childhood, and she kept reliving moments, from holidays to Sundays together, as if she could see new motivations behind everything her parents did. Had they been in love, or was her father a convenience? Had he fallen in love at first sight with her beautiful mother, and Delilah had taken advantage of him?

She remembered a particular day when they'd gone fishing, all three of them. Her parents had laughed with each other. Her father had put her up on his shoulders when they walked, helped her bait the hook, looked at her with pride when she caught a tiny fish. It was hard to tell if her mother had been having a good time or simply throwing pebbles into the stream to read signs in the ripples, something Emily knew Delilah believed in.

She began to realize that her questions would drive her crazy if she didn't do something about them. The box of diaries and yearbooks seemed to be shouting at her each time she stepped into her room, so on her last night at the boardinghouse, she gave in and opened it up before going to bed. She sat cross-legged on the mattress in her old nightshirt and pulled out the diaries first. To both her relief and disappointment, they were from her mother's middle-school years. No secrets to be found. And she would hardly need to research the names of boys Delilah had a crush on at thirteen.

The yearbooks from the late seventies and early eighties weren't that much more informative—no hearts drawn around a certain boy's photo, no declarations of love. But that wouldn't have been her mother's style. When Emily had once whined about finding nothing to do in high school, her mother had actually confessed she found one club she enjoyed—the 4-H club. That had made Emily giggle, for she was a child of the city, and she hadn't been able to imagine her mom on a farm. It was easier to imagine now, for her mom had grown up right next door to a working ranch. And though Delilah had the Wiccan appreciation of nature, loving anything to do with meadows and streams and forests, she'd chosen San Francisco to raise her daughter, a contradiction Emily had never asked about.

She paged through the yearbook until she found an outdoor picture of the 4-H club members. Her mom was prominent, with her long curly hair blowing across her cheek, her eyes luminous and mysterious as she looked into the camera. Emily stared into that face and felt the same old frustration and sadness and the terrible yearning of a child wanting to be loved by her mother.

She took a deep breath and turned the page. She began to read the lines scrawled by Delilah's friends. One girl's name was repeated all four years, with more than one mention of "best friends." Cathy Lombardi. Perhaps she still lived in Valentine Valley. Emily had never heard her mother mention the name, so she doubted they'd remained friends. Delilah's San Francisco friends were all women who frequented her store, who believed in the goddess, like she did.

By morning, Emily had decided to go talk to Cathy. She knew if she left town and never returned, her mother's secrets would haunt her. She had to know the truth about her real father, even if she didn't act on it.

When she returned from her morning run, she whipped up a special breakfast for the widows, scrambled eggs and a selection of her favorite breads and coffee cake, some of which she'd baked the previous night.

Mrs. Thalberg was the first to enter the kitchen, and she paused on the threshold to shake her head. "I knew this day was coming. You're moving into the apartment."

Emily gave her a hug. "I am. I hope you don't mind."

Mrs. Thalberg sighed. "Renée warned me that you were almost ready, so I can't say it's a surprise."

"You'll come visit me, won't you? Although believe me, it's very bare bones. Nothing as wonderful as the Widows' Boardinghouse."

"Then why don't you stay?" The old woman seemed to search her face.

Emily hesitated. "I'm thirty years old, and I've never lived on my own. I went from my mom's house to sharing a dorm, to getting married. The couple months since my divorce don't really count. I think it's time I give it a real try."

Mrs. Palmer bustled around them into the kitchen, followed by Mrs. Ludlow, taking her time with her walker.

"Sounds like the perfect reason," Mrs. Palmer said. "Rosemary, even you can't dispute such common sense."

Mrs. Thalberg sighed and patted Emily's arm. "It sounds like an exciting time in your life."

"Exciting?" Emily said, giving a short laugh. "I don't know about that. It's pretty scary to start over again."

"Now you're being modest." Mrs. Ludlow slowly sat down at the table. "I think you're very brave."

"It's brave to do something important that you don't *have* to do," Emily countered. "I have no choice. I think that's called desperation."

The widows laughed, and although Emily joined them, she wasn't joking. They all gathered around the table, and after they oohed and ahhed over her cooking until she was blushing, she needed to change the subject.

"I've been going through my mother's yearbooks," she began slowly, buttering a slice of pumpkin bread. "Before I leave town, I'd like to talk to people who were friends with my mother. Cathy Lombardi wrote in every yearbook. Does she still live in town?"

"Cathy? Of course she does!" Mrs. Thalberg beamed. "She's the secretary at St. John's Church, and her married name is Fletcher."

A church secretary? The woman's photos made her seem like a refugee from the sixties, with her tie-dyed shirts, headbands, and colored glasses.

"She's there every day," Mrs. Ludlow said. "I'm sure she wouldn't mind if you dropped by."

"I will. Which church is it?"

"The Catholic one on Third and Grace, just the next

block over from your building," said Mrs. Thalberg. "Now before you get going," she added, when Emily started to rise, "we have some things we've been collecting for you."

Emily was surprised and even embarrassed when the widows handed her several bags filled with linens. "Oh, you didn't have to—"

"Now why should you waste your money buying new towels and sheets?" Mrs. Thalberg demanded. "We've lived so long that we have plenty, and we're happy to share."

Emily felt herself blinking back tears as she looked at the three widows. "I don't know what to say. You've been so kind to me, accepting me into your home and treating me like family."

It was like she had grandmothers—three of them.

Mrs. Thalberg patted her arm. "You *are* like family, my dear. That's how we felt about your grandmother."

"I'm going to miss you all, but I will certainly come visit, and I hope you'll do the same."

"I've been waitin' for a tour ever since you got here." Mrs. Palmer rubbed her hands together with glee.

And this was the moment Emily should have told them about the interest from Leather and Lace, but she decided against it. She didn't want to risk spoiling her last morning with the widows, especially when Mrs. Thalberg so graciously insisted she would drive Emily and her possessions into town. Or perhaps she wasn't giving the widows enough credit, but Nate's concern wouldn't quite leave her.

Chapter Ten

St. John's Church was built of stone, with a tall spire that topped town hall. Though it looked majestic and conservative, Emily had to laugh, because right across the street was the Mystic Connection, the new age store the old men had been grumbling about. She wondered what the priest thought of the Wiccan priestesses who might frequent the shop.

The rectory and the church office were next door to St. John's, and when Emily entered, the woman at the front desk rose with a smile.

"You must be Emily Murphy," the woman said, coming around the desk and holding out her hand. "I'm Cathy Fletcher. Mrs. Palmer gave me a call."

She should never trust the widows with an actual secret, Emily thought with resignation. She shook hands with Cathy, a plump woman with a matching skirt-and-sweater outfit. Short, curly brown hair framed her face, and she wore stylish glasses. No longer a rebel teenager, Emily thought with amusement.

Cathy gestured to a chair and sat down beside her.

The rectory looked to be a converted Victorian home, complete with a two-story foyer that was outfitted for the receptionist.

"Mrs. Palmer tells me you're Delilah's daughter," Cathy said.

"Had she already changed her name in high school?" Emily asked ruefully.

Cathy laughed. "She loved that name, but no, it wasn't official. Mrs. Palmer told me about the change, and that you came to town to sell the old store because your mom died last year in a car accident. I was so sorry to hear that."

"Thank you."

"It feels like a part of my childhood is gone." Cathy sighed.

"Did you keep in touch with my mother?"

Cathy took a deep breath and straightened her skirt over her knees. "Not for long although I sometimes like to think that if we had e-mail back then, we would have remained friends. Letters can be hard to write. Plus, I went to work right away as a secretary—I took business classes in high school—and your mom . . ." Her voice trailed away.

"Yes?" Emily didn't know how to ask about the pregnancy without adding more gossip to Valentine's rumor mill.

"Your mom felt . . . oppressed by small-town values and nosiness. I might have flirted with the idea of being a wild child, but when it came down to it, I just didn't want to leave."

"Did she ask you to go with her?"

Cathy frowned. "No, and perhaps that's part of the reason we drifted apart."

"But you said you didn't want to leave."

"I guess it would have been nice to know she wanted me to. And then she got pregnant and married so fast, and that new life really changed her."

Emily withheld a sigh of frustration. It sounded like Cathy didn't know that Delilah had gotten pregnant before leaving Valentine. "So she told you about me?"

"Oh, yes." Cathy smiled. "She said she was grateful your father loved her enough to marry her even though they hadn't planned on you so quickly."

"Did she sound happy?" Emily asked wistfully. She shouldn't ask—she knew how her mother felt. Her mother had confided her ambivalence about being a mother on the eve of Emily's wedding.

"Happy? Don't take this the wrong way, honey, but when you're eighteen and pregnant, I can't imagine you can be happy right away. She was scared for her future, but your dad supported her. The last letter I got from her was when your dad died. She didn't want me to worry, said she was using the insurance money to begin her own business to support both of you. Imagine—a new age store. I thought it so appropriate. Sadly, she never answered my next letter. By then I was married and pregnant, and we both just got so busy with our lives." She sighed, a small smile lingering on her mouth. "But look at you. Obviously, Delilah succeeded in raising a wonderful daughter."

"That's nice of you to say." Emily leaned forward. "So tell me about you and my mom. I'd love to hear a couple stories. Were there other good friends I can talk to?"

"Good friends from high school? No. Delilah and I . . . well, we were different, but then you've seen the pictures."

Cathy laughed, as if she'd long ago made peace with her past. Emily envied her.

"Delilah and I had each other, and that was fine for us."

"She mentioned the 4-H club."

"Oh, she did a few things with them for the fun of it, but always claimed no one else really understood the two of us. But then again, I'm kind of embarrassed just remembering how we used to behave."

Cathy launched into several stories about how they rebelled against the music of the early eighties and wore bell-bottoms to the prom. It really did seem like Delilah and Cathy against the world. The two didn't even date all that much, at least according to Cathy. By the time Emily left, she tried to tell herself that perhaps she wasn't meant to know the complete truth. But now that she'd given in to her curiosity, she couldn't just abandon the search.

Emily awoke in the morning and lay still, listening. She was alone in an apartment she owned, a rare, heady feeling. Valentine Valley might have been a small town, but she could still hear noises outside her window at dawn—cars heading off to work, the faintest sounds of voices as several people walked past. She wasn't the only one who was an early riser.

But there wasn't a single honking horn, just the distant, muted sounds of a new day. She could get used to this.

After her run, she went to take a shower, only to realize she hadn't remembered a shower curtain. Laughing at herself, she took a quick bath, feeling awkward because it had been years since her last. The towels were soft, and had hand-sewn embroidery along one end. Those women were so thoughtful!

She spent part of the morning purchasing several sheets of drywall and all the accessories she'd need—including a shower curtain. She held back on the tools because of Nate's offer. Was she simply supposed to call him up and remind him? But she didn't have to. As if she'd summoned him, he marched into the restaurant, bearing a toolbox and other supplies, a man who worked with his hands and knew how to get things done. A little shiver of delight worked its way up her spine. How was she going to get any work done when she wanted to gape at him?

She put her hands on her hips and demanded in disbelief, "How did you know I might need you?"

He grinned. "Hal called me. I picked up your drywall, too."

"He said he would deliver the panels." She felt annoyed, as if Hal thought she couldn't take care of things herself. "You didn't need to—"

"It wasn't out of my way." After donning work gloves, he walked back toward the entrance, saying over his shoulder, "Surely you didn't want to inconvenience Hal?"

"Inconvenience?" she muttered. "I spent my money there."

When Nate returned, hefting the first panel of dry-wall, she pointed to where she wanted it, then stood back and admired the view without guilt. She'd never really thought about how enjoyable it was to watch a man work with his hands. Her ex-husband had always hired men to do any repairs or renovations.

As Nate made a few more trips to his pickup, she consulted her notebook lists, so she wouldn't delay him. He put down the last panel and straightened, and she found herself studying the width of his back too much. She was only human. As long as she looked but didn't touch . . .

When he met her eyes, she had a friendly smile waiting. "Thanks so much, Nate. I made a list of the tools I need, so if we could separate them out, you can be on your way."

"On my way? You're kidding, right? I'm hardly going to let you borrow my tools without making sure you can handle them properly."

"But I've watched a ton of videos online. I'm perfectly prepared."

He chuckled. "Sounds like you're ready to bake a cake."

"There can be a lot of preparation to bake a cake!"

"Look, Emily, I'm here to show you what to do. Neighbors help neighbors in Valentine Valley. It'll go a lot easier if you just accept my help."

Something uneasy seemed to flash across his face before he glanced away.

"Did you buy yourself some work gloves?" he asked.

She hesitated, wanting to protest some more, strangely excited and nervous that they would be spending time together. But if he kept assuming he knew what was best for her, she was going to have to set him straight. She'd already spent ten years letting a man sway her decisions. She was in control of herself now, knew what was important in her life. Having let herself go head over heels for Greg, she would never make that mistake again.

But she couldn't deny that watching him was a pleasurable sensation all on its own. When he squatted to show her how to pry away the baseboard from the damaged wall, she bit her lip and concentrated on his words, on his gloved hands, so she wouldn't have to look at the way his jeans tightened over his broad thighs.

Horseman's thighs.

Oh, God, she'd been reading too many historical romances, she thought, holding back a laugh.

But like a good historical-romance heroine, she had goals for her future to focus on. She took the pry bar, awkwardly inserted it, pulled the wood away from the wall, then moved to the next section. Later, she rose to move a panel of new drywall away from where she'd be working next.

"Hold on there," Nate said, coming up behind her. "You're too skinny for that kind of work."

She drew in a breath when he put a finger in the belt loop at the back of her jeans and tugged.

"I think you need to eat better," he continued.

She hadn't been eating as much, trying to conserve

her money. Did it show? That was it—she was going to have to get a job.

"Oh please," she said loftily. "The way everyone in Valentine keeps trying to feed me, I won't be fitting into these jeans soon."

He was still standing too close, looking down at her, his face almost puzzled. What was he thinking? She hadn't said anything outlandish or daring. His eyes continued to study her face, narrowing, and she felt the very air between them begin to shimmer with a growing tension that had nothing to do with renovations and everything to do with seduction. A distant part of her ordered her to be strong, but she felt herself sway toward him, and he lifted a gloved hand as if he might touch her face.

And then he stepped back. "Okay, it's my turn to feed you." He pulled off his gloves and tossed them onto the bar.

She was blinking and dazed and barely able to speak. "W-what are you talking about?"

He tugged off her gloves, and with unerring aim, threw them beside his own. "We're going out for lunch."

"I made a sandwich." But it was obvious he suddenly wanted to get away from her, and she was thankful that at least one of them hadn't been mentally incapacitated.

"We're working up a bigger appetite than that. The Halftime Sports Bar has a BLT so huge you can barely bite into it."

"And is that supposed to sound appetizing?" Even though it did. "Look, Nate, it's a nice gesture, but I have so much to do. You go on."

"Now that you're living on your own, my grand-mother can't watch over what you eat."

"So she put you in charge? Did she call you the moment I left?"

When he hesitated, her mouth dropped open. "She did! Good Lord, those widows called Cathy Fletcher before I could get to her, too. Your grandmother is a wonderful woman, but she's nosy—gee, I wonder where her grandson gets it from."

"Cathy Fletcher?" He frowned. "Hey, wait—nosy? I didn't call Grandma; she called me. And what about Cathy?"

She'd hoped his defensiveness would make him forget her slip, but no such luck. She lifted her nose in the air. "I'm interested in St. John's. My grandparents were Catholic, so surely they were parishioners there."

He studied her face as if he didn't know whether to believe her. "Whatever. We're going to the Halftime. It's just down the street. My treat."

She glared at him, feeling indignant. "You've done too much, Nate."

He tipped her chin up until she looked him in the eyes. "It's a BLT, Em," he said softly. "If you want, you can pay."

He shortened her name just like his sister did, and it almost hurt her inside that he could treat her so fa-miliarly, and she could feel so desperately in need of that. Somebody treated her kindly, and she fell apart. Words tumbled out of her that she hadn't planned. "Then perhaps—perhaps you can give me your ideas on where I can find a part-time job around here."

He frowned, but said, "No problem."

But maybe it was a problem. She didn't want help, then she asked for it. He must think she was crazy. But he was standing too close, looking at her mouth. It was her turn to be the sensible one, so she quickly stepped away. "A BLT, huh? What if I'm a vegetarian?"

"You ordered a burger at Tony's Tavern."

The flush of heat she felt just looking into his eyes only intensified. "Oh, right, I keep forgetting about that."

"I don't," he said shortly, and went by her to wash his hands at the sink behind the bar.

What was that supposed to mean? she wondered with exasperation. Well, she was just going to ignore it, as she was trying desperately to ignore the awareness that crackled between them whenever they got too close.

Chapter Eleven

Nate scrubbed his hands far longer than he needed to, trying to get control of himself. *What the hell am I doing?* He put his hands on her jeans like he was allowed to touch her. And every conversation they had seemed to lead back to that night at Tony's, even if it was only in his thoughts.

She'd made it clear that she was leaving town. Was that some kind of challenge to him, one he couldn't control? After all, he didn't want a relationship with her either—of course that made her the perfect woman to date, no strings attached. Couldn't he just be friends with a woman? he thought with disgust.

Yet here he was, teaching her about drywall, taking her to lunch—touching her. He hadn't felt so out of control in a long time, and he knew what happened when he started to care too much. He'd screw up her life, and she'd hate him for it. And he'd hate himself.

But the alternative was to cut her out of his life, and he just couldn't do that. Or he could treat her like one of the women he occasionally dated—even though he wasn't dating her. He'd keep it light on the surface, no deep talks, no intimacy.

And he was hardly manipulating her life—he was lending her the tools she needed, showing her how to use them. That wasn't forcing himself or his ideas on her.

Taking a deep breath, he turned around, only to find her missing. He walked through the swinging door into the kitchen, but she wasn't there either. He heard the tapping of her feet down the steps, and she came in the back door a moment later. She'd changed into a flowered top that flattered her without being too revealing.

She blushed. "I needed my purse," she said, a bit defensively.

He arched a brow.

"And that shirt was dirty and sweaty. I wasn't going to wear it to lunch. I happen to like the people in this town, and they don't need to see me at my worst."

"You've certainly met enough of them," he said over his shoulder as he walked into the front of the building.

"Through no fault of my own, believe me. I thought I was going to clean, sell, and be out of here, but life had other plans."

"Don't you know a lot of people in San Francisco?" he asked, as they left the building, and he waited for her to lock up.

"Well, of course, but I'd built a life there. We did a lot of entertaining."

Scout bounded out through the open window of the pickup.

Emily gaped. "That was impressive."

Nate whistled, and Scout came to heel.

"He's very well trained," she said.

"He has to be. He's a cattle dog, with a lot of responsibility. He's good at getting animals to do what he wants."

"And humans, too?" she asked, smiling. "He has you wrapped around his paw, going everywhere with you." She looked at the people they passed on the street. "But then again, lots of people have dogs around here. Hal didn't even mind Scout inside the hardware store."

"And he's coming into Halftime with us, too."

"Oh." She gave the dog a surprised look.

The Halftime Sports Bar was just a block down Main Street, and unimpressive from the outside, with neon signs the only decoration in the two windows that flanked the glass door. But inside, there were comfortable chairs and tables, flat screen TVs with perfect views from anyplace you sat, a huge old wooden bar that had to be there from the nineteenth century, and sports memorabilia hanging all over the darkly paneled walls. There was always something to look at.

Julie, the daytime hostess, was a redheaded college student who always had a teasing wink for him and a pat on the head for Scout. She was too young for him but took the rejection good-naturedly. As she led them to a table, Nate nodded one by one to the people he knew and didn't respond to Julie's curious gesture toward Emily. Sometimes he could see why Emily's mom had wanted to leave.

As she sat down, Emily smiled at Julie, who handed her a menu.

"You won't be needing that," Nate said.

"So I'm supposed to order the BLT," she said dryly.

Julie walked away, saying over her shoulder, "It's delicious."

"I think I'll look through the menu anyway," Emily said to him pointedly.

He raised both hands. "I've eaten here a lot, but you don't have to take my recommendation." He let her scan the menu in silence, and when she at last put it down, he said, "So about the entertaining you used to do. You just liked throwing parties for no reason?"

"I love to throw parties, but there was often a reason. We entertained my husband's partners."

The mysterious husband. Nate felt uncomfortable about his own curiosity. "What kind of partners?"

"Greg's a corporate lawyer at an important firm. He liked to make a good impression, and I liked entertaining." She gave him a wry smile. "By all outward appearances, we complemented each other well."

Their waitress, Linda, approached, setting down a glass of ice water for Emily and a Dale's for Nate.

"Thanks, darlin'," he said, taking a swig.

Linda, a working mom of school-age kids, gave a laugh. "We all know what you like to drink, Nate. Have you been out on the bike much yet?"

"Up at Mushroom Rock. It's not too wet up there."

Emily looked between them, amused and wide-eyed.

"You must be Emily," Linda said, looking her over with open friendliness. "I'm Linda."

"Nice to meet you," Emily said.

"What can I get you?"

Emily sighed and smiled. "A BLT and a small salad, please. Ranch dressing on the side. And a Diet Coke."

Nate grinned. "I'll take the same, Linda, but hold the Diet Coke and the salad and give me fries instead."

When Linda had gone, Emily said wryly, "Must be nice to have a job that burns lots of calories."

"You bet." He took another sip of beer. "You've spent so much time alone here that it kind of surprises me you like being with a bunch of people at parties."

"I didn't think I came off as shy," she said wryly.

He chuckled, and again the memory of standing between her thighs bent over a pool table rose between them.

She cleared her throat. "I'm focused on a single purpose here, but in my real life, it really makes me happy to entertain. I love to cook and decorate, all those girly things that must make a cowboy like you squirm."

"I don't just squat on my haunches eating steak grilled over a campfire."

She laughed. "Glad to hear it."

"Although I enjoy that, too."

"You're the outdoor type?" she said, hand pressed to her chest, batting those sky blue eyes at him.

"And you're the elegant hostess. What else did you do with yourself?"

Some of the humor left her eyes. "I volunteered a lot of my time. I didn't have a job."

Surprised, he said, "That's rare nowadays."

"It is. My mom was pretty disappointed. But . . . I thought I knew what I wanted—and what Greg wanted. I was happy for a while there."

She looked wistful and sad, and there was a part of him that wanted to know how she'd been hurt, what her ex had done to her. Had Greg wanted some other woman? That seemed hard to understand. But more focused questions would only increase the hurt in her eyes—and make him know her too well. Not good.

Emily sighed, regretting how easily Nate made her pour out things that were none of his business. Had he been disappointed she hadn't been ambitious enough to work these last nine years? Many men expected a woman to share equally in paying the bills. But he didn't seem to judge her, and she was grateful. Or else he was hiding his thoughts well. He was good at that, she suspected.

Was he good at keeping secrets, too? So far, she didn't think he'd said one word about what they'd done together—even though the whole town knew *something* had happened. But he'd been a gentleman so far and forgiven her for leading him on. And she'd forgiven him for taking advantage.

He looked over her shoulder and briefly frowned.

She turned and saw that an older man had just come through the door and removed his cowboy hat. He had graying brown hair that matched his mustache, and the lean ranginess of a man who worked the land, dressed in tan work pants and a denim jacket. When the stranger spotted them, he gave a faint smile and approached their table.

Nate stood up, and whatever reservations he'd first had faded into an affectionate smile. "Hi, Dad."

Emily straightened with eagerness but tried not to

show it. Nate had kept his private life off the table, including info about his family. She imagined he even regretted that she'd befriended his sister. He was being far smarter than she was. But still . . .

Nate towered over his father, gesturing to Emily. "Dad, this is Emily Murphy. Emily, Doug Thalberg."

"Nice to meet you, Ms. Murphy," Mr. Thalberg said, his voice gruff and worn.

They exchanged a firm grip, and she liked the way he regarded her steadily, pleasantly. She couldn't even read curiosity in his expression—and that would make him as unreadable as his son, which would make sense.

"You here for lunch, Dad? You could join us."

"Thanks, but no, Deke Hutcheson is meetin' me. But I'm early, so I'll be glad to join you for a beer"—he crinkled his eyes at Emily—"if I'm not intrudin'."

"Not at all," Emily said.

Linda was already on her way carrying another Dale's, along with Emily's salad, and Mr. Thalberg took a seat.

"No offense, Ms. Murphy," he said, "but I don't recognize you. Did Nate meet you in Aspen?"

This was just another confirmation that Nate didn't tell anyone—even his family—about her. But why wouldn't Grandma Thalberg have mentioned her? Was the old widow trying to keep Emily hidden so that Nate would feel less family pressure? Before she could explain who she was, Nate answered for her. Biting her tongue at his presumption, she poured some of the dressing over her salad.

"Emily is only visiting Valentine, Dad. She's Agatha Riley's granddaughter, come to sell the building."

Mr. Thalberg's eyes focused on her. "Dot's daughter."

"Dot?" Emily echoed, smiling with bemusement before taking the first bite of her salad.

"A nickname. She hated it. Changed her name to Delilah, I know, but I couldn't break the habit. We'd been friends too long. I was sorry to hear about her passin'."

"Thank you. I know you must have remained friends through the years since Nate told me about the money you lent her. I promise I'll pay you back as soon as the property sells."

Mr. Thalberg glanced at Nate so quickly that Emily almost missed it, but it gave her a strange feeling. Yet how could she say, *Why that unreadable look at your son?*

"No problem," Mr. Thalberg said. He and Nate took matching drinks of beer.

"My mother left Valentine right out of high school." She hesitated, uncertain how to phrase her question. "It seems . . . strange that you would lend her money years later."

"She had the buildin' as collateral, and I knew where I could reach her. I was lookin' for an investment at the time, and her store expansion looked promisin'. Why not help her?"

"Did she say why she didn't just sell the building here?"

"No. Perhaps she wanted to give you a reason to return someday."

Emily laughed with faint bitterness. "She didn't speak well of her time here, but you probably know that."

"Maybe she wished things had been different." Mr. Thalberg sighed. "But she never told me. Sorry."

Deke Hutcheson came limping through the door, and Mr. Thalberg stood up, taking his beer.

"Nice to meet you, Ms. Murphy."

"It's Emily, please, especially for an old friend of my mother's."

Mr. Thalberg nodded and glanced pointedly at Nate. "See you at home."

Deke waved at them both but followed Mr. Thalberg to a table. Linda brought over their BLTs at that moment, leaving Emily's to the side so she could finish her salad.

"Those are huge," Emily said. "I'll be taking half home for another meal."

"Not me." Nate took a big bite and closed his eyes in bliss.

She studied him for a moment, eating the last of her salad, then taking the first delicious bite of her BLT, thinking about his ability to keep quiet, and the way even the town elders regarded him with respect. His sister loved him, so that counted for something, too. Emily liked the easy camaraderie between him and his father. He understood families.

"Nate, I have something personal to tell you. Could you keep it between the two of us?"

He paused then swallowed his food. "Of course."

"I . . . misled you about how I knew Cal Carpenter."

She told him about the letter from her grandmother and the old woman's bombshell about Emily's paternity.

He blew out a breath and sat back to study her. "I'm so sorry."

"I tried to ignore it at first, figuring—what could I do? I loved my father and—" She broke off, the lump in her throat suddenly making speech difficult. Swallowing several times, she finally continued. "But ignoring it just makes it haunt me more."

"You questioned my dad about her," he said, his eyes widening. "Did you think he and your mom—"

"I never even considered it. I knew my mother. There's no way she would have gone to your dad about a loan if she was keeping his baby a secret. She was a private person in many ways, and that would have been inviting trouble."

"So you're positive we're not related," he said with faint amusement.

"And why would it be a problem if we were?" she asked innocently.

He didn't say anything at first, only looked at her with doubt and intensity, enough to make her squirm.

"As for my father," Nate finally said, "he's not the kind of man to let a woman leave town right after he's slept with her. He's too honorable. Once he cares about you, he never stops."

"And that would have meant he had an affair," she said quietly.

"No, it wouldn't have."

She frowned. "But you're older than I am. Your parents weren't married?"

"My father is the kind of man who would fall in love with a woman even though she had MS and a five-year-old kid. He adopted me. My biological father left us right after my mom's diagnosis."

Emily's heart gave a lurch as she watched Nate continue to eat. Was he trying to pretend it didn't still hurt? "Oh Nate," she said softly.

He glanced up at her. "No puppy-dog eyes. It was the best thing to happen to both of us. He was . . . scum."

"And Doug Thalberg adopted you." She sat forward, intrigued. "I'm considering adoption myself. I would love to talk more with your parents."

He frowned. "Maybe." He gestured to Linda for another beer.

She studied him in surprise. Most men would express some curiosity that an unmarried woman her age was considering adoption. She wouldn't have answered with personal details of heartbreak that would only make him pity her, but she'd learned not to repress the memories of her baby's death. But it was as if the discussion of his parents' personal situation had made him . . . shut down. Was that why he'd winced when his father walked in? He didn't want Emily talking to him?

She should be offended, but instead, she was intrigued. His new coolness was like a blazing warning sign, but she'd started this conversation, and she was going to finish it.

"I could use your advice," she said, after taking a sip of her Diet Coke.

Another frown. "About adoption?"

Not likely. "No, about my grandmother's letter.

Every older man I see, I find myself wondering. I need to know the man's name."

They were interrupted by Linda, who brought another round of drinks.

With her elbow on the table, Emily rested her chin in her palm. "What makes this difficult is how much my father loved my mother."

"And that's part of the reason this hurts so much," Nate said.

She eyed him. "Wow, cowboy, that was insightful."

He took a big bite of his sandwich and chewed, not agreeing or disagreeing.

"My mother," she began, then paused for a moment. " 'Mother' isn't the best word for her. After my father died, she was wrapped up in her store, then in her succession of men. I was third in line."

She was waking up all the twisted emotions she thought she'd put behind her—the hurt, the anger, the despair. And love? Could she still have a spark of love for a woman who had kept the truth from her all these years? Emily thought of her own mistakes, and knew she was just as flawed as anyone else. But a lie like this . . .

"I can't be surprised she kept this terrible secret," she said softly. "The night before my wedding, she told me she hadn't wanted to be a mom so young, and when my dad died, the responsibility was overwhelming, making everything worse. She'd made mistakes. At the time . . . at the time I was furious with her for laying that on me just before my big day, and I didn't understand how a woman couldn't want her own child. But I might have misjudged what she was trying to say to me. I think she was apologizing in her way, and giving me a warning that life doesn't always end up as we want. Maybe I also wasn't seeing the clue in her words, about her 'mistakes.' I need to discover what I can." Now that time had passed, and she'd carried her own child, it was also far easier to imagine how her mom had felt when eighteen and pregnant—afraid and penniless. But her mom had never gotten past the ambivalence about her pregnancy.

Nate pointed at her with a french fry. "Then tell me how I can help."

"I talked to Cathy Fletcher, her high-school friend."

"Ah, so it wasn't just interest in St. John's that sent you there."

She shrugged and smiled. "Cathy assumed Mom got pregnant in San Francisco, so I didn't correct her on that. No point in letting the whole town know."

"And you trust that I won't do the same?"

She studied him, trying to come up with a flippant reply, but couldn't. "Yes."

He wiped his mouth with a napkin and sat back, his expression unreadable. It was almost as if . . . he didn't like being trusted. He was probably trying to keep the boundaries intact between them since she was doing such a poor job.

"If you're asking my opinion," Nate said, "I'd go to the source, Doc Ericson. He's been here forever. If your mother consulted him, she might have told him the father's name in confidence."

Emily straightened in surprise. "I didn't even think

she might have gone to a doctor. It's a good lead, thank you."

"I'll introduce you."

She started to protest.

"Of course you can make an appointment yourself," he interrupted. "But with privacy laws nowadays . . . you might have to bring proof of her death or something, and maybe I could just persuade Doc to help."

She let out her breath, feeling reluctant. "Okay, good point."

"I have another lead. You said you were looking for part-time work, right?"

"Just remember, I'm not working for *you*!"

He looked at her like she was crazy. "Trust me, I'm not asking. But a job has been staring you right in the face—at Monica's Flowers and Gifts."

"She has two employees."

"I'm not talking about Karista."

"But Mrs. Wilcox has been sick," Emily protested. "Monica would never fire someone over that."

He leaned across the table and spoke in a confidential tone. "Did you ever think that Mrs. Wilcox is too kindhearted to leave Monica in a lurch, even though she might be ready to take a break?"

"No!" she whispered, looking around as if someone would overhear them in the bustling sports bar. "How do you know—oh, wait, the Widows' Boardinghouse and Gossip Mill."

He grinned. "Good one. But I'm not revealing sources. I could talk to Monica for you."

Though she should be amused at how easily he tried

to take charge, she found herself stiffening. "I'm perfectly capable of speaking to Monica myself."

His smile grew lazy. "I'm relieved."

After a glance at the check, he tossed some money on the table. She'd already pulled out her wallet, and they had a momentary staring match. With a sigh, she let him have his way.

As they walked out of the Halftime, Scout at Nate's heels, she gave Nate a sideways glance, knowing she'd become his project, and she was only encouraging him by asking for his help. If it had been pity, or thinking he had to help the "little people," she'd have put a stop to it immediately. But it wasn't. She guessed it was Nate's very nature to help everyone he could, but that was difficult for someone like her, who wanted—needed—to do things on her own.

She glanced over her shoulder as the door closed behind them, and saw Mr. Thalberg watching them. She gave a wave, and he answered with a pleasant nod. He'd raised a lost boy into a fine man. He hadn't been a biological father to Nate, and it hadn't mattered one bit. Love and respect were what mattered.

Nate paused, looking over his shoulder back inside the Halftime. "I forgot about something I need to discuss with my dad. Can I meet you back at your place in fifteen minutes?"

"Nate, you've shown me enough to finish out the day, and perhaps several days' worth. Why don't you go back to your own work?"

Standing there on the street, he looked down at her, indecision in every line of his tense body. That tension jumped to her like lightning, and she couldn't help wondering if there was more to his need to help her— and it set off alarm bells in her head.

"Go, Nate," she said, giving his shoulder a friendly push. "I'll give you a call when I reach a renovation impasse. Text me about Doc Ericson when you get the chance. And thanks for lunch. Now go on. Daddy's waiting."

It was his turn to roll his eyes, and she gave him a grin as she turned and walked back down Main Street. Her purse swung and bumped against her hip as she walked, and she knew with certainty that he was watching her.

Chapter Twelve

Nate stood on Main Street, admiring the cute sway of Emily's ass as she walked away from him. People were watching him, he knew, but a man had a right to look at an attractive woman.

But did he have a right to keep coming around when his body was telling him he wanted more from her?

Scout was watching him, his head cocked to one side with confusion.

"Nope, we're not going with her, buddy. I'm giving you every mixed signal today. Let's go see Dad." He and the dog went back inside the Halftime and approached his father's table. He nodded to Deke. "Can I borrow my dad for a sec?"

Deke frowned as he forked his salad around his plate. "Sure thing, kid. It'll give me time to find the fried chicken I know was buried in here somewhere."

Nate walked back to the bar and found two empty stools at the end. Before he could think how to broach the uncomfortable subject, his father did it for him, as straightforward as always.

"Did you lie to that girl, Nathaniel?" he asked mildly.

Nate winced. "'Lie' is a lot stronger word than's necessary."

"She thinks I still own the lien on her property. Why didn't you tell her you bought it?"

"At the time it came up, she and I were pretty upset with each other," Nate began slowly.

"You're talkin' that first night when you two were settin' the town gossips afire?"

"Yeah, that night." Nate sighed. "I didn't know anything about her except that she was down on her luck. And I didn't want her to think . . ."

His dad put his hands on his hips. "That you're more than a dirt-poor cowboy?"

"Something like that." But not really. He waited for his dad to cuss him up one side and down the other.

But his dad just studied him for a moment, his gaze unreadable. "You're a grown man, Nate. I'm not tellin' you what to do."

Nate felt strange, wondering why his dad didn't interfere a bit more where Emily was concerned. Did he know something Nate didn't? "Why did you invest in something so risky as a new age store, Dad?"

Doug shrugged. "Why not? Dot had collateral and had already proven she could make a success of the store. She wanted to expand. Perhaps you get your good head for investments from me."

They grinned at each other.

Nate didn't like keeping secrets from his dad, and this new one Emily had confided in him was important. His dad had known Delilah after all, and Nate hoped Emily would want to hear Doug's opinion.

"You see, Dad, Emily has this problem. She just found out that her mom was actually pregnant with her when she left town."

Doug arched a brow. "I never heard that."

"No one did, so this is just between us. It was Agatha Riley's info, and Emily just found out about it. She's going to ask Doc Ericson if he's got the name of the father."

Doug put a hand on his shoulder. "Don't let her have you believing I might be on a boyfriend list."

Nate smiled. "She says you're not, that her mom never would have come to you for money if she was keeping something that big from you."

"I'm sure you're relieved," Doug said dryly.

It was Nate's turn to shrug. "It shouldn't matter—she won't be here much longer."

"You tell yourself that, son. And you go ahead and help her as long as you need to."

Nate stiffened. "I'm not at the ranch as much as I should be, but I'm able to keep track of a lot of the paperwork by phone and e-mail. It's just that she doesn't know what the hell she's doing even though she insists she doesn't need help. I have to show her how to use my tools, or she might break 'em."

Doug slowly smiled. "Are you tellin' me or yourself?"

"You," Nate said irritably.

"Then don't worry. We can do with less of your time

until the hay's ready to be cut. Frankly, your mom and I were sayin' it's been rather peaceful on the ranch lately."

"You're talking about what's been going on between me and Josh."

Doug shrugged. "You're both adults; you'll figure it out. Unless you want advice."

"Nope."

"Why am I not surprised."

There was a note taped to the front door of the restaurant in Monica's scrawled hand, sending Emily to the alley, where she found a sturdy coffee table with only a few scratches. She ducked into Monica's workroom from the back door, going past the big walk-in coolers with their explosion of colorful flowers, and the worktables with racks of ribbon spools and containers of wire and other supplies.

In the showroom, she waited while Monica finished with a customer, then said, "A coffee table?"

"It's not from me," Monica said, leaning back against the counter and crossing her arms over her chest. "Brooke left it. She said it was in storage after the boardinghouse renovation. Oh, that reminds me." She reached beneath the counter for a bag and handed it over. "It couldn't be left in the alley."

Emily peered inside at a bundle of white eyelet cotton fabric. "What's this?"

"Curtains. It appears the widows are concerned you're letting the whole town see in at night. I'm assuming one of them handmade them for you, since Mrs.

Ludlow asked me to measure my own front window to compare the size. Hope you have a plain rod across the top, just like I have."

"That is so incredibly generous," she murmured, staring down into the bag. She was still so amazed by how the residents of Valentine Valley were going out of their way to help her. She felt . . . cared for, rather than another anonymous face people passed by in the big city. "You're *all* so generous—and that includes your Mrs. Wilcox."

Monica frowned. "What does she have to do with it? Poor lady is in bed again today."

"Which leaves you with the bulk of the work during the daytime. Nate seems to think Mrs. Wilcox would like a rest but is too concerned you'll need her."

"That's ridiculous! She knows she can tell me anything."

Emily shrugged. "I'm only telling you what Nate told me."

"Did he give you any brilliant solutions? Because if he's wrong, and I hurt her feelings by suggesting a long vacation . . ."

"His brilliant solution is one that would help me, too." Emily took a deep breath. "If it's okay with Mrs. Wilcox—and you, of course!—I could take her place part-time until I go home. It'll give her a break, and me a little spending money and—"

Monica threw her arms around her. "And me someone reliable to help out so I'm not trapped here twelve hours a day. This is perfect!" She stepped back, still holding Emily's shoulders. "But are you sure you're not trying to do me a favor out of some misplaced sense of gratitude? I know how important it is for you to sell quickly and move on."

She almost winced, for that made her sound so self-centered. Was that how she came off? "No, Monica, you'd be helping me so much—you know that. Certainly, I haven't been successful at hiding my financial problems from you guys."

Laid-back Monica actually giggled. "I'm so happy! Not about your financial problems, of course—which I can relate to, because I've been there before—but that you'll be working with me."

"Will we get anything done?" Emily laughed. "So how much do you want me to work?"

"I'll have to talk to her, of course, before making something permanent. But what do you say to fifteen to twenty hours a week during the day? I can be very flexible."

"So can I. I think this will work out."

They grinned at each other.

"I have an appointment with a bride in fifteen minutes," Monica said, "so I should probably get out my paperwork. Let me talk to Mrs. Wilcox and get back to you. Then we'll arrange a training day—it won't take long."

"Just let me know," Emily said, taking her package of curtains and heading out the back door. She was really looking forward to working with customers and hanging out with Monica several hours a day. She didn't like being alone so much. She would have to re-member that, when she narrowed down her major—to find a career where she worked with other people.

When her phone beeped, she found a text from Nate waiting for her. They had an appointment with Dr. Er-icson at eight in the morning. The little thrill that shiv-ered through her just seeing Nate's name on the screen was something she'd have to deal with eventually.

The next morning, Emily changed clothes three times before deciding on what to wear—just to ask questions of a doctor! She felt like an idiot even as she knew the doctor wasn't the reason she was wearing sundress, sandals, and summer sweater, even though it was rain-ing outside.

When she heard a horn honk in the alley, she scooped up her pink raincoat and purse, then dashed outside. She opened the passenger door and got in, meeting Nate's gaze, before deliberately looking out the passen-ger window. She heard the soft drumming of the rain on the roof, felt the damp mugginess from keeping the windows up. It was like a warm little world inhabited by the two of them. Far too seductive, making her feel overheated and dismayed all at the same time.

After letting her off at the front door to the doctor's office, he parked around back and met up with her inside the vestibule.

"The doctor opens early," she said, feeling awkward.

"No, but he did today, for us." Nate glanced down at her as he rapped on the inner door. "I didn't think you'd want other patients seeing the two of us at a doctor's appointment together."

Her eyes went wide, for it had never occurred to her—and then she started to laugh, covering her mouth when the door creaked open.

Dr. Ericson was a short, spry man with a white mane of hair. He gestured them into his small waiting room, which was mercifully empty, and then through another door into his book-lined office. A pair of skis rested in a corner.

"You haven't put those away yet?" Nate asked, gesturing to the skis.

The doctor shrugged. "A man can hope. I'm thinking about skiing the Fourth of July bowl. My nephew can take me up on his snowmobile. I'm too old to be skinning up a mountain."

Emily glanced at Nate. "Skinning?"

"It's a way to ski uphill when the lifts aren't running," he explained. "You put skins on your skis, and they let you go forward, but the friction keeps you from sliding backward."

"Oh," she said, nervously looking back at the doctor.

"Sorry about my manners," Nate said. "Doc Ericson, this is Emily Murphy."

They shook hands.

"Have a seat," Dr. Ericson said, keeping his shrewd eyes on her. "Nate didn't say what this was about, only that you needed privacy. Not privacy from him, I take it."

She shook her head. "It's nothing to do with Nate.

I could have come alone, but he knew you, and . . . I thought it would help smooth the way."

The doctor steepled his fingers and regarded her over them, waiting.

"My mother was Dorothy Riley, and she grew up here."

He didn't look surprised. "I've heard who you are."

"I'm just so popular," she said lightly, then realized she was rubbing her damp palms on her skirt and stopped herself.

"It's too bad you and your mom didn't continue to visit," Dr. Ericson said.

"Having finally spent some time here, I agree. But . . . my mother didn't seem to have any good memories of Valentine, at least as a teenager. I recently learned that my mother was pregnant with me *before* leaving Valentine rather than afterward. My mom died last year, so I can't talk to her. Could you look in your records and see if she came to you about this, if perhaps she mentioned the name of the father?"

He slapped his hands on the desk, startling her. "Don't see why not. She was your mom, after all, and privacy laws don't really matter now that she's dead. But I'll have to dig through the old files in the storage room. You two amuse yourselves. Nate, keep your hands off my skis."

When he'd gone, Emily sank back in her chair and let out a heavy breath.

"You thought he wouldn't help?" Nate asked.

"I was worried your legendary charm might not work on an old man."

"My 'legendary charm'?" He grinned.

She grinned back. "All a person has to do is walk around town with you. I've never seen so many women burst into smiles at just the sight of a man. What did you do for that kind of welcome?"

He wiggled his eyebrows suggestively, and she laughed.

"Oh, please, not that young hostess at the Halftime," she said.

"No, but she keeps trying. I like 'em a little older than twenty."

"Let me guess—twenty-one?"

"Naw, my sister used to babysit Julie and some others her age. I'd feel like a pervert."

"And that's the only reason?"

He slouched in his chair and sent her a dangerous look. "I like a woman with a little more experience."

She felt a pleasurable tension seep into her bones.

"Life experience, that is," he added, flashing those dimples at her.

"Oh, you must mean divorced. My lucky day. I'm glad my bad judgment gives me an edge over perky college students."

His laugh was a low rumble, and they kept looking at each other until Dr. Ericson marched back into the room, holding a folder in one hand.

"Damn, I'm organized," he said with satisfaction, spreading open the folder.

Emily held her breath, shocked to find that she hoped her grandmother was somehow wrong, that Jacob Strong was her dad, that everything could go back to the way it was.

Chapter Thirteen

Nate reached to take Emily's hand, then stopped himself. He saw both courage and fear in her face and knew that regardless of what had happened in his past, he didn't have to brace for the unknown like she did.

Doc lifted his head and somberly narrowed his black eyes at Emily. "I remember your mom and her case quite well, but I wanted to confirm my memory before saying anything. She was definitely pregnant before she left town."

Emily's shoulders slumped. He couldn't look away from her face, pale now, with a hint of tears she didn't let fall. But . . . hadn't she already known this? Or had some part of her still not wanted to believe?

Her voice trembled as she said, "Is there any mention of my—of the father?"

Doc shook his head. "I remember asking, but she refused to tell me even though I insisted that a young man deserved to know the truth. She said she'd do what was best, and that was the last I ever heard from her.

Did see her in town once or twice when you were little, but that was all."

Emily nodded, biting her lip, then managed a rueful smile. "If you don't know the father's name, I'm not sure how to find out. There was only one close friend, and she didn't know about the pregnancy."

"Guess you've got a mystery."

Color was returning in splotches to her face, and her voice took on an edge of anger. "My father—the man I thought was my father—died when I was little. But I loved him, and I remember him. Do I really want to know if my mom lied to him as well as me, if she used him? She wasn't the best mom in the world, but this makes her out to be . . . some kind of monster."

"Or a frightened teenager," Doc said neutrally.

"She wasn't a frightened teenager for long," Emily said bitterly. "She could have told me many times over the years. But then she always thought she knew best."

Nate wondered if Emily was remembering her mom's little talk on her wedding night. Had Delilah meant to spill the secret then and changed her mind?

"Could she have been protecting you?" Nate asked.

She regarded him impassively. "Or protecting someone else? Probably herself. It would have been inconvenient to deal with it all, with the emotions she caused." She wiped a hand down her face and forced a smile for Doc as she stood up. "I'm sorry. You don't need to hear all this."

Doc Ericson came around the desk and took her hand. "Anytime you need to talk, I'm here. Sometimes a neutral person can help make things clearer."

"Thanks. What do I owe you for the appointment?"

He waved a hand. "Nothing. I didn't do anything but answer one question."

"You're very kind." She slipped her purse over her shoulder, and said to Nate, "I'm ready to go."

She was quiet when they got in the pickup, and although he put the keys in the ignition, he didn't start it up. Should he say something? Comfort her? They were trying to keep each other at a distance, but this was so big.

And then she started to cry, big tears sliding down her cheeks, and he felt absolutely helpless. He drew her into his arms, and she clung to him, her face pressed into his chest. Rubbing her back, he whispered the only words he could, that it would be okay.

At last, her sobs quieted, and only the occasional shiver swept her body. With a sigh, she relaxed against him and let him stroke her hair.

"You're good at this," she murmured at last.

"Yep, women cry a lot when they're with me."

She glanced up at him in bemusement.

"With gratitude," he finished solemnly.

She chuckled and pulled away, leaning her head back against the seat and closing her eyes.

"Do you feel okay?" he asked.

She shrugged. "I—I don't know what I feel. I finally have to accept it, you know? It's like everything I thought about myself is turned upside down. I'm angry with my mom, I feel sorry for my dad—and then I wonder if he knew. I mean, come on. Wouldn't you know if a woman had a full-term baby seven months after you met her, or however long it was?"

"Maybe he was so in love, he didn't count the months—or he didn't care, especially once he saw you."

"Damn, you say the sweetest things," she said ruefully.

"Or maybe he knew from the beginning, and agreed to everything, but died before he could tell you the truth. And your mom . . ."

"Go ahead, find a good excuse for her," she said bitterly.

"Maybe she loved him, too, and when he died, she only wanted you to remember the best about him."

She rolled her eyes. "Now you're giving her too much credit. You didn't know her. She was a selfish woman, and whatever excuse she made to be able to sleep at night, believe me, it was all about *her.*"

There was nothing he could say to that, but he silently thanked God for the parents who raised him.

"So what are you going to do now?" he asked. When her eyes filled again, he regretted the question immediately. "I'm sorry. It's none of my business."

"No, no, please, I'm the one who's sorry, dragging you into this mess, crying all over you. Thank God it's raining, so you can explain your wet shirt." She sighed, turmoil clouding her eyes.

"Jacob Strong was your dad, whatever else you find out. You have memories of him, just like I have memories of my biological father. Believe me, you can thank God your memories are far better than mine."

She studied him intently, and he knew he'd said way more than he meant to, but her pain seemed to bring words out of him he hadn't planned.

Emily wanted to ask him so many questions but knew she was only looking for a distraction, and there was that dismay in his eyes again before he'd turned to start the pickup. He didn't want to talk to her about his past—he didn't want her to know things about his family. She understood that, but he'd just given her the realization that something far worse than a divorce had happened to his family.

"You're right, he was my dad," she said softly. "And I'll never know the truth of my parents' relationship. But I can know the truth of my paternity," she added, her voice becoming flat and impassive.

"But you can't solve it right now, not on an empty stomach. My grandmother asked you and me to come to brunch this morning, and since I forgot to tell you in advance, we'll just pretend I did."

She had to smile. "How did they know we'd be together this morning—I know you wouldn't tell them about our doctor appointment. Imagine what they'd think about *that* information."

He gave an exaggerated shudder. "Grandma knows I'm helping you with the renovations. Brooke has a big mouth. I got the invitation when I stopped in yesterday to fix the light switch."

"Did you find little scratches like someone had used a screwdriver to sabotage it? Your grandma might be pretty devious."

They glanced at each other and smiled, even as Nate drove out of the parking lot.

"I hope you don't mind," he said, "but I talked to my dad about your mom. He confirmed that they were just friends, by the way."

"I can't believe you actually asked him." She could only imagine the awkwardness of *that* scene.

"I didn't ask him—he volunteered the information. And he won't tell anyone."

"I know that." She should be angry that Nate hadn't asked her permission first, but she wasn't. Frankly, it freed her up to talk to Doug Thalberg herself eventually. Sighing, she said, "I guess I'll have to figure out what to do next about my real dad. I'll go through my mom's things again."

"And maybe you can go back to Cathy Fletcher and see if she can give you the names of some boys they hung out with."

"She said they didn't date much."

"But you know better now." He hesitated. "And I don't like hearing you say your 'real dad.' You know Jacob Strong was your real dad, too."

She stared at him in surprise, feeling her eyes sting and her throat close up. Hoarsely, she said, "Cowboy, you better stop being so nice to me, or I'll start thinking all you ranchers have soft underbellies."

He rolled his eyes, but she thought his face might actually be getting red. Doug Thalberg had rescued a woman and her son and helped mold Nate out of his love.

Sheesh, she was going to make herself cry again.

The sun had come out by the time they reached the Widows' Boardinghouse, letting them eat at a picnic table on the back porch. She spent a pleasant hour telling the ladies all about what had been going on, from her renovations, to the lovely curtains, to her new job at Monica's Flowers and Gifts. All uncomplicated topics.

"Has anyone shown interest in buying your place?" Mrs. Thalberg asked.

To Emily's surprise, Nate clamped a hand on her knee. She glanced at him, trying not to laugh. Guess he didn't want her mentioning Leather and Lace. "The real estate agent has contacted me, but he won't know anything until I'm ready to show the place."

So Nate thought he could control the conversation, did he?

She looked at his grandma with wide-eyed interest. "Mrs. Thalberg, I finally met your son yesterday. Such a nice man."

Mrs. Thalberg grinned. "You're a sweet girl to say so."

"Nate's pretty quiet about his family although I do talk to Brooke, as well. I haven't met his brother yet."

"That's a surprise," the old woman said, narrowing her eyes at Nate, who dug into his pecan pie without looking up. "They've always been close, of course, working side by side twelve hours a day. Josh is six years younger, and he used to follow Nate everywhere."

Nate winced as he washed down his pie with a sip of lemonade.

"Josh wanted to be just like his brother," Mrs. Thalberg continued. "Once he tried to ride Nate's horse and got himself thrown. Broken arm, too, but not the first broken bone he'd have, working on the ranch."

"If I recollect," Nate drawled, "I was the one who got in trouble for his broken arm, which wasn't fair, considering I was nowhere near the barn when it happened."

"That's how it is with family," Mrs. Palmer said brightly. "We're responsible for each other."

"I never had any brothers or sisters," Emily said, feeling wistful.

And then for the first time it occurred to her that she actually might. Nate was watching her as if he knew what she was thinking. She wasn't ready to go public with what she knew, because that was what would happen if she told the widows. They'd make lists and go interview every man of the right age, a Valentine spectacle.

Because they cared, she reminded herself in wonder.

"You should have seen Josh's reaction when Nate went off to college, and he couldn't go," Mrs. Thalberg said, shaking her head. "He was twelve, and a handful, as boys are at that age."

"They don't grow out of that," Emily said dryly.

The widows twittered with laughter, and Nate rolled his eyes.

"It's hard to be the only man at a hen fest," was his response. "Grandma, isn't there something that needs fixing?"

"Don't you want to hear how Josh moped for days after you left?" Mrs. Thalberg demanded. "He even ran away, saying he was going to Colorado State with you."

He went still. "I didn't know that."

Mrs. Thalberg patted his hand. "Your mom probably didn't want to worry you. We found him that night, camping on his way to Ft. Collins, him and his dog and his horse."

Nate smiled faintly. "That was a good dog."

"Enough reminiscin'," Mrs. Palmer said. "Emily, now that you're workin' at Monica's—"

"I haven't started yet."

"Well, when you do, give me a call, and I'll come in and talk about a flower order for the preservation committee. We like to congratulate each business when they open or finish renovations after usin' the grant money."

"That's really nice of you. I'll call."

"She makes it sound so subtle and tasteful," Nate said. "It wasn't always flowers they offered for grand openings."

Mrs. Thalberg laughed out loud.

"Nathaniel Thalberg," Mrs. Palmer said with mock indignation. "Your teasin' is uncalled for."

"Oh, come on, don't you remember when the toy store opened? You had free giveaways for the kids—"

"To encourage the parents to attend and become payin' customers!" Mrs. Palmer interrupted.

"But you gave away cap guns! Nobody even uses them anymore. I don't know how you found them."

Mrs. Ludlow sniffed. "We were harkening back to childhood memories."

Nate leaned toward her. "It deteriorated into a disaster when all the kids were firing cap guns in the store, and the too-sensitive smoke detectors went off, sending everyone running out onto Main Street."

"And the sprinklers?" Emily squeaked.

"Not enough smoke to set them off. The smoke detectors had to be recalibrated."

"We were lucky," Mrs. Thalberg said, wiping tears of laughter from her eyes. "The bill for water damage could have put the committee out of business."

Emily found her gaze trapped in Nate's as they at first shared their amusement, until it changed into something intimate. By the time they were in the pickup, intimate had turned into smoldering. She enjoyed his company too much, his sense of humor, his thoughtfulness to his grandmother. He was luring her in without trying to. It was so seductive to feel desirable, to know that she could affect him as much as he affected her. He didn't look at her as he drove, but his eyes were narrowed and his jaw clenched. It was as if he realized that every time they were alone, the passion between them burned just a little brighter, a little hotter.

In the shade of the alley behind her building, he stopped so suddenly, it sent her purse tumbling to the floor. Swearing, he reached for it at the same time she did, and they bumped heads. As they both turned to apologize, their gazes met and held, and suddenly, she couldn't seem to catch her breath. Before she knew it, their mouths came together in a fierce, hot kiss that burned away her fake shell of friendly indifference, turning her into a woman greedy for passion. His hand cupped her head and she arched even farther toward him, both restrained by their seat belts.

Gasping, she pushed away and gaped at him, her mouth damp, her heart thundering in her chest. "My God," she whispered.

"I didn't mean—"

"I shouldn't have—"

He held up both hands. "Stop. I don't want to fight this anymore."

"Fight . . . what?" she whispered, still trembling and aching with need. She needed to hear him say the words. He tasted so good, and she wanted more, like he was chocolate candy she shouldn't have but craved.

"You and I get along," he said at last.

She choked on a laugh. "Sexy. Don't make me swoon too much, cowboy."

He groaned and tipped his head back. "We're hanging out a lot. It'd be stupid not to enjoy it. We said no dating, but I think if we keep the ground rules clear, we could enjoy ourselves together in something that's not work or duty or with friends." He turned off the ignition, unbuckled his seat belt, and faced her. "There's a lot of other stuff between 'just friends' and a committed relationship."

"Go ahead and explain it to me." She was staring at his mouth. "But be quick."

He closed his eyes as if for control, and she felt

wickedly content that she affected him as much as he did her.

"We could just date casually," he said in a husky voice.

She knew he was trying to seem *very* casual, but after that kiss, it was too late. His gaze was openly traveling down her body, and she was glad she wasn't wearing the raincoat. She unbuckled her seat belt, and he watched her like she was doing a striptease.

Her brain was having a heated debate, ping-ponging between letting her know this might be a mistake and slyly whispering that she could control something so harmless as dating.

She couldn't lie to herself—she liked his kisses, liked the way he was looking at her, as if he'd been resisting showing his interest and now couldn't get enough of the sight of her. It made her feel like a desirable woman, something the last few years of her marriage had taken away—she'd thought for good.

His eyes narrowed when she didn't say anything. "Well, Em? Tell me what you think."

"I—" She glanced away, suddenly realizing that her doubts and fears were bubbling to the surface. "I'm not sure I know anything about dating, Nate. And that's the truth. As for that first night when we kissed, alcohol had a lot to do with it."

He made a dismissive sound. "I don't believe that for a minute. Or is that just what you've been telling yourself?"

"Maybe." She looked down, picking at a thread in

her sundress. "You have to understand. I had crushes on boys in high school, and the occasional date, but when I met Greg in college, I fell hard. We both knew we saw marriage in our future."

He reached for her hand, and she let him, enjoying too much the way he gently rubbed her fingers. His own were rough with calluses, large and very male.

"Then think of this as an experiment," he urged, obviously trying to win her with his dimpled smile.

She softly laughed. "An experiment? But aren't you the master at dating? Won't it be beneath you to try to teach a neophyte like me?"

He began to tug on her hand. She had no choice but to come up on her knees, even as he leaned back against the driver's door. He put up the armrest so that nothing separated them on the bench seat. He gave another tug until she was forced to put her other hand on his chest to brace herself or fall into his lap.

"I don't think I'll be bored," he said huskily, threading his hand into her hair and cupping her neck to draw her closer. "Let's find out. Kiss me, Em."

He spoke those words so close to her that she felt his breath on her mouth. Those green eyes held her, challenged her, intrigued her. She leaned in for the kiss, and admitted to herself that he'd been right—alcohol had had nothing to do with the attraction that simmered between them.

She kept the kiss light, playfully teasing his lips with her own, learning the soft touch of him, exploring the way each kiss heightened her rising need. She hadn't felt this way about a man in so long, eager and desperate, afraid and fearless all at the same time.

She lifted her head and stared at him, still only touching with her hands and nothing else. "Were you bored?" she whispered.

He groaned and closed his eyes as he leaned his head back against the window. "If you get a little closer, you'll see how not bored I am."

Then he lifted his head and kissed her, not giving her a chance to change her mind. He held her head to his, deepening the kiss, his mouth hot and open on hers. When his tongue teased hers, she groaned, and could have easily tumbled into his lap for more.

She lifted her head again, gasping. "Okay, okay . . . you've made your point."

"I don't think so."

He tried to pull her against him. This time she pushed away, and he let her go.

"Hey, I'm a neophyte, remember?" she said, feeling shaky and still full of yearning. "I think this is going too fast for me. We haven't even been on a date—and don't tell me brunch with your grandmother counts."

He winced. "No, that was certainly no date."

"Well, I'm glad to hear it. A girl expects a lot when a cowboy asks her out."

His slow smile almost made her change her mind about kissing him some more.

"A lot? Should I feel threatened by your expectations?" he asked.

"Probably not. The way every woman smiles at you,

it seems you've met a few dating expectations," she said dryly, sinking back to her own side of the pickup.

He linked hands with her again, his smile banked into earnestness. "I'm glad you're giving this a try, Em. There's more to life than figuring out your past or your future. You can live in the now, just like I try to do."

"The now, huh?" She grinned, but inside she couldn't help her curiosity. Was he hiding from something in his past, or didn't he want to confront the future? Or a little of both? She was intrigued enough to want to find out.

He nodded. "The now. No expectations but enjoyment."

"I don't think I've ever met anyone as bossy as you, Nate Thalberg."

"Someone had to take charge and speak the truth about what was happening between us. I couldn't have taken another moment working side by side on renovations."

"So you're saying that now you'll feel free to seduce me instead of teach me to drywall?"

"Heck, no. I'm just saying that now I can be patient, knowing that I'll have my shot."

He raised her hand and placed a soft kiss on her palm that sent shivers up her arm.

"We can have fun together. You won't regret it, Em."

She looked into his eyes, and although she was flattered and excited, she also felt a trace of fear. He was so . . . overpowering. Would she be able to date without entangling her emotions? Other people did. And she had strong motivation to keep things casual—college in the fall.

"Let me show you what we do for fun in these mountains," he said. "It's spring, the runoff is fast into the river valleys, the perfect time for whitewater rafting."

She widened her eyes. "Are you kidding? That sounds scary, not fun. The movie theater is showing a forties romantic suspense film festival. It would give us so much to talk about."

"Since when have we lacked for conversation?"

She laughed and batted her eyelashes at him.

"Then we compromise," he continued. "Let's do something outdoors as a first step. Let me take you hiking. The view from these mountains has to be seen."

"It's a deal. But you have to teach me to drywall first."

"Blackmail. You play dirty. I like it." He leaned in and gave her a quick kiss. "Now I have to get back to the ranch. We'll talk."

She felt like one big cliché, floating as she went inside her building and changed into old clothes. She glanced at the box of her mother's things, then deliberately turned away from it.

The second-guessing about Nate began as she pried baseboard and trim. She was taking a chance, knowing it might hurt her in the end.

But if this was a mistake, she had damned well better enjoy it along the way.

Chapter Fourteen

Early the next morning, Emily removed the last of the damaged trim and baseboards, then showered and dressed for her first day's training. She was at Monica's Flowers and Gifts by ten for her first official tour and description of her duties—taking care of customers, placing orders, preparing simple flower arrangements, making bows, and, of course, dealing with the local craftspeople about their consignment items.

And through it all, Emily watched Monica at work, the way she knew so many of her customers and their tastes, or if they were tourists, the way she sensed how they wanted to be approached and made them feel at ease. Young lovers out for a stroll popped in for an impromptu rose. Expensively dressed older couples from Aspen, looking to spend a simple day together, toured all the little Main Street shops, intrigued by the crafts on display.

While Monica dealt with a bride's mother about flower arrangements for a wedding shower, Emily washed the little china plates, with their tulip-and-daffodil pattern, on which Monica served the day's pastry treat. The coffee cake was delicious, of course, but Emily frowned as she considered it, knowing that Monica ordered her desserts from the pastry chef at the Sweetheart Inn.

When the door jingled with the customer's departure, Monica sat down on the little wrought-iron chair by the dessert table. "Whew! Mothers of the bride can be so picky."

"Isn't she your cousin?" Emily said, glancing toward the door.

"And that's why I feel free to comment. It will be a lovely wedding if Angela calms down. Hard to believe my cousin has a daughter old enough to marry." She shuddered.

Emily grinned, then gestured to the coffee cake. "Sweetheart Inn?"

"Yep, and delicious."

"Of course. But can I make a suggestion? I love to bake. Why don't you let me whip something up for you? Why should you pay those exorbitant prices from the inn?"

"I pay it because it's the only game in town. But I must say, those tarts of yours were scrumptious."

Emily grinned and sat down opposite Monica. "I've been working on my high-altitude baking since I arrived."

"So now my customers will be test subjects?"

"Hell, no, you will. If you don't like it, I take it back. I just . . . I just really miss cooking for people. Almost makes me want to move back to the boardinghouse. Those ladies were very appreciative."

"Wow, okay, okay, we wouldn't want you to give up your freedom just to keep baking. I'll pay you, of course."

Emily shrugged. "Just the ingredients. I'm not a professional although I did bake desserts for a friend's catering business in San Francisco. Nothing full-time, just when she was swamped." She cut a slice of cake. "But regardless, this shouldn't go to waste."

"Dessert before lunch—my idea of being a grown-up."

While they dug into the cinnamony goodness, Emily studied her friend, who'd seemed . . . not quite herself this morning, shadows beneath her eyes, her smile a bit strained.

"Monica," Emily said hesitantly, "is something wrong?"

Monica shot a surprised glance at her, then gave a distracted smile. She opened her mouth to answer, but then stopped at the sound of someone in the back room and put a finger to her lips.

Into the shop came a young black woman with close-cropped hair, dressed elegantly in pants and a silk blouse. Emily saw the resemblance at once, the cheekbones of a model, and caramel-colored skin.

Monica stood up. "Hey, Missy—Melissa, I'd like you to meet my friend, Emily."

Emily stepped forward to shake hands with Monica's sister, who didn't flinch at her childhood nickname. "Nice to meet you, Melissa."

The woman's smile was friendly and engaging, but then as a reporter, she dealt with the public all the time.

"You're the one doing all the renovations yourself, right? Monica bragged about you."

"She shouldn't have. I'm such a klutz that I have to learn everything I do each step of the way."

"And who better to help than Nate?" Melissa grinned at her.

Monica winced her apology.

"He knows a lot about renovations," Emily said neutrally. "He's been kind enough to take time out of his busy schedule to help."

"That's our Nate," Melissa said cheerfully. She glanced at her sister. "I'm heading over to Mom and Dad's. See you there for dinner?"

"I'll be there."

"Bye, Emily," Melissa said, sliding on expensive sunglasses as she went to the door. "Don't work too hard."

When she'd gone, Monica went to the glass door, and after watching her sister walk away, let out a heavy sigh. "She's staying with me, which she usually never does. Mom is beside herself, considering she renovated Missy's old room."

"Well, Melissa probably didn't realize it was for her. And you're her twin—don't you think she'd want to spend time with you?"

Monica frowned, and said in a softer voice, "It's so . . . uncomfortable now. It makes me want to cry."

Emily put an arm around her, which Monica accepted for a moment, before straightening and moving behind the counter. "She took over my second bedroom with enough luggage for a monthlong stay."

"You know how the weather can change here. She probably wants to be ready for anything." Emily hesitated. "How's it going so far?"

Monica shrugged. "Okay. I tried to show her the things I've changed in the flower shop, but she only pretended interest. The fact that she looks down on what I do . . ." Her voice dropped to a whisper, "It really hurts, Emily."

"Oh, Monica." Emily felt helpless in the face of her friend's pain. "I'm so sorry."

Monica wiped away a tear and put on a fake smile. "I've got to go to the bank. Do you mind keeping an eye on the store on your first day? I'll bring back lunch, too."

"Uh . . . lunch hour? Isn't that a busy time?"

"Sure it is, but you'll do fine. The cash register walks you through any purchase, and you seemed to pick that up easily. If they want to place a large order, have them make an appointment with me. Here's the calendar. Most people just want to pick out some flowers for whatever occasion is happening that day, and often, they know exactly what they want. If not, show them some flowers. Just check the price list to give them a ballpark figure. And play up the crafts and plants— they make great gifts! If you're really stuck, remember, I'll be back in half an hour. People will understand."

Monica hurried out, as if she might break down in front of Emily and didn't want to. It made her think again that she might have her own sister out there. She was almost glad when a customer walked in. While the older gentleman sampled a piece of coffee cake, she wrapped up a half dozen roses for him in a fancy white box. By the time she was done, a younger man in his twenties was hovering near the displays at the front of the store. He was tall and lean, in cowboy boots and jeans, a typical outfit in Valentine. He wore a leather vest over a t-shirt, and it seemed to go with the stubble on his face.

When she came up behind him, he swept off his cowboy hat and turned to face her. She could have stopped in her tracks at the tousled brown hair that framed storm cloud gray eyes. He was too handsome by far, straight nose, full mouth, even with a scar that curved on his chin.

"Afternoon, miss," he said, nodding to her.

Colorado cowboys were so polite. "May I help you?" she asked.

He hesitated, his hands curling the edge of his hat.

"Flowers for a girlfriend?" she suggested.

He shook his head. "No girlfriend. Guess I was looking at all the crafts you have here."

"Everyone in Valentine seems so talented. You'll be able to find a gift for anyone."

"It's not so much a gift I'm looking for. Thought I'd ask about how to submit something to be sold in your store."

"I see." She gave him a frank smile. "I'm sorry, but it's my first day, and I haven't been taught about the consignment part of the business. Monica should be back in fifteen minutes or so. Would you like to wait for her?" When he hesitated, she realized she didn't want to let him go so easily. "What do you make?"

"I tool leather—creating designs and patterns," he

added, when he saw her clueless look. "I've made frames, wallets, belts, and saddlebags, to name just a few."

"Do saddlebags sort of look like purses?"

He smiled. "Sort of, but don't tell a ranch hand that."

"Leather purses tooled by a handsome cowboy? I think those would sell, too."

"Depending on my talent," he added dryly.

"Well, of course, but I didn't think you'd be venturing into the flower shop if you didn't think you had talent."

His smile spread into a grin, and she found herself wondering how many hearts he'd broken.

"So do you want to wait for Monica?"

"Naw, I'll catch up with her later. I want to see the look on her face when I bring a sample by."

"So you know her?"

"'Course. She was just a couple years ahead of me in school."

Emily found herself wondering if Monica could use her own cowboy distraction right around now. Nate was working wonders on Emily's frame of mind. She had barely thought about her hunt for her father all morning as she looked forward to a drywall session with him.

"Then come on back when you're ready," Emily told the cowboy as he walked to the door. "Can I tell her who stopped by?"

"Now that would ruin the surprise." Grinning, he slipped on his hat and tipped it toward her. "Afternoon, miss."

Emily watched him walk down the street, shaking her head. You didn't meet men like that in San Francisco—what a shame.

That evening, when darkness began to creep over them, Nate was answering e-mails in the ranch office. At last he sat back and let his mind wander tiredly—and it immediately went to Emily. He'd see her in the morning, and he was eager for it.

He could be careful. It wasn't as if he was unaccustomed to dating and enjoying himself, ending it when the urge to smother the woman with his opinions and his help started to prove too attractive.

With Emily, his help was concrete—it was about her renovations, or her search for her dad. His opinion wasn't important, so much as practical advice. Now if she started asking what major she should focus on in college, he was backing away like she was dynamite. He'd talked careers before, with terrible results, and not just with his college girlfriend.

He turned off the office lights and went out into the night, standing still for a moment as his eyes adjusted. He saw the lights on in the horse barn and knew it had to be his brother. Josh had converted an old tack room into a leatherworking shop and spent a lot of his spare time there. On his way through the barn, Nate petted the horses, who all dipped their heads out of their stalls to greet him with soft whinnies. Scout was a favorite with the horses and remained behind to greet his friends.

Nate followed a stream of light across the floor, then leaned his shoulder against the doorway to watch his brother. Josh was using shears to cut a piece of leather into a strange shape that Nate didn't recognize. But he knew talent when he saw it, and his brother had that.

Josh suddenly glanced up, his face creasing into a curious smile.

Nate looked around the workshop at the goods in various stages of work, from pieces of unadorned leather to braided rope to the beginnings of a vine of flowers etched into a long piece of leather. "What will that be for?" Nate asked, gesturing to the last item.

"The frame of a mirror."

Nate nodded, impressed. "I know I've told you before, but you're really good."

Josh glanced up. "Thanks."

"So what's the plan for all of this?" Nate asked.

"There has to be a plan?" Josh asked, studying him with amusement.

"My thought was, you're so talented that it's a shame you only create things for yourself or the family. Lots of other people would be interested, especially in a tourist town like Valentine has become."

Josh cocked his head. "What if I'm not interested in becoming a businessman? I'm a cowboy, a full-time job."

Nate didn't like how he was suddenly feeling defensive. "You don't have to become a businessman. You can hire people to do that work for you. But you have to come up with a business plan, a guide for what you expect to do with this."

"That's what *you'd* do, big brother," Josh said quietly. "You like the business side of things."

"Well . . . yeah. It's part of having a business."

"You're making my leather tooling about more than it is. It's what I do for enjoyment."

Nate's defensiveness morphed into irritation. "I don't just work, you know. I can enjoy things, too."

"Seems to me you're turning even Emily Murphy into work—drywalling, I hear? Sexy."

"How did you know—" Nate broke off.

Josh grinned in a knowing way, and that made Nate want to stick out his chest, and say, "Oh yeah?" like he was twelve.

But he wasn't going to go bragging about what he and Emily had recently shared just to prove to his brother that he had all the different parts of his life under control.

Nate gritted his teeth. "I came to tell you that I'll be gone part of tomorrow morning."

"Drywalling."

Nate groaned as he turned to leave.

"Hey, where you going?" Josh called, all innocence. "You can't take a joke? Or I'm hitting too close to the truth?"

"I'm blowing off a morning's work," Nate called over his shoulder. "Guess after all the pestering you've been doing, that should make you happy. My irrigation ditches are all yours."

Josh grumbled, and Nate felt a little bit better.

Emily was just finishing breakfast the next morning when her doorbell rang. Unlike her city apartment, there was no intercom for her to discover who was at the door. Wrapping her robe tighter about her waist, she ran down the stairs, opened the door into the hall, and stepped to the back door, thinking with exasperation that it was only seven thirty in the morning.

Through the door window, she saw Nate. "It's drywall day," he called, his voice muffled.

She smiled, feeling little prickles of pleasure warm her. Unlocking the door, she opened it, then blushed when Nate gave her a slow grin as he looked down her scantily clad body.

"Now that's the way a man wants to be greeted."

She hugged herself about the waist, wishing her robe reached at least to her knees. But why was she nervous? It wasn't as if Nate was going to demand she undress for him.

Although that sounded exciting . . .

"I'm sorry I'm not ready," she said. "I guess we never decided on a time."

"I'm used to working by dawn—I thought I was giving you too *much* time."

She cocked her head. "We'll have to be more explicit with our schedule. You can wait in the restaurant while I shower—"

"Naw, that's okay, I'll come up."

He came toward her, and she was forced to step back, or he'd have run right into her. He was carrying a bag and a paperboard container with two cups.

He paused, and his smile dimmed. "Running away from me already?" he asked quietly.

He seemed strangely solemn all of a sudden.

"Running away? I'm trying to stop myself from giving you a kiss. Thought I'd seem a little desperate since we haven't even had a date yet—and drywalling doesn't count."

His white teeth flashed in a grin. "Just as long as you're not getting skittish all of a sudden." He leaned down, his mouth near hers, but not quite touching. "So can I kiss you?"

She answered by pressing her lips to his, letting her hand touch his chest, feeling all breathless and light-headed. They didn't dive into the kiss with tongues and heat, but she felt like they did.

"Mmm," he murmured, rubbing his cheek against hers, inhaling the scent of her hair. "What am I here for again?"

"Coffee?"

He chuckled and stepped away, looking cute and re-gretful. "Do you like coffee?" he called over his shoulder as he headed up the stairs.

"Sorry, no," she said, closing both doors and following him up.

Nice view, she thought, watching his long legs.

"More for me, I guess."

It was her turn to chuckle as she emerged into her apartment behind him. "No problem. I'm used to people assuming. Guess I'm a rarity."

He walked down the hall past the bedrooms and the galley kitchen, into the living room that overlooked Main Street.

"Not as much damage up here," he said.

"A bit," she said, looking at the scraped wood floors and the dings in the walls. "But I'd rather take care of the big stuff downstairs first."

"Go ahead and shower while I eat."

"Okay, okay, I'm sorry I didn't know to hurry."

She disappeared into her bathroom and set a land speed record for showers, firmly putting aside daydreams of his joining her. She was moving way too fast, if only in her own imagination. When she emerged from her bedroom, she found Nate looking out the front window as he munched a bagel but not standing too close.

"Afraid someone will see you up here?" she asked innocently.

He glanced at her. "Not at all."

"So I'm not a secret?"

"That we're dating? Why would I do that?"

"I don't know. I don't know you all that well, do I?"

But she knew enough to like him, to trust him with some of her deepest family secrets. And that was a little scary.

"That's why we're dating," he said smugly. "To get to know each other."

"Oohh, so that's the reason."

"That's one of my reasons. What are yours?" he asked, his voice lowering to a deep rumble, leaning sideways into her until their arms brushed.

Oh, she liked the sound of his voice too much.

"Because you promised to teach me to drywall, and I felt like I owed you."

"So you're dating me out of pity and gratitude?" he demanded, tossing his bagel onto the bag and advancing on her.

She gave a little squeak as she escaped toward the

back door, but he caught her around the waist. Nate was so tall and broad behind her, and she felt absolutely delicate.

Feminine, too—and desired. She felt his mouth behind her ear.

"Tell me the truth," he whispered.

She shivered. "Oh, all right, you're just so hot, cowboy. Now can we get to work?"

He let her go and patted her butt. "That's more like it. Have a bagel. You need your strength."

She munched on breakfast and followed him downstairs, listening to his detailed instructions about drywalling, trying not to let her eyes linger on his broad shoulders or flexing biceps. They worked side by side for an hour, while her mind followed tangents that turned darker and more troubling. He seemed so competent at everything, so well liked, so at ease with himself. He knew exactly what he wanted, whereas she was a nearly broke, divorced woman without a skill to her name. Sometimes he made her feel so unaccomplished though she knew he didn't mean to. She told herself that at least he admired her determination to learn how to make the repairs herself.

He might want to date her to get to know her, but what would he find—a woman who was so messed up she didn't know what to do next with her life, still grieving past sorrows? How was that any fun for anybody?

She told herself to get under control. He didn't need to know all her fears and doubts; this was supposed to be fun. And she was *allowed* to have fun.

Sometimes she didn't need reminding, especially

when his gaze roamed slowly down her body, making her feel like she wanted to straighten up and tuck loose strands of hair behind her ears—or maybe slouch bonelessly onto the nearest horizontal surface and pull him to her.

Okay, okay, this was enough togetherness for one day. The long morning of listening to his instructions while trying to keep from kissing him had taken its toll.

"Nate, you've done enough for one day. Surely you're needed on the ranch."

She was achy in muscles she hadn't used in a while, while he looked fresh and fit.

"I guess my brother's been taught enough of a lesson," he said.

"Excuse me?"

Nate grinned and shrugged. "He was ribbing me last night. He's got this leather-tooling hobby he does for fun, and has this stupid idea I don't do *enough* for fun. So since he thinks I work too hard, I gave him my morning chores. I'm sure he's sorry he ever opened his mouth."

A cowboy who did leather tooling? she thought with curiosity. Now that couldn't just be a coincidence.

"So I'm your new project to prove to your brother you're not all about work?" she asked lightly, watching him wash up in the sink behind the bar.

"You're a lot of things," he mused, walking toward her. "But proving something to my brother? Naw, I'm hardly thinking about him when I'm looking at you."

He pulled her into his arms and she came up against his body, feeling his arms around her, the heat of him seeping pleasantly into her. "You must like your women all dirty and perspiring."

"Hmm."

He kissed her then, leisurely, masterfully, until her heart was trembling along with her knees, making her grip his t-shirt to keep from collapsing.

He gave her another quick kiss, then grinned with satisfaction. "When are you free to go hiking?"

"I'm working for Monica tomorrow afternoon, but the following day it's just the morning. How about after lunch?"

"It's a date. How did your first day at the flower shop go?"

A handsome cowboy told me about his art and made me curious. "It was great. I'm a natural with customers," she boasted, arching an eyebrow playfully. "Monica said I could bake for her. I'll be going to the grocery store later today."

"Good for you." He leaned down over her. "Now don't I get another reward for all my hard work today?"

And then he kissed her, and every thought, every trouble or apprehension, fled her mind.

When they both came up for air, he leaned his forehead against hers. "I'm not certain I can wait two days to see you."

That made her feel wonderful—and uneasy all at the same time.

Chapter Fifteen

Emily spent the next two days in a fog of romance. Gorgeous cowboy Nate was desperate to date her. It made her want to hug herself and dance around her apartment. He was the perfect antidote to her low self-esteem after the way Greg had discarded her when she couldn't give him a biological child. She was a woman in charge of her life, a woman who felt confident enough to date but didn't *need* a man to be content.

By day, she plodded along ripping down damaged drywall or worked in the flower shop; in the evening, she baked for Monica, chocolate mousse cake one day, a peach cobbler the next. More furniture kept appearing—a plant in a lovely ceramic container from Monica in honor of her first day, the perfect decorative touch on the coffee table beneath her front window; a lamp to read by; then, to her surprise, a love seat that was well used but in good condition. She didn't feel so . . . temporary anymore. Her brief sojourn in Valentine Valley was becoming part of her journey, not an ordeal she had to get through.

On the day of her afternoon hike with Nate, she attended the Music to Eat By program at the community center with Brooke and Monica. It was an old, converted, brick factory building, with conference rooms as well as a large banquet hall that could be used for wedding receptions. On the huge deck, overflowing with potted plants and vines laced through trellises, a bluegrass band played their guitars and harmonized beautifully for the crowd of twenty to thirty who'd gathered to eat lunch purchased from the Silver Creek Café. All the local restaurants took turns being the vendors for the Music to Eat By crowds. While eating her Chicken Caesar wrap, Emily followed the other two into the banquet hall, browsing the display booths set up to promote Valentine tourism: cooking-for-two school, a string quartet available to hire along with other musical groups, and romantic picnic baskets made to order.

"This is so cool!" Emily said. "What a great way to promote businesses that don't have a storefront. It's such a generous way to help other people."

"They promote people like me, too," Monica said, gesturing to the potted flowers and plants as they walked back onto the deck.

"You do such beautiful work," Emily gushed.

Brooke rolled her eyes. "Oh, please, let's not get started."

They took a seat at a picnic table vacated by a young family.

"Then we can talk about Emily's creative talents," Monica said, giving Brooke a fake frown. "Already, she's good at putting an arrangement together, choosing interesting combinations of color and flowers. She's the best hire I've made in a long time."

"I'm the only hire you've made in at least two years," Emily said, laughing. She glanced around at all the people talking softly or swaying to the music. "Monica, I'm surprised you didn't ask your sister to join us."

"Yeah, you haven't mentioned her much," Brooke added, watching her friend closely.

Monica shrugged, her smile fading. "She's doing some writing for an assignment while she's here. It's hard for her to get away from work completely. It's just such a challenging career," she added brightly.

Brooke scowled. "You imitate your sister well, but maybe you're taking what she says too seriously. Perhaps it's not about you but about her own excitement for her job."

"I can't help taking it personally," Monica said glumly, setting down her quesadilla wrap half-eaten. "I can no longer tell what she's even thinking when she says some of this stuff. Emily, be glad you don't have a sister."

Emily blurted, "I don't know—maybe I do."

Brooke cocked her head. "What does that mean?"

Though she hadn't intended to, Emily told her friends all about the revelation of her biological father and how Nate had been helping her.

"Never knew my brother was so sensitive," Brooke said dryly, even as she studied Emily. "So . . . how are you taking this? It must be hard."

"It is," Emily said, her voice subdued. "I loved my

father though I only knew him a few years. To think my mother lied to me all this time, and . . . and . . . I can't even yell at her about it, or demand answers. I'm all on my own."

"You know we'll help any way we can," Monica said. "And trust me, sisters aren't all bad. I couldn't have imagined growing up without Missy. We were the best of friends, and she made every step of high school bearable."

"And you could have a sister or brother right here in town," Brooke said, looking around the crowded deck.

"It's . . . unnerving," Emily admitted. "I really debated just forgetting the whole thing, but I can't seem to manage it. Nate has had some good ideas, so we'll probably discuss it today."

"Today?" Brooke said, perking up. "He's working with you?"

"Actually, it's a date," Emily said.

"Oooh." Monica gave her arm a little shove. "No more 'we're just friends'?"

"We're still friends," Emily insisted. "But now we're dating." She drew air quotes around "dating."

Brooke snorted her laugh. "Let me guess—my brother suggested that."

"It was a mutual decision. Neither one of us wants to get too involved."

"But he's helping you find your father," Brooke said dubiously. "Seems pretty involved to me."

"That's the friendship part. The dating part is . . . I don't know. Today's our first date. He wanted to go rafting, and I refused."

"Oh, you don't know what you're missing," Monica said, shaking her head. "Springtime down our rivers is so exciting."

"Maybe, but I'll leave rafting to you athletic mountain types. I suggested the movie festival."

Another snort from Brooke.

Emily laughed. "And that was pretty much his response. We're going hiking. Good thing I've been running and renovating, so maybe he won't have to wait for me too much on the trail." She felt her phone vibrate in her pocket. Apologetically, she said, "Let me get this text. Nate said he'd let me know what time he'll be free."

"We moved irrigation dams this morning," Brooke said. "The next hayfields have been flooded. He should be available."

Emily read the text and responded before looking up. "Nate's already in town. I told him we were almost done eating."

Five minutes later, Nate came up the stairs to the deck, and Emily's stomach did a little flip-flop that was part nerves, part anticipation. They were changing their relationship, and that could be bad or good. She chose to see it as good—something fun to fill her days until it was time to head back to school.

It took another few minutes for Nate to work his way through the crowd, what with everyone needing to talk to him about something or other. Scout got several rubdowns, and he accepted them as his due.

"Your brother is a popular guy," Emily told Brooke.

"He knows everybody," Brooke answered, a hint of pride in her voice.

Nate sat down and looked around at the three women, a grin on his face. "I'm the luckiest guy here."

His sister groaned, and Monica made a funny face.

"What a sweet compliment," Emily said, smiling at him.

"That's it, time to go," Brooke said, getting to her feet and tossing the second half of her veggie wrap in front of her brother. "I can't even finish this, you make me feel so sick."

"Enjoy your afternoon." Monica waved good-bye.

"What did I say?" Nate demanded in a baffled voice.

"Nothing. They know we're spending the afternoon together, that's all."

He stared at Brooke's sandwich. "And to make my *sister* lose her appetite—that's saying something. Oh, well, shouldn't let it go to waste."

Emily laughed as he dug in.

He swallowed and winced. "No meat."

"Nope."

He shrugged. "It's good anyway."

They sat in companionable silence, finishing their wraps and listening to the music. Nate bought another one, and they split a piece of cheesecake full of caramel and chunks of chocolate. Another Sweetheart Inn dessert. Scout sat down in front of Emily and watched her plate with the same concentration he reserved for a stray calf.

Emily licked her fork and closed her eyes. "God, this is so good."

"Decadent. And aren't you amazed a cowboy like me knows those big words?"

They ended up driving a half hour down valley to Mushroom Rock, where the cliffs rose above their parked car. The path through red earth wound slowly up, back and forth through trees and rocks, before reaching the summit, where rocks jutted out like a finger into the sky. The entire valley spread out before them, and Emily swayed dizzily, staring at the snow-topped mountains across from them. She kept wanting to put Scout on a leash, but Nate had him well trained. A simple command called him back to his master's side. But usually, Nate let him sniff every bush and leave his mark.

"Let's go out onto Mushroom Rock," Nate said, gesturing toward a narrow path that led out onto the promontory.

"Out there?" she squeaked, clutching his arm. "The view isn't any different."

"But then it feels like it's all around you. Come on!"

He led the way, and she wished she could close her eyes as the sides of the cliff plummeted down either side of the path. But at last they found a rock to sit on, and her vertigo eased enough for her to enjoy herself again.

"Oh, Nate, this is just incredible," she whispered. "We feel so . . . above the whole world."

"We hiked a thousand feet higher than the valley, so we're pretty high up."

He opened his backpack and handed her a bottle of water, which she drank from greedily. He poured some into a little portable bowl for Scout. Next he opened a Ziploc bag.

"Trail mix," she said. "Yum."

"GORP."

"Excuse me?"

"Good Old Raisins and Peanuts."

She laughed. "And M&Ms, too."

They ate and drank contentedly for a while, nodding at another hiker who passed them to go out onto the very tip. Emily shuddered and briefly closed her eyes.

Nate laughed at her. "So tomorrow I help you put up new drywall."

"If you're able. There're certainly other things I can do if you're . . . moving dams, or whatever Brooke said."

"Hayfields have to be flooded to help the crop grow. Every morning and evening we move portable dams and flood a different section of each field. You know that hailstorm we had yesterday morning?"

She winced. "You were out in it?"

"You bet. Those things sting. I'll be glad to get away and only do drywall."

"Thanks, Nate."

They ate more GORP, and Emily was so hungry from the hike, she thought she'd never get enough food again. She fed some nuts to Scout, who'd long ago mastered the look of quiet desperation. Then she told Nate she'd revealed the search for her dad to Brooke and Monica.

"I've been procrastinating," she admitted. "I keep wondering if I'm passing my dad on the street. I never had my mom's attention, and my husband, well, you can see what he thought of me. Part of me is worried that if my biological father rejects me, too, I don't know if I can handle it. Maybe I'm just a coward."

Nate put his hand on her knee. "No. If you were, you'd be huddled in an apartment in San Francisco, or maybe you'd still be married to that jerk."

"No, he left me, not the other way around."

"I'm sorry to hear that."

She nodded but didn't elaborate. She couldn't share with anyone the terrible hurt Greg had inflicted on her.

"I don't care about him," Nate said. "You're not a coward. You're trying to find a new way to support yourself, and you eventually want to adopt. You can't tell me that's not a brave thing for a single woman to do. How can your biological father not be happy about the way you turned out?"

"Thanks," she said, turning to smile at him.

They looked into each other's eyes for a moment, and then she leaned in to kiss him, letting her hand cup the roughness of his cheek. Suddenly hungry for more, she opened her mouth to him and let every other awareness fade away.

Until they heard the hiker going by them back up the trail.

She broke away and felt her face get hot. "Sorry."

"Don't be. I'm sure he's jealous as hell of me."

Laughing, she leaned her head against his shoulder. "This has been a great day. You were right—it's done me good to get away from work."

"Then we need to plan to get you out again. The mountain biking is fantastic around here. I usually bike these trails we just hiked."

She gaped at him. "These *dangerous,* narrow trails? I feel queasy just imagining doing them at high speed."

He grinned, flashing his dimples. "It's fun."

"No, thank you. I have a better idea. I haven't seen Aspen yet."

"Then it's a date. Everyone should see Aspen."

"Well, that was easy. There must be some daredevil part of the town you're hiding from me."

"Nope. I have time to make you try something riskier eventually. And I will."

He looked deeply into her eyes, and she thought of all the risky, athletic things she could do with him—in bed. But she was getting ahead of herself, she thought, eating another handful of GORP. Nate chuckled softly, as if he knew what she was thinking.

Admitting to Nate that she felt like a coward where her biological father was concerned spurred Emily to action. The next day, she stopped by St. John's to see Cathy Fletcher, her mother's high-school friend. Once again, she didn't reveal her mother's pregnancy, but with careful questioning, she got Cathy to reveal the names of two boys who occasionally hung out at the Riley family store when Delilah worked after school.

They were no longer boys, of course. Steve Keppel was now the building and grounds supervisor at the Royal Theater, according to Cathy.

She'd already met the other man—Hal Abrams, the owner of the hardware store. She didn't want to make Cathy suspicious, so she didn't ask any detailed questions, but her mind was buzzing. She tried to remember everything about Hal, but he'd been quiet compared to the coffee-drinking ranchers. He had sandy-colored hair, and hers was strawberry blond. That wasn't too different.

Cathy didn't think Delilah had actually dated either of the boys, but obviously she'd been with *someone*. Unless her mom had been forced—no, Emily wasn't going there. Her mom freely got involved with men throughout her life, and she'd started in Valentine Valley. She'd never had any hang-ups where men were concerned. There wasn't one particular type, either. She'd dated construction workers and lawyers, even a professional baseball player once. Men had been captivated by her easy charm and her pointed interest in them.

There was one other person Emily could turn to with her questions before approaching her possible dads directly—Doug Thalberg. He'd known her mother well enough to lend her money. Surely he might be able to hazard a guess about the identity of her father, or perhaps confirm Cathy's suggestions.

And Monica offered her the perfect opportunity the following day when Emily showed up for work.

As Emily set out her carrot cake, Monica breezed in from the workroom and groaned. "You are going to make me fat."

"But think how happy you're making your customers."

"I don't know. This used to be an occasional thing for me, but with you here, I'm starting to hear from people how much they look forward to sampling. Are they even buying when they come in, or are they just getting fat themselves?"

Emily laughed. "No, they're honestly buying. I sold that lovely ceramic vase Mrs. Ludlow painted."

"Oh, good, because that's been here a while, and I was starting to feel guilty whenever Mrs. Ludlow asked about it. She'll get a nice check when I do the monthly consignment payout." She glanced at the carrot cake again. "You know, Missy was down here late last night. She'd left the apartment to make a call on that smart phone that never leaves her hand. When I came down to work on the Thalberg arrangements, I caught her eating several of yesterday's mini cupcakes. You'd have thought she was committing a crime. God forbid a sister have hips. We're not alike in *that* department."

Emily smiled, but it faded as she studied Monica. "Are things any better between you?"

Monica shrugged. "Mom keeps us busy when we're together, visiting family, shopping in Aspen. You've been a big help letting me get away. I'm feeling guilty that you're not able to work on your renovations as much."

"Don't be. Now that the drywall is up, and that cracked wall mirror gone, I've been able to start the prep work before painting." She hesitated. "But I didn't mean to sidetrack from you and Melissa."

"There's no me and Melissa anymore, so let's not discuss it. We're two people with different interests, and living with her is helping me come to terms with that."

That didn't sound like they'd made any progress at all, but Emily knew it was time to drop the subject.

Monica briefly consulted the large calendar on the counter. "You up for doing a delivery for me this morning?"

"Of course!" Emily had already driven Monica's minivan adorned with the flower-shop logo.

"Several arrangements have to go to the Silver Creek Ranch. I think Mrs. Thalberg's sister is coming to visit, and she wants fresh flowers to liven the place up." Monica eyed her. "I assume you don't mind visiting Nate's family? His dad's waiting for the delivery."

Emily grinned. "It's such a hardship, but I'll bear it."

"I made up the arrangements last night, so they're waiting in the coolers out back. Let's go load them in the van."

Soon Emily was on her way to the ranch. It was the first really warm day of late spring, and she'd worn a sleeveless flowered dress and sandals for work, so she felt presentable for the Thalbergs. Maybe she'd get to meet Nate's mother. She didn't call Nate and tell him she was coming out—it was for work, after all. And if she was honest with herself, she didn't want to hear if he sounded upset about it. They were getting along so well, it would hurt her if he still didn't want her near his family.

So much for keeping things casual when she already knew he had the power to hurt her. Well, she'd always felt things too deeply; she would have to get over it. She didn't need a man's approval anymore.

After crossing the First Street bridge, she glanced down the road toward the boardinghouse, realizing how much she missed the chatter of the widows every morning. She would have to invite them to dinner, now that she had enough places for everyone to sit!

She was sort of surprised at herself, wanting to entertain in an apartment that was so tiny. But it was . . . hers, and she wanted to invite people in and show them what they meant to her.

She followed the winding dirt road to the ranch house, a two-story building made of rough logs, with porches wrapping around both levels. The roof was bright red, matching several of the barns. It was well cared for, and lots of spring flowers grew in the land-scaped beds surrounding the house. Several barns rose behind in the distance, as well as other small buildings.

She backed the van up near the front porch, but before she could even bound up the steps, Doug Thalberg was coming through the front door.

"Emily, it was so kind of you to bring the flowers for my wife."

"It was no problem, Mr. Thalberg. And it's my job now." She smiled at him and was relieved when he smiled back. "Is your wife at home?"

"Nope, but she told me where she wants the flowers."

Though she was disappointed, Emily didn't show it, helping Mr. Thalberg to bring the flowers inside. Two arrangements were in vases, and another was a big spray that he put in the hearth of the stone fireplace that dominated the log-walled room.

"This is beautiful," Emily said, looking around.

The upholstered dark furniture was lightened by throw pillows in greens and reds. Huge bookshelves were built into the wall on either side of the fireplace.

The wood floors had several small rugs in various patterns of green.

"We've remodeled over the last hundred years, of course, but this room was part of the original homestead."

"How incredible that you have such family history," she said wistfully.

"You do, too, Emily. You just don't know it yet."

She hesitated. "Nate mentioned that he told you about my predicament. Would you mind if I ask you a few questions?"

"Not at all. Let me get some lemonade, and I'll meet you on the front porch. It's too beautiful to waste a spring day inside."

She stepped back outside and sank onto a comfortable wooden rocker with a cushion on the seat. She rocked gently, staring across the fields with hay rippling in the breeze, and toward the looming mountains. The peace of such a view could quiet the troubles of any soul.

He returned with a tray containing a pitcher of lemonade and two glasses. After pouring them each a drink, he sat down beside her, and neither of them said a thing for a few minutes.

"Mr. Thalberg, your land is simply stunning."

He gave her a small smile. "God's land, you mean. You can't help but believe in Him when you live in the Rockies."

She found herself glancing at the one barn she could see. "Is it always this quiet?"

He grinned at her from beneath the brim of his hat.

"No, ma'am. But my kids are up on our grazin' allotment in the mountains, repairin' fence. It's a job that never ends. The elk migratin' through do some of the damage, along with roamin' cattle. There's age and weather conditions as well."

"I can only imagine what the snow must be like up there in the dead of winter." She shuddered.

"Are you a skier?" he asked.

"Not regularly, but I've done it a few times."

"You'll have to return and give our mountains a try. Nate's quite the expert on skis or snowboard."

"I'm not surprised. He seems an expert at a lot of things. He gave me a crash course in drywall. And the work he did at the boardinghouse was just amazing."

"You should see his cabin."

Not just yet, she thought. "Your mom did some bragging about it. She's very proud of all her grandchildren."

They sat quietly for several minutes, as the breeze blew in the scent of growing hay.

"Those questions I mentioned," she began at last.

He nodded politely.

"I talked to Cathy Fletcher about my mom having a boyfriend, but she said Delilah didn't date much. Well, obviously there had to be someone," she said dryly, "so I wondered if there were any boys who hung at the store, who might not have been officially 'dating' my mother. She thought of Hal Abrams and Steve Keppel. Do those names spark any memories?"

Mr. Thalberg frowned as he rocked. "They both still live in town, of course."

"I know, but I hate to just approach two strangers and say, 'Are you my father?' Knowing my mother, she didn't tell him she was pregnant. It'll be a terrible shock."

"Well, not terrible," he said, giving her a faint smile. "When a man does the deed, he knows there's a chance, even with all the precautions in the world."

"Did my mother . . . talk about those men to you?"

"Sorry, no, but I do remember them hangin' out on Main Street a lot their senior year. The store was pretty popular with all the kids, includin' me. There's even another name you might add to your list. Joe Sweet."

She frowned. "I've heard that name before."

"His family owns the Sweetheart Inn and Ranch. They have their fingers in a lot of the businesses in town."

"You mean through the preservation fund?"

Mr. Thalberg chuckled. "Nope, that's for people who want to donate anonymously. They've never made any secret of the fact they're rich enough to invest when they want."

"Is that a bad thing?" she asked doubtfully.

"Not at all. I'm just tellin' you how it is. Joe spent some time chasing after Dot. I didn't think she ever chose one of those boys, but obviously she did."

"So you can't help me narrow the list down from those three men?"

"Sorry, no. Dot never spoke of any of them to me."

Emily nodded her disappointment and took another sip of her lemonade, reminding herself that at least she had another name to research. She'd talk to Nate for more personal details about each of the men.

She heard a crackling sound, then, "Dad?"

Mr. Thalberg unclipped a radio from his belt and spoke into it. "Yeah, Nate?"

"We've got a problem up here and we could use your help. Several dozen cows and calves escaped through a hole in the fence before we could repair it. We're searching now, but we're on horseback. You want to bring an ATV up here and give us a hand?"

"On my way."

"We're at the Pinelands."

When he put the radio away, Emily smiled ruefully. "Guess I'll be going."

He gave her a grin. "Ever ridden an ATV?"

Her eyes widened. "No. But I'm expected back at the flower shop."

"We'll call Monica, but she won't mind. This'll be your first ATV lesson. Come on."

Chapter Sixteen

Nate rode his horse across the grassy pasture. Off in the distance, the ground sloped away, with clumps of pine trees huddled around meandering creeks. The tops of the mountains rose up all around him, as if gathering all the meadows into its arms.

If only the cattle could have stayed gathered, he thought wearily. He was used to chasing them, of course. They could be damned ornery. But up here in the mountains, once free of their grazing lands, they could be mixing with someone else's herd, or stumbling down a steep drop and breaking a leg.

The radio at his waist crackled as Josh and Brooke took turns calling in their reports.

Nate keyed his radio. "Anyone check where Jackson Creek meets the pond?"

No one had, so Nate rode that way, whistling for Scout to go on ahead. The other ranch dogs were working with Brooke and Josh, and they could find cattle even better than experienced ranch hands.

At the sound of an ATV in the distance, he twisted

in his saddle to see if it was his father. Relieved, he waved a hand, then frowned as something seemed . . . different. He saw arms around his dad's waist, and then a head peeking over his shoulder.

He recognized that wind-whipped strawberry blond hair trailing from beneath her helmet. What was Emily Murphy doing with his dad? Nate was used to keeping his private life separate from the women he dated—it had been that way ever since college. Now as they pulled up on the ATV, and he saw Emily's wide-eyed excitement, he considered the way he'd always compartmentalized the people he was close to. But it was necessary. No one got hurt that way.

But he couldn't frown long, seeing Emily's happy grin. She waved to him, and he smiled and waved back. He saw the relief she couldn't hide, and that took him aback. Did she think he'd be angry with her? He felt a bit defensive, then looked deeper, wondering if he'd made her feel that way.

His dad cut the power as Nate rode up beside him. Apollo showed no fear of the big machine, having spent his life around farm equipment. Scout jumped up on the rack behind Emily, his regular perch. She laughed and ruffled his fur, and something in Nate's gut gave a funny squeeze.

Doug gestured with a thumb at Emily behind him. "She was making a flower delivery when you called. Thought she'd like a ride."

Nate leaned on the pommel and grinned at her. "If I'd have known you liked four-wheeling, I'd have suggested a backcountry adventure."

"I thought I could trust your dad to give me a more sedate ride than you, but I was wrong! I didn't know a person could drive so fast!"

Doug glanced over his shoulder, wearing his usual small smile beneath his mustache. "Wait until we ride through a creek."

"What?" she cried, her eyes glinting mischievously.

"Now you know why I made you borrow some of Brooke's clothes," Doug said.

Nate glanced down Emily's legs and saw that she'd had to stuff the extra long material into waterproof boots. "New boots?"

"These are your mom's. Her feet are more my size. Hope she won't mind."

"Nope, she'll be glad we had an extra pair of eyes."

Emily let relief flood through and settle her nerves as she watched Nate sober as he told his dad the various lands they'd already searched. She was still surprised and dismayed at how much Nate's opinion of her mattered. It didn't bode well for their simple dating—or more likely her reaction to it.

She couldn't stop staring at him, with his cowboy hat shielding his eyes, the Carhartt jacket covering a flannel shirt, and fringed chaps over his jeans. The scarf at his neck was bright red and fluttered in the breeze. She was so busy admiring his fine form that she almost jumped when the ATV motor roared to life beneath her.

Mr. Thalberg glanced at her with amusement, and she gave him a sheepish grin. Her legs still trembled after the half-hour ride from where they'd left the pickup. Perhaps she was going to be sore tomorrow, but it was worth it.

Nate rode off ahead of them, and Scout jumped down and bounded after his master. Mr. Thalberg turned and went another way, and she clung to him as he raced through the meadow, high grass whipping against her legs. She turned her head and watched Nate, inhaling at the beauty of the scene as he headed across the meadow, the mountains framing him, the sky so blue above the snowy peaks. She felt almost hungry at the powerful way he moved so effortlessly with his horse.

For the next hour, Emily listened in awe at the coordination between the Thalbergs as they searched for each cow as if it were a member of the family—but of course, the sale of those cows was their profit at the end of the season. Nate's voice over the radio was one of cool composure as he coordinated the rescue. Emily gasped with delight and awe when Mr. Thalberg veered toward the thundering cattle, who obediently changed their direction, swarming together almost like bees. Nate, Josh, and Brooke rode from different directions, adding cows and calves to the growing herd.

When every cow was accounted for and guided back through the damaged fence, shared grins appeared on Thalberg faces. Josh and Brooke dismounted and went to work with the spools of barbed wire that had already been stacked near the damaged fence. Josh smiled and tipped his hat to her, and she touched the brim of her helmet in reply.

To her surprise, Nate frowned at her, and she gave him a wide-eyed look of puzzlement, as if she didn't know what was going on. But she knew—Nate Thalberg might be a little jealous over her. She felt giddy.

Then she sobered—she didn't want him to be jealous.

The sky slowly darkened as speeding clouds caught up with the sun. Emily looked overhead in surprise. Where had the beautiful day gone?

"We'll let you finish here and get your horses back to the trailer before there's too much rain," Mr. Thalberg called. "See you at the ranch."

Emily looked back as they rode away to see Nate staring after them momentarily before dismounting and going to help his brother and sister. The rain began in earnest then, and she was glad for the heavier clothing Mr. Thalberg had insisted she wear. Once they were in the pickup, he blasted the heat, but she was still chilled through.

Back at the ranch house, she hurried into the bathroom in the hallway near the bedrooms. After discarding her wet clothes in a heap, she hopped into the shower and let the hot water soothe her. As she toweled off, she could tell by the voices echoing through the house that the others had arrived home. And then she realized that her dry clothes were in Brooke's bedroom. She swore silently under her breath.

Nate opened the bathroom door. "Hey, Josh, I left my—"

She gave a little shriek, thankful he only saw her naked back before she yanked the towel higher and wrapped it around her.

"Jesus, I'm sorry," Nate said, making no move to

shut the door as his gaze took in her towel-clad body. "I thought Josh had arrived before me."

She rolled her eyes. "No knocking in the Thalberg household?"

He grinned. "Well usually, but I did hear the water shut off, and just assumed."

That cocky grin slowly died, and she felt as if she were wearing nothing at all, the way his gaze lingered on her damp skin. She should stop him; she should kick him out. But she stood still, basking in his admiration, wishing he'd come in and shut the door.

At last he cleared his throat and spoke in a husky voice. "Guess I'd better let you finish."

"Oh, I'm finished," she said, slipping by him, shivering as she brushed against his body. "I'll be in Brooke's room, so you might not want to accidentally walk in there."

His chuckle sounded a bit strained, but she didn't look behind to see. She finished dressing quickly, and although Brooke invited her to stay for lunch, Emily felt too guilty for abandoning Monica, so she headed back into town before Nate emerged from his old bedroom.

Nate worked hard all day, trying to rid his mind of the tantalizing glimpse he'd had of Emily. She'd been damp from the shower, her supple back bare of tan lines after winter. He'd had just a side glimpse of the roundness of one breast, and the image lingered.

He had dinner with his family, and when Brooke

and Josh headed back to the irrigation dams, he hung back a moment, bringing the last of the dishes into the kitchen.

His mom stood at the sink, her cane resting against the counter beside her, her hips swaying a little to the radio she always played when she worked in the kitchen. She had his dark hair though she now had to color it to keep it that way, but her eyes were brown. Sometimes it made him sad that his green eyes were from the father he didn't want to remember. Same with his height. His mom barely came up to his shoulders, but her exuberance always made her seem larger-than-life. She'd been dealt several terrible blows in her youth, but you never knew it to talk to her. When her MS flared up, she was the first one to wander the hospital, talking to kids in the pediatric ward or sitting with chemotherapy outpatients. There were times in her life she had to use a wheelchair, but she got up every day looking forward to whatever chores she could do.

Now, as he set the dishes in the sink, she glanced at him with amusement. He immediately grew wary.

"So I missed meeting your Emily," Sandy said.

Nate sighed. "She's not *my* Emily. She's a friend I'm helping out."

"A friend?"

"Well, yeah. I know she stopped by today, but it was because of the flowers you ordered."

His mom raised an eyebrow, but his father was the first to comment. "She had questions about her dad, of course. I told your mom all about it."

"Hope she didn't make you too uncomfortable,"

Nate said, feeling more and more awkward. "It was probably good you weren't here, Mom, or she might have grilled you, too."

" 'Grilled'?" Sandy echoed. "Having a conversation has now become an interrogation? It almost sounds like you're warning me away from her."

"Not true," Nate insisted.

"If I didn't know better," his mom continued, her mouth turned up with repressed laughter, "I'd think you were in charge of who I can visit with."

"Of course not." But he didn't know how to explain his uneasiness, even to himself.

"You better get going, Nathaniel," she said, nodding to the back door, "before I dissect whatever you're not saying."

He left quickly, hearing his mom and dad's laughter.

After he and Josh had finished irrigating that evening, he took another shower back at his cabin and drove into town. He wasn't sure what he meant to do, but he felt restless. Normally, he might meet a few guys at Tony's Tavern and play pool, but the memories of Emily on that pool table were a bit too vivid. He could go dancing at the Outlaws and not lack for partners, but there was only one woman he wanted to concentrate on tonight.

He found himself parked in the alley behind Emily's building, not knowing quite how he got there. This was probably a bad idea. Scout whined softly, as if sensing his uncertain mood.

"You stay here, buddy."

He left the windows cracked open and rang the bell

for the apartment. When he heard her voice, something inside him felt eager and randy and surprisingly uncertain about his welcome. He took off his hat.

She opened the door and smiled at him, her hair in soft waves about her shoulders. She wore workout shorts and a clingy t-shirt, and hell, he didn't think she was wearing a bra. It took everything in him to keep his gaze on her lovely, expectant face.

"Nate, twice in one day?" she said, cocking her head.

"This one's my idea, but earlier today, that was all your fault."

She sighed. "Your father was very persuasive, saying no one should visit Colorado without riding an ATV."

"And now you've done it. Next time, you'll have to see it all from horseback."

"Another date?"

"You're not going to suggest a trip to the local history museum?" He was kidding, but her face lit up.

"I'd forgotten all about it! I love museums."

He winced and ran a hand through his hair. "It's really small. And I know the local history by heart."

"Then you can elaborate on the skimpy displays."

He let his gaze roam down her body, saw her nipples tighten for him, felt himself getting hard. "Speaking of skimpy displays . . ." He thought she might cross her arms over her chest, but she didn't.

"Isn't it kind of late for early-rising cowboys?"

He looked into her sky blue eyes, opened his mouth, but nothing came out. He felt like a horny teenager again.

Her gaze softened. "Come on up." She glanced past him. "No Scout?"

"Nope."

She hesitated as if waiting for an explanation, then gave him a small smile. He followed her up the stairs, admiring her lean runner's thighs displayed by the shorts. Along the hall that ran past the bedrooms, he saw a framed photo of the Elk Mountains in winter, then another mountain picture in the living room, the high peaks of the Maroon Bells rising over the lake.

He arched a brow at her, and she blushed.

"Garage sale," she explained. "Your sister is a master at haggling."

There was a throw rug before the small couch and an upholstered wooden chair facing it. Though still spartan, the apartment was starting to seem more homey. He glanced at her swiftly, then away. What was wrong with him? He was usually the one so at ease, the one in control. And he *needed* that control, knowing his own weaknesses. But tonight . . .

"You must think I'm crazy to be decorating something that's so temporary," she said hesitantly.

"Not at all."

"It's just that . . . I like how it feels, having my own place. It's mine, and I want it to look a certain way, without anyone's influence. Valentine has helped me discover that." She smiled and shook her head. "Can I get you something to drink? I have Dale's."

"My favorite beer," he said.

"After you ordered it, I thought I'd give it a try. Go ahead and have a seat."

She moved past him, and he inhaled her scent, saw the jiggle of her breasts, felt his control beginning to slip. He wanted her, he wanted to taste every part of her. Instead, he forced himself to sit down gingerly on the little couch, in case it creaked under his weight. Nothing happened, so he relaxed a bit, but not completely. He had a hard-on the size of Montana, and felt like a lumbering, growling bear in her pretty little apartment.

She emerged with a couple beers, and he didn't say anything, just watched her set them on the coffee table. She gave him a curious stare but didn't speak as she returned to the galley kitchen. This time she brought out a bowl of chips, salsa, and napkins. As she leaned over, the t-shirt gaped a bit, and he could almost see farther down her chest. To his disappointment, she straightened, put her hands on her hips, and studied him. Her breasts gave a bounce that was his undoing.

"Nate, what—"

He reached forward, caught her hand and drew her toward him, sweeping her legs out from beneath her and cradling her in his lap. She gasped, but didn't protest, just looked up at him all wide-eyed.

"I've wanted to do this all day, heck for weeks," he whispered, and lowered his mouth to kiss her.

To his relief, she flung her arms around his neck, which pressed her breasts against his chest, making him groan. He deepened the kiss, felt wild about her taste, and wanted to touch her everywhere. He licked and nipped his way down her neck, buried his face in her hair, used his hands to explore her lean back. He cupped the curve of her ass before moving up inside her shirt, along her ribs. Her heart pounded hard against his, and she seemed desperate as she cupped his face and brought their mouths together again. They kissed as if they'd never kissed before and might never again. She tasted like the sunrise to him, the promise of something new, fresh and full of possibilities.

And then his hand captured her bare breast, and her ragged moan made him shudder. He kissed her even as he trailed his fingertips across her nipple, over and over until she squirmed in his lap, gasping. Then he pinched her lightly before soothing her again.

He lifted his head and stared into her glassy eyes. "I want you, Em. Let me take you to bed."

She rested her trembling hand on his chest. "I want you, too, but . . . it's too soon for me." She gave him a crooked smile. "We've only had one date."

He groaned. "Doesn't fixing fence count?" Her soft laugh made her breast jiggle in his palm. "Damn, you feel good."

"So do you. Kiss me again."

They kissed for a long time, and when her warm hands crept up under his shirt, he was the one who stopped it.

"Okay, okay," he whispered huskily. "If you touch me much more, I can't make any promises."

Her eyes were soft with tenderness, even as she slid from his lap to sit beside him on the little couch. They were pressed together along their arms and legs, and he kept her hand in his.

They remained silent for a little while as he worked to get himself under control. He looked at the book beneath her lamp, a romance with a racy cover. The apartment was saying more and more about her. He liked being with her, whether it was putting up drywall or hiking up a mountain. And if she needed to wait until she was comfortable at the thought of sex with him, he'd be okay with that.

"So you're not mad I came to the ranch today?" she suddenly asked.

He heard the hesitation in her voice, and it caught him by surprise, as he remembered this afternoon and her look of relief that he hadn't been angry with her. "Why would you think I'd be mad?" he asked hesitantly, knowing he might be mad—if she were someone else. He worked so hard to hold women at a certain emotional distance, to not let them close—to keep them from being hurt.

Her gaze lingered on their joined hands. "Nate, you don't exactly have a reputation as a man who brings women home to the family on a regular basis. And you might have thought it an . . . intrusion that I was there when you hadn't invited me."

"You made a flower delivery, Em," he said. "And then my dad invited you for a ride. I'd never expect you to say no. But . . . I know what you're saying, and I admit, my reputation isn't without cause. It's been pretty deliberate."

"I get that impression," she murmured, watching him.

He looked into those blue eyes, and knew he had to tell her the truth. "It's because I know myself pretty well. I hurt women, Em. I don't mean to, but it happens, and not just to women I'm dating."

Though she'd stiffened at his first revelation, now she looked bewildered. "Nate, I know you're not after any kind of commitment. I'm not either—I'm leaving Valentine soon. But surely the women around here know that you're not interested in marriage. You made it very clear up front. And they still let themselves be hurt that you keep things casual?"

"That's not why they get hurt," he said, running his hand through his hair even as he leaned his head back against the couch.

She said nothing, only continued to look at him expectantly.

He had never talked about this with a woman, hell, with anyone. But he took a deep breath. "I . . . don't know when to stop, Em," he murmured. "When people need help, I . . . help them. Over and over again, until they don't know when my *helpful* suggestions are doing more harm than good. I don't know either, until it's too late."

He looked at her at last, braced for the worst, for her laughter or her disbelief. But she was studying him with intensity, with compassion.

"Tell me what happened, Nate," she said at last, taking his hand.

He pulled away and stood up, beginning to pace. "The usual," he said shortly. "Bad breakup with a girl I loved in college. Romantic baggage and all that. I learned my lesson."

"One bad breakup in college?" she asked with quiet disbelief. " 'Romantic baggage'? Don't trivialize whatever happened. She doesn't deserve that."

He winced and closed his eyes, remembering Lilly's face, the uncompromising fury and bewilderment in her voice when she called to tell him she wasn't coming back to school, that she didn't love him anymore. "I didn't see what I was doing," he said, his voice harsh. "Over and over I helped her with every aspect of her life, from her classes to her homework, to what sorority she might enjoy. I never let her do anything on her own, to the point that she depended on me, and when I couldn't be there, I let her down."

Emily came and stood in front of him. "So you're saying she resisted all your helpful advice."

"No, never."

"You were helping her when she asked for your advice, and that was wrong?"

"I was *smothering* her," Nate said, feeling the cords in his neck go taut as he ground his teeth together. "I should have seen what was happening. But I didn't, until she dropped out of school because she felt like such a failure."

Emily put her hand on his arm and he let her, though he felt tight with tension.

"Nate, that wasn't all your fault. It sounds like she didn't know what she wanted. I've been there—we've all been there. To blame you was wrong."

"I know what you're saying, Em, but if it was just that, then okay. But it kept happening over the next couple years. It's like I couldn't distance myself, I couldn't see where other people ended, and I began. And it wasn't just the women I dated. My cousin came to visit for a summer to work on the ranch, and he was so lost on what he wanted to do with his life. He followed me around like my word was gospel, and we mapped out a plan together because I thought for certain he wanted the discipline and life of a soldier."

She winced.

"You can see it coming, though I didn't," Nate said bitterly. "He *hated* the military, almost got himself dishonorably discharged, but held it together until his enlistment was up. Good old Nate jumped right in to solve every problem." He stared down at her. "Sound familiar?" He waited for her to deny it, but when she hesitated, he could only sigh. "I fight it, Em, and I win that battle now."

She put up a hand. "Stop talking and listen to me. All I wanted to say was that I can see your kindness, Nate, and how much you care about people. But you haven't stepped over your bounds with me, and I won't be letting you. I spent years of my life ignoring the warnings I kept telling myself—I'll never do that again. I make my own decisions, and I have enough 'romantic baggage' that started in college, all of my own making. And if you lend me tools or your knowledge, or kiss me senseless, it's because I'm allowing it. And your girl-friends and your cousin? They didn't know themselves yet, and I'm sure they learned to stand on their own two feet. I did."

"It's nice of you to say that, Em." But he didn't believe he was blameless.

"Then we're okay?" she asked.

"We're okay."

To his surprise, she leaned against him and rose to

her tiptoes for a kiss, as if he hadn't just warned her off.

"Guess you better go," she said. "Scout will be worried."

At the door, he cocked his head. "Aspen?"

"Aspen," she answered dreamily, surrendering to another kiss. Then her eyes snapped open. "Aspen! Our next date."

He chuckled. "What about tomorrow?"

"I have to work until after lunch. You could pick me up at two, unless you think that's too late. I can skip painting for a single day."

He couldn't stop touching her, fingers caressing her waist, or down her soft arm. He almost forgot what they were talking about, so he linked their hands together. "That's fine. We can wander town for a few hours, then have dinner." He bent down to kiss her one last time. "See you tomorrow," he whispered against her lips.

When Nate had gone, Emily leaned against the door and contemplated what he'd told her. It would be so easy to feel like a giddy teenager again. But she was a mature woman of thirty who knew her own mind, and he was a mature man who'd made mistakes and wouldn't repeat them. All the better for her. His attention, his sweet consideration of her feelings, and the way he made her feel like the most desirable woman ever to inhabit the planet . . . those things were a balm to her spirit. The fact that he had such a weighty reason not to go any further reassured her.

But she felt sorry for him, too. He was still hurting about things that weren't all his fault. She'd tried to tell him, but she guessed he didn't believe her, not after long years of thinking the worst.

With a sigh, she sank onto the love seat and let her mind drift back to the moments spent in Nate's arms. Then she shook herself, saying aloud, "Get yourself together, Emily Murphy. Emily Strong. Whoever you are."

She might have had a different last name, if things had turned out differently. That put her back to the three men who might be her father—and if she were honest, there could be other candidates, but she couldn't think about that right now. She'd almost told Nate about them, but decided to stand on her own two feet for a while and do her own investigating. Good thing, too, after what he'd just confided. There were only three likely men, after all, one of whom she'd already met. When she went in for more paint supplies, she would talk to Hal Abrams, try to get a feel for him. As for the other two men—she'd have to subtly ask questions.

She thought of the yearbooks then, and went to look at the black-and-white pictures of each. Fresh eager faces, and Hal Abrams looked different without a beard. Neither he nor the other two men seemed familiar to her at all, as if their genes might be part of hers. She couldn't believe there was nothing here to give her a clue. With a groan, she flipped open one of the middle-school diaries and riffled the pages, Delilah's handwriting a blur of schoolgirl penmanship. But right at the end, just before the book closed, she saw different ink, different writing.

Surprised, she opened it back up to the last written

page. It was Delilah's handwriting, but not the same. And the date—the date was April of her senior year. For some reason, she'd added an entry to her old diary. Even the page before was dated four years earlier.

Excited, nervous, Emily spread the book wide on her lap and began to read. It was about a boy, and her mother almost gushed about meeting him in secret down by the creek, or in a barn. But she never said his name! Over and over, she melodramatically mentioned his blue eyes seeing into her soul.

Blue eyes, just like Emily's, but not her mom's. There was only the one entry. Closing the book, she put her hand against it, and said, "Thanks for the clue, Delilah. At least it's something."

Brooke and Monica would be a good place to start. She was already relying on Nate enough, and it was obvious *he* didn't want her to lean on him. It seemed . . . confusing to turn to him for entertainment, for renovations, for . . . hell, for foreplay, then consult him about her biological father. She wouldn't get too dependent on him. He'd be hurt as badly as she would. She'd spent the last ten years being dependent on a man who'd given her every indication that he was dependable— until the worst happened.

She refused to go back to that woman who couldn't seem to leave her bed last year. She was going forward one step at a time, and that was all she could ask of herself.

Chapter Seventeen

The next morning, Emily was in the back room of the flower shop making bows when Monica called out, "Em, there's someone who wants to talk to you."

Emily came through the door, then stopped in surprise on seeing Josh Thalberg standing at the counter, carrying a closed box.

"Hi, Josh," Emily said, staring with interest at the box.

"Josh said you hadn't been formally introduced," Monica said doubtfully, "and I was to do the honors."

Emily smiled at Josh, who returned the smile in a slow, aw-shucks way that was endearing. "We spoke once, but without exchanging names. And then I saw you at the ranch," she said to Josh. "We never did get to say two words to each other yesterday."

"Damn cows," he said, nodding.

Monica spread her hands wide. "Ookay. Emily Murphy, this is Josh Thalberg."

Josh put the box on the counter, and they shook hands. "Nice to finally meet you, Emily."

"You, too." She gestured to the box. "Can I help you with something?"

He gave Monica an apologetic glance. "Emily and I discussed selling my work on consignment, and I wondered if you'd mind if we continued?"

"No problem," Monica said. "I've got an arrangement to work on. Thanks for your business, Josh. Em, I can answer any questions later." Then she disappeared into the workroom.

Emily smiled. "You might regret wanting to work with me. I'm pretty new at all this."

"I thought it was only fair to show you my work since you were the one who persuaded me to give it a try."

"I didn't drag you in off the street—that was your idea. But let's stop praising each other and see what you've got."

He opened the box, and one by one set his work on the counter.

She gasped at the leather-framed mirror, intricately tooled with a Western desert sunset. "Oh, Josh, you're so talented!"

He didn't say anything, only brought out several frames tooled with mountain cowboy life, as well as leather journals and wallets done in flowers and vines, and belts with stamped geometric patterns. Lastly, he showed her two purses, one covered in daisies with a long strap, and the other a clutch with a swirling pattern. "These last two are what I've been working on since you mentioned them."

"That quickly?" she said in surprise.

"I already had the leather. Just had to cut it out and

begin work. I looked through Brooke's closet for ideas in regard to size, then did some research on the Internet. Do you think these will sell?"

The stitching was done in leather to look Western, but it was meticulous and snug. The inside was well lined. "Josh, these are so unique. I think you'll be pleasantly surprised how well they'll sell. We'll have to talk about the price you should ask for. Your Internet research will probably come in handy there. But first—how the heck do you have time to do this? It seems ranch life is twenty-four hours a day. Do you have any kind of social life at all?"

He shrugged and seemed to redden a bit as he stared out the window. "I like to keep busy. There's something about this work that just . . . calls to me. And the family knows and respects the time I give myself."

She found herself wishing she could ask Nate about Josh's talent but didn't know if that was going too far. She was consulting him about her most personal problems, but she shouldn't want the same from him.

"Emily, you have another visitor," Monica called from the showroom.

Again? Emily put aside her pen after recording the last of Josh's crafts as she sorted through them. It couldn't be Nate, when they would be seeing each other that afternoon. She walked into the showroom and saw a short middle-aged woman with black hair framing her face. She held a cane in one hand, and her eyes fastened on Emily with interest.

Emily glanced at Monica, who grinned, and said, "Emily, this is Sandy Thalberg."

Nate's mother. Curious and excited at the same time, Emily put out a hand, but to her surprise, Mrs. Thalberg gave her a big hug. Flustered, but pleased, Emily laughed. "Mrs. Thalberg, it's so wonderful to meet you. I'm sorry we didn't get a chance to meet when I delivered arrangements yesterday."

"I was disappointed, too," Mrs. Thalberg said, studying Emily with friendly eyes. "Please call me Sandy. Otherwise, I won't know if you're talking about me or my mother-in-law. She and Brooke always speak of you fondly, as do my boys."

Emily highly doubted that Nate and Josh said much about her at all, but she didn't bring that up. "Your whole family has been so welcoming. And I wouldn't have had a clue about my building renovations without Nate's help. Please, have a seat," she added, gesturing to the wrought-iron chair near her pastry display.

"You've got to try Emily's croissants," Monica gushed.

"My mother-in-law raves about your baking," Sandy said, taking a seat and accepting the croissant Monica handed her on a napkin. Sandy took a big bite, then hummed her approval.

Emily knew she was probably blushing.

"Oh, Emily, my family was right about your cooking," Sandy said, even as she licked a crumb from her lip. "I've come here to ask you to Sunday dinner, but after eating this, I'm worried my cooking will pale in comparison."

Emily saw Monica give her a wide-eyed glance, and inside, she felt a little thrill of her own, followed quickly by concern for Nate's reaction. "Mrs. Thal—Sandy, you're too nice."

"Well, I try to be, but I don't have to try about this. I guess I'll ask you to dinner and take my chances."

Emily smiled, knowing she was too curious to refuse. Nate would just have to understand. "Thank you so much. I'd love to come. And please, I'd like to contribute. Let me bring dessert."

"Then I'm off the hook for having to compete with this." Sandy ate another bite, watching her. "I hear you helped herd the cattle."

"No, I clung for dear life to your husband, while he herded the cattle." Emily laughed. "It was a wild, exciting ride."

"It's not a job for the faint of heart," Sandy said, shaking her head. "You have to love it, and love the life. The long days can be grueling, but being together as a family makes everything worthwhile."

Emily could have melted inside at the warmth and contentment in Sandy's voice. After a terrible beginning as a young woman, she'd found everything she ever wanted, children, a home. Emily wanted to change her life, too, and for just a moment, she imagined doing it here, in Valentine, with those mountains standing guard, and the wide-open, vivid blue sky proving that anything was possible. She felt suddenly empty imagining those mountains replaced with towering concrete.

She found herself blurting, "I've learned so much in the few weeks I've been in town. Life in Valentine Valley is so different from San Francisco."

"I hope you consider that a good thing." Sandy lowered her voice as Monica went to wait on a customer.

"It's made me see things in a different way. Frankly, I've felt more relaxed here, more at peace with the decisions I've made. I was pretty unhappy when I got here, but now I know things will work out."

"Because you'll make it happen." Sandy smiled. "Sometimes all we can hope is to be at peace with our decisions, especially after a bad marriage. I'm not sure Nate told you, but I can relate to your problems."

"Yes, Nate mentioned your first husband. I'm so sorry you had to go through that."

Sandy's husband left her because she had been diagnosed with MS—not too different from Greg's leaving her over not being able to have children. And in that moment, it all rushed back on Emily, the sadness, the emptiness. But it didn't overwhelm her. Suddenly, she realized that Sandy had touched her hand and now gave it a supportive squeeze.

They smiled at each other.

The flower-shop door jingled as it was opened, and Nate strode in. Dressed in jeans and a polo shirt, hat in his hand, he came up short when he saw the three women, and his gaze focused on Sandy touching Emily's hand.

Monica chuckled and escaped into the workroom.

"Hi, Nate," Sandy said, grinning up at him.

Emily thought her eyes sparkled with mischief, and Emily sat back in her chair to watch Nate's reaction.

"Hi, Mom," he said, then glanced at Emily. "I'm early, I know. Sorry."

Yet his look told her he was glad he'd come early.

Emily gave him an innocent smile. "No problem. Come have a croissant with your mom while I get ready to leave."

Nate watched Emily as she sauntered into the work-room looking way too satisfied. He put his fists on his hips and studied his mom. "Well?"

"Well what?" she asked innocently. "Oh, Nate, you need to try these croissants."

"I'm saving my appetite. I imagine Emily told you why," he said dryly.

"Actually, we didn't talk much about you at all. I take it you and Emily have a date? Where are you taking her?"

"Into Aspen."

"That makes sense. She shouldn't travel all this way and not see it. Who knows if she'll ever get back here?"

That made Nate grit his teeth, but he hid his reaction with a pleasant, "So what brought you into town? Where's Aunt Marilyn?"

"I came to meet Emily. Marilyn wanted to relax this morning after the trip yesterday. We're spending the afternoon at the spa up valley. Have you ever had one of their massages? I feel so alive afterward."

Nate didn't want to hear spa stories. "You came to meet Emily? Why?"

"Because I didn't get to meet her yesterday. And since you've been spending so much time with her, I thought I should meet the woman who could pull you away from work." She shrugged her shoulders as if it all made perfect sense.

Had she allied herself with Josh about his spreading

himself too thin? She of all people knew what he could accomplish if he set his mind to it. "So now you know she's a nice woman and a friend. Are you satisfied?"

Sandy laughed. "I am, now that she agreed to come to dinner Sunday."

Nate briefly closed his eyes on a sigh. "You didn't think you should talk to me about it?"

She waved a finger at him. "About who I invite to dinner in my own home? Nope. And why would I think there's a problem since you spend so much time with her?"

Feeling tense, he answered, "There's not a problem, Mom."

"And she's Brooke's friend, too. And your grand-mother's. Even Josh seems to know her."

That didn't help his tension.

Nate lifted both hands. "Fine, fine, I get it. I'm look-ing forward to dinner already."

"That's good," she said, rising slowly to her feet and reaching for her cane. She patted his cheek. "So don't break up with her before Sunday, or it might be awk-ward for you."

He opened his mouth but thought better of trying to explain things. "Yes, ma'am."

She lifted her head, and he leaned down to kiss her cheek.

"Have a good time today," she said.

Her grin made him grin in return. "Thanks."

But after his mom left, he remembered the way she'd been touching Emily's hand when he arrived, the seri-ous, sad looks on both their faces. The memory lingered with him, even while he tried to get Monica to open up about her sister's tense visit; then it briefly fled his mind when he saw Emily, wearing a short skirt and a V-necked top that showed more of her breasts than he was used to seeing.

She blushed. "Monica loaned this to me, said I needed to blend in in Aspen."

"No," Monica countered, "I said she needed to show herself off *to* Aspen."

"So it's all about Aspen, and none of it for me?" Nate demanded. He put his arm around Emily and gave her a quick kiss. "I forgive you. I don't care about the reason as long as I can enjoy the looking."

"Well, now that you have his forgiveness," Monica said dryly, "all is right with the world."

Emily was still chuckling when she hopped up into the pickup. "No Scout?"

"He stayed home today. I wanted you all to myself." When they left Valentine behind and were driving along Route 82, he said, "I noticed that you and my mom were looking pretty serious when I got there. Everything okay?"

She looked out the window for a long minute, the breeze blowing her red-blond curls about her pretty face. Her expression was briefly pensive before she sighed and gave him a small smile.

"Your mom and I have a lot in common, and not just you," she said quietly. "We both had lousy marriages to men who weren't what they seemed."

Nate kept his eyes on the road. He hadn't imagined that the two women could so quickly touch on such a sensitive topic when they'd just met. Could women just look at each other and know when they shared something? He knew how his father had treated his mother but had assumed that Emily's husband had been restless, or had decided he wasn't in love. Comparing Emily's situation to his mom's made it seem so much darker and complex. He gripped the steering wheel tighter at just the thought of Emily being hurt.

"So Greg lied to you?" he asked.

She hesitated. "Not really. I knew what he wanted in life. I just never imagined he would go looking for it without me."

"You mean he had an affair?" He felt guilty even asking, in the face of her pain.

"No. Nate, don't worry about it. It's in my past, and it's too beautiful a day to think about sadness. So, do you have plans for Aspen, or will we just see what happens?"

Nate had to force a smile, when he really wanted to know every detail of what Greg had done to her. He felt the strong pull of sympathy and compassion and knew where they could lead to. They were only dating, he reminded himself. He wasn't going to learn everything about her. Because if he kept feeling this way, he was going to have to end it between them. And Emily would thank him for it.

Emily was relieved when Nate dropped the subject of her ex. The fact that he was curious meant he still didn't always succeed at keeping his distance, and she wasn't going to be another person he regretted being with. He didn't need to understand her or her past. She was escaping painful memories, starting a new life, finding a new Emily.

And this Emily showed off a lot of cleavage, she thought ruefully. Glancing down at her chest still made her start with surprise, as if she hadn't finished dressing. She'd dressed much more conservatively in San Francisco, and not because Greg had tried to control what she wore. She just had a different sort of life then.

Now, it gave her pleasure to see the way Nate couldn't take his eyes off her, and once she even had to remind him that he was driving. It took twenty minutes to reach Aspen, where he parked the car, and they wandered hand in hand through the small town. Victorian gingerbread homes gave way to impressive mansions that perched on the hillsides through the valley. But the town itself still clung to its cozy village charm. He took her on a gondola ride up the mountain so that she could gape at the incredible view of the green valley spread below her and the snow-topped mountains all around her. They window-shopped the little boutiques on the Cooper Avenue Mall, a touristy area where a little creek ran through a tree-shaded boulevard. She gaped at the clothing prices and insisted she didn't need to try anything on. He even begrudgingly followed her into the little history museum, where she learned all about the nineteenth-century mining that had begun the transformation of a remote encampment to the eventual mecca for the world's wealthy. For dinner, he took her to a small, candlelit restaurant, where the chef came out to greet him like an old friend. Nate later explained that he and the chef had common friends in an organic farmer down valley, but Emily thought he was leaving things out. She didn't blame him.

On the trip back to Valentine, the darkness enveloped them in the truck cab, and Nate took her hand. "Would you like to come back to my cabin for a drink?"

She glanced at him without surprise. She enjoyed being with Nate, and found his notion of dating much easier than she'd imagined. There was no pressure, for she knew he wasn't looking for a wife. She'd spent her life longing to be someone's wife, looking for the family and stability she'd never had. And look where that had gotten her! If she didn't go to Nate's cabin, was she still protecting herself? How was she supposed to live a new life like that? Maybe she was being too cautious, too careful. It was time to be as sexually casual as everyone else in the twenty-first century.

"Since you haven't answered my question," Nate finally said, "should I take it back? Maybe I'm rushing you."

As they turned off the highway, heading toward the deeper darkness of the mountain silhouettes, she unbuckled her seat belt and slid beneath his arm. "No, you're not rushing me. I'd love to see your place."

She felt his hand in her hair, and she could have purred at the pleasure of it. She wasn't going to think about anything else but him and the night and the passion they'd felt combust between them since the first moment they met.

Silver Creek Ranch was dark beneath the starlit sky as they rode between the hayfields and the creek. When the pickup turned into a driveway, a spotlight came on over a garage. Nate's cabin was made of logs, old, she could tell, but kept in good shape. Scout was waiting just inside, and he joyously greeted them before running past into the night.

"Is there a fence to keep him in?" she asked dubiously.

Nate shook his head. "He knows his way around. Sometimes he's gone for hours."

"Will he need to be let back in?"

He met her gaze. "He'll wait on the porch until I come for him."

"Ah, how handy."

"I know how to train a dog."

Inside, he'd opened up the main living area into one room, with a kitchen and its island in one corner, dark cabinets gleaming with silver touches. As he flipped on more accent lights, she realized that the focus of the room was a pool table.

She arched a brow at him, and he grinned.

"I never hid my enjoyment of the game," he said, going to the wet bar at the end of the kitchen counter. "Would you like a glass of wine?"

"Anything white would be fine." She kept staring at the pool table, remembering. She heard soft music turn on, something sensual in rhythm and blues.

He brought her a glass of wine, then stood at her side as she took a sip. "Every time I look at this table, I remember."

"Good or bad memories?" she asked, glancing at him with amusement.

"Both, I guess. You were . . . wild that night, and I enjoyed every minute of it. And then it was over, and I never got to see how the game ended."

She set down her wine. "Then we should play another game."

He put down his own glass. "I'll win," he said softly, reaching out to touch her bare shoulder, just a fingertip that gently traced.

She shuddered and briefly closed her eyes at the electric sensation. "You won't be the only winner." She grinned at him. "So rack 'em up, cowboy. But first take off your shirt."

His smile was briefly interrupted with surprise, and she took satisfaction in that. No point being too predictable since she was becoming a new Emily.

Nate sailed his hat onto the glass coffee table, leaving his black hair tousled, then slowly pulled off his shirt, his gaze fixed on her. Her mouth went a little dry at all that lean muscle earned working hard for a living. Even though he had the faintest farmer tan on his lower arms, it was obvious he worked without a shirt when he was overheated.

Speaking of overheated . . . she felt suddenly too warm beneath his smoldering regard. She didn't want to play pool; she wanted him to sweep her into his arms as if he couldn't resist her anymore. Instead, he sauntered to the pool table and racked the balls, just as she'd stupidly asked. Ah, but he had to bend over the table . . . and reach for things . . .

"Emily?"

To her surprise, she realized he'd been holding out a

cue to her, and she'd barely noticed, so focused was she on his broad chest scattered with dark hair.

"Oh . . . sorry."

When she reached for the stick, he closed his hand over hers, bringing her closer, until her bare arm brushed his bare chest.

"I think you need a lesson," he murmured against her hair. "May I?"

"Please."

Then started the most pleasurable, slow-building foreplay of her life, as he used his hands to position her body, to guide her arms, to lean her over the edge of the table to position her cue just right. Her pulse pounded so hard she could barely hear the music. When she was trying to make a shot, he was right behind her, and she gasped when his hips brushed her backside.

"Concentrate," he whispered evilly.

She glared at him over her shoulder, then her trembling hands ruined the shot. But it didn't matter, for he leaned his hips into hers, pressing her against the table. He buried his face in her hair, kissing her neck, caressing her arms and back, then pulling her shirt up over her head. He reached around to cup her breasts and guide her back against his body. She sagged in his arms as he gently rubbed her nipples through her lace bra, playing with her, tormenting her. Her moans were plaintive, and his answering groans let her know he felt just as turned on as she did. When he unsnapped her bra, she let it fall down her body. He turned her about and stared down at her with so much hunger she felt like a sex goddess. Feeling provocative, she leaned back on the table, bracing herself with her arms behind her, her breasts practically lifted in his direction.

With another groan, he gathered her against him, skin to skin, her nipples gently abraded by the hair on his chest. Then, just like before, he lifted her until she sat on the edge of the table. When he pressed between her thighs, this time her skirt rode up. And then they were kissing, his hands filled with her breasts, his tongue taking possession of her mouth. She lost track of everything but the feel of him beneath her hands, the sleek heat of his skin, the ripple of muscle down his stomach, the roughness of his face at the end of the day.

He kissed his way down her neck, arching her back, and she wantonly let her hair spill all around the table, crying out when his lips found her nipple. He nipped and licked and drew her deep within his mouth, leaving her shuddering and gasping, pressing herself hard against the long ridge of his erection.

"Let me take you to bed," he whispered harshly.

"Why not right here?" she whispered back, still arched and offering her breasts.

He groaned and shuddered, and she felt him cup her buttocks with both big hands. The slide of her panties down her thighs was erotic, until the feel of his fingers lightly stroking her made her realize that everything before had led up to this, this burst of sensation and need and desperation.

"Nate, please," she whimpered.

But he seemed in no hurry, staring down at her half-naked body with hooded eyes, his fingers moistening the deeper he played with her. With his other hand, he caressed her breasts. She trembled and shuddered with each touch, holding her breath as he came closer and closer to what she really wanted.

He circled her clitoris, making her practically sob. She came at once, shuddering in his arms as he reached down to hold her.

"Jesus," he whispered hoarsely.

"It's been a long time." Her voice was shaky with satisfaction. "Now take off your pants, and let's rack some other balls."

His laugh was partially a groan, and she heard him fumbling in his pants pocket before he yanked off his clothes. He was quick with a condom, and before she could even reach for him, he thrust home swift and sure.

She felt the deep fullness, the pressure of him already unfurling a new burst of passion. Joined so intimately, he leaned over her, hands braced on the pool table on either side of her body, his eyes pinned to hers.

"You . . . all right?" he asked, his breathing coming deep and quick.

"Better than that." She reached to play with his nipples, to stroke every part of his bare skin she could reach.

Eyes closed, he accepted her touch, quivering, his erection pulsing inside her as if longing to be unleashed. Perspiration broke out on his forehead, he bit his lip, yet he held himself still as she explored him.

Then, with a groan, he pulled out and surged back

in. She felt electric, her skin tingling with sensitivity. Every thrust of his body brought her closer to bliss again, and when at last she exploded, he let himself go, harder and faster and deeper until his upper body collapsed on top of her.

Chapter Eighteen

Nate felt as if his body were no longer under his control, so sated and exhausted were his muscles. And then he realized that Emily was sprawled on an uneven table beneath him.

He came up on his elbows and cupped her moist, flushed face. "Are you okay? Did I hurt you?"

Her smile was sleepy and satisfied and indulgent. "I'm more than *okay.*"

She was so small, he lifted her right off the table, and she laced her ankles behind him and held on tight. It was only a few steps to the leather couch, and he was able to sink back, never leaving her body. Her short skirt pooled around her hips, an erotic sight.

"Jesus," he whispered again, her breasts right before him like ripe peaches. He took them in his mouth, felt her body clutch him from deep inside. He was still hard, and moved in her slowly, even as she laughed, and then gasped again when his tongue flicked her nipple.

"So do you use that pool table a lot?" she asked, clutching his head to her.

"You're the first." She tasted sweet, and he could smell the scent of her skin, elusive and floral.

"So pool tables are our shared destiny."

He chuckled and leaned back against the couch to look up at her. He couldn't keep his hands off her breasts, and she watched him with a faint, amused expression, even as her eyes went dreamy.

At last, she slid to the side, and he excused himself to take care of the condom. When he returned, she was already in her bra, the skirt tugged back into place.

"Emily—"

"I should go," she interrupted, her voice laced with reluctance. "I'm . . . I'll feel too close to you if I spend the night. Neither of us wants that."

He pulled on his jeans but didn't protest. Yet he found himself wanting to touch her, to soothe her, but she pulled her shirt over her head, then straightened it over her breasts.

She gave him a reluctant glance. "You'll think this strange, but you're only the second man I've ever made—had sex with."

"I'm not surprised, considering how young you were when you married." Had she meant to say "made love"? That she'd changed her words made him feel confused even though she was calling sex what it was.

She smiled. "Trust you to understand how . . . strange this is for me."

He watched as she looked around, and he found her purse and handed it to her. "Does this change things for you?"

"You mean can we still date?"

She came up on her tiptoes, and he leaned down. Their lips met softly, briefly, once, twice. He would have gone on kissing her, but she stepped away.

"Yes, Nate, I'm not done with you yet. I still have a couple months before classes start, and you've proved too much fun."

He followed her to the door. " 'Too much fun'? I'm not sure how to take that."

She looked over her shoulder, smiling, even as her gaze drifted down his chest. "That you're irresistible, and I'm only human."

"Then don't resist me. Let's get together again."

"All right." She opened the door, and Scout came bounding in, happily bouncing between them. "He's all yours, Scout."

"Wait, you don't have a car," he reminded her. He slid on his shirt and a pair of shoes, then followed her out to the truck, Scout trailing behind. He and his dog drove her home, and the silence was companionable and easy. He kept glancing at her as she leaned against the headrest, calm and faintly smiling.

When he would have escorted her inside, she touched his arm. "I'm okay. You can watch me open the door and guard against the Valentine criminal element." Then she laughed. "Does the sheriff even have anything to do around here?"

"Cattle rustling."

Her eyes sparkled as she left his truck. When she unlocked the door, she blew him a kiss and slipped inside.

Nate watched until he saw her bedroom light go on above the alley. He gripped the steering wheel tightly, disappointed she hadn't invited him up. It was seldom he wished for an evening not to end, so he tried to laugh at himself. But it wasn't easy. He was feeling the old pull too strongly, the one that always got him in trouble.

Emily looked out the window, moving the curtain only briefly, curious why Nate still hadn't left. At last he put the truck in gear and slowly drove down the alley, and she pressed her face against the glass until his taillights disappeared.

This fling with Nate was supposed to be fun, to make her feel better, to start a new chapter in her life. And it had, to a degree. Every moment of the day had been enjoyable. They laughed at the same things, even liked the same foods—not that those were all you built a relationship on.

Yet . . . who was she kidding? Dating wasn't a simple concept. Nate was using her for a good time, and she was using him . . . to forget. Always, lurking beneath her day was the reality that her future was murky, that she had yet to find a place for herself in it. Her past, everything she thought she wanted in life, was just as illusory. Every decision she'd made, every goal, had ended up wrong and full of heartbreak. Though it helped her to pass the time with Nate, in the end, she had to remember she was still alone. And she wanted it that way for now—she had to prove to herself that she didn't need anyone else.

And she had a dad out there somewhere, a dad with blue eyes. He could be part of her future—if he wanted her.

* * *

In the morning, while Emily tried to carefully remove the paint that her tenants had splattered all across the lovely mahogany bar in her restaurant, she waited for Brooke's response to her text.

Instead of a text, Brooke strode through the door at midmorning, wearing cowboy boots and jeans beneath a heavy rain slicker.

"It's terrible out there," she said, shaking off the rain as she stood just inside the door.

"Drape your coat over my only unbroken chair."

Brooke grinned as she did so. "Thanks for getting me away from the ranch. Josh and Nate were working on mechanical stuff for the swathers."

"You've lost me," Emily said, pounding the tin lid back in place on the paint remover.

"Something about carburetors and oil changes. Swathers cut hay. It's almost time, but this rain certainly doesn't help."

Brooke followed Emily into the kitchen while she washed up. "No more flooding the fields?"

"Hope not. And I can follow directions in the shop, but that's about all. And they're bickering about a meeting Nate's supposed to attend although he says he can finish helping Josh first—and Josh thinks Nate should just leave. I think they were happy to see me go since they weren't interested in my opinion." Brooke smiled. "So what's going on?"

"My biological father. I could use your help. I have three names now, and I've put off researching them long enough."

"Researching? Can't you just introduce yourself?"

Emily winced. "Hi, my name is Emily. Did you bang my mother thirty years ago? And are your eyes blue because she gushed about them in her diary?"

Brooke laughed. "Okay, I get your point. Nice clue, by the way. What's your plan?"

"I just want to . . . see them first. Okay, see their eyes. I've already met Hal Abrams—"

"Mild-mannered Hal is a contender?" she asked, eyes wide.

"Yeah, but that only confirms my doubt. He seems like a nice guy."

"And he's been with the same woman since high school, and they have one son."

"Well, he hung around my grandparents' store, flirting with Delilah, so he might not be all that innocent."

"Or those other guys were simply the friends he hung out with."

"I know, I know. And eventually I'll ask the questions I need to. But today . . . I just want to see them, see if I get some kind of sense or intuition."

"And get close enough to see their eyes."

Emily sighed. "That'll be fun. And I'd feel stupid hanging out alone, waiting for a glimpse. That's where you come in. You're going to show me the sights."

"Like the hardware store?" she asked doubtfully.

"No, we'll start with the Royal Theater, then maybe the Sweetheart Inn."

"So tell me names," Brooke said, leaning forward with interest.

"Cathy Fletcher and Doug Thalberg suggested them.

The first is Steve Keppel, building and grounds supervisor at the Royal Theater."

Brooke frowned. "Keppel . . . He has twin daughters a couple years younger than me, and a son younger than that, maybe still a teenager. He's divorced."

"Okay. At least when I get around to questions, I won't be upsetting his wife." Three kids—were they her siblings? It seemed unreal.

"Who's the next suspect?"

"Joe Sweet."

Brooke whistled, eyebrows raised. "Not divorced— pretty happily married, or so it's always seemed. He's part of a very big, very powerful family in this valley. Several sons in their twenties and a teenage daughter."

More potential siblings, Emily thought, feeling a little daunted. What was she getting into? How many people would be affected? Maybe she should call the whole thing off.

"Stop it right there," Brooke said sternly. "I can read your face so easily. This isn't your fault. And they would want to know the truth."

"Even if it disrupted their lives?"

"It's not like you're twelve years old looking for a place to live," she said patiently. "You just want to know your father. And these guys—they're good men. They'd want to know you."

Emily took a deep breath and let it out. "Okay, okay, I'm not backing down. Let me get changed, and we'll take a walk to the theater."

"Wear your rain boots and carry an umbrella," Brooke said glumly.

* * *

The Royal Theater had been built when the town was in the middle of the silver boom in the late nineteenth century. The detailed décor had been gilded until it shone, all against a red-and-cream background, and the town had certainly kept up repairs. Emily was so busy gawking at the elaborately painted ceiling of the lobby, with cupids smiling down from heavenly clouds, that she almost forgot why she was there.

"I don't see him," Brooke said as she surreptitiously scanned the room.

About a dozen other people lingered in the lobby, looking at the giant framed posters that represented the movies being shown in the upcoming romantic-comedies film festival, as well as the newly released movies.

"Can we just wait?" Emily asked. "I'm a tourist, after all."

"There's usually a tour every morning and afternoon during the season. Let's check the schedule."

It was hung next to the box-office window, and the young woman inside smiled at them.

"Can I help you, Brooke?" she said through the glass separating them.

"No thanks, Naomi, my friend might be taking the tour today."

"It starts in another hour." The chubby blonde smiled at Emily.

"Thanks!" Emily smiled and stepped away, then whispered to Brooke. "You're as bad as your brother, knowing everyone in town."

"Sometimes it's bad—but sometimes it's good." She

turned back to the box office. "Hey, Naomi, any repairs going on today, or can we take a look at the stage while we wait?"

Emily held her breath.

"Go on in," Naomi said, popping a quick bubble of gum. "The crew is doing some seat repairs, but that shouldn't bother you."

"And we won't bother them," Brooke responded brightly.

She led Emily through the lobby, past many curtain-framed double doors that were stationed around a long, curved hall. Every so often, wide, carpeted staircases led up to what must be the balcony.

"Maybe we should go up and peer down," Emily suggested.

"Coward." Brooke kept walking until she reached an open door. Inside, they passed beneath the over-shadowing balcony, and the theater soared up to a high ceiling, swirls painted in gold just like the lobby. Several private boxes were stacked atop each other along the side walls. Down the long aisle, a wide, empty stage held several boxes and pieces of equipment along the edge. Four men were scattered through the auditorium, attending to seats that were in various stages of repair.

Brooke boldly walked halfway down the aisle, then sat down. Emily slid in beside her, feeling nervous.

"Don't worry, lots of people come to gawk," Brooke said in a soft voice. "There's a lot of history here. You really should take the tour sometime. Can-can dancers from France made a special stop here in the silver boom days."

But Emily was only half listening. "Do you see Steve Keppel?"

Brooke looked at each man, then shook her head. "Not here."

"Damn." Emily started to stand up.

Brooke pulled her back down. "Where you going? He's their boss. He'll check in eventually. That way we won't have to look even more suspicious tracking him down."

Fifteen minutes later, when Emily thought she'd memorized everything on the walls, a man in jeans and a button-down work shirt walked down the main aisle, right past them.

Brooke squeezed her arm, and whispered, "That's him."

Though his hair was faded and thin on top, Steve Keppel was a redhead. Emily thought of her own strawberry blond hair—could this be her father? Her stomach twisted in knots as she continued to study him. Besides a slight paunch, he had the broad frame of a man who worked with his hands for a living. He talked to each employee doing repairs in a polite, un-emotional voice. No kidding around, no cracking jokes. He looked down the aisle toward someone in the back, and she thought his eyes were dark. Too dark. But she wasn't close enough to be certain. Her gaze stayed glued to Steve, who walked down to the stage and began going through boxes.

"One of his daughters dated Josh, now that I think about it," Brooke said slowly. "I think he complained that her dad was a stickler about curfews. A real straight arrow."

"Doesn't sound like the kind of man my mom preferred," Emily replied, sighing. "People do change, of course. And there's the hair. And did his eyes look dark to you?"

Brooke glanced at her. "The hair doesn't look like your color, so it's hardly proof of anything. But yeah, I thought his eyes seemed dark, too. Do you want to go talk to him?"

"No. It just feels wrong. Let's go find Joe Sweet." As they stood up and walked up the aisle, past a couple of gawking tourists, she added, "Thanks for not pushing the issue, Brooke. I need to take things at my own pace."

"And that's why you didn't go to my brother about this." Brooke grinned.

As they walked through the lobby, Emily shook her head. "No, that's not it at all. Nate respects whatever I ask him to." She didn't meet Brooke's eyes, feeling a high-school blush heat her face. She was hardly a teenager hiding her first sexual encounter, but her intimacy with Nate seemed too private and special to be shared right away. Especially with his sister. "It's just . . . I need to rely on myself."

Brooke laughed. "I understand, believe me. On to the Sweetheart Inn. If it was a beautiful day, I'd suggest walking, but in this rain, let's hop in my Jeep."

Like everything in Valentine Valley, the inn wasn't too far away. Emily had often seen its windows reflecting the sun during the day, and its lights twinkling at night, seeming to float above the town on the slopes of the Elk Mountains. They entered the grounds from Mabel Street, and Emily admired the lush gardens and trees, giving her a feeling of remote peacefulness. The inn itself was three floors of elaborate white-sided Queen Anne, with levels of gables and turrets, towering chimneys, and several covered porches trimmed with sunburst details in the corners. A few stained-glass windows added color. Daffodils and tulips bloomed everywhere, and banks of forsythia bushes were bursts of yellow among the greenery.

"Wow," Emily breathed, as they drove past the inn and toward the parking lot off Bessie Street.

"Beautiful, huh? The original Sweets were miners who hit it rich, then came here to Valentine to expand into ranching. Joe's dad built a modern ranch house nearer to their fields, and his mom turned this old place into an inn. Not as pricey as in Aspen, but the most expensive place in town. The most elegant restaurant, too."

"And the pastry chef," Emily said, remembering how everyone ordered his work.

"Oh no," Brooke suddenly said, pulling into a parking spot and looking over her shoulder. "I just saw Joe's truck heading down the road."

"Are you sure he was in it?" Emily asked with disappointment.

"I'd recognize that blazing white Stetson anywhere. Should we follow him?"

"That won't accomplish a look into his eyes."

"Well, there's a family portrait in the lobby of the inn. Do you want to see that?"

"Yes!" Emily's frustrated disappointment turned into eagerness. Maybe she'd have an answer sooner than she thought.

After parking, they walked across the long porch, where baskets of impatiens hung like Christmas decorations. Inside, the "lobby" must have been the original front parlor, now decorated with a collection of antique stained-glass lamps on mahogany furniture. A wide staircase led up to the next floor. The front desk resembled an old-fashioned bar, where a young man waited on guests. On the far side of the lobby, she could see the elegant restaurant through closed French doors.

But it was the portrait that captured her interest, and she didn't need Brooke to point it out. It dominated the wall just to the right of the entrance, a huge sprawl of many generations of a family. They'd been photographed outside against a backdrop of green bushes and trees, making them look like a colorful flock of birds—very happy birds.

Scanning the several men in the photograph, Emily whispered, "Which one's Joe?"

Brooke silently pointed to a middle-aged man, lean and fit. The Stetson was tipped back on his head, just revealing blond hair lightened white. Above his confident smile were Paul Newman blue eyes that made Emily gasp.

"I thought his eyes might be blue," Brooke mused. "But I didn't want to get you excited for nothing."

Emily nodded and kept studying his open face, the contentment she could sense beneath the surface. There was family all around him, and she wondered if the dark-haired woman beside him was his wife, and which were his kids. But always her gaze returned to his face, while her heart beat an excited yet terrified rhythm to her thought of *Are you my dad? Is this my family? My* huge *family?*

She backed away from the portrait, knowing that Brooke was studying her closely. "We can go now."

Though Brooke started to talk about the Sweet family on the drive back to the restaurant, Emily stopped her, still too dazed.

In the flower shop, Monica was in the workroom, arranging cut flowers in a wet foam base in a basket. She looked up and smiled. "What have you two been up to today?"

Emily eased onto a stool. "I . . . I think I may have found my father."

Monica gasped and listened avidly as Emily and Brooke recounted their adventure.

"You don't want to look into Hal's eyes?" Monica asked.

"I already did once, and I certainly wasn't blown away. I don't even remember them. But a high-school girl gushing about blue eyes—Joe Sweet was the perfect target for that."

"What's next?" Brooke asked, rubbing her hands together.

"I guess I'll go introduce myself eventually, hear

what he has to say. But not yet. I've got a name—let me just absorb it."

"I think you need a distraction," Monica continued. "I'm taking my sister to a hockey game tonight."

"A hockey game?" Emily echoed in surprise.

"There are lots of rinks in these mountains, and a lot of leagues. I need to amuse my sister with something that doesn't involve me hearing about her running from protestors in the Middle East."

"It sounds like a dangerous job," Emily said.

Monica sighed. "It is. And I know she's brave. But it's not the only kind of job. So wear some warm clothes. We leave at six."

Chapter Nineteen

After a lunch shift at the flower shop, Emily worked on the damaged finish to the restaurant bar, glancing at her cell phone too much. Nate was working all day, she knew. He certainly didn't need to call her right away. But she was surprised how much she longed to hear his voice, how much she wanted to feel his arms around her and bask in the admiration he so openly showed her. She hadn't felt so excited in years, and it was wonderful and scary all at the same time. She found herself hoping the hockey game would end early, so she could meet up with Nate.

She got a text from Brooke at six sharp, and met her and Monica in the alley. All of them wore jeans and long-sleeve shirts and carried fleece or denim jackets.

"I thought your sister was going?" Emily said to Monica.

Monica rolled her eyes. "She's coming. She didn't bring the right clothes for a rink, so she's going through mine."

They sat in the Jeep and chatted for another ten min-

utes until Melissa came outside, looking cool and un-
hurried, still elegant in jeans and a silk blouse. Monica
grumbled something under her breath, and Emily bit
her lip to keep from smiling.

When they reached the rink in Aspen, Emily bought
a hot dog and Diet Coke before donning her fleece
jacket to leave the warm lobby.

"So is this a local college team?" Emily asked
Monica. "Do you know the players?"

"Sure I know the players. The Valentine Massacre
is an adult rec league team. You're dating one of the
stars."

Emily's mouth dropped open, and she hurried ahead
of the women toward the boards surrounding the
rink, where Plexiglas windows protected them from
the puck. She saw several dozen men skating around,
warming up, shooting at the goal, bumping into each
other.

Then someone slammed into the boards right next
to her, and she flinched back. The man pulled off his
helmet, and she saw Nate, his hair already damp with
sweat.

She spoke loudly near the crack between the Plexiglas. "Your sister didn't tell me you were on the team."

He leaned against the boards and slowly smiled at
her, green eyes glittering, making it very clear he was
remembering what they'd been doing last night. She
felt a wave of heat sweep over her and wondered if she
was giving off steam in the cold rink.

"I'll talk to you after the game," he said, then winked
at her.

She melted into a smile that made her feel positively glowing, then followed the other women up into the bleachers, filing past a few handfuls of people who'd come to cheer on friends.

"Woo-hoo, did you see that smirk on Nate's face?" Monica called to Brooke.

Emily blinked and tried to appear innocent as she took a seat next to Melissa, who eyed her with interest, popping a cheese-coated french fry into her mouth.

Brooke sat down on the end, jostling Emily. "I saw it, and believe me, I know damn well what it meant. Someone's been holding out on us."

Emily munched her hot dog and just looked back and forth at them. They waited impatiently while she chewed and swallowed. "I'm not sure what you expect me to say."

"Dish it out, girlfriend," Monica said. "The truth."

Emily opened her mouth, then embarrassment made her hesitate. She wasn't used to talking about something so private. Nate probably wouldn't appreciate it if she—

"Look at her," Brooke said with a snort, "she can barely get the words out, and her face is as red as a tomato."

"Leave the girl alone," Melissa said mildly. "She doesn't have to tell you busybodies everything."

"Busybodies?" Monica echoed, rearing back as if affronted. "Are you my grandma? And *you're* the one who heard Nate's truck in the alley late last night."

"I didn't bring it up to her, did I?" Melissa said with exasperation.

They sounded like sisters, not distant acquaintances, Emily thought, feeling relieved for them. Maybe things were starting to get better.

"You brought it up to me, leaving me all wondering," Monica grumbled.

"You didn't tell *me*!" Brooke shot back.

"Okay, okay, you need to give this a rest." Emily felt like another black-and-white-striped referee. All she needed to do was lace up a pair of skates and hold them all back from fighting.

They looked at her expectantly.

And again, she felt her face go all hot. "I can't just . . . talk about it!"

And then they laughed, even Melissa.

When a whistle blew, Emily was vastly relieved. She watched the game, glad there was no outright fighting, the one thing she usually hated about hockey. And Nate was pretty good—fast on his skates, deadly with his aim, absorbing the occasional blow to his body when a defender got ambitious. She didn't understand the rules, but it didn't really matter. She found herself cheering when the score got too close, then giving a final whoop when Nate's team won.

They waited in the lobby for the men, along with several other women Emily was introduced to. The players appeared, their hair slicked back from showers, carrying huge duffel bags stuffed with equipment.

"Hold your breath if one of those bags is open," Brooke whispered. "The smell will kill you!"

Emily expected Nate to treat her as casually as always, but, instead, he gave her a smacking kiss and kept his arm around her. Monica and Brooke rolled their eyes knowingly, and all Emily could do was grin and shrug.

More food was ordered, and everyone sat down at tables to eat. Emily found herself next to Tony of Tony's Tavern fame, and he grinned and held out his hand.

"Maybe we should meet properly—I'm Tony De Luca."

She laughed. "Emily Murphy."

"See you two are still kissing."

Would she ever stop blushing? "Guess we are."

"Hey, Dad!"

To Emily's surprise, a boy of maybe ten or eleven came running up to them. He was overheated, his brown bangs damp, chocolate smeared on his cheek as he held out his hand.

"Dad, can I have some quarters?"

Tony groaned. "I gave you everything I had when I got here, Ethan. Didn't your mom have any for you?"

"You know she doesn't like me playing the games here."

Emily said, "I have a couple quarters, if it's okay with you, Tony."

"You don't have to do that," he said, but didn't seem upset at her interference.

She reached into her wallet and held out some coins. With a quick "Thanks!" Ethan grabbed the coins and took off with the other boys.

Emily eyed Tony, who shook his head. "So you're a dad."

"A single dad," he said with a sigh. "His mom and I split a couple years ago."

That perked her interest. "Do you find it hard being a single parent?"

"Sure, sometimes."

"I'm thinking of adopting. I'd love to talk to you sometime about what it's like raising a child by yourself."

But was he truly alone, when he had everyone in Valentine? He must have all the support—and nosiness—he could ever need.

"I share custody with my ex, so it's not quite like doing it by myself, but I'll answer any questions I can."

"My ex wanted kids, too," she said ruefully. "But I found out that was all he wanted from me."

Nate walked over just in time to hear this, and he stared at Emily, surprised she'd reveal something painful so easily. He told himself it was good that she could talk about the past instead of keeping it inside; but to his discomfort, he realized he wanted her to talk to *him* about those things, not Tony.

Why was she so determined to adopt if both she and her ex had wanted kids? It wasn't like she was ancient. Or did she just not want to marry again? That should make him feel relieved, but it didn't. It was as if every wall he'd built up around himself these last few years was starting to crumble. Emily was getting to him in ways he thought he'd long been on guard against.

He couldn't let this happen again, couldn't risk hurting Emily. And deep inside, part of him began to turn to ice.

"Hey, Nate," Tony said, looking curiously between Emily and him.

Nate wondered what his face had revealed. He forced a smile. "Nice goal in the third period. You saved us."

"Thanks."

Another teammate called out, "Hey Nate, how's the rodeo prep going? You doing like I said, and taking bets on the bronc riding?"

"Why should I, when you know I'm going to win?"

There was booing and cheering all mixed up together, and he saw Emily watching him with curiosity. He almost slid an arm around her waist, knowing he'd be aroused by the flare of her hip and the warmth of her all pressed to his side. But he stopped himself, and was relieved when she said she was going home with the girls.

"I came with them, Nate." Her tone was apologetic.

"She's our date," Brooke said, spreading her hands wide. "Girls' night out."

He nodded, forced a smile. "I'll give you a call tomorrow."

Wearing a saucy smile, she said, "I'll look forward to it."

And he watched her go through the double doors out into the night, not realizing Tony had come to stand beside him.

"So it's like that," Tony said mildly.

Nate shrugged. "Guess you could sort of tell the first night that we were interested in each other."

"Guess I could. Don't enjoy yourself too much. I'll try to pretend I remember what it's like have a free social schedule and time to pursue a woman."

"Kids'll do that to you."

"Seems like Emily wants 'em, but without a husband."

Nate eyed his friend. "She's mentioned it."

"Guess you should feel relieved."

Nate smiled but didn't say anything. He *should* feel relieved. But he didn't.

"Tony's a nice guy," Monica said, as they drove back to Valentine.

Emily looked out the window at the solid darkness of the mountains blotting out the stars. She thought about young Ethan, running toward his father, his face alive with excitement and mischievousness. The slumbering ache inside her awakened as she remembered her brief motherhood.

And the way she controlled her grief was reminding herself that she'd taken control, that she was going to make a happy family life happen. She was already making good friends who could be like sisters to her.

Then Brooke launched into the story about spying on Steve Keppel and believing that Joe Sweet might be Emily's dad, all for Melissa's benefit.

"If you're hesitant to talk to him outright," Melissa said, "maybe there are hospital records you don't know about. Were you born here?"

"San Francisco."

"Oh."

"Guess we'll have to handle this with our own small-town ways," Monica said dryly.

Emily saw Melissa press her lips together and look out the dark window.

"You know, Em," Monica continued, "you could think about this from another angle, from people's motivations. Maybe Joe would be thrilled to know he has another child, and you're worried about approaching him for nothing."

"Listen to Monica," Melissa chimed in. "She's always been good at reading people."

Monica stared at her over the seat. "Is that a compliment?"

"Of course it is. You should go back for your master's in psychology. Those were always your best classes."

Emily couldn't miss the hurt that flashed briefly in Monica's eyes.

"I use my skills with people every day," Monica said between gritted teeth. "What about you?"

"What do you mean? We're twins; I certainly have people skills as well, and I use them."

"From everything I hear, you're only with people at work. Sounds to me like you lead a lonely life."

Melissa stiffened. "That's not true."

"Okay, no squabbling, kids, or I'll have to stop the car," Brooke said mildly, looking into the rearview mirror to meet Emily's eyes.

"I heard the guys mention a rodeo," Emily said, changing the subject.

"The Silver Creek Rodeo," Brooke said. "My family's been running it for decades. You mean you haven't heard about it?"

"I've seen the posters—who could miss them?" But

Nate had never told her, and now that he'd confided in her, she understood why. But after all their intimacy, it was hard for her to still feel casual about him, which should be a blinking Caution sign for her to pay attention to.

"It's only a few weeks away," Monica said. "You can't leave before then. It's the highlight of early summer around here."

"I'm a champion barrel racer," Brooke said, holding up her arm to flex a muscle.

Monica laughed. "And so modest, too."

Brooke continued as if she hadn't spoken. "Josh and I do a little team roping, although Nate and Dad often beat us. Emily, there's even a baking contest. I'll forward you the info."

Emily nodded but figured she'd talk to Nate first.

As she was getting ready for bed, Emily heard her doorbell, and when she looked out the window, she saw Nate's pickup in the alley. With excited anticipation, she wrapped a robe around herself to hurry down the stairs. After she opened the door, he stood looking at her, his expression so intense that it took her breath away. Then he swept her into his arms.

"Damn, but you looked so good tonight," he said into her hair.

Between kisses, she laughed. "In my jeans and fleece?"

"In your robe, I don't care. I couldn't stop thinking about you. I couldn't wait—"

He slammed the door behind him and carried her upstairs. And then they were undressing each other, her tugging loose his shirt, him pulling free the belt of her robe.

"Emily."

He said her name between a whisper and a groan, and her blood hummed with pleasure and need. They fell naked on her bed, and it was like a scene from a movie as they kissed and caressed and rolled about with abandon.

"I can't get enough of the taste of you," Nate murmured, exploring her body with his lips and tongue.

She lay there, quivering and feeling worshipped, gasping as he spread her thighs and with the torture of his tongue made her beg for him. When her orgasm practically shook her off the bed, he came up on his hands and stared down at her, dazed.

"I'll be right back," he said hoarsely. "In my pants—"

"Hurry," she panted back.

He grinned down at her like a pirate anticipating plunder, all dark-haired and wicked-eyed. With a giggle, she pushed him away, and when he returned with the condom, helped him put it on. She took over, mounting him, controlling both of their pleasure. His grin faded and they stared into each other's eyes as their bodies, their very wills, took hold, sweeping away lighthearted play, leaving them desperate and yearning and overcome.

Only when she was collapsed at his side, staring stupidly up at the ceiling, was she able to think rationally. "I have ice cream."

He gave a hoarse chuckle. "You should have said that before. It might have made things interesting."

"Instead of boring?" she asked sweetly.

He slapped both hands to his chest as if she'd shot him. When she sat up, he said, "No clothes allowed."

"But I think my front curtains are open!"

"No clothes."

Giggling foolishly, she crept down the hall, ducked into her galley kitchen for chocolate ice cream and two spoons, then dashed back to her bedroom. Nate was waiting for her, propped up on pillows against the headboard, still naked. She skidded to a halt, her mouth open, and almost tossed aside the ice cream. Damn, he looked good, all lean, long muscle.

He was watching her just as intently, and she was as unembarrassed as if he'd been looking at her nude forever. It was daunting—it was exhilarating—it was confusing. So she opened the ice cream and took a spoonful, her gaze never leaving him.

"You can be my second dessert," she said.

He laughed and patted the bed, then scooped her against his side. They shared the ice cream, feeding each other or themselves, and when a dollop landed on her breast, he licked it off.

"Wait, wait," she said, laughing, putting her fingers over his mouth. "I have something to ask you. I heard you and your friends talking about the rodeo. Brooke explained that it's your family tradition."

"Yep." He slowly licked his spoon, and he wasn't watching her face, as if he anticipated licking other things.

It would have been so easy to melt into a chocolate puddle beneath him.

"I'm surprised you never mentioned it," she said curiously.

"I didn't think you'd be interested," he said, "and I wasn't sure you'd still be here."

"The girls will probably pressure me to enter the baking competition. Are you okay with that?"

He smiled, but for some reason, she wasn't certain it reached his eyes.

"Why wouldn't I be?"

"We're . . . just dating. This is your family event or tradition or whatever, and if you felt I'd be intruding . . ." She felt like an idiot, worried about his reaction when it was a public event anyone could attend. Much as she wanted to keep things casual, it was starting not to feel that way for her, but she couldn't let him know that. Maybe the sex had changed things since she'd always considered herself an old-fashioned girl. But she had to grow beyond that girl.

"I was simply waiting to see if you'd still be here for the rodeo before I asked," Nate said. "I'd like you to come."

"Then it's a date." But she still felt awkward, and he must have sensed that, because he cupped her cheek and leaned forward to softly kiss her.

"Sorry," he murmured against her lips.

"It's really okay," she murmured back, then forgot about the ice cream.

Chapter Twenty

Saturday evening, after the flower shop closed, Emily was making a cheesecake to take to the Thalbergs for dessert the next day, when Monica rang the bell and came up to join her.

Monica looked at the batter with its chunks of brownie pieces and nuts. "Oh, please, can I have the bowl, Mom?"

Emily laughed. "If you're a good girl."

"I came up to tell you that Nate stopped by at lunch. Did he catch up with you later?"

Emily frowned. "No, no messages."

"He saw his brother's handiwork in their new special display."

"What did he say?"

"He seemed surprised, like Josh hadn't told him. And Josh apparently didn't tell him he was taking you to lunch." Monica blinked her big brown eyes innocently.

Emily waved a hand, then licked batter off her finger before it spread anyplace else. "There wasn't a plan. It was a spur-of-the-moment thing."

"Okay. Think that's a good idea, when something's going on between those two?"

"A good idea?" Emily echoed, confused. "Josh is a client. Why would Nate care?"

"I don't know. But I thought you seemed a little upset about not knowing about the rodeo. And since he didn't call you, maybe he's a little upset you didn't tell him about Josh."

Emily opened her mouth, then slowly closed it. Was dating truly getting this complicated? She was trying hard not to involve Nate too deeply in her life—how could he possibly object?

Monica looked around the kitchen. "You baked more than one dessert?" she asked incredulously.

Emily glanced at the brownies and the raspberry torte with a little guilt. "I couldn't decide."

"They're all good—everyone says so. You could sell them."

Emily blinked at Monica, then around her kitchen, still orderly in the middle of a baking explosion. Sell her desserts? "You mean . . . to a bakery?"

Monica met her gaze in surprise. "Well . . . you could sell them yourself."

"My own bakery?" she asked in disbelief. "I don't know anything about running a business."

"Why can't you learn?"

"You don't understand—my mom's business took up most of her time, and so I stayed as far away from it as I could."

"I thought you said men took up the rest of her time."

"Well . . . they did."

"Would you make that mistake?"

"Of course not! But this isn't about my mom. Do you have any idea how much real estate costs in San Francisco? I couldn't just . . . open a business."

Monica rested her chin on her fist and watched her with interest. "Who said anything about San Francisco? You own a building right here."

"But . . . this isn't my home," Emily said, bewildered. "I'm not staying here. And I've got Berkeley in the fall." But in that moment, she thought of making heart-shaped cakes and gooey Valentine's Day treats. But that would mean changing every plan she had for herself, flitting to whatever new idea struck her fancy—and that seemed too much like her mom.

"Okay, forget about *where* you have a bakery," Monica said. "Is it something that interests you?"

"I—I never thought about it. I just like to bake. I'm not a trained pastry chef. No one would buy anything from me!"

"Then maybe you should think about it first. Nothing else has occurred to you, right?"

"I'm going back to college to figure that out," she said, feeling stubborn and uneasy. "Not culinary school."

"And you like college," Monica said dubiously.

"I'm older and wiser now. And smart, too—did I mention that? I know lots of people back home, a whole network of people who'll help me make a decision." But some friends hadn't been so easy to reach the few times she'd called. Maybe they really were Greg's friends instead of hers.

"Should I be sorry I brought this up?" Monica asked.

Emily shook off her panic. "No, no, of course not. But I'm not a chef, I'm not a businessperson. I don't know what I am," she finished, looking away.

She felt Monica touch her arm.

"It's okay, Em," she said softly. "There's no rush."

"No rush? I'm thirty years old!" she whispered fiercely. "Ever since—since Greg left me, my life has been turned upside down. I've really had to look at myself, and realize how poorly prepared I let myself be, all in the name of love and family."

"Those aren't bad motives, honey."

"I wasn't thinking about my future—I let Greg take care of me. And Nate," she whispered. "It would be too easy to let him take care of me. I'm pathetic."

Monica took her shoulders and gave her a little shake. "Stop that! It's not true. I've admired your determination from the first. You came to a strange town with very little money. You had a little help with your renovations, but *you've* done the majority of the work. Some people might crawl into a hole instead of look for a dad who's a stranger to them—not you."

Emily was surprised to feel tears slide down her cheeks.

"And as for Nate—he's been your friend. Friends help each other. He helps *everyone.* Trust me, he doesn't need to do that for sex."

Emily found herself choking on a laugh. "Is that supposed to make me feel better?"

"I don't know, but it made you laugh."

And then Monica hugged her, and Emily hugged her back, her eyes still dripping tears.

Early Sunday afternoon, Nate went to the ranch office and sat down at the computer. There was still so much left to do before the rodeo. First, he went into the spreadsheet showing the livestock he'd ordered from the stock contractor—and found nothing.

He gaped at the computer. You couldn't hold a rodeo without bulls and broncs to ride. Could he really have forgotten something so important? He never forgot anything!

He should go talk to his father, but he went to look for his brother instead, the brother he always confided in. Maybe between them they could fix this if it wasn't too late. Nate stormed out of the office, checked in the house for Josh, then out in the barn. The door of the converted tack room was ajar, and he walked by Brooke in her horse's stall without saying a word. Scout slunk in with her instead of following him. Then he spotted Josh bent over his workbench, using a tiny knife on a long strip of leather.

"I need to talk to you," Nate said urgently.

Josh slowly straightened, eyes concerned. "About what?"

"I just went to look at the status of the rodeo stock—Josh, I forgot to order it." He slapped a hand to his forehead. "I don't know what happened."

Brooke stepped into the doorway and looked between them uncertainly. "Nate?"

He grimaced at her. "Brooke—"

"Calm down," Josh interrupted, setting down his knife. "Everything's okay."

Nate groaned and said to Brooke, "It's not okay. The rodeo might not go on because I forgot to order—"

"I ordered it," Josh said simply.

Nate gaped at him. "The stock? For the rodeo?"

"Is ordered. I was curious, looking through all the prep that you do for this event, and I noticed your usually meticulous spreadsheet wasn't filled out. So I called and took care of it. I got it all in a notebook, and just didn't log it into the computer yet. Sorry to scare you."

Nate leaned back against the worktable and closed his eyes. "You don't have anything to be sorry for. You saved my ass."

Josh grinned. "Someone had to."

Nate popped him in the shoulder, and Josh did the same back.

Brooke rolled her eyes. "How old are you two?"

Nate felt positively elated with relief. "Obviously, I'm not old enough. I can't believe I made such a mistake."

"You're human," Josh said simply.

"And now you'll probably say I told you so, that I'm spreading myself too thin," Nate said in a glum voice.

"Nope, you draw your own conclusions, big brother. But I've always got your back."

Josh bent over his etching, Brooke whistled and returned to her horse, and Nate stood there, wondering if he'd overextended himself by getting involved with Emily—too involved.

* * *

That night at dinner, with Nate's whole family gathered around, including Grandma Thalberg and Aunt Marilyn, Emily seemed like a pretty, bubbling flower in their midst, smiling and laughing, and looking so at ease.

Nate felt anything but. It was as if he didn't know himself anymore, his feelings for Emily, his confusion over what Josh had been saying. He wasn't used to feeling confused about anything.

And then she smiled at him, and he saw her in her pretty sleeveless top and flowered skirt, looking beautiful and happy, her hair a mass of red-gold curls, as if she took special care just for him and his family. He had to tell her the truth, that he was getting too close, that he'd hurt her. He'd already almost hurt the ranch. He had to break up with her, just as he'd done with so many other women over the years. But this time, this time, he felt the hurt, too.

Emily had a lovely evening with Nate's family, even if Nate, though smiling and occasionally cracking jokes, seemed a bit preoccupied. On the drive back to her apartment, she didn't know how to ask him if anything was wrong—didn't want to force him to talk when he wasn't ready. After all, he wasn't the one who'd invited her to the big family dinner. But she had to say something.

"Brooke and I went to the Royal Theater the other day. And no, it wasn't for a film festival. I'm saving all those for you."

His white teeth glimmered in the darkness of the pickup. "And I'm so grateful. That Bette Davis was some hot chick."

She laughed. "Actually, we went so I could spy on Steve Keppel."

He glanced at her. "Why?"

"Because Cathy Fletcher gave me his name as one of the teenagers who hung around at my mom's family store."

"Aah," he said, nodding. He pulled into the alley behind her building and stopped the car, watching her with interest. "And do you think he's a possibility?"

She shrugged. "He has red hair, but his manner seems so . . . serious. And Brooke said he was a stickler about curfews, hardly the kind of guy my mom would choose."

"But people change."

"You sound like your sister, but yes, you're both right. I just didn't get a . . . gut feeling about him. And then there are the eyes."

He smiled. "The eyes? A window to the soul?"

Laughing, she said, "I found an entry in my mom's diary after all, just one, from her senior year. Although she didn't write his name, she focused on her boy-friend's incredible blue eyes."

"So that's where you get them," he said quietly.

She smiled and reached for his hand.

"And did you talk to him?"

"No, not yet. His eyes seemed too dark. Then there's Hal Abrams, whom I've already met."

He nodded. "Any gut feeling about him?"

"No, and I don't remember his eyes behind his glasses, so they couldn't have been all that memorable. We went to see Joe Sweet, another of the guys, according to your dad."

"My dad?"

His head tilted back in surprise, but he didn't release her hand, which made her relax.

"Yep. But Joe was headed out of town, so I didn't even get to see him. Brooke told me about the painting in the lobby."

"You don't have to say anything more. Even I've noticed his eyes. You think he's the one?"

"Maybe. I think so. I don't know," she added in a rush. "I'll have to talk to him."

"One of the players on my hockey team is his son, Will."

Emily's mouth dropped open. "Really? I wish I had known. Although it would have been strange to see him and wonder if he was . . . if we were related."

"I know the family pretty well, and I have business with Joe." He squeezed her hand. "Can I answer any questions?"

"Come on up and have a beer while I pick your brain." She grinned. "Aren't we lucky you don't still live at home? Maybe you're one of those guys who doesn't want his mom to know the hours he keeps."

Nate smiled, but he seemed . . . restrained, which echoed his behavior all evening. She let it go, fighting every impulse to ask him to confide in her. He followed her upstairs, and she brought out his favorite beer and the brownies she hadn't taken to the ranch. As they settled side by side on the love seat, she listened to his summary of Joe.

"He's not your average rancher," Nate said, leaning his head back on the couch. "He's actively involved in a coalition of organic farmers, and he's their rep to a lot of the restaurants in the valley."

"Organic farming? Now that sounds promising."

His hand very gently stroked her thigh, up and down, making her brain feel fuzzy. "What else?" she asked.

"He's a writer of local history, too, kind of a bohemian guy with a lot of interests."

"Oh, better and better. He definitely would have appealed to my new age mother. I'll go to the Sweetheart Inn. Maybe I'll have better luck running into him with all his family around."

Nate didn't offer to introduce her, which surprised her—and didn't. He thought his involvement would somehow hurt her, she knew, and he had a right to his feelings. But she shouldn't let herself feel so . . . forlorn about it.

She pushed away any of her doubts and remembered that she was making a new family, including good friends she'd never neglect, and a baby sometime in her future. She smiled as she imagined Brooke and Monica as doting aunts, the widows acting as the best kind of grandparents. There was so much love here in Valentine Valley.

The bakery idea floated to the surface of her mind. She saw happy people enjoying meals together over food she'd created. Then she quickly submerged it.

Nate's fingers dipped between her thighs and trailed higher.

Oh yes, and she had Nate—for now. She wished she could be like him, content with his life, knowing just what he wanted and what worked for him. He was watching her, his face all serious, his green eyes unusually dark as they studied her. And then they drifted to her mouth and flared with heat, and she felt an answering shiver of pleasure.

"Guess what I got yesterday?" she said in a low voice. "A persuasion gift from Leather and Lace. They want me to remember they have first dibs when I put the building on the market."

Though the corner of his mouth turned up, he still searched her eyes with an intensity that confused her. She touched his face with her fingertips, smoothing along his brow, then dipping into the dimples in his cheeks. He caught her fingertip in his mouth and lightly bit.

"Do you want to see it?" She leaned against him, whispering near his ear, "There's a lot of lace," then gently bit his earlobe. "And leather."

With a groan, he turned her across his lap, and said hoarsely, "I can't resist you."

She sank into his kiss, so she wouldn't have to think he'd showed any hesitation.

But the widows did hear about the gift the next evening, when Emily had them over for dinner, along with Monica and Brooke. Emily gave everyone a tour of the restaurant, blushing with pride at all the praise, realizing what an accomplishment it had been to turn that disaster she'd seen the first night into a building any business would be happy to buy. The widows discussed the varied businesses that might go there, while she served dinner buffet style since she didn't have a big enough table. She could picture a boutique restaurant, or maybe an exclusive shoe store, or even a bakery— run by somebody else, she told herself. And the more she looked around at these dear ladies, so concerned about her and the town, the more she felt she couldn't go on keeping the secret about Leather and Lace's interest. So she told them, then tried not to wince as she awaited their reaction.

After a momentary, bemused silence, Mrs. Thalberg asked, "Do they have a website?"

Soon, they were crowded around Emily's laptop, oohing and aahing over the sometimes tasteful, sometimes raunchy, Leather and Lace catalogue.

Emily was shocked and delighted by their open minds and couldn't help saying, "You know, Nate wasn't certain you'd approve."

"Young men can be so conservative," Mrs. Palmer drawled, rolling her eyes.

As they debated the function of several of the garments—Emily kept her lips pressed together to keep from roaring with laughter—she served the raspberry torte she hadn't taken to the Thalbergs. That launched a whole new discussion about the overworked pastry chef at the Sweetheart Inn, and all the upcoming summer weddings. Emily frowned at Monica, as if she had set the whole thing up.

After Brooke drove the widows home, Monica stayed to help Emily clean up.

"Okay, do you have a confession to make?" Emily demanded sternly.

Monica frowned, looking confused. "About what?"

"There was a lot of talk about having only one pastry chef in town. You're the only one I discussed it with."

"I said nothing. Scout's honor," she added solemnly. "But . . . have you given it any more thought?"

Emily sighed and sank down on the love seat. "When I made that flower delivery to St. John's today, I sat there in peace for a while, hoping to find answers, but I'm just as clueless as ever. Then a wedding party began to arrive, and I found myself wondering where their reception would be, and about the cake—and I've never done a wedding cake in my life!"

"You know you don't *have* to do wedding cakes," Monica said, sitting in a chair opposite her. "That's kind of a specialty, I think."

Emily crossed her arms over her chest and frowned.

"Stay open-minded, Em."

"I've *been* open-minded, but I have to go home. I start school in the fall, and I can't just throw it away because of one different idea. I'm not that . . . flighty. Getting the money to start my own business would be hard, and how could I support a child never knowing if I'd make enough to cover the bills that month?"

Monica nodded sympathetically.

"I'm enrolled at Berkeley," Emily insisted. She rose to her feet to continue taking dirty dishes to the kitchen, refusing to meet her friend's curious eyes.

Chapter Twenty-one

Wherever he was, whatever he was doing, Nate couldn't get the image of Emily in that little lace number out of his mind. Not that he'd let her wear it for that long, but still . . . The lingerie stood for something—for Emily leaving. She might have a buyer for the building, then she'd be gone. Maybe he could wait until then to break up with her. That had been the plan all along.

But he was hurting her already. He knew she thought he'd go to the Sweetheart Inn with her. It was one thing to help her to take concrete steps to find her father, and another to be there while she met him. It would be a momentous, emotional moment for her, and he didn't want to influence her opinions or decisions.

Tuesday morning, just after sunrise, Nate and his brother and sister were already up in the White River National Forest, riding their grazing allotment, looking for sick cows, broken fences, or evidence of coyotes or other predators. It was usually a peaceful time, with the weather breezy and cool on the mountain, the smell of pine as well as the grass so necessary to the herd.

And so far they'd seen nothing unusual, were able to talk casually about a new saddle Josh had been commissioned to decorate, or the barrel racer coming to challenge Brooke. Nate enjoyed this time immensely, the feel of his horse beneath him that linked him to his ancestors and the land. He loved what he did.

"So Emily's going to dinner tonight at the Sweetheart Inn—alone," Brooke suddenly said.

Nate's peace was shattered, and he glanced at her with a frown. "I know."

"I thought you two were dating," Josh said curiously.

"We are, but this isn't a social evening."

Brooke sighed and guided her horse around a tree stump. She briefly explained to Josh about the chance that Joe Sweet was Emily's biological father.

Josh whistled. "This must have been tough for her. And you helped?" he asked Nate, eyeing him with amusement.

Nate shrugged, feeling grim.

"You are so easy to read," Josh said, shaking his head. "You've been rattled by one little mistake for the rodeo."

"Little?" Nate echoed icily.

Josh ignored him. "It's not because you've been with Emily. I can tell you want to go with her tonight, so why are you resisting?"

Nate didn't answer, and knew Brooke was eyeing him in the way of little sisters who are about to savor something to use over a big brother's head.

"Don't sacrifice a good relationship for work, Nate," Josh continued quietly.

Apollo shook his head and danced sideways, giving Nate a welcome distraction.

"Look, we're dating, we're not in a relationship," he said at last. "We'll be ending it soon, and it's better that she not get used to confiding everything in me."

"Hey, she's got me, too!" Brooke said. "But I think I understand where you're going, and I don't like it. You want to break up with her already, don't you?"

"That's between me and Emily," Nate said impassively.

"Why?" she asked, as if she hadn't heard him. "You're having fun, so's she."

"It's not always about fun, it's about people not getting hurt."

"And he doesn't mean himself," Josh told her.

Brooke snorted. "I already knew that."

"Thanks," Nate said dryly.

"Wait," Josh interrupted, standing up in his stirrups. "Is that fence near the creek leaning sideways?"

"Must be elk again," Nate said. "Brooke, write it down."

"How does the girl become the secretary?" she asked with sarcasm, pulling a little notebook out of the breast pocket of her vest.

"It's because you're the youngest, not because you're a girl," Josh told her.

They guided their horses along an overgrown path, tall grass slapping their chaps.

"Back to Nate," Brooke said, putting away her notebook.

Nate winced. "Must we?"

"So you think Emily's going to get hurt," she continued thoughtfully. "Is she falling in love with you?"

To his surprise, just the thought made his chest hurt. "No, it's not about that." He hesitated, then said in a low voice, "It's just . . . I'm going to hurt her. I always do."

He spurred his horse to a trot, not wanting their pity or to answer questions.

Josh caught up with him. "Nate, you've got these habits where women are concerned, and never once have you even been tempted to go beyond the ten-date rule. After all these years, you might have grown up a bit. We all do. Don't you think you should start trusting yourself? Emily is making you behave differently—doesn't that tell you something?"

"*I* think it should tell you something," Brooke said from the other side, her tone superior. "You don't want to break up with her, and you're fighting as hard as any calf on the end of a rope. Take her to dinner. And if you just want to call it a date, then fine. But don't give up because of what *might* happen. Emily's not like the other women you've dated. She's strong, and she's growing stronger every day. I think you've met your match, and it scares you silly."

"Now that's enough," Nate said with exasperation. "While you've been jawing, you missed another sagging fence."

"Fine, Josh and I will go check out the fence post, while you call Emily. Take her to dinner. She shouldn't be alone when she meets her dad for the first time."

"Is that a yearling on the wrong side of the fence?" Josh suddenly called out.

"I'll get her before you will," Brooke challenged.

Nate watched his brother and sister ride off at a gallop. *Scared silly?* Of falling in love? How was he supposed to know what love felt like? He always thought he'd positively know when it was time to settle down and start a family. He didn't want to imagine it could involve feeling so ambivalent and hopeful, worried and excited, all at the same time. Was he really falling in love?

That would screw up everything. But he called Emily and asked if he could accompany her to the inn. Though she hesitated, she said yes at last. And he felt relieved, like he'd made the right decision. Now he would have to be very wary and aware, to remain neutral, to be her support and not influence her.

That evening he picked her up to take her to dinner at the Sweetheart Inn, and for the short drive there, he couldn't stop looking at her, her hair caught up at the back of her head, the blue dress hugging her curves tastefully but provocatively—at least to him. She wore strappy sandals that showed off her cute feet. Cute feet?

Emily kept looking at him, too, not quite hiding her confused expression. He hadn't really explained why he wanted to take her to dinner, and she hadn't asked. Maybe she really had wanted him to come support her, and he was just a jerk.

As they passed the front desk of the inn, he exchanged a nod with the slim, older woman who was waiting on a customer.

"Who's that?" Emily asked softly, when she went to examine a mixed set of vases on several shelves.

"Eileen Sweet, Joe's mother. She's the one who turned this place into an inn, and now runs it with her daughter Helen."

He saw Emily's gaze dart back to her, wide-eyed with interest.

"Maybe she's your grandma," he whispered.

She elbowed him. "None of that, Nate Thalberg. We're here to look around, not speculate."

"Look around? We're having dinner."

He saw her glance at the open French doors leading to an elegant formal dining room, its low lighting emphasized with candles everywhere.

"I'm sure it's expensive. We could just explore and look for Joe."

"We can eat and see if Joe's here just as easily. The family is always wandering through the dining room. Come on." He took her elbow and led her toward the restaurant. "And as for the money, I asked you out, so it's my treat."

"Couples take turns paying, and since this was my idea and for my benefit—"

"Who says it's for your benefit?" he drawled. "You're puttin' out later."

The laughter in her eyes made him begin to relax at last.

The Sweetheart Inn Restaurant could rival one in any elegant, Old World hotel. It was situated in a corner addition to the house, with windows filling two long walls, emphasizing spectacular views during the day. He could hear the muted sounds of someone playing the piano. They followed the hostess past tables dressed in white cloth, with fresh flowers and candles as decorations.

When they were seated and opening their menus, Emily whispered, "So was the hostess a Sweet as well?"

"Yep, Theresa, Joe's niece. She's pretty involved with every aspect of the inn. I think they're grooming her to take over someday."

After giving their order to the waitress, Emily put her chin on her hand and studied Nate. "You look pretty good for a cowboy," she said in a low voice.

He glanced down at his casual slacks and button-down shirt. "Uh . . . thanks."

"You fit right in here, even though I could swear some of these elegantly dressed people came up from Aspen for the day. I think I've seen that woman over there in a movie."

He smiled and took her hand, and the usual thrill zapped right up his arm and seemed to burn in his chest, a comforting warmth sometimes, a blazing inferno of desire at others.

She gave him a bright smile, and said, "So tell me more about Joe. If he was someone my mom was attracted to, what would drive her away?"

"You mean besides being pregnant at eighteen?"

"Besides that," she answered wryly. "If Joe really is my da—biological father, why do you think she didn't tell him? She had to feel so alone, so frightened. And apparently he's not a mass murderer or anything."

"For one thing, your mom seemed like a rebel, according to you. Joe's family has been here over 130 years. Some people consider them our leading citizens."

"That's a lot to live up to," she mused. "And something that Delilah wouldn't have wanted. She valued her independence."

"Even when there was a baby involved?"

She hesitated. "Even then. She liked to do things her own way. She only married once, even though I know she received several proposals in her life."

"She told you that? Seems like it would be getting her little girl's hopes up."

"I was a teenager before she mentioned those kinds of things, and by then, too cynical about her wild ways. I was relieved each time she declined. She would have been miserable having someone to answer to."

"Were you?" he asked quietly.

She blinked at him. "Miserable about answering to someone? No, not often. Greg wasn't demanding of me. And I trusted him—my mistake."

Emily seemed relieved when the sommelier approached to pour their wine, and Nate let the topic go. He hadn't meant to start it anyway. Then the waitress arrived with appetizers they hadn't ordered.

"Compliments of Mrs. Sweet," she explained, smiling at Nate.

"Give her my thanks," he said. "Is Joe around tonight?"

"Sorry, I haven't seen him."

Emily shook her head after the girl had left. "You're a charmer even with the older women, but then I've seen that with the widows."

He smiled and saluted her with his wineglass. After taking a sip, he said, "Since it looks like you might be disappointed again about Joe, I have an idea. I'm going to book a room."

"Oh, no, Nate, we can't do that."

"Then you can explore to your heart's content as a guest and not feel like you're intruding. You'll meet more of the family."

She opened her mouth, then slowly closed it, as if she were considering the idea.

"And if you're going to protest about money again, I don't want to hear it. The rooms are all priced differently, and some are small but reasonable, especially since it's still early in the season. The front desk can get us anything we need, like toothbrushes—and you won't be needing anything to sleep in."

He realized that making her happy was truly important to him, which was why he was so worried about doing something to hurt her. He finally had to admit that this was more than dating—he found himself wanting to tell her things about himself he'd never confided in another woman. He trusted her—but that didn't mean he trusted himself.

Before he realized what he was doing, he told her about forgetting to order stock for the rodeo.

"So Josh thinks I'm overextending myself," Nate finished tiredly. "And before you get all worked up, it doesn't have anything to do with you. He'd been bugging me about this long before you came to Valentine Valley."

She smiled briefly. "Whew. Guess you know me well enough by now to know I'd be worried about just that. But okay, if it isn't me, then you need to look at

yourself. If Josh believes you're overextending yourself, then that means you're doing more work than he
does. So he's a slacker?"

"Of course not! He works as hard as anybody. He's
just . . . enjoying pissing me off lately."

"Then he thinks you do way more than you need to.
Why do you go above and beyond?"

"I just . . . do what's necessary to keep the ranch
running. And I want my mom and dad to enjoy getting
older rather than worrying about the little stuff."

"Ah," she said, tilting her head. "So it's about your
parents. You're the oldest child. Makes sense."

He sighed. "I don't like that there's a part of my mom
that feels bad for me because of what her first husband
did. She's always saying that because we were on our
own for a while, I learned way too early to do things
myself, to . . . I don't know."

"Protect her? Help her?"

He shrugged.

"Or maybe there's something else going on," she
said quietly. "You're adopted, after all, and you weren't
an infant when it happened. But what if your problems
are connected to Doug? You've been a great right-hand
man to him."

He frowned at her. "He raised me to be what I am.
I'd do anything for him."

"With all the stuff you coordinate around the ranch,
are you still trying to prove how much you love him,
love the ranching lifestyle?"

Nate opened his mouth, but an answer didn't come.
After a moment, he murmured, "I didn't like how

stressed the family became when I went to college. I always thought Dad believed I was choosing another life instead of his."

"Did you want to?"

"Never, not once," he said, shaking his head. But hadn't there been moments since when he regretted being pulled away from a conference call about the breeding program he'd invested in, or a new method of getting organic produce into the most markets, just to do chores that other people could do? But he *loved* the satisfaction of those chores, of making the ranch succeed.

"Maybe you're still trying to prove your loyalty to the ranch by being everything you think you should be. Josh knows you well enough to see you're feeling torn."

Nate stared at her thoughtfully. Were his problems at the ranch all because he knew deep down that he was being drawn toward the business end of the ranch, and he was fighting it? "Okay, Doc," he said instead. "I'm not used to being dissected."

"It's good for the soul," she insisted. "And after all, aren't you the one who thinks he's always *doing* the dissecting?"

He reared back, pretending she'd slapped him. "Ouch."

They smiled at each other.

As her salmon and his steak were served, Emily studied Nate's face, which she was growing to know too well. He wasn't only the easygoing cowboy he presented to the world. He'd had heartache as a little boy, and she knew it was probably worse than he was saying.

But she'd given him something to think about, and she wouldn't harm the evening by pushing anymore.

So while they ate, she told him about his grandmother's reaction to Leather and Lace, and the newest garage-sale treasure, a scarred old blanket chest, she'd found for her bedroom. She'd come to realize she loved decorating something to suit her own simple tastes, not Greg's more expensive ones.

When Nate asked about the painting she'd been doing in the restaurant, she mentioned she was almost done, and they both got quiet. She didn't want to think about the painting because when she was finished, she'd be selling and leaving. That was the plan, and it was a good one. But there was an ache inside her that didn't have a name, something she couldn't look at too closely.

After dinner, when she gasped over the dessert tray, and Nate mentioned to the waitress that Emily baked, she found herself being escorted back into the kitchen to see the area where the pastry chef worked. She almost turned down the tour, but her refusal might make Nate wonder why, and she didn't want to explain the crazy idea she and Monica had been batting around, the one that kept reappearing in her mind just before she went to sleep, disturbing her dreams.

The pastry area was a separate room off the hot kitchen, with its own walk-in refrigerator and freezer, and a stand mixer as tall as she was. Utensils hung from hooks within easy reach. Stainless-steel shelves were filled with sheet pans and trays, every size base for cakes. The upper shelves overflowed with ingredients like sugars from around the world, and various imported fine chocolates. She gaped at them, imagining what she could create, suddenly longing to do so. She stood outside a glass-walled cooler filled with the finished products for the evening's guests, sumptuous cakes and pies and chocolate decadence. Another set of shelves on wheels contained unrefrigerated pastries, scones, and breads. Nate seemed to keep studying her, and she felt uneasy and vulnerable. She hated worrying if every decision she made was the right one.

It was a relief when he took her to their room, with its fireplace and curtained four-poster bed. Their little balcony overlooked the mountains they couldn't see at night, and she thought about the decadence of sitting there in the morning.

Nate came up behind her and put his hands on her shoulders. "You seem quiet."

She glanced back at him, resting her hands on top of his for a moment. Then she turned into his arms and kissed him, not wanting to talk about anything else.

When Nate suggested a dawn hike to the hot springs up behind the inn, Emily practically had to be dragged out of the comfortable bed. But when she saw the little built-up rock pool along the bank of a tumbling stream, steam rising in the flickering light between the trees, she gave a little gasp. There was even a little bench, and an overflow of bushes and plants and flowers for privacy. Nate stripped and waded in, while she looked back down the path in indecision. But upon hearing his satisfied sigh as he settled into the hot water, she took off her clothes and joined him.

They relaxed for an hour, enjoying the sun and the steam and each other, before returning to the inn for breakfast on the stone terrace.

They'd only just sat down when Nate called, "Joe!"

Emily stiffened and turned her head to see a lean man wearing a white cowboy hat raise his hand to Nate and smile. As he walked toward them, Emily studied him and saw a good-looking older man with a day's growth of light stubble on his face. And those eyes, as clear and bright as if they could see past the horizon. He swept off his hat when he saw her, displaying his unruly white-blond hair, long enough to brush his collar.

"Hey, Nate," Joe Sweet said good-naturedly.

Emily just stared at him.

"Joe, I'd like you to meet Emily Murphy." Nate hesitated, then without asking how she meant to proceed, added, "Her mom was Dorothy Riley."

An immediate change came over Joe's face, cheerfulness turning into wary interest. He studied her with an intensity that made her feel all charged up and strange inside. *Oh, God, it's all true.*

"That's a name I haven't heard in a long time," Joe finally said, nodding to her. "Emily, it's nice to meet you, although I think I met you once when you were a little girl."

"You did?" She swallowed and gestured to a chair. "Would you mind joining us?"

Joe kept looking at her, and she kept looking at him, and she didn't know what she felt—was she supposed to experience a bang of revelation? An instant yearning? Instead, she simply felt anxious and intrigued all at the same time.

Nate signaled for the waiter, who filled all their coffee cups. "You want coffee?" he asked Emily in surprise.

She stared at her cup. "Oh, of course not." She smiled distractedly at the waiter. "Could I have a glass of orange juice, please?"

When he'd gone, she watched Joe put cream but no sugar in his coffee. "So you . . . met me?" she began cautiously.

He smiled at her. "One of the rare times your mom came back to town. You were only a couple years old at the time. Cute as a button then, and you've grown into a pretty young woman."

She smiled nervously at his compliment. He couldn't possibly know he was her father, not by the way he was acting.

"Mr. Sweet—"

"Joe," he said affably.

"Joe." She was almost glad when her orange juice arrived, and she took a sip. Nate said nothing, letting her take the lead. Joe seemed to realize she needed a moment, for he remained silent, too. "Joe, I don't know if you know this, but my mom died last year."

His face clouded over. "I heard about the accident. You have my condolences, young lady. No one should die so young."

She nodded. "Thank you. When I returned to Valentine to sell the building I inherited from her, I discovered that she'd lied to me my whole life. The man she married when she left here wasn't really my dad."

His sympathetic expression faded into confusion.

She rushed on. "I recently discovered she was pregnant when she left town at eighteen."

Now Joe's skin turned pale, mottled with red. "Son of a bitch," he murmured. "Oh, sorry."

"Don't worry about it." Emily stared at him, not certain what he was thinking. Was he angry?

Whatever struggle was going on inside Joe's head, he seemed to shake it off with a sigh. "How'd you get my name?" he asked. "It's obvious you came to speak to me."

"Doug Thalberg said you used to hang around my grandparents' store. You weren't the only one, of course, and I still have two men to talk to."

"Forget about them," he said flatly. "I was dating her."

His gaze was sharp on her face, as if he needed to examine her every feature. She felt a little faint with nervousness.

"You were?" she whispered. "Did you . . ." And then she couldn't go on.

"I didn't know she was pregnant," he said, running a hand down his face. "She broke it off, and she left town. When I saw her again—with you—she knew what I was thinking. She—she lied about your age, right to my face. Said she was happily married to your dad, and I believed her. Why would she do that?"

"I don't know." Emily barely saw Nate wave away

the waiter, so focused on Joe was she. She gripped her orange juice, shaking so badly she almost spilled it, then sat back and fidgeted with the napkin in her lap. "In some ways, I never understood my mother. We didn't exactly . . . get along. I didn't like the way she ran her life, and she thought I was crazy for getting married young—just like her." She added that last part with faint sarcasm.

And still they stared at each other.

"I think—" Joe broke off and cleared his throat. "I think she never liked it here, and didn't want to be forced to stay."

Emily nodded gravely.

"And she didn't like my family," he continued, a trace of bitterness in his voice now. "She thought they were too concerned with us and what we did. She didn't like that the ranch and the inn were so important to me, often saying they were more important than she was." He winced. "But that's no excuse for . . ." He gestured toward her. "For *this*."

Emily flinched.

Joe's eyes went wide, and he reached toward her, but stopped before touching her hand. "That came out wrong. I'm sorry. I just don't know what to call this— this situation between us. I mean . . . I think you're my daughter."

He didn't sound angry so much as bewildered and hesitant, and something in Emily relaxed the tiniest bit.

"Until a couple weeks ago," she whispered, "I had the memory of a wonderful man as my dad, even though he died when I was seven. I'd feel better if we had a DNA test just to make sure. We really don't know who else my mother might have . . ."

And then she trailed off, because she couldn't stop looking at him, and he seemed to be feeling the same thing.

"No problem," he said in a husky voice. "But I think . . . I think . . . you look like my mom."

Emily was almost shocked when a tear rolled down her cheek. And then he touched her hand, and he was trembling as much as she was. Her mind, which had been so focused on him, started reeling. It was true—she really had another family, brothers, a sister.

She drew her hand away. "I . . . I heard you're married, right?"

He nodded, not looking offended by her withdrawal. "My wife's name is Faith, and we've been together thirty years."

"Right after my mom left?"

He winced and glanced at Nate. "Faith was a good friend and helped me realize what true love was. We have three sons and a daughter."

He kind of stumbled on the last word, and she smiled awkwardly, wondering if he would someday include her as another daughter when he talked about his family.

Her family. Three brothers and a sister. She'd wanted nothing but a close family her whole life, and had failed time and again, first with her mom, then with her own marriage. And now there were all these new people.

Joe looked . . . okay with it so far, even eager, but how would his wife feel? His children? Would that make him change his mind about his own feelings?

It seemed overwhelming, all these people she was now connected to in Valentine, Nate and Joe, Monica and Brooke, the widows at the boardinghouse—so many people, so many new ways to be hurt. It was suddenly too much.

Joe cleared his throat. "Maybe . . . maybe you could come to dinner sometime."

She stood up hastily. "I—I don't know. I'll be leaving town soon—oh, but of course, I promise I'll visit, and we can get to know each other. But—but I can't stay, not really. I grew up in San Francisco, and my life is there."

Nate was staring at her, his expression impassive as she foolishly babbled. Was she hurting him, or would he be relieved when she left? She didn't want to hurt anyone—including herself.

"Nate, I'm really not too hungry, and I promised Monica I'd work today. Do you mind if we leave?"

Joe got to his feet, too. "Emily, it was nice to meet you."

He put out a hand, and she slowly took it. He cupped hers in both of his and smiled at her. Her throat felt so tight she didn't think she could swallow, but she managed a smile in return.

"We'll talk again when you're ready," Joe said. "You let me know."

She nodded and hurried away without a backward glance, hoping Nate was following.

Chapter Twenty-two

When Emily arrived through the back door of the flower shop, Monica looked up from an arrangement she was designing.

"Well, well, well," Monica said with interest. "I never saw your lights go on last night after your big dinner with Nate."

Emily gave her a wry, tired grin. "He booked a room. That is such a beautiful place."

Monica continued to study her. "Well?"

Emily sat down on a stool. "I guess you're not talking about Nate."

"Did you see Joe?"

"We talked." Emily had to swallow again. There was a lump in her throat that wouldn't seem to go away. She'd had it during the quiet ride back here, during the distracted kiss she gave Nate before leaving him. She sighed. "Joe says he was dating my mom, and that she lied to him about me. He says he's my dad."

Monica's face briefly lit up, then she seemed to control her reaction. "So . . . how does that make you feel?"

Emily had to chuckle. "You sound like a psychiatrist."

"Well, I'd have to be blind not to be able to tell you're upset. Aren't you glad to know the truth?"

"It won't be official until the DNA test." She sighed. "But he thinks I look like his mom."

Monica squeezed her hand.

"I only saw her briefly at the front desk last night, so who knows. As for glad? Relieved, maybe. He seems like a nice enough guy, and Nate likes the family, so they have to be okay."

"Nate would know."

Emily frowned at her but didn't want to get into it about Nate.

"So what are you going to do now that you know?"

"Do? I—I don't know. I'm not going to fall apart if that's what you mean. I've had a couple weeks to come to terms with the fact that my dad . . . my dad wasn't who I thought he was. But he considered himself my dad, and that's good enough for me."

"Of course it is!"

"As for Joe, I have to be a pretty big complication in his life. His wife will probably be upset, and maybe his kids, too."

"Upset? Over something that happened when he was a teenager? I think that's a little harsh."

"Having a kid you never knew about? Some people could be pretty upset. And he's angry at my mom for lying to him."

"And probably sad that he got to miss out on helping to raise you," Monica added gently.

Emily fought against the tears that filled her eyes. She couldn't think about that. "I don't want them to consider me some kind of responsibility now. They don't owe me anything."

"Emily, listen to yourself! You're talking like there's a balance sheet, and things have to add up. Life isn't that easy. How would you feel if you had a child you didn't know about?"

Just the thought gave her a painful squeeze through her chest. "Oh, Monica, I just don't know what I'm supposed to do now," she whispered.

"I'll give you the cliché answer: Take it one day at a time. There's no right or wrong here. Just a group of people trying to get to know each other."

"A group—do you know how many kids he already has?" Emily asked with exasperation.

"You make five."

Emily hastily stood up. "I can't think about that now. Let's talk about something—anything—else. Is Melissa still here?"

Monica groaned. "It's been *forever*. She keeps saying she's got all this vacation time coming, and she's still able to do some writing from here, and I know she's begun seeing some old friends, but—damn, I want my apartment back."

Emily smiled. "I admire your patience. Are things . . . better between you?"

"A bit. I've given up hope that it'll ever be what it once was, but if we can make the holidays less tense, I'll be content."

Emily's cell rang, and she glanced at it. "It's Nate."

"Gee, he only just dropped you off, right? Guess he can't get enough of you."

"Or he feels sorry for me."

Monica rolled her eyes. "Take the call. I think I have a customer."

Emily stared at the phone, then sent it to voice mail. She couldn't talk about this anymore. Ever since she'd arrived in Valentine Valley, she felt like the butt of everyone's pity. She could handle this on her own.

The next day, after a lunch shift at the flower shop, Emily was painting behind the restaurant bar when she heard a knock at her front door. She popped up and saw a man outside, his face shadowed by the building. Wiping her hands on a clean rag, she came around and realized that Joe Sweet had come to call. Her stomach did a little spasm. She'd done a good job putting him out of her mind. Perhaps it hadn't been so easy for him to do the same.

She opened the door and smiled tentatively at him. "Hi, Joe."

He circled his cowboy hat slowly in his hands, even as he nodded at her. He studied her too closely, too eagerly, and Emily felt her shoulders stiffen.

"Hi, Emily. Mind if I see your place?"

She stepped back, and, as he came inside, she found herself relieved that no one else was with him. *Relieved?* Shouldn't she be curious? She had brothers and a sister! And a stepmother . . .

"This place looks a lot different than I remember it,"

he said, looking around. "I didn't eat at the last restaurant."

When he seemed almost apologetic, she laughed. "When you have a place like the Sweetheart Inn, why would you eat anywhere else?"

"Oh, believe me, I eat at a lot of different places. I'm pretty involved in the restaurants around here."

"Nate said you're a proponent of organic farming?"

His eyes lit up, and he started talking about healthy eating and slow food, and what pesticides did to the environment. Emily let him ramble, interested in spite of herself and grateful he was filling what would probably be an awkward silence.

"I've been overseeing a garden I helped build at the high school. It's never too soon to stress the importance of good food to teenagers." He started circling his hat in his hands again.

"You seem like a busy man, yet you make time for kids. I like that." She found herself wondering what her childhood would have been like with him in it. No, she wasn't going there. The past couldn't be changed.

"Do you have kids?" he asked.

She hesitated, not wanting to explain her baby's death before she had ever taken a breath. "I'd like to someday, though. Sadly, I've already been divorced."

"I'm sorry to hear that."

She gave him a tour of the kitchen, then took him upstairs.

He grinned. "I like what you've done with the place. It seems homey."

She'd really created that feeling all by herself, she thought with wonder, then heard herself saying—and meaning it, "It's been good to be here."

He looked out the front window. "You can't see the park from here, but you know the pavilion?"

She nodded.

"The ladies of the preservation fund have been working with me on putting a farmer's market there this summer. Nate's been pretty involved with it." He glanced at her with a hint of speculation.

"I don't know how he has the time," she said blandly.

"Time, money—he gives whatever he can. He's active in the preservation fund."

Is he? she thought, trying not to show her curiosity. It was none of her business. But at least he was using his money for good, helping make Valentine better for everyone. Because you couldn't tell by his old pickup and basic denim wardrobe that he might be worth something more substantial.

"And then there's the rodeo," Joe continued.

She wasn't making this easy for him, but she didn't know how to do that. "It'll be my first."

"You'll have a good time. All the women wear their finest Western gear, even if they're not competing."

"I hear I can enter the baking contest."

"Well that's good! Not sure you can beat my wife's apple bread, but you can try."

She laughed, finding herself slowly relaxing in his company. "Then I better not enter the bread competition. So what kind of Western gear should I wear on the big day?"

He looked down at her feet in flip-flops. "Do you have cowboy boots?"

"No," she said regretfully.

"I could help you choose them. There's a store in Aspen with a great selection."

She studied his face, the way he tried not to appear too hopeful, and felt a sudden tenderness that made her blink against tears. "I'd like that."

"Do you want to go right now? I have some time, if you do."

She hesitated, feeling a bit silly and awkward, but touched, too. "Okay, let me wash up and change."

He grinned, and she found herself grinning back. It was a start.

Emily spent the next couple days working as hard as she could. Occasionally, she would glance into her closet at her new cowboy boots, which Joe had insisted on buying for her. They were tooled with daisies up the side, and she felt like a cowgirl in them—like a real resident of Valentine Valley. The time spent with him had been confusing and cautious, but there were moments where they forgot the new reality between them and just chatted. Yet every time he started talking about his family, she found herself steering the conversation away though she wasn't sure why.

She had another revelation while spending time with Joe. She had at first been offended by his offer of the cowboy boots—though she hadn't told him. Then it had dawned on her that she'd been so busy trying to be Miss Independence, that it had never occurred to her that that was how people, how *family,* showed they cared. It had happened so seldom in her life, she hadn't been able to recognize it for what it was.

Maybe Nate didn't recognize it either, she mused, wondering . . .

Valentine Valley filled up with rodeo crowds. Emily had never seen so many cowboy hats in her life. She and Nate shared an occasional meal, but the rodeo that weekend began to take up more and more of his time. It was a good thing. She had to keep reminding herself not to imagine things were too deeply felt, that there might be more to the softness in his eyes than friendship and enjoyment. They couldn't have more than that even if she wanted it. Nate didn't.

Her building was done at last—bare of furniture on the first floor but ready to be whatever the new owners wanted it to be. She called the real-estate agent, and he toured the place for the first time, whistling his admiration. After taking pictures, he promised to get back to her soon about whether the owner of Leather and Lace wanted to see it before making an offer. When he'd gone, she stood in the middle of the restaurant and felt . . . melancholy, wistful, as if this building had been another stage in her life that she was soon to leave behind.

Luckily, preparing for the rodeo baking competition kept her mind off anything too weighty. She settled on a chocolate mousse cake, and baked two, one for the judges, and one to be auctioned off later in the day for the Valentine Preservation Fund.

Just after dawn on the morning of the rodeo, the

clouds broke, signaling a beautiful mountain day. Emily showed up with her entry and walked the ranch grounds, gawking at the colorful tents fluttering in the breeze, and the profusion of food vendors. She made plans to come back and sample the food, fried dough, sausage and peppers, and her favorite, cotton candy.

Crafters and leather artists displayed their wares. She noticed Josh wasn't among them, but she was able to meet several of the women who sold their crafts on consignment at the flower shop, and blushed at their praise for her ability to hand-sell their goods. She'd helped these people earn a living with their talents, and it made her feel good.

Little boys and girls were dressed as cowboys, complete with chaps and spurs and little Stetsons. Emily later found out they were competing in a sheep-riding contest—who could stay on the longest, just like the big cowboys riding a bucking horse. Spurs jingled from cowboy boots as young men arrogantly strode through the grounds, ready to compete. More than one person called a hello, and she realized how many people she'd met in just a few short weeks.

And everywhere were the animals, of course. Many competitors brought their own horses for the barrel racing, calf roping, and team roping. Dogs roamed the grounds, occasionally wrestling for dominance, then barking in merry packs. In pens, the cattle lowed in deep baritone voices, as if warning all the competitors to expect a challenge.

At the baking-competition tent, she stayed to help

Sandy Thalberg coordinate the entries. She got whis-
tles from more than one cowboy, and she felt positively
pretty in a sundress and cowboy boots—nothing like
you'd see on the streets of San Francisco. She was
dying to know what Nate thought but knew he must be
crazy busy so didn't seek him out. But every time she
heard his deep voice over the loudspeakers that echoed
through the valley, she felt a little thrill of excitement.
And then his voice was gone, and Josh's took his place.
Emily exchanged a curious look with Sandy, who only
shrugged her shoulders and went back to work.

A half hour earlier, in the ranch office, Nate looked
out the window at the lightening sky and scowled. He'd
printed out several lists and talked to all the event co-
ordinators. He still had some more announcements to
make, but he was waiting for the last document to print,
then he'd follow his prescribed list, making sure everything got done.

"Nate?" Josh ducked his head in the door. "Where
the heck are you?"

"I'm coming," Nate said, standing near the printer
impatiently. "Are the bulls in the holding pen?"

"Of course. You already delegated that task."

"Right, sorry."

"You know, big brother," Josh said, half-sitting
on the edge of a desk and studying Nate, "I bet you
wouldn't know how to enjoy the day if you weren't running the whole thing, being everything to everybody."

"Of course I would," Nate said absently. "It's a great
event, and everyone has fun."

"I don't think you're capable of having fun."

Nate frowned and came around the desk, brushing by his brother. "What are you talking about?"

Josh grabbed his arm. "A challenge. I dare you to hand me those papers, that microphone, and all the control. I'm not worried it won't get done—I'm saying you won't be able to stop yourself from interfering."

"Josh, you're making a point, fine, I get it. But not today."

"Yes, today."

Josh made a grab for the clipboard as Nate attached the papers. Nate resisted.

"You gonna turn down a challenge, big brother?" Josh asked softly, with an air of danger and a gleam in his eye.

Nate finally looked at his brother—really looked at him. And heard him. He thought of Emily's conclusions about him trying to prove himself.

He didn't have to prove how much he loved the ranch. Everyone knew.

"Okay," he said suddenly, letting go of the clipboard. It banged against Josh's chest from his pull.

Josh slowly smiled. "Really?"

"Really. I can let it go. I trust you."

"I never doubted that," Josh said, eyeing him.

Nate smiled. "Go on. Go have fun."

After Josh had gone, Nate left the office, took a deep breath of the warm air, scented with hay and cattle and the smell of grilling sausages.

Brooke ran up to him. "Hey, I need—"

"Go talk to Josh. I'm taking the day off."

"What? But Nate . . . you *love* the rodeo." Her voice sounded bewildered.

He shrugged. "I'm not going anywhere. Now hurry! The first event starts in an hour, and there's still a lot to do."

She left, shaking her head and muttering, and Nate was trapped for another ten minutes, turning away everybody and their brother asking endless questions about the rodeo. He referred them all to Josh.

Then he saw Emily step out of the baking tent, and their eyes met and held. Her slow, sexy smile made his insides twist, and she did a little twirl in her yellow polka-dotted dress. When he saw her cowboy boots, a surge of hope took him by surprise. They were just boots, but they made him think . . . was she considering staying in Valentine Valley? Where was his worry about breaking up with her? It was no longer there, as if he'd let a lot of things go when he gave over control.

They met in the shade of the stands, and he kissed her long and hard.

She swayed in his arms and stared up at him in pleased surprise. "That was quite the greeting."

"It's those boots—I'll never be able to resist you now."

They heard Josh's calm voice on the loudspeaker, and Emily studied Nate's face.

"Is that your doing?" she asked slyly.

He grinned. "Nope, it's his. Josh challenged me, and I never go back on a challenge." He kissed her nose.

"What kind of challenge?"

"The kind where I'm a participant, not a coordinator."

"Really?"

"Don't sound so surprised," he said dryly.

Josh ran by them at full speed. Nate didn't even turn his head to see where he was going.

"Impressive," Emily said, nodding. "I might actually believe you're capable of this."

"Glad someone does."

"So you'll be forced to keep me company all day, and explain everything I'm watching."

"Except when I'm competing with Dad. The team roping's next. Dad's the header, I'm the heeler."

"So you rope each other?" She grinned.

"No, a steer," he said, laughing. "Gotta catch him around the horns, then the hind legs. When he's taut between us, time's called."

"Sounds exciting!"

"You can watch with my mom." He lowered his voice. "Afterward, we'll find somewhere more private to watch the events."

She gave him a wicked smile and squeezed his arm against her.

He looked back at the barn. "The hayloft? We'll be able to see over the competition fields from the window up there."

"And we'll be alone."

"For a while anyway. Then I've got to show you how a man line dances at the big dance in the truck shed tonight."

"The truck shed?" She covered her mouth as if hiding her laughter. "I knew about the dance of course—I made some beautiful flowers for the tables. But no offense, isn't the truck shed where you house all the big equipment?"

"You bet. But the ladies have been getting it ready for a country dance, complete with lanterns hung like it's the Old West."

"Sounds romantic," she warned. "You up for that, cowboy?"

"Yes, ma'am."

Chapter Twenty-three

Later that night, Emily invited the girls back up to her apartment to sample some of the goodies that she hadn't ended up entering, and to celebrate her winning the grand prize blue ribbon in the baking competition. She sat back on her love seat, watching them make small talk with each other, feeling a contentment with other women that was new to her. She savored it quietly as she ate her cookie-dough mini cupcake in two delicious bites.

Melissa pulled a chair over to her. "So did you think any more about the college stuff we discussed?"

Emily opened her mouth, but before she could answer, Monica said, "I think Emily has a career path she'd like more than college. She should stay here and open a bakery."

Brooke gasped, then clapped her hands together. "That is *perfect*! When did you come up with that?"

Emily tried to speak again, but this time, Melissa

interrupted. "A bakery?" she said, frowning. "Emily, you're enrolled at *Berkeley.*"

"And is there something wrong with a bakery?" Monica asked her sister in an icy voice. "God knows you're always quick to show me how you feel about a mere flower shop."

Melissa's brown eyes went wide. "What are you talking about? Your flower shop is cool, and I like how you've brought in the local craftspeople."

Monica gaped at her. "Missy, you're lying to yourself if you think you've ever given me the impression that you approve of what I'm doing. I know it's not a big high-powered job like yours, but it's tearing me up inside that you think I don't measure up."

Emily and Brooke stared at each other helplessly but let the argument between the sisters play out.

"When did I ever say you didn't measure up?" Melissa hopped to her feet as if she could no longer stay still. "I've always been proud of you. It's you who didn't like what I did, wouldn't even come with me to DC after college."

"What do you mean come with you?" Monica echoed, throwing her hands wide as she met her sister nose to nose. "You knew I loved Valentine and wanted a life here. And you made sure I felt bad about my choice compared to yours!"

Melissa burst into tears.

Monica glanced at Brooke as if looking for help, but Brooke could only shrug and urge her silently with her hands to do something.

"Why are you crying, Missy?" Monica asked in a softer voice.

"I never wanted you to feel bad," she said, between sobs.

Emily helplessly handed her a tissue, and she took it to blow her nose.

"Then why were you always talking up your job and the city?" Monica asked plaintively.

"Because . . . because . . . I wanted you to come with me!"

Monica's mouth fell open.

"We went to . . . college together," Melissa continued, gasping out her words, "and I just assumed we'd go have our careers together. But then . . . but then . . . you went home, and I went to a city where I didn't know anyone, where I didn't have my twin . . ." She gave another sob and buried her face in several more tissues she pulled from the box. "And I've been so lonely!"

Monica started to cry, too, then they were both holding each other, rocking. Emily stared at them, feeling touched and even frightened, because now she had a sister, too. And how could they ever be so close since they hadn't grown up together?

"I was even jealous," Melissa said, lifting her head to smile weakly at her sister. "You were so happy."

"But—I thought you were happy, too, flying all over the world, covering the stories you thought so important."

"I *am* happy with my job. But I'd rather be home more, which is why I took so much time off, I guess.

And when would I ever have time for a man? I've met guys I was attracted to, but it's hard to be the power sister in a couple, and most lose interest fast."

"Well, do you see me with a man? A laid-back life doesn't always bring on the bliss. I guess there's good and bad in both our lives." She took Melissa by the shoulders. "But Missy, why didn't you tell me this from the beginning? We lost *years* drifting apart."

"I know, I know," Melissa said, blowing her nose again. "I just felt so weak and foolish and didn't want you to know."

They stared at each other, smiling slowly, tears starting up again, and then they were hugging as if they'd never let go.

"Maybe I'm glad I don't have a sister," Brooke said wryly.

Emily sighed. "Guess I do now. Do you know her?"

"Well, I've met her occasionally, but Em, Stephanie's only seventeen years old."

"A teenager," she said with a groan.

Emily glanced at Melissa and Monica, sitting side by side and talking about, of all things, some guy Melissa met back in Washington, completing each other's sentences, laughing at things no one else in the room got.

"Was it always this way?" Emily asked Brooke.

She shuddered. "Worse. Are you sure you want to meet your sister?"

Emily took a deep breath. "I think it's time."

"What about this bakery idea?" Brooke watched her closely.

"I've . . . considered it. There are a lot of reasons I don't think it would work."

"Really? Tell me my brother isn't any of those reasons."

"No. And he doesn't know, Brooke, so don't tell him."

"But Em—"

"I'll handle this, I promise."

The day after the rodeo, Nate hung up his cell before putting it in his pocket. He took a few quick notes so he wouldn't forget the business discussion, because lately, his mind strayed to Emily if he didn't focus. His secretary, Gloria, Monica's aunt, glanced at him briefly but didn't ask any questions. They were alone in the ranch office, and he spun his chair slowly until he could look out the big picture window at the Elk Mountains. The word "majestic" must have been created for mountains. They called to him even now, with their remoteness, their sense of adventure. It had always been about freedom for him, and the quiet stillness in his mind as he skied fast down a hill or controlled the jarring turns on his bike.

But since Emily had come to Valentine Valley, being alone didn't have the allure it once did. He found himself thinking of things he would show her, or tell her about. She never left his thoughts anymore, and he was filled with a sort of . . . peace because of it.

He was a man who knew the value of family and knew how much Emily longed to experience it. Here she had a dad who couldn't wait to get to know her, yet she kept him at a polite distance. But then she'd always held part of herself back. Nate wanted to know everything about her. He'd tried to break up with her and couldn't make himself do it. He'd spent ten years honing his discipline, and mastered the ability to keep himself from getting too close to people he might hurt—but he'd still let himself fall completely under her spell.

He'd fallen in love with her, and for a moment, the realization made him pause, as if he'd feel worried by this new closeness with a woman. But instead, something lightened inside him, something eased. It felt right. Emily was intelligent and fun, determined to succeed on her own, trying to find the path of her life in the midst of uncertainty and chaos. He knew she'd been betrayed over and over, yet she had gotten back up and was stronger for it. She was a woman who'd stand up against him when he was treating her wrong—how had he not seen that?

He loved her. The thought felt bright and shiny, complete with a different kind of hope for the future that he'd never felt before. He wanted to be with her; he wanted to make her part of him.

Could he convince her to share the last of her secrets, trust him, if he'd share his?

Emily wasn't surprised when her doorbell rang that night, and she opened it to find Nate leaning in the doorway, giving her that special, intimate smile he was so good at. The welling of warmth and happiness his face alone inspired in her took her by surprise, and for a moment, she resisted, knowing without a doubt that leaving him would hurt. But whether she stayed or left, one of them would be hurt.

She couldn't stop herself from letting him kiss her, tucking herself beneath his arm as they walked up the narrow stairs side by side. She laughed and tried to push him away, but he wouldn't let her.

When they were settled on her love seat with two beers, he studied her thoughtfully, and she grew uneasy.

"So what's going on, Nate?" She twisted on the small sofa, one knee bent along Nate's side so she could face him.

"I meant to introduce you to an important woman in my life yesterday, but I never got the chance."

She raised her eyebrows in surprise.

"Gloria's my secretary. I hired her about five years ago when I realized the work I was doing was keeping me off the ranch. It may seem funny to an outsider, but I love working with my family on property we've owned for more than a hundred years."

This was important, and she felt a sense of distance, as if this moment loomed larger-than-life.

"It doesn't seem funny at all," she said quietly. "I lo—really enjoy that about you."

His smile seemed twisted with amusement and tenderness, and she could have lost herself in those vivid green eyes.

Nate finally cleared his throat. "About ten years ago, it began to be obvious that the ranch was in trouble. We're small, and easily affected by a bad season, whether it's a winter that lasts too long or a drought that affects our only hay crop of the year. In other parts of the country, they can have several cuttings a year, but up in the mountains, the season isn't long enough for more than one. Anyway, my dad had some money set aside. Knowing diversification was a way for a small ranch to survive, he gave it to me to invest. I probably bragged too much when I got back from college about all I'd learned in my business classes."

Emily touched his hand. "Or he trusted you."

She expected Nate to shrug off her compliment, but he didn't, only studied her with a seriousness that made her feel almost nervous.

"Thanks." He squeezed her hand. "This ranch is everything to my family, and the heritage of the land and the trust my father and grandfather placed in the next generation to protect it . . . well, I couldn't let go of this place. I couldn't risk it failing. So I took the money and I invested it, just a little here or there, testing my theories on where we'd earn the most. And I discovered I seemed to have a knack for what would make a profit— bull genetics, organic produce in Aspen's restaurants, rodeo stock, a winery on the Western Slope, even the stock market."

She gave him a warm smile. "So you have a head for money. Why am I not surprised?"

"I guess I do. I invested for myself as well, and I've done pretty good."

"Pretty good?" she echoed, amused.

"Pretty good."

He smiled at her almost abashedly, and the warmth she felt for him curled right up inside her as if to stay.

She felt a little jolt of fear, which she pushed down, as if squashing it would make it go away.

"So I have some money," he said, a trace of resignation threading into his voice. "To help my dad simplify things, I bought out some of his own investments . . . like the lien on your building."

"I take it you don't mean recently."

He shook his head.

She should be angry that he'd misled her, but she knew him so much better now, understood that he had fears he wouldn't acknowledge, that his past had affected him just the same as hers had.

"You don't have anything to say?" he said, warily studying her face.

She took a sip of her beer. "I guess whether it was you or your dad owning it, your family still did, and I'll be repaying the debt."

His eyes narrowed. "But I deliberately—"

"I know," she interrupted. "You didn't know me, Nate. I was some chick you'd gotten drunk with in a bar and who you'd now discovered was so broke she couldn't afford a night in a motel. I don't blame you for protecting yourself or your family. If I only thought you a cowboy, you could be certain I wouldn't demand anything of you—that you wouldn't get too close."

He briefly rubbed his fingers over his eyes. "That sounds pretty bad."

She took his hand again. "It wasn't. I'm not angry."

"But maybe you're disappointed I didn't tell you any of this sooner."

"No. You're a private person, Nate, and you were

honest with me about that. I've heard about your involvement in the preservation fund."

"You have?" he demanded. "Who—"

"It isn't important. You do the best you can for the people you believe in, and you don't want anyone's thanks, so you keep it private. The fund lets you help, while keeping your distance, not risking guiding a person a way they might not want to go, right?"

He winced. "I never thought of it like that. I kept parts of my financial life private for other reasons. A lot of my dad's friends wish the town wasn't changing, that their ranching lives would stay the same, that newcomers would never find our little peaceful corner of the world. The preservation fund bothers some of them, and I didn't want them throwing my involvement back in my dad's face. But Em, it bothered me they couldn't see the future, that Valentine would die without new blood and new investments to make it attractive."

She smiled. "Not everybody can see the future like you can. And as for keeping things private—I like that about you. My ex would donate to charities and make sure his name was prominent every time. I blinded myself to a lot of things about him, rushed into marriage without considering the important stuff. But I'm older and wiser now."

He looked at her with a poignant sadness that made her turn away.

"You were right about my biological father affecting me," he said at last in a quiet voice. "He left my mom when she was ill, but the worst of it was, he cleaned out every bank account and used up the credit cards before he left."

Emily couldn't hold back a gasp. "Oh Nate." She imagined Sandy as a young abandoned mom with a frightened little boy, no money to buy food or pay the bills. "Your mother is such a brave woman. But your own wariness about people makes so much more sense."

He stared at her in surprise, then bit by bit, tension seemed to leak away from him, as if her words had answered questions he'd never known he had.

"You know, we have something in common," she continued, picking at the label on her beer bottle. "Your first dad left your mom because she was ill. Greg left me because I couldn't have children."

She didn't look at him, afraid she'd burst into tears. When he put an arm around her, pulling her against his warm, solid side, to her surprise, she didn't feel as devastated as she once had.

The words just started tumbling out of her. "I could get pregnant, you see, though it took a long time. But then I'd have a miscarriage, two or three months in."

"Oh, Emily," he said raggedly.

"My third pregnancy went much farther, but then in my seventh month, the baby died. The doctor said I'd be unlikely to ever have children." She swallowed hard but didn't look at him. "When I came home from the hospital, Greg said he wanted his own children, that he didn't want to adopt. So he left me."

And then Nate pulled her into his arms, and she

clung to him, but her eyes were dry, her emotions full of sadness but also a rising determination. She pulled away to look into his eyes.

"So you can see why I plan to adopt. I want a family, and biology doesn't matter to me. Greg was an ass, and if we'd shared any kind of true love, he couldn't have treated me that way. But we matched so well, wanted the same sort of traditional life. I let that blind me to the kind of man he really was, let myself make excuses when I sensed he might not measure up."

Nate still looked at her as if she might crumble to pieces any moment, and he wanted to be her rock.

She smiled tremulously and cupped his face with one hand. "It's okay," she insisted. "The worst of the betrayal is past me now. Trust me, anger has a way of pushing out the grief. It was bad at first—I almost lost myself in depression, never leaving my bed for days. I feel like such a fool now. I let him make me feel like less than a woman because I couldn't give birth. You'll really think I'm an idiot when I tell you I refused Greg's guilt money, wanting no connection to him."

"I don't think you're an idiot." Nate touched her hair, her shoulder, her hand, as if he couldn't stop.

"It didn't work for me, Nate. Marriage, I mean. You're telling me deeply private things, and I'm doing the same for you, but . . . I don't think of myself as anyone's potential wife. I stand on my own now."

Chapter Twenty-four

Nate was as startled as if she'd slapped him. They'd been confiding their secrets; he'd never felt so close to a woman, wanted so much just to be with her and love her and make her happy for the rest of their lives. But she didn't want the same. He shouldn't be so surprised. She'd been up-front with her intentions—just as he had, he thought wryly. But he thought things had changed between them, deepened. They had—he couldn't mistake that. But whereas he accepted it, anticipated a future they could share, she was putting on the brakes. She'd suffered a betrayal at the lowest moment in her life, when the promise of a new little baby had died. And he didn't know what to do, what to say, to prove himself. Or if she was even ready to hear it.

"I hope you're not implying that every man is as stupid as your ex-husband," he finally said. "Most of us are glad to adopt—I owe my life to such a man."

"I know that."

She wouldn't meet his eyes; he could feel her retreating bit by bit, as if she feared she'd said too much and wished she hadn't. He didn't want her to regret confiding in him, didn't want to make everything worse by pleading with her to look at him for the man he was, not in the shadow of her ex-husband.

But he knew she was afraid of being hurt again, by him and her new father and his family. And she would leave him, leave Valentine, rather than risk such betrayal again.

"I'm sorry to be so blunt," Emily whispered at last. She studied his face with earnest worry. "Maybe I never should have said—"

"No." He took her shoulders in his hands. "I want to know everything about you. Believe me, I'm grateful for your trust." He wanted to tell her he loved her, that he always would, that he'd never do anything to harm her—but she didn't want to hear it, and he felt bewildered and battered trying to think of a way to change her mind.

"You probably want to go now," she said, a touch of forlorn trembling in her voice.

"No, I don't. I want to be here with you. We don't have to say anything more. It will be enough for me."

She settled against him with a sigh, tucking her head beneath his chin, curling her knees up until they rested across his thighs.

He was lying to himself, he thought, squeezing his eyes shut. He wanted more. He wanted everything with Emily. If he told her how he felt, she'd just think he was trying to fix everything like usual. He'd spent his life making things happen, but he couldn't force her to love him.

* * *

Joe's wife, Faith, called Emily the next morning and invited her to dinner that night. Emily thought the woman sounded a bit too cheerful but was glad Faith was trying. For a moment, Emily almost refused, feeling overwhelmed at the thought of them all staring at each other around a table. There would be expectations none of them—including herself—might be able to meet.

But then she thought of Nate, and his concern, and the tenderness in his eyes he no longer hid from her. He'd want to see her tonight, and she wasn't certain that was a good idea for either of them. They'd gotten too close, and she was still leaving. After everything she'd revealed to him, she was surprised he hadn't fled from her apartment and her past and all the ways he thought he could fix her. It would be just like him to try hard to make everything better. She was grateful he hadn't.

So she accepted Faith's offer, hoping to make Joe happy, for he'd been just as wounded as Emily had by Delilah's lies.

Their ranch home was larger than the Thalbergs', but there the similarities ended. Everywhere were touches of the bohemian lifestyle Nate had hinted at, from tarot cards on a table to crystals hung in every window. Faith must be a patron at the Mystic Connection, the new age store in town. The paintings on the walls were medieval or mystical or brimming with abundant nature: flowers, waterfalls, or mysterious forests. Emily saw a cluttered office as she followed Joe and Faith down a hall into the living room, books scattered around a computer, and she remembered Nate's mentioning that Joe liked to write.

Faith wore a gauzy multicolored, loose gown, her frizzy silver-streaked black hair pulled back from her freshly washed face. Emily found herself charmed by the woman's forthright manner. As she led Emily into the living room, she gestured to her children with pride, and they all stood up, as if Emily were a business client. She felt hot with embarrassment and nerves.

Three young men—Emily's brothers—stood around their sister, almost as if she needed protection.

"Emily," Joe said, "these are our children, Will, Chris, Daniel, and Stephanie."

Stephanie was a pretty girl, with her father's crystal blue eyes and bright blond hair that she wore in a ponytail. Suspicion and wariness twisted her expressive face, and Emily's hopes began to sink. Joe had said he'd told his children about her, but he'd never explained how badly Stephanie must have taken it. Emily had made a terrible mistake coming so soon, but it was too late to change it. Stephanie looked as pale as winter frost.

Emily's tension had coalesced into a little ball of pain in her stomach, and she was certain she wouldn't be able to eat anything. Her very existence had caused this poor girl grief. She was tempted to leave but knew that would make it seem as if she had been chased away.

Thankfully, the three young men eyed her curiously but without dismay. Will was taller and broader than his dad, with sandy blond hair, frank, hazel eyes, and a cleft in his chin centered in a square jaw. Chris's hair was lighter, as were his pale blue eyes. He was built more like his dad, leaner and compact, though with the same chin as his brother. Daniel, still in college, had inherited his mother's darker hair and gray eyes. He sported several tattoos on his arms and wore a silver stud beneath his lower lip. But his smile was curious and friendly as he nodded a greeting.

All three men could have been just as suspicious as Stephanie, upset that their lives had been disrupted by an old secret, but one by one they shook her hand and gave her a polite, even curious, smile, which she returned though her lips trembled. These were her brothers. She didn't know what to think, but she wanted to be happier rather than so nervous and uncertain.

Will and Chris must have realized her mood, because they shared a look before Will said, "So you're my big sister."

Emily gave him a faint smile.

"How sad for you, Will, that you've lost all your 'oldest child' privileges," Chris said dryly.

Emily actually chuckled, and she almost covered her mouth with surprise.

"What privileges?" Will demanded indignantly. "I had to babysit you."

Will's good-natured disgruntled look encompassed both his brothers and sister. Stephanie's lips twitched as if she fought a smile. Then she looked at Emily, and her eyes went cool again. Emily sighed. She wished she could join in the bantering, but words stuck in her throat, and her chest felt tight with unshed tears. Staring at their faces as they teased each other, she wondered what it would have been like if she'd known them as children. She was a sister, but a stranger. It seemed so insurmountable to ever be more.

They were her family now, but it felt all wrong. She'd longed for this her whole life, but how could only occasional visits back to Valentine mold them into the close family she'd dreamed of? Was she making a mistake in leaving?

"Kids," Faith said, obviously assessing Stephanie's mood—and perhaps Emily's—"come finish helping me in the kitchen so your dad and Emily can talk."

Stephanie glared at Emily over her shoulder as she followed her brothers out. She caught her dad's frown and looked guilty, hunching her shoulders.

When they were alone, Joe said, "I'm so sorry about Stephanie's behavior."

Her eyes went wide. "No, oh please, this isn't her fault."

"I guess I should have told you she was having a hard time with my past," he said solemnly. "But . . . I didn't want you to misunderstand. This really isn't about you but about me. Guess I'm not her perfect father, you know? She always thought of herself as Daddy's little girl."

Emily didn't know what to say as she stood there awkwardly in the middle of their living room.

"I feel badly that you have to go through this. I wish—well, I could wish for a lot of things, but the past is the past, and we can only live for the future."

Emily couldn't help wondering what he wished for—that he'd never slept with her mother? That she'd never been born? Or should she give him the benefit of the doubt and hope he meant he wished he'd known about her all along?

"I don't know how to say this, so bear with me." Joe put both his hands on her shoulders. "I've thought a lot about the renovations you've been doing, how hard you're working on your future." He smiled at her, but there was uncertainty in his eyes. "I haven't been able to help you grow up, and it really makes me sad. Could I—would you let me help you now? I know you have plans to go to college, and I've helped my sons with their tuition. Would you let me do the same for you?"

Emily was surprised and confused, but she managed a smile. "Joe, that is such a nice offer, but I can't accept."

"Emily—"

"No, please, I understand that you just want to help, but it would make me feel like I searched for you only for money, instead of the truth."

"I wouldn't think that."

"Maybe not, but I would. There's no guilt here, nothing to make up for. None of this was our fault. I thank you so much for the offer, but I just can't accept."

He studied her face for a moment before nodding, and Emily let out her breath.

"You've gotten your way right now, young lady," Joe said with mock sternness. "But we might revisit this subject in the future."

She laughed, feeling some of her discomfort ease. "We'll see."

To her surprise, he smiled at her with a tenderness that made her heart ache. He leaned down and gave her a quick kiss on the cheek.

"I've been wanting to do that," he whispered. "My daughter."

Feeling moved and choked up, she watched as he laughed at himself and turned away to wipe his eyes.

These people were strangers, but they were family, too, people she'd be connected to for the rest of her life. She knew she was lucky, that another family might keep her on the outside, an unwelcome surprise. But Joe obviously cared about her. It was a good start.

The doorbell rang, and Joe went to get it, returning with Nate. Emily couldn't even be surprised.

"Sorry I'm late," he said, handing over a bottle of wine to Faith, who came out of the kitchen to greet him, wearing an affectionate smile.

The four younger Sweets followed their mom, and it was obvious by their grins that they all knew Nate well. Emily felt better already—Nate to the rescue, she thought, biting her lip against a smile. His instincts were good, and she was grateful.

Nate kissed Faith's cheek, shook hands with all three young men, hugged Stephanie, then Emily. He stood at her side like they belonged together.

Emily arched a brow at Joe, who spread his hands wide, as if saying Nate's arrival wasn't his suggestion. Perhaps Faith was just as interested in matchmaking as she was in meeting Emily. Faith and Grandma Thalberg must know each other.

Emily knew that everyone saw them as a couple, and the hurt she expected to feel about that didn't happen. Her longing for a normal family had caused her so much pain, and this new family could do the same. But how could she live her life afraid?

When Stephanie begrudgingly passed her a basket of rolls at dinner, Emily met her eyes and saw that wariness, that fearfulness of being hurt, just like she'd been feeling. But just because Emily was afraid didn't mean she could pretend these people weren't important to her.

"Wait until you see what Emily's done with her building," Joe told his family, smiling at her.

She glanced at Stephanie to find her continuing to eat, but at least she wasn't turning away because Emily was the center of attention. "I had a lot of help," Emily insisted, "including the Internet."

"And Nate," Will said, cutting a slice of pork chop and popping it into his mouth.

Nate only grinned as he dug into his mashed potatoes.

Will and Nate were friends, and men did their best to annoy each other, she knew. In a friendly manner, of course.

She smiled as she considered Will. "Yes, Nate helped. And I'm grateful. I'm sure he'll be relieved when I'm out of his hair." That caused another scary jolt of unease as she thought of leaving Valentine—leaving him.

Nate gave her an unreadable glance as he said, "You know that's not true. I've enjoyed every minute."

Stephanie gave a little snort, then covered her mouth with her napkin. More than one person chuckled, including Emily.

Faith eyed her curiously, and Joe just smiled and shook his head, as if Emily amused him.

"Regardless of who helped," Joe said, "I know you've done the majority of the work yourself. Drywall, wooden trim, and all the plastering and painting. It's as if you were readying it for yourself. You come from a long line of businesswomen, after all."

Emily stared at him in surprise, then spoke too quickly, "No, I don't know anything about business. Have you been talking to Monica?"

"Monica?" Nate echoed, looking way too curious.

Emily found them all staring at her with interest, especially Nate. She wanted to make up something, but he was looking at her with such sweet intent, so concerned for her. He'd shared everything about himself with her. She found herself blurting, "Monica thinks I should open a bakery."

Nate's eyes went wide with surprise. She couldn't look away.

Joe and Faith spoke over each other. "Great idea!" "We could use a bakery in Valentine."

"It's . . . silly," Emily said at last, her appetite gone as she stared down at her half-eaten pork. Even she had to question why she was so reluctant to consider the idea, when her subconscious couldn't seem to let it go. "My life is in San Francisco. I'd love it if you'd all come to visit me soon."

"But what are you going to do there?" Stephanie asked.

Emily lifted her chin and didn't look at Nate, reciting the words she'd kept telling herself for the last few months. "I'm going back to college with the money I'll make from selling my building. I need to find the career that's right for me. You're going to college, right?" she asked, hoping for some kind of connection with her new little sister.

But Stephanie looked at her as if Emily were an elderly woman with no business joining the young people. Emily sighed.

Nate drove her home and remained silent for the ten minutes it took to drive off the Sweetheart Ranch and back into town. Emily kept twisting her fingers together, wondering what he was thinking. He didn't seem angry or sad or . . . anything. Whereas she was a jumble of emotions, and suddenly so tired of thinking.

He followed her upstairs to her apartment. When she went to get him a beer, he caught her arm.

"Emily, talk to me."

For a moment she stared at his hand, then up into his face. His concern eased something inside her, and she knew he only wanted what was best for her.

Softly, he asked, "Are you going to run away from Valentine Valley, just like your mother did?"

She caught her breath, wanting to deny it, but suddenly knowing she couldn't.

"Please tell me you're not running away from me," he continued hoarsely. "I know from the beginning we talked about ending things, but I've changed my mind."

Slowly she said, "I swear, this isn't just about you, Nate. It seems I've spent my whole life trying not to be my mother. Maybe—maybe I've been trying to *prove* it, first with my marriage, and now—now with this need to start my life over. I think—I think I'm more like her than I imagined, taking too many risks."

"Is that so bad?" Nate asked earnestly. "She made mistakes, some bad ones, but you won't do the same."

"I chose Greg, didn't I?" she shot back.

"You chose him as a young girl in college. You're not that girl anymore. You take smart risks now, coming here to restart your life, when you could have played it safe in San Francisco."

"My mom struck out on her own, leaving everything behind," Emily whispered. "She never thought anything through, and I was trying to be so careful to be different from her. She jumped from relationship to relationship, taking such terrible chances. I can't accuse myself of that," she said wryly, "not with two men in a decade."

"See, you've learned from her mistakes."

"Yet maybe I missed the point. I didn't *want* to take chances. I wanted movies, where you wanted white-water rafting. I resisted anything scary you tried to tempt me with." *I resisted falling in love with you,* she thought, knowing it was too late. "I was trying to be so independent, thinking that if I stood on my own, I couldn't get hurt again. You were the perfect partner in crime for me, asking nothing of me, promising that both of us would remain unscathed, the same as always."

He took her face between his hands. "I'm asking now, Em. Stay. Give us a chance to see what we have. Give Valentine a chance."

Valentine Valley was the town of her dreams, where families were interconnected, where everyone knew each other, where love was renewed—or begun. Had the romantic spell of Valentine really woven itself about her?

Perhaps the biggest risk she would ever take was staying right here, getting to know her new family, and trying to be her own woman—her own boss, she thought, thinking with new excitement about the bakery. How could she call herself an independent woman if she left town because she was afraid of being hurt again? Could she start her own business with the talents she'd been given, or the ones she'd inherited?

"If you leave here," Nate said, "you'll just be another lonely person in a big city."

She thought of Melissa and felt again the woman's pain.

"People know you here—*I* know you," he continued quietly. "You could have a life here."

She took a deep breath. "With you?"

Nate was the biggest risk of all, standing there patiently waiting for her to make the move. There was a new openness to him, as if he was finally ready to take chances, if she would let him. He had discovered long ago what he was meant to do with his life. He had a quiet confidence, a belief in himself and his town, and mostly in his family.

Did he want *her* to be part of his family?

He thought he had everything together—but he

needed her, she knew. She saw things about him he'd never known about himself. And he was part of Valentine Valley, too. She'd been fighting being a part of it from the beginning.

"I love you, Emily," he whispered, cupping her face, kissing her gently. "I'll never hurt you."

She stared up into his eyes, and everything fell into place, as if her journey here had taught her, brought her to this moment. "I love you, too."

And then she was crying and smiling and kissing him. He let out a whoop and twirled her around.

"Okay, okay," she said, when at last she was safely on the ground. "I'll stay and give this place a try."

"So you'll open this mysterious bakery you've never mentioned to me?"

"I guess you'll have to get over the loss of Leather and Lace."

"But what will you bring on our honeymoon?"

She stared up into his beloved face, no longer the lonely, sad woman she'd been on her first rainy night in Valentine. She'd found a new strength inside her, and she would use it to love Nate as he deserved.

"On the honeymoon? Why, I don't plan to wear anything at all."

They shared a grin.

Epilogue

In autumn, colorful leaves swirling through brisk air,
Emily's bakery, Sugar and Spice, had its opening day.
A long glass display case ran the length of the room,
and a second glass cooler for her cheesecakes and other
refrigerated goodies stood perpendicular to it. She already had orders to bake for two engagements and a
baby shower.

Now she stood behind the glass counter where
the bar had once been, staring with quiet joy at all
the people who'd come to wish her well. Monica and
Brooke were still arranging the flowers that bloomed at
every little table in the coffee corner, while Josh set out
the leather key rings he'd tooled with her cupcake logo
for the first day's customers. The widows had asked to
help out, and they were her new part-time employees,
wearing matching aprons they'd designed themselves
with the logo ASK US WHY WE'RE SUGAR AND SPICE.
They kept "forgetting" to take them off whenever they
went to lunch or dinner.

Nate was the first one to see that she'd come out

of the kitchen, and the smile he gave her made tears spring to her eyes.

"Em, come show them!" he called.

There was a general cry of delight when Nate dragged her forward by the hand so they could all see her lovely pear-cut diamond engagement ring.

Her sister Stephanie gaped at it, then at her. "Oh my God, it's beautiful!"

Emily smiled at her little sister. "You better get used to it. Your job as maid of honor will be to polish it every time you see me."

Stephanie blushed and laughed, glancing at her parents, who beamed back at her. After a slow start, Emily was making progress becoming friends with her teenage sister. Joe wiped his eyes with a hankie when he thought no one was looking, and his mom, Eileen, covered her trembling smile.

Emily slipped her arm through her father's. "Dad, you'll walk me down the aisle, won't you?" It was the first time she'd called him that, and it felt right.

That set up another chorus of "awws" until Grandma Thalberg pulled her away.

"Emily, you'll never guess! The Valentine Valley Preservation Fund committee has agreed to set aside some money to help Leather and Lace open their store after all—but don't tell Nate!"

Emily laughed. "Oh, Grandma, he already knows. Don't breathe a word, but he's become a long-distance customer. Aren't I the luckiest woman in the world?"